PRAISE FOR IAN HAMILTON AND THE AVA LEE SERIES

PRAISE FOR THE WATER RAT OF WANCHAI

WINNER OF THE ARTHUR ELLIS AWARD FOR BEST FIRST NOVEL

"Ian Hamilton's *The Water Rat of Wanchai* is a smart, action-packed thriller of the first order, and Ava Lee, a gay Asian-Canadian forensic accountant with a razor-sharp mind and highly developed martial arts skills, is a protagonist to be reckoned with. We were impressed by Hamilton's tight plotting; his well-rendered settings, from the glitz of Bangkok to the grit of Guyana; and his ability to portray a wide range of sharply individualized characters in clean but sophisticated prose."

— Judges' Citation, Arthur Ellis Award for Best First Novel

"Ava Lee is tough, fearless, quirky, and resourceful, and she has more — well, you know — than a dozen male detectives I can think of... Hamilton has created a true original in Ava Lee."

— Linwood Barclay, author of *No Time for Goodbye*

"If the other novels [in the series] are half as good as this debut by Ian Hamilton, then readers are going to celebrate. Hamilton has created a marvellous character in Ava Lee... This is a terrific story that's certain to be on the Arthur Ellis Best First Novel list."

— *Globe and Mail*

"[Ava Lee's] lethal knowledge... torques up her sex appeal to the approximate level of a female lead in a Quentin Tarantino film."

— *National Post*

"The heroine in *The Water Rat of Wanchai* by Ian Hamilton sounds too good to be true, but the heroics work better that way... formidable... The story breezes along with something close to total clarity... Ava is unbeatable at just about everything. Just wait for her to roll out her bak mei against the bad guys. She's perfect. She's fast."

— *Toronto Star*

"Imagine a book about a forensic accountant that has tension, suspense, and action... When the central character looks like Lucy Liu, kicks like Jackie Chan, and has a travel budget like Donald Trump, the story is anything but boring. *The Water Rat of Wanchai* is such a beast... I look forward to the next one, *The Disciple of Las Vegas*."
— *Montreal Gazette*

"[A] tomb-raiding Dragon Lady Lisbeth, *sans* tattoo and face metal."
— *Winnipeg Free Press*

"Readers will discern in Ava undertones of Lisbeth Salander, the ferocious protagonist of the late Stieg Larsson's crime novels... she, too, is essentially a loner, and small, and physically brutal... There are suggestions in *The Water Rat of Wanchai* of deeper complexities waiting to be more fully revealed. Plus there's pleasure, both for Ava and readers, in the puzzle itself: in figuring out where money has gone, how to get it back, and which humans, helpful or malevolent, are to be dealt with where, and in what ways, in the process... Irresistible." — Joan Barfoot, *London Free Press*

"*The Water Rat of Wanchai* delivers on all fronts... feels like the beginning of a crime-fighting saga... great story told with colour, energy, and unexpected punch." — *Hamilton Spectator*

"The best series fiction leaves readers immersed in a world that is both familiar and fresh. Seeds planted early bear fruit later on, creating a rich forest that blooms across a number of books... [Hamilton] creates a terrific atmosphere of suspense..." — *Quill & Quire*

"The book is an absolute page-turner... Hamilton's knack for writing snappy dialogue is evident... I recommend getting in on the ground floor with this character, because for Ava Lee, the sky's the limit." — *Inside Halton*

"A fascinating story of a hunt for stolen millions. And the hunter, Ava Lee, is a compelling heroine: tough, smart, and resourceful."
— Meg Gardiner, author of *The Nightmare Thief*

"Few heroines are as feisty as *The Girl with the Dragon Tattoo*'s Lisbeth Salander, but Ian Hamilton's Ava Lee could give her a run for her money... Gripping... [Ava is] smart, gutsy, and resourceful."
— *Stylist UK*

"With Ava Lee comes a new star in the world of crime-thrillers... Hamilton has produced a suspenseful and gripping novel featuring a woman who is not afraid of anything... Captivating and hard to put down."
— *dapd/sda*

"Thrillers don't always have to be Scandinavian to work. Ava Lee is a wonderful Chinese-Canadian investigator who uses unconventional methods of investigation in a mysterious Eastern setting."
— *Elle* (Germany)

"Ava has flair, charm, and sex appeal... *The Water Rat of Wanchai* is a successful first book in a series, which will definitely have you longing for more."
— *Sonntag-Express*

"Hamilton is in the process of writing six books and film rights have already been sold. If the other cases are similar to this first one, Ava Lee is sure to quickly shake up Germany's thriller business."
— *Handelsblatt*

"Brilliantly researched and incredibly exciting!"
— *Bücher*

"Page-turning till the end of the book!... Ava Lee is the upcoming crime star."
— *dpa*

"Exciting thriller debut with an astonishing end."
— *Westdeutsche Zeitung*

"Seldom does one get a thriller about white-collar crime, with an intelligent, independent lesbian and Asian protagonist. It's also rare to find a book with such interesting and exotic settings... Readers will find great amusement in Ava's unconventional ways and will certainly enjoy accompanying her on her travels"
— *Literaturkurier*

PRAISE FOR THE DISCIPLE OF LAS VEGAS

"I started to read *The Disciple of Las Vegas* at around ten at night. And I did something I have only done with two other books (Cormac McCarthy's *The Road* and Douglas Coupland's *Player One*): I read the novel in one sitting. Ava Lee is too cool. She wonderfully straddles two worlds and two identities. She does some dastardly things and still remains our hero thanks to the charm Ian Hamilton has given her on the printed page. It would take a female George Clooney to portray her in a film. The action and plot move quickly and with power. Wow. A punch to the ear, indeed."

— J. J. Lee, author of *The Measure of a Man*

"I loved *The Water Rat of Wanchai,* the first novel featuring Ava Lee. Now, Ava and Uncle make a return that's even better... Simply irresistible." — Margaret Cannon, *Globe and Mail*

"This is slick, fast-moving escapism reminiscent of Ian Fleming, with more to come in what shapes up as a high-energy, high-concept series." — *Booklist*

"Fast paced... Enough personal depth to lift this thriller above solely action-oriented fare." — *Publishers Weekly*

"Lee is a hugely original creation, and Hamilton packs his adventure with interesting facts and plenty of action." — *Irish Independent*

"Hamilton makes each page crackle with the kind of energy that could easily jump to the movie screen... This riveting read will keep you up late at night." — *Penthouse*

"Hamilton gives his reader plenty to think about... Entertaining."

— *Kitchener-Waterloo Record*

PRAISE FOR THE WILD BEASTS OF WUHAN

"Smart and savvy Ava Lee, Toronto forensic accountant, returns in this slick mystery set in the rarefied world of high art... [A] great caper tale. Hamilton has great fun chasing villains and tossing clues about. *The Wild Beasts of Wuhan* is the best Ava Lee novel yet, and promises more and better to come."

— Margaret Cannon, *Globe and Mail*

"One of my favourite new mystery series, perfect escapism."

— *National Post*

"You haven't seen cold and calculating until you've double-crossed this number cruncher. Another strong entry from Arthur Ellis Award–winner Hamilton."

— *Booklist*

"An intelligent kick-ass heroine anchors Canadian author Hamilton's excellent third novel featuring forensic accountant Ava Lee... Clearly conversant with the art world, Hamilton makes the intricacies of forgery as interesting as a Ponzi scheme."

— *Publishers Weekly*, STARRED review

"A lively series about Ava Lee, a sexy forensic financial investigator."

— *Tampa Bay Times*

"This book is miles from the ordinary. The main character, Ava Lee is 'the whole package.'"

— *Minneapolis Star Tribune*

"A strong heroine is challenged to discover the details of an intercontinental art scheme. Although Hamilton's star Ava Lee is technically a forensic accountant, she's more badass private investigator than desk jockey."

— *Kirkus Reviews*

"As a mystery lover, I'm devouring each book as it comes out... What I love in the novels: The constant travel, the high-stakes negotiation, and Ava's willingness to go into battle against formidable opponents, using only her martial arts skills to defend herself... If you want a great read and an education in high-level business dealings, Ian Hamilton is an author to watch."

— *Toronto Star*

"Fast-paced and very entertaining." — *Montreal Gazette*

"Ava Lee is definitely a winner." — *Saskatoon Star Phoenix*

"*The Wild Beasts of Wuhan* is an entertaining dip into potentially fatal worlds of artistic skulduggery." — *Sudbury Star*

"Hamilton uses Ava's investigations as comprehensive and intriguing mechanisms for plot and character development."

— *Quill & Quire*

PRAISE FOR THE RED POLE OF MACAU

"Ava Lee returns as one of crime fiction's most intriguing characters. *The Red Pole of Macau* is the best page-turner of the season from the hottest writer in the business!"

— John Lawrence Reynolds, author of *Beach Strip*

"Ava Lee, that wily, wonderful hunter of nasty business brutes, is back in her best adventure ever... If you haven't yet discovered Ava Lee, start here." — *Globe and Mail*

"The best in the series so far." — *London Free Press*

"Ava [Lee] is a character we all could use at one time or another. Failing that, we follow her in her best adventure yet."

— *Hamilton Spectator*

"A romp of a story with a terrific heroine."

— *Saskatoon Star Phoenix*

"Fast-paced... The action unfolds like a well-oiled action flick."

— *Kitchener-Waterloo Record*

"A change of pace for our girl [Ava Lee]... Suspenseful."

— *Toronto Star*

"Hamilton packs tremendous potential in his heroine...A refreshingly relevant series. This reader will happily pay House of Anansi for the fifth instalment." — *Canadian Literature*

PRAISE FOR THE SCOTTISH BANKER OF SURABAYA

"Hamilton deepens Ava's character, and imbues her with greater mettle and emotional fire, to the extent that book five is his best, most memorable, to date." — *National Post*

"In today's crowded mystery market, it's no easy feat coming up with a protagonist who stands out from the pack. But local novelist Ian Hamilton has made a great job of it with his Ava Lee books. Young, stylish, Chinese Canadian, lesbian, and a brilliant forensic accountant, Ava is as complex a character as you could want... [A] highly addictive series...Hamilton knows how to keep the pages turning. He eases us into the seemingly tame world of white-collar crime, then raises the stakes, bringing the action to its peak with an intensity and violence that's stomach churning. His Ava Lee is a winner and a welcome addition to the world of strong female avengers." — *NOW* Magazine

"Most of the series's success rests in Hamilton's tight plotting, attention to detail, and complex powerhouse of a heroine: strong but vulnerable, capable but not impervious...With their tight plotting and crackerjack heroine, Hamilton's novels are the sort of crowd-pleasing, narrative-focused fiction we find all too rarely in this country." — *Quill & Quire*

"Ava is such a cool character, intelligent, Chinese-Canadian, unconventional, and original...Irresistible." — *Owen Sound Sun Times*

Also in the Ava Lee Series

The Disciple of Las Vegas
The Wild Beasts of Wuhan
The Red Pole of Macau
The Scottish Banker of Surabaya
The Two Sisters of Borneo
The King of Shanghai

THE WATER RAT OF WANCHAI

AN AVA LEE NOVEL

THIS EDITION INCLUDES:

THE DRAGON HEAD OF HONG KONG

THE AVA LEE PREQUEL

IAN HAMILTON

This edition published in 2014 by
House of Anansi Press Inc.
110 Spadina Avenue, Suite 801
Toronto, ON, M5V 2K4
Tel. 416-363-4343
Fax 416-363-1017
www.houseofanansi.com

19 18 17 16 15 2 3 4 5 6

Library and Archives Canada Cataloguing in Publication

Hamilton, Ian, 1946–
[Novels. Selections]
The water rat of Wanchai ; and, the dragon head of Hong Kong / Ian Hamilton.

(An Ava Lee novel)
The water rat of Wanchai was previously published in 2011.
Issued in print and electronic formats.
Water rat of Wanchai ; and, the dragon head of Hong Kong.
ISBN 978-1-77089-811-0 (pbk.).—ISBN 978-1-77089-812-7 (html)

I. Title. II. Title: Dragon head of Hong Kong. III. Series: Hamilton, Ian, 1946– Ava Lee novel

PS8615.A4423A6 2014 C813'.6 C2013-907049-4
C2013-907050-8

Cover design: Gregg Kulick
Text design and typesetting: Alysia Shewchuk

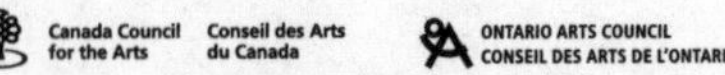

We acknowledge for their financial support of our publishing program the Canada Council for the Arts, the Ontario Arts Council, and the Government of Canada through the Canada Book Fund.

Printed and bound in Canada

For La

CONTENTS

THE DRAGON HEAD OF HONG KONG

THE AVA LEE PREQUEL

(1)

SHE SAW HIM WHEN SHE STEPPED OUT OF THE elevator. He was at the far end of the hall near her office, a small figure sitting on the floor, his arms wrapped around his legs and his forehead resting on his knees. He didn't seem familiar until he looked up in response to her approaching footsteps.

"Mr. Lo?" she said.

His eyes were bloodshot and had dark circles underneath. There was dry saliva at the left corner of his mouth, and it appeared as if he hadn't shaved for a few days. She thought he had been drinking or crying, or both.

"I needed to see you," he said in a hoarse voice as he struggled to his feet.

Ava Lee unlocked the door to her one-room office. "Come in," she said.

He followed her and sat in one of the two chairs she had for visitors. She sat behind the metal desk, which was next to a filing cabinet. That was all the furniture she had. There was no pretence that this was anything but a small business. Her accounting firm was only five months old, and the few clients Ava had were either friends of her mother or people attached to them. Mr. Lo's wife was a frequent mah-jong companion of Jennie Lee.

"You seem troubled," Ava said.

"I'm ruined," he said, shaking his head, his eyes averted.

"Mr. Lo, things can't be that bad."

"I can't get the guy in Hong Kong to pay me."

"Kung Imports?"

"Yes, him, Johnny Kung."

"I thought you had stopped shipping chicken feet to him when he fell behind in payments. And, when he did pay you, for making all those deductions from your invoices for what he claimed were quality issues."

"He talked me into sending another three containers."

"Good grief. So how many does he owe for now?"

"Nine."

"What is he giving you as his reason for not paying?"

"I don't know. He won't talk to me. He isn't answering emails. He isn't taking my phone calls. I'm not even sure if his office is still open."

"Two months ago you expressed some reservations about him, when the quality claims kept increasing."

"I did."

"But you still sent him another three containers?" Ava asked, and then saw the pain her words caused flash across Lo's face. "I'm sorry, I don't mean to second-guess you."

"That is something I'd better get used to — I'm going to hear enough of it from my wife. Kung owes me a million dollars, and half of that money was loaned to me by my brother-in-law."

Ava knew of Mrs. Lo only from her mother, who described her as a ferocious mah-jong player. Her mother didn't use words like *ferocious* lightly. Ava felt a twinge of sympathy for the small middle-aged man sitting across from her.

"Is there nothing you can do?" she asked.

"Like what?"

"Have you thought about getting a lawyer, or going to a collection agency?"

"A lawyer would take too long and I don't have that kind of time. I did contact a collection agency in Hong Kong, but when I mentioned Kung's name, they backed off."

"What did they offer as a reason?"

"They said they had done the dance with him before and that it was a waste of effort," Lo said, his voice breaking.

"Why a waste?"

"He's slippery. He moves money in and out of different company accounts and banks."

"And you had no idea he operated like that when you started doing business with him?"

He grimaced. "He was recommended to me by the brother of a friend."

"Mr. Lo, I have tremendous sympathy for you," she said. She didn't want to deride the Chinese tendency to value even a tenuous family connection more than proper due diligence when it came to doing business. "What I'm not sure about is why you have come to see me."

"When I was thinking about becoming a client, one of the things that convinced me to go with you was that my wife told me you weren't just an ordinary accountant," he said.

"She was paying too much attention to my mother," Ava said.

"So you aren't a forensic accountant?"

"Actually, I am trained as one, and I did work as one for

a while, but all I provide here is more traditional, straightforward accounting services."

He slid forward in the chair until his knees were touching her desk. He stared at her. "But you know how to track money, right?"

"Yes, that was part of my training."

"So help me, please," he said in a rush. "Find my money. I'm sure Kung has sold off the containers. The money is somewhere."

"Mr. Lo, even if I can locate the money, how do you expect we'll get our hands on it?"

His chin slumped onto his chest and he stared at his feet. "I don't know, but I can't just do nothing. I can't leave things the way they are. The pressure at home from my wife and from my brother-in-law is going to be unbearable. But I know that if I tell her you're looking into it, it will buy me some time."

"I honestly don't know enough about how things operate in Hong Kong and China to be of much help."

"Please."

Ava sighed. "Look, I'll make some phone calls tonight to some people who do know how things work there. I can't promise you any more than that."

"So you aren't saying no?"

"Or yes."

"That's good enough."

How desperate is this man? she thought. "Okay, so we'll leave it at that. I'll contact you sometime tomorrow and let you know what I've decided to do."

(2)

AVA WAS WALKING HOME TO HER ONE-BEDROOM apartment on Leslie Street, just south of Highway 7. She lived in Richmond Hill, a northern Toronto suburb with a large Chinese population. She would have preferred to live in the city centre, but when she had returned to Canada after graduating from Babson College in Wellesley, Massachusetts, her entry-level salary from the multinational accounting firm that hired her couldn't support a downtown lifestyle. So for practical reasons, Ava had located in the north. It wasn't entirely a hardship. She was spared the agony of what would have been an hour-long commute from the city to the office; there were at least fifty Chinese restaurants within a fifteen-minute walk from her apartment; and her mother's house was only a slightly longer walk away.

Her mother had asked Ava if she wanted to move back into the family home. Ava thought about that for less than ten seconds before saying no, and her mother seemed relieved. The two were close but they were different, and they both understood that living together for prolonged periods of time wasn't healthy for their relationship.

Among other things, Jennie Lee was a night person who thought nothing of dusk-to-dawn mah-jong games. When Ava was growing up, it wasn't unusual for her mother to be coming home as Ava headed out for her daily morning run.

Ava's job with the multinational had lasted for just over three months. Her resignation was mutually agreed upon. She had a strong mind and found it difficult to take instructions blindly from people who knew less than she did. Even when working alone she found it tough to follow corporate guidelines and regulations that she found inflexible and often wanting. And the firm wasn't about to let her operate as she saw fit.

She interviewed for other jobs and was offered several, but she immediately got cold feet at the thought of being locked into another bureaucracy. And the jobs that wouldn't encumber her independent nature tended to be mundane, involving more bookkeeping than accounting. Jennie Lee had come to her rescue. Not only did she suggest that Ava set up her own company, she had already lined up a handful of clients, including Mr. Lo, whose business was the most interesting.

Mr. Lo had been quite cocky when Ava first met him. He had found a poultry farm in rural Ontario that wasn't exporting its chicken feet and had no idea of their real value. Lo was able to buy them at about half the going market rate. He had been doing this for six months before Ava became his accountant. Lo had managed to talk the farmer into signing a one-year contract, with a right-of-first-refusal clause for a second year. Lo wasn't stupid; he knew the farmer would eventually be contacted by other buyers and that his price would go up. His aim was to ship as much as he could in that first year.

Lo had started slowly and carefully. At first he had three Hong Kong–based customers, but it turned out the supply wasn't large enough to meet their demands. Any one of them could have taken all the production, and they each agitated to do exactly that. Kung Imports finally offered him a premium above his price and convinced Lo to drop the other clients. In the beginning, Kung paid by wire transfer upon receipt of the bills of lading. Those terms were modified to payment after customs and health department clearance, and that's when the trouble started. Every shipment seemed to be held up by the health department, which refused to release the products to Kung for sale — or so Lo was told by Kung. Eventually some shipments were released and paid for. But because Lo kept shipping more product and because those shipments were being tied up by the health department, the unpaid invoices began to accumulate.

Ava had advised Lo to stop until the accounts were settled, but his contract with the farmer was nearing the end of its first year and he was anxious to export as much product as he could. When she asked him what kind of man Kung was, he replied, "I met him in Hong Kong. We had several dinners and he took me to his club on the Kowloon side. He showed me around his warehouse and his office. It's a big operation. He looked like a guy I could trust."

"What about your friend's brother, the one who recommended Kung to you? What does he have to say about this?"

"He said he met Kung socially and never did business with him."

"Will he call Kung for you?"

Lo shook his head. "He said he didn't want to get in the middle."

It was six o'clock when Ava opened her apartment door. It was about eight hundred square feet and furnished with old couches and chairs from her mother's basement and garage, and a few items she had cared enough about to bring back from Wellesley. She went into the bedroom to change. She slipped off her white button-down shirt and a pair of black cotton slacks she had bought at the Brooks Brothers store on Newbury Street in Boston. She had never worn Brooks Brothers before going to work, but now it was basically all she ever wore for business. She thought the clothes imparted a professional image. She also didn't have to tax her imagination every morning when it came to clothing choice.

She hung the shirt and slacks on the closet door to air and put on her Adidas training pants and a plain black T-shirt. When she returned to the living room, she saw that the message light on her phone was blinking. That surprised her. Her mother and most of her friends called her cellphone. She dialled the access code, expecting to hear a sales pitch.

"Ava, this is Mummy. Call me when you can," Jennie Lee said. "I tried your cellphone. It's off."

Her mother sounded upset, and it was with some nervousness that Ava dialled her number.

"*Wei*," the familiar voice said.

"Mummy, is everything all right?"

"Your cellphone is off."

"I know. I just realized that I turned it off during lunch with Mimi and left it in my purse all afternoon. Is that why you're calling?"

"Of course not, Ava. Did you meet with Hedrick Lo this afternoon?"

"Yes, I did."

"Did you make him any promises?"

"Like what?"

"Did you tell him you would help him get back some of the money he is owed?"

"No. He asked me to, but all I said was that I would have to think about it."

"Well, that isn't what he's telling Jessica Lo."

"That son of a bitch is twisting my words," Ava said and then paused. "I'm sorry, I didn't mean to be rude about a client."

"Jessica is saying worse things than that about him," Jennie said. "Jessica says he's an aggravating man at the best of times, and right now she says the times are not very rosy. How bad are his problems?"

"Mummy, I'm not sure I should be sharing that kind of information with you."

"You aren't a lawyer or a doctor. I didn't know accountants had to swear an oath of secrecy."

"We don't, but there are ethical boundaries."

"Jessica sent him to you, and all the money that he's been using to finance his business is from her and her family."

Ava heard her mother take a deep breath and pictured her dragging on a cigarette. "What has he told her?"

"Not much, and that's the problem. He came home this afternoon looking worried, and when she pressed him, he told her there were some issues with the client in Hong Kong. He said he was having trouble getting fully paid but that she wasn't to be concerned because you were looking after it."

"Good God."

"So it isn't true?"

"Some of it is."

"Ava, how much money is involved?"

"Enough."

"Poor Jessica," Jennie said. "Ava, do you think you could actually help Lo?"

"I'm trained to find money that's gone missing, but finding it and getting it back are two different things. In Canada I could take someone to court. He was shipping to Hong Kong. I have no idea how their law works."

"I can tell you one thing," Jennie said. "There's no such thing as bankruptcy there."

"What do you mean?"

"I mean you can declare bankruptcy, but that doesn't mean the people you owe money to will just go away," Jennie said. "Beyond that, I don't know. The person you should talk to is your father. There isn't much that he doesn't know about doing business in Hong Kong and China. I'm sure he would love the chance to discuss it with you."

"Maybe I will. If not for Mr. Lo, then for future reference."

"Oh, Ava, please do it for Lo if you can," her mother said suddenly. "Jessica's family is high-powered and successful. They've been looking down on Lo for years. This little venture of his has improved his status with them, and it would be a shame if it fell apart. If he loses the money they put into the business, they'll make the rest of his life a living hell."

"Did Mrs. Lo tell you that?"

"Yes. Despite her complaints, she does care about him, almost more than about the money. And her reputation — her face — is tied up with his."

"I'll tell you what, I'll call Daddy. I'll make up my mind about what to do after I talk to him."

"Normally he leaves the house after eight o'clock. Don't call him until then. He won't be able to have a conversation."

"I understand," Ava said.

(3)

MARCUS LEE WAS THE FATHER OF AVA AND HER older sister Marian. He was also the father of four sons from his first wife, and the father of a son and daughter from a third wife. The marriage to the first wife was legal; his second and third were traditional and more form than substance. He still lived with the first wife in Hong Kong. Jennie Lee had been shipped off to Canada when Marian was four years old and Ava was two. The third wife had appeared much later, had given him two more children, and was now living in Australia.

It was, by Western standards, a strange family structure. But in Hong Kong it wasn't that unusual among the wealthy for a man to have more than one wife and family. There were rules of engagement, and as long as everyone followed those rules, the system worked.

Jennie had been working in a company that Marcus owned when they met. They fell in love, embarked on their marriage of sorts, and the girls followed. She knew from the outset that he would never leave his first wife, and that his sons would inherit his estate when he passed. She thought she could manage the situation, but her emotions eventually got the best of her. When things got really bad, Marcus sent her to Vancouver. She lasted two years there before the cold and the dampness got to her. Then she and the girls moved to Toronto and settled in Richmond Hill.

Oddly, the distance between Marcus and Jennie saved their relationship. They talked every day on the phone and he spent two weeks a year with her. He loved the girls, and he supported them and Jennie in a style that was comfortable if not luxurious. He had bought her a house, paid for a new car every three years, provided a monthly allowance, and covered the expenses of the girls' private-school education and extracurricular activities.

To Ava's knowledge there had never been another man in Jennie's life. As far as her mother was concerned, Marcus was her husband and he had her complete loyalty. Similarly, both Marian and Ava never thought of him as anything but their father. That they saw him for only two weeks a year wasn't that much different from the lives of their Chinese friends at school. There were, Ava realized later, a great many second and third wives in Toronto. Her mother said that Toronto's most elite private schools would be half-empty without their offspring.

When Ava was in her late teens, her relationship with her father began a subtle change. Instead of communicating with her through Jennie, he would call her directly. He had a keen interest in her education, making quiet comparisons between her progress through the accounting programs at York University and Babson and the educations his sons were receiving. She knew Marcus often spoke to Jennie about his other children, but she found it awkward when he did so with her. Still, she listened politely and didn't ask if he was as open with his first wife and four sons when it came to the subject of his Canadian family.

Ava looked at her watch and saw that it was too early to call Hong Kong. She reheated some noodles with shrimp in the microwave and sat on the couch to watch television. The couch had come from her mother's basement. Marian had lost her virginity on it. Ava had lost hers in her dorm, to the captain of the women's soccer team, when she was a freshman at York University.

Hong Kong was twelve hours ahead of Toronto, so Ava waited until eight thirty before she phoned, figuring that her father would be in his car by then, working his way down Victoria Peak to his office in Central. She dialled his cell.

"Hello, sweetheart," he said after two rings.

"I hope this is convenient," she said.

"I'm in the car."

"So you can talk?"

"Of course, but it's rather strange for you to call like this. Has something happened to Mummy?"

"No, she's fine. I have a business problem I wanted to discuss with you."

"This has to do with your new business?"

"Yes."

"Mummy said it was going well."

"Well enough, but I have a client who has a problem," she said. "He's been shipping containers of chicken feet to Hong Kong and the buyer has decided to renege on paying the invoices."

"My knowledge of chicken feet is restricted to ordering them in a restaurant."

"My client is owed a million dollars."

"Hong Kong?"

"American."

"That's serious."

"He's asked me to try to locate the money. That's something I'm trained to do, but I have no idea what legal remedies are available to us in Hong Kong if I do find it."

"Has the importer been making quality claims?"

"How did you know that?"

"It's the oldest con game around. They say there's a quality problem with the shipment and use that as an excuse not to pay or to heavily discount. Of course, they suck in the exporter by paying in full for the initial loads before the claims start. But once they start, they escalate. And if your client doesn't buy the lies and decides to sue, the importer throws the claims at you and keeps you tied up legally for months. Once he thinks he's exhausted the law, he just stops negotiating and disappears."

"Have you gone through something like this?"

"No, but I can send you to ten people who have."

"What do they do about it? My client has gone to collection agencies, but none of them seem to want to take it on."

"Is the importer triad?" Marcus Lee asked quietly.

Ava paused. "I have no idea."

"That's one possibility. The other is that he's just smart. It isn't hard to set up a company in Hong Kong and then in Guangzhou and Shenzhen and move around the goods and the money. The law gets complicated."

"I'm told he's smart."

"Then it will be difficult."

"What if I find the money? Is there anything I can do to claw it back?"

"Ava, you're getting into some dangerous waters."

"Daddy, I'm only asking what's possible."

"Normally — and I'm telling you this second-hand, you understand — finding the money is the least important part of the equation for the people here who are expert at collecting debts. The first thing they want is the debtor. Once they have their hands on him, the money — or what's left of it — has a way of coming home."

"I see."

"Do you?"

"I think so."

"It isn't the kind of thing you want to be involved in."

"What do they charge to collect a debt?"

"Ava!"

"I'm just asking."

He paused and Ava expected him to put her off. "Thirty percent," he said.

"Wow."

"I know it sounds like a lot, but it's the going rate," Marcus Lee said. "So what are you thinking of doing about this client of yours?"

"He needs help."

"And you're trained to provide it," Marcus said, and then paused. "I have to say I was a little surprised when your mother told me about your new venture. Never mind that all those years at York and Babson equipped you to do more. All I kept thinking was how bored you must be. You've always struck me as a girl who has a very low threshold for boredom."

"I wouldn't do this because I'm bored," Ava said, surprised that her father could read her so well. "I would only do it if I thought I could help Mr. Lo."

(4)

SHE DIDN'T SLEEP WELL. HER CONVERSATION with her father kept circling around her head. He was right; she was bored. All those years of education were being wasted doing basic accounting for people who could do it themselves if they bothered. And the amount of money Lo had lost wasn't insignificant, she told herself. It was certainly worth an effort to recover it. Then she smiled. Even if she got back only a tenth of what was owed, she wanted to go after it, as long as Lo was prepared to pay at least her expenses.

She called him at nine o'clock. "Mr. Lo, this is Ava Lee. I've been thinking about Kung Imports. Could you come by my office around ten?"

"Are you going to go after him?"

"Is ten okay?"

"Does this mean you've decided to do it?"

"I need to talk to you before I make my final decision, and I don't want to do it over the phone."

"I'll be there."

"And just in case, please bring all the contact information you have for Kung. I want every phone number, every address, and the names of everyone you know who is acquainted with him. If you have any photos of him, bring those too."

Lo showed up on time and sat in the same chair he had the day before. But this was a different man. The desperation was gone from his eyes and his demeanour seemed, if not confident, at least composed.

"My wife sends her regards, and her thanks for taking this on for us," he said.

"We need to discuss my terms before that becomes a reality."

"I'm sure they will be reasonable," he said. "Besides, at this point you're my only option. I can't imagine what you might ask for that I can't agree to."

Ava stared at him across the desk, not sure if he was being sincere or if he was in some sly way appealing to her sense of fairness. "You do understand that I'll have to go to Hong Kong. I can't do this from here."

"Yes."

"And you will have to pay my expenses."

"*Momentai.*"

"I won't go crazy, so don't worry about that."

"I'm not worried," he said, and paused. "Would you object, though, to using some Marco Polo miles I have, to book your flight on Cathay Pacific?"

"No, I guess not."

"And the hotel I stayed in last time was a good deal for Hong Kong."

"As long as it's clean and well situated."

"It's both," he said. "Once I know when you're leaving, I'll book it for you."

"Thanks," Ava said, keenly aware that, only option or

not, Lo was already negotiating. "Now there's the question of my fee."

"What do you want, some daily rate?"

"I thought about that and decided against it. I mean, I could spend two weeks traipsing around Hong Kong and not recover a dollar, and you'd be out of pocket even more money," she said. "I think the fairest thing is for me to take a percentage of whatever money I can recover."

"Do you have a number in mind?" he said carefully.

"I made some phone calls last night. The people I spoke to told me that collection agencies in Hong Kong normally charge thirty percent."

His face fell.

"Mr. Lo, you told me you contacted some collection agencies there. Is that number inaccurate?"

"No, but there weren't any expenses involved."

"You weren't their client, and you are mine. So, given the nature of our relationship and the expenses being paid, I am proposing that I keep ten percent of what I collect."

"Do we deduct your expenses from that?"

"No."

"I wasn't being picky," he said quickly in response to her firm tone. "I just wanted things to be clear."

"And are they?"

"Yes."

"Well then, you should book me on the earliest possible flight to Hong Kong and organize the hotel. Now, did you bring the information I asked for?"

He slid a large brown envelope across the desk. "Everything I have on Kung is in here."

(5)

THE CATHAY PACIFIC PLANE BEGAN ITS SLOW and steady descent to Chek Lap Kok airport almost an hour before it was scheduled to land. This would be Ava's fourth trip to Hong Kong. The other three had been with her mother and sister to visit Jennie's family and friends there. They hadn't seen Marcus — or at least the girls hadn't. Jennie had left them alone in their hotel room on two nights, saying that she had mah-jong games. Marian believed her. Ava didn't.

"Will you see your father?" Jennie had asked when Ava told her that she was going to Hong Kong to try to help Hedrick Lo.

"I don't have any plans to. I'm there on business."

"Still, you won't mind if I tell him that you're there?"

"No."

"What hotel did you book?"

"The Oriental Crocus."

"I've never heard of it. Is it part of the Mandarin Oriental chain?"

"Hardly. It's a three-star hotel in Mong Kok."

"Why did you choose that?"

"I didn't. Mr. Lo did. He's paying."

"He's cheap."

"He told me he's stayed there himself and it isn't so bad. The office of the importer he was working with is nearby, so it's convenient."

"He probably wants to save money on taxis. Or did he actually tell you to take the MTR?"

"Mummy, you're the one who asked me to help him."

"I know." Jennie sighed. "It's just that the idea of you going to Hong Kong alone is kind of odd. You've never been there without me. I want to feel that you're safe, and a three-star hotel in Mong Kok doesn't sound secure."

"You know I'm perfectly capable of looking after myself."

"I still worry."

"Don't, and don't harass me when I'm there either, or ask Daddy to check up on me. I'm going there to work. I don't need to be babysat and I don't need any distractions."

Jennie became quiet, and Ava knew her mother was probably offended by her directness and her tone. This was how many of the conversations between them ended — Ava declaring her independence; her mother acting hurt; Ava saying, "I'm sorry, I know you love me"; and Jennie replying, "I know, and I also know you will do exactly whatever you want to do regardless of what I say." This time Ava added, "I do promise that if I run into any serious problems, I'll call Daddy."

Ava had taken a limousine to Pearson International Airport to catch the Cathay flight. It departed at ten thirty in the evening and, after crossing the international dateline, would land her in Hong Kong at six in the morning two days later. She spent most of the day of her departure fussing about what to take with her. Her travel experience was limited to holidays, when she packed casual clothes, and major upheavals such as moving from Toronto to Wellesley, when she took just about everything she owned. This was her first extended business trip and she was unsure about what to pack. She finally decided to restrict herself to business wear and her running gear. Four Brooks Brothers shirts, two pairs of black slacks, a pencil skirt, two pairs of pumps, slippers, underwear for a week, and her cosmetics bag filled a suitcase. She stuffed her running shorts, socks, and T-shirts into a carry-on and wore her running shoes, track pants, and jacket to the airport.

Because it was a last-minute booking, Ava was assigned a window seat in the rear of the economy section. She shared the row with an elderly Chinese couple, who told her they were going back to Hong Kong for Chinese New Year in March. Ava asked why they were going four weeks before the actual event.

"To visit with friends," the woman said in Cantonese. "Our children are in Toronto, but we still miss our Hong Kong friends."

Ava was fluent in Cantonese. It was the language spoken in her mother's house six days a week. Mandarin was Sunday's language, and Ava spoke it passably after ten years of Saturday classes and Sunday practice.

The flight took sixteen hours. After learning everything she could about her seatmates in less than an hour, Ava retreated to the video programming and then fell asleep. She woke somewhere over the Pacific with a burning need to pee. The Chinese couple had fallen asleep with their legs stretched out. The seats in front were pushed back as far as they could go. Ava would have to be part contortionist to slip between the seats and the couple and get to the aisle.

She was five feet three inches tall and weighed about a hundred and fifteen pounds. If she'd been larger or less lithe, she wouldn't have made it out and back without stepping on the elderly couple.

When she had settled back into her seat, she tried to sleep again, but it was already morning in Toronto and there was no convincing her body that it was otherwise. She reached into her bag and pulled out the paperwork that Lo had given her. There were multiple addresses and phone numbers for Kung Imports. Disconcertingly, the purchase orders didn't have a company address on them, other than "Mong Kok." There were phone and fax numbers and an email address on the POs, but Ava had tried them before she left Toronto. No one answered the phone or responded to her fax or email. She checked the wire transfers that Kung had sent to Lo. They had been issued by a bank in Shenzhen, not Hong Kong. Why hadn't she noticed that before? Well, for one thing, her job had been to make sure the money added up. It was Lo's responsibility to make sure he wasn't getting cheated.

The last thing she looked at was two pictures of Lo with the man he said was Kung. They were in a nightclub or karaoke bar. The men were sitting on a couch in front of a small round table that held several glasses and a bottle of Johnnie Walker Blue Label Scotch. Ava was no expert on Scotch, but she knew that Blue Label was the premium brand. Two women in evening dresses were draped over the men's shoulders; one of them had her tongue in Kung's ear. Both men had silly grins splashed across their faces. Ava had no idea how tall Kung was, but he was broad across the shoulders, and burly. He had a full head of black hair that was combed back, and his face was round and fleshy under the eyes and the jaw. The shape of his face was oddly out of sorts with a rather delicate nose and thin lips. *What an odd-looking man*, Ava thought.

She put the photos and the other paperwork back into the envelope and took out a pen and a Moleskine notebook from her bag. On top of the first page she wrote KUNG — LO and then detailed every fact she thought was relevant. Her plan was to find Kung and discuss the accounts payable situation in a professional, businesslike manner. If that didn't work, she would threaten him with lawsuits. If that failed, she would call on the banks with his purchase orders and Lo's invoices in hand and see if she could get their co-operation. Beyond that, she wasn't sure what else she could do.

As the plane continued to glide towards Hong Kong, Ava looked out the window and saw the first hint of morning sun. It peeked out from just beyond the horizon, the South China Sea glimmering under the light it cast. The sea was alive with ships. Ava counted more than twenty in her immediate view. Hong Kong was one of the world's largest container ports; the traffic below was waiting to enter the harbour, steaming towards it, or already fully loaded and headed out to another destination. The plane was flying low enough now that, among the massive tankers, freighters, and container ships, Ava could pick out sampans and what looked like fishing boats. It was, she thought, all so exotic — almost romantic — and it reminded her of how different life was in this part of the world.

There was nothing romantic about Chek Lap Kok. Within forty minutes of landing, Ava had disembarked, cleared Customs and Immigration, and collected her bag and was walking to the express train that would take her to Kowloon. The airport was built on reclaimed land on Lantau Island, to the southwest of Hong Kong. It replaced the old airport, Kai Tak, which had been situated on Kowloon Harbour.

The first time she had landed at Kai Tak she was ten, just old enough for it to make a lasting impression. Her mother had put her in the window seat and Marian in the middle, but as the plane weaved its way through the mountains that encircled the city, they had pushed against her so they could share the view. The South China Sea was beneath them and to the west; a long strip of a runway that jutted into the harbour was in front. To the east was Kowloon, its office and apartment buildings so close to the airport that Ava felt she could reach out the window and pluck laundry from apartment balconies.

Kai Tak was as congested as the neighbourhoods that surrounded it. The lineups at Immigration seemed endless. Baggage took forever to reach slow-moving carousels. Then there was the walk into the arrivals hall, where families and friends were crushed so close to the exit door that Ava was afraid she'd lose her mother in the melee.

"I love this airport," Jennie Lee had said, gripping her daughters' hands. "The instant you step through these doors, there's only one place in the world you can be."

Well, that's not true anymore, Ava thought, as she neared the train station. Chek Lap Kok had sister airports in Singapore and Kuala Lumpur, and she was sure more would follow. Modernization had become a mania in Asia.

She spotted an ATM outside the station and withdrew $5,000 Hong Kong, just less than $1,000 U.S. Then she waited ten minutes for the train that would take her over the Tsing Ma Bridge, a dual-decked structure that stretched one and a half kilometres over the Ma Wan Channel, more than sixty metres above the major shipping lane in and out of Hong Kong. The train was on the lower deck of the bridge. Above, three lanes of traffic moved in each direction. It never ceased to amaze Ava how efficient it all was.

It took only twenty minutes to get to Kowloon. Ava exited at Olympic station. The Mong Kok neighbourhood was to her east; to her south was Tsim Sha Tsui with its five-star hotels, expansive malls, and breathtaking view of the Central district of Hong Kong, across Victoria Harbour.

The air was cold and damp when she walked out of the station. Winter in Hong Kong was bone-numbing. Few of the homes — more than ninety-five percent of them apartments — had central heating, and inside and out the chill was pervasive. She took a cab to the Oriental Crocus. Mong Kok was fully alive with the morning commute, and as the cab inched eastward on Cherry Street and then north on Tong Mi Road, she began to wish she had taken the MTR.

Mong Kok was a working- and middle-class neighbourhood of modest-sized office buildings and older apartments lined up along narrow streets, interspersed with storefronts and restaurants that catered strictly to the locals. The driver had seemed to know where he was going when Ava mentioned her destination, but he still almost drove past the hotel. Its façade was no wider than two small storefronts, and if Ava hadn't spotted the name above the doorway they would have missed it. The moment she did see it, she wished she hadn't allowed Mr. Lo to make the reservation. On her trips to Hong Kong with her mother they had always stayed at the Mandarin Oriental in Central — a true five-star hotel that epitomized unobtrusive luxury. The Crocus was merely unobtrusive.

She walked into the lobby and was relieved to see that it was clean and airy. The hotel had nine floors and her room was on the eighth. When she opened the door, she felt a surge of regret. The room wasn't much bigger than a jail cell. It had a double bed, a small dresser, and a folding table and chair. She knew she would have to slide her luggage under the bed if she wanted room to turn around. She unpacked, putting her clothes in the dresser, pushed her bags under the bed, and then headed to the bathroom for a shower.

When she came back into the room, she sat on the bed and thought about what to do. Part of her was tired and the idea of crawling under the duvet was appealing, but she remembered from her previous trips how necessary it was to try to stay awake if she wanted to avoid serious jet lag. She reached out and took Lo's envelope from the table. She had printed out a map of Mong Kok and had marked where Kung's office was. It didn't look like more than a ten-minute walk from her hotel. It was time to put Plan A into action.

(6)

KUNG'S OFFICE WAS IN THE SERENITY BUILDING on Bute Street, which was a few blocks south off Tong Mi Road, close to the Nathan Road intersection. Ava knew of Nathan Road. It was one of the major north–south routes in Kowloon, and its southern terminus on Victoria Harbour was in the heart of Tsim Sha Tsui — home of the original Peninsula Hotel and some of the best shopping in the world. In Jennie Lee's mind, no trip to Hong Kong was complete without high tea at the Peninsula and a day spent shopping in the neighbourhood. Ava and Marian both lacked their mother's shopping gene, but they had gone with her and in the process got to know the south end of Kowloon.

Bute Street wouldn't hold Mummy's interest for a minute, Ava thought as she trudged along. It was all noodle restaurants and discount shops on the ground floors, with apartments in need of repair on top. The Serenity Building was just as shabby. It was six storeys of nothing but offices, and its grey stucco exterior was flaked and broken from street level to as far up as she could see.

The building lobby didn't inspire confidence either. Its

tiled floor was sticky and littered with cigarette butts. To the left of three elevators she saw a company directory. Kung Imports was listed as an occupant of suite 612.

As she stepped out of the elevator that had creaked and groaned all the way to the sixth floor, she found herself staring at one double door. She glanced right and left and saw nothing else. There seemed to be only one office on the floor. A computer printout was tacked to one of the door panels. When Ava drew close to it, she saw that it listed the companies that were, presumably, inside. There were at least ten, and all of them seemed to be involved in the import or trading business. She thought about Mr. Lo, talking about how impressive Kung's offices were, and wondered if he had actually been here.

She opened the door and found herself looking at a sea of desks. They ran from the door to a row of glass-panelled offices along the far wall, from one side of the room to the other. Most of the desks were occupied, and a steady buzz of one-sided phone conversations filled the air.

"Can I help you?" a woman's voice said.

Ava turned and saw a middle-aged woman wearing an orange T-shirt seated behind a desk. To her left were four empty chairs and a beat-up wooden coffee table.

"Is this reception?" Ava asked.

"I guess so," the woman said, pointing at a small sign on the corner of the desk that did indeed read RECEPTION. Next to it was another that read FAN YING.

Ava was wearing black slacks, black pumps, and a plain white button-down shirt, but she felt decidedly overdressed. Everyone else seemed to favour jeans and an eclectic mix of casual tops. She walked over to the woman. "I'm looking for Kung Imports."

"You mean you're looking for Johnny Kung," the woman said.

"Yes," Ava said.

"He isn't here."

"Then can I see someone else who works for the company?"

"There's only him."

"What, no secretary, assistant, or bookkeeper?"

The woman pushed her chair back and swivelled to the left. "See that empty desk over there in front of the last office? That desk is Kung Imports. That's all there is. We have close to thirty companies that rent offices and desks. They come and go. Kung Imports went, along with whatever records there were."

"Would you know where?"

"No."

"I see," Ava said, feeling flustered by the woman's abruptness.

"You're the third person in the past two weeks who's come here looking for him. I told them the same thing."

"And why did they say they wanted to see him?"

"They didn't, but from the looks of them there's money involved."

"How do you know that?"

The woman stared at Ava. "How old are you?"

"What does that matter?"

"Besides the fact that you're a woman, you seem a bit young to be in the collections business."

"What made you assume I was?"

"They're the only people who ever want to see Kung."

"Well, that's not my case," Ava said softly.

"No?" the woman said.

Ava took several small steps forward until she was at the desk and then leaned over. “Mrs. Fan, I’m here because of my sister,” she whispered.

“And why is that?”

“She’s been seeing Johnny Kung. Now she can’t find him.”

The woman shrugged.

“Auntie, my sister is nineteen years old. She met Johnny in a karaoke bar. He set her up in a small apartment in Hung Hom. Now he’s gone.”

“That’s normal enough.”

“Do you mean for Johnny?”

“For men in general, but Johnny is as general as any man can be.”

“Well, that doesn’t matter, because none of this is normal in my family. My sister was a student at the Polytech until she met him.”

“Then what was she doing in a karaoke bar?”

“She wasn’t a hostess, if that’s what you’re implying,” Ava snapped. “She had a part-time marketing job with a liquor importer. She went to the bars to promote their products. She said she was sampling Johnny Walker Blue Label when she met him.”

“I didn’t mean to insult your sister.”

“She’s beyond insults now. He hasn’t paid the rent in two months and she’s three months pregnant. The only reason I want to find him is to get him to live up to his responsibilities.”

“I’m sorry. I would help you if I could,” the woman said.

“Isn’t there anyone in here who might know where I can find him?” Ava said.

The woman hesitated and Ava saw her glance towards Kung’s empty desk.

"Please, Auntie," Ava said.

"Wait here for a minute," the woman said, rising from her chair.

Ava watched her walk towards and then past Kung's desk and enter one of the closed-in offices. A moment later, the man who was inside looked in Ava's direction. Ava hoped he wouldn't come out to talk to her. She was feeling self-conscious enough about the lie she had spun. She'd had no idea she could lie that well, but then, she had never really tried before.

Whatever they were talking about in the office, the conversation was getting more animated. It made her uncomfortable to watch. She sat in one of the chairs, out of their line of sight.

When the woman returned, she was carrying a piece of paper in her hand. "Here," she said, thrusting it towards Ava. "That's the name of a hotel in Shenzhen. My boss thinks that's where Kung is most likely to be."

"What makes him think that?"

"It's his normal hole in the ground when the collection boys are after him. He's in Shenzhen often enough that he even has an office there."

"How many collection boys are chasing him now?"

"Nosy little thing, aren't you?"

"I'm sorry, I know it's none of my business. I'm really grateful for your help."

"One more thing. My boss says that he doesn't use his real name when he's there."

"What name does he use?"

"If I knew that, I would have told you already."

"Yes, of course."

"Now, good luck to you."

(7)

SHE LEFT THE OFFICE ON BUTE STREET, DISAPPOINTED that Kung hadn't been there and discouraged by the reality that was Kung Imports. What had Kung shown Mr. Lo that convinced him he was dealing with a legitimate company? *Surely not that office*, she thought. But then, who knew what Lo had been told and what his state of mind was. Maybe he went there the morning after a night at the karaoke bar.

She was pleased with herself, though, for getting a lead. It was still early in the day, and it occurred to her that she probably had time to get to Shenzhen to check it out. Ava knew of the city but had never been there. Until 1979 it had been a small village at the very edge of Hong Kong's northern border with China; then it became the first of the special economic zones established by the Chinese government to attract foreign investment and create jobs. Premier Deng himself had travelled there to make the announcement. When questioned about cozying up to capitalists, he said, "When you own a cat, what does it matter if it is black or white? All that matters is that it catches mice." The village was now a city with a population that neared ten million. That was a lot of mice, and Ava had to assume Kung was one of them.

When she got back to the Oriental Crocus, she went directly to the check-in desk. "I need to go to Shenzhen today. Where can I catch a train and how long will it take?" she asked.

"You can get the train at the Mong Kok East MTR. It takes about forty-five minutes to Lo Wu station, which is the entry point from Hong Kong into Shenzhen," a young woman said.

"Thanks," Ava said, turning to leave.

"Excuse me," the woman called after her. "Do you have a visa for China?"

"No."

"You'll need one, but you can get it at Lo Wu when you arrive. The only problem is that the lines can be very long and slow. I thought I should warn you."

"Thanks again."

Ava rode the elevator to her room to collect her passport and the two photos of Kung that Lo had given her. She looked at the bed and quite suddenly felt an urge to sleep. She fought it off and headed downstairs.

"Now, where exactly is the Mong Kok East MTR?" she asked the same woman.

The station was a five-minute walk from the hotel. The morning rush hour was over, and she was able to buy her ticket and work her way onto the platform without getting pushed and jostled. She had experienced rush hour once, with her mother and Marian. It was something she never wanted to go through again. Getting to the train had been hard enough, but then they had to fight to get on it, her mother holding onto their hands for dear life, and survive being so tightly squeezed together that Ava couldn't move her arms.

The train to Shenzhen arrived half-empty and Ava was able to find a seat. At the first stop, Kowloon Tong, the train filled, but there was enough room for people to stand, so she could follow the train's progress through the New Territories and towns such as Tai Wai, Sha Tin, Tai Wo, and Fanling.

When Lo Wu was the next scheduled stop — by her watch, about five minutes away — she saw the other passengers begin to stand and move towards the exit doors. She had no doubt that when the train stopped, they would be making a mad dash towards the Chinese immigration booths. Part of her was tempted to join them, but then the thought of how unpleasant it would be to get caught up in the melee prevailed. She was one of the last people off the train.

It took twenty minutes to get to an immigration officer. He looked quickly at her passport and then directed her to a door with the words VISA APPLICATIONS above it. Thirty minutes and twenty dollars later she emerged with a five-day visa stapled into her passport.

There were two things she noticed immediately when she walked out of the station and into the city: everyone was speaking Mandarin, and Shenzhen seemed to be one gigantic construction site. She had been prepared for the Mandarin but not for the extent of the city's development. Stunned, she stood on the sidewalk and counted the cranes that were in plain view. When she got to forty, she stopped.

She walked to the taxi stand and got into a long, snaking line that was orderly and moved quickly. When she climbed into her cab, she was barely seated before it was moving. "The Good Luck Hotel," she said.

The driver's face fell. "So near," he said.

Ava pulled a Hong Kong $100 bill from her purse. "Here, will this make up for it?" she said.

"No renminbi?"

"Just Hong Kong."

He sighed and took the money from her.

The cab left the station, drove past two stoplights, made a right turn, and pulled up in front of the Good Luck Hotel. "If I'd known it was so close, I would have walked," Ava said.

The driver grunted.

She slid out from the back seat and stood in front of a large grey box dotted with small windows. If it weren't for the name on the sign, the hotel could have been mistaken for an office tower, or even a factory. She glanced both ways down the street. The aesthetic appeal wasn't any better. She had read that Shenzhen was a city that had been thrown together in a hurry rather than planned. It was all about function and purpose. The quality of city living was an issue for another day.

She walked through the revolving doors into the hotel lobby. It was as plain as the exterior, with a bare brown tile floor, a Styrofoam-panelled ceiling, and walls that lacked any decoration. It did look expansive, but that was mainly because it was sparsely furnished. There were only four sofas, ten chairs, and six coffee tables in an area that was about fifty metres long and thirty metres wide.

It was just past eleven thirty and the lobby was crowded. Three lines of people were checking out and two lines of people stood in front of empty desks that said CHECK IN. Ava didn't like their chances of seeing their rooms anytime soon.

Her plan had been to show her photos of Kung to hotel staff to see if anyone recognized him. There was no doorman and the front desk staff were busy, but there was a young man leaning on the baggage counter. Ava walked over to him. He stood erect as she drew near. He was no more than five foot six and rail thin. Ava wondered how he managed to lug the suitcases, some of which must have weighed as much as him.

"Do you need help with your bags?" he asked, smiling.

"No, but my uncle may. I've been waiting for him for about ten minutes and haven't seen him. Tell me, did you see him leave?" she asked, holding out one of the photos.

He shook his head.

"Have you seen him at all over the past few days? I was told he was staying here, but I haven't actually heard from him."

He took the photo from her and appeared to study it. "I don't recognize him, but I'll keep my eyes open now. This is a good vantage point because everyone has to walk by. Why don't you give me your phone number and I'll call you if I see him."

"I don't think that's such a good idea," Ava said, taken aback by his obvious flirtation.

"This isn't my real job, you know. I'm an engineering student at the university. I do this for pocket money."

"Thanks all the same," she said. "I'll sit on the other side of the lobby and watch for him myself."

Any ideas she had about sitting disappeared as soon as she got a good look at the couches and chairs. People were squeezed into every inch of them, and others hovered, waiting for an opening. Ava took up position against a wall that gave her a clear view of the hotel elevators and most of the lobby. To her left was a restaurant that had a long lineup of people, most of them with suitcases. She thought about eating but didn't have the patience to stand in line. Besides, she didn't want to risk missing Kung.

After leaning against the wall for half an hour, she was bored and tired, both states being aggravated by the fact that she wasn't convinced Kung was even in the hotel.

She crossed the lobby again. The bellboy greeted her with a smile.

"I've changed my mind," she said quickly. "I do want you to call me if you see my uncle. The only problem might be that my number is international."

"I can use one of the hotel phones, but it will cost me money."

"How much do you need?"

"Two hundred renminbi should be enough."

Ava took a Hong Kong $500 note from her purse. "Here, this will cover it and pay you something for your trouble. And if you do think you see him and it turns out to be him, I'll pay you another thousand."

"You must really like this uncle of yours."

"Never mind about that," she said, handing him one of her business cards. "My mobile number is the one on the bottom."

"I think you should leave me his photo as well. It'll help me and I can maybe show it around a bit. I mean, I want to be sure that I pick out the right guy."

"Yes," she said, without any feeling of confidence.

Ava left the hotel to go back to the train station. The weather had been gloomy when she arrived, but now the sky was visible through patches of cloud and the sun flickered. As she walked, she became even more conscious of the surrounding construction activity, with its constant noise of cranes in motion and pounding piledrivers that she hadn't heard from the taxi. She also hadn't noticed how many people wore face masks. Halfway to the station, she understood why they did. Her nose began to itch; she blew into a tissue and saw that her mucus was tinged black. As the sun lit the area, she saw that the air was filled with sparkling floating dust particles.

When she got to the station, she went immediately to the washroom. She blew her nose again, brushed her hair, and washed her hands and face. Walking any distance in Shenzhen wasn't something she planned to do again.

The posted schedule said that the trains ran every ten minutes to Mong Kok. Ava headed for the platform but was stopped just short as passengers were funnelled from the main terminal into a series of enclosures like cattle pens that opened onto the platform. When Ava complained to the woman standing next to her, the woman said, "You don't take this train often, do you."

"No."

"Well, if they didn't have these holding areas, everyone waiting for the train would be crowded as close to the platform edge as they could get. The people on the arriving train would find it almost impossible to get out. When the train gets in and all the passengers have disembarked, the doors here open and we can get on. It's a very efficient system."

Three minutes later Ava witnessed the system at work. After the train disgorged what looked like thousands of people, she watched as thousands more ran from the holding area towards it. She could hardly imagine the chaos if the two human waves ever collided.

She walked rather than ran to the train and was still able to find a seat. Five minutes later she forced herself to stand. Her jet lag had returned and she was struggling to keep her eyes open. Being on her feet helped, but she began to worry about what she would do when she got back to the hotel in Mong Kok. There was no way she could stay in her room without succumbing. As she contemplated her options, her phone rang. Her senses were so dulled that she didn't recognize the ring at first.

"*Wei*," she said.

"This is Pang from the Good Luck Hotel. You gave me your phone number."

"Oh, yes."

"I just saw your uncle."

"What?"

"He walked past me as he was heading out."

"Are you sure it was him?"

"If it wasn't, it was someone who looked exactly like the person in the photo you gave me."

"So he's a hotel guest?"

"I think so. I showed his photo to the guy who works the bell desk full-time and he said he had seen him coming and going for a few days."

"That's great," Ava said.

"So what are you going to do now?"

"What do you mean?"

"You owe me more money."

"Of course, of course I do. I'm on the train heading back to Kowloon. I need to get off and reverse my course. Are you going to be there?"

"Till six."

"Okay, then we'll hook up in about an hour," Ava said,

and felt a sudden surge of energy. “Tell me, did your colleague happen to know what name my uncle is using at the hotel?”

Pang became quiet and Ava realized that her question must have sounded ridiculous to him.

“I mean, you know he’s not really my uncle, don’t you,” she said.

“Yeah, I figured that.”

“So, do you have a name?”

“No, but I found out a couple of other things that you should know.”

“And those are?”

“He’s never alone. According to my friend, Chew, he has two tough-looking guys with him. And you’re not the only person asking questions about him.”

(8)

SHE EXITED THE TRAIN AT FO TAN, CROSSED THE platform, and five minutes later was on her way back to Shenzhen. When she reached Lo Wu station, this time she noticed how easy it was to leave the train, and any last doubts about the use of the pens vanished.

"I'm only going to the Good Luck Hotel," she told the cab driver when she got outside. "But I'll pay you a hundred Hong Kong."

He nodded. She climbed into the back seat, her mind full of thoughts about Johnny Kung. *So I've found him*, she thought. *Now what do I do?*

Pang waved at her as she walked through the front door of the hotel. Beside him, an older, shorter, rounder man stared at her. She went over to them.

"This is Chew," Pang said.

"Hi," Ava said, trying to ignore Chew's eyes, which were locked on to her chest. Ava did have larger breasts than was usual for a Chinese woman, and in China they seemed to generate keen interest.

"I showed him the photo and he recognized your guy," Pang said.

"He's been here for at least three days," Chew said.

"Is he here now?"

"No."

"You mentioned that there were other people asking questions. Who were they?"

"I have no idea, but they're in the lobby now."

"Where?"

"Don't turn around right away, but when you can, look towards the sofas. There's a little bald guy sitting by himself to the left; he's got tattoos on both arms. Then look further left and you'll see another guy by the door, with a ponytail and a wispy beard. He's also got tattoos. They're a team, I think."

"Why do you suppose that?"

"They take turns sitting and standing."

"Triad probably," Pang said.

"What makes you think that?" Ava asked.

"The tattoos. They're almost like a uniform."

"The guys with the man you're looking for have them too," Chew said.

"Triad?"

"Could be—just different gangs."

"You need to be careful," Pang said.

"Thanks for the advice," Ava said, and turned to Chew. "What kind of questions were those men asking?"

"They had a picture, like you, and they wanted to know if I'd seen the guy. That was a few days ago, so by now they've seen him for themselves. They've been in and around the hotel ever since, but I haven't seen them approach your guy. That's a bit strange, don't you think?"

"I have no idea," Ava said. She went into her bag and took out Hong Kong dollars. "Here's your thousand, Pang, and I'll give Mr. Chew here five hundred for his help. Does that work?"

"Sure," Pang said.

When Chew said nothing, Ava pressed the bill into his hand. "Thanks again," she said.

Ava crossed the lobby towards the man on the sofa. He was slumped to one side, his elbow sunk into the sofa's arm, his chin resting on his palm. *He looks bored*, she thought. She stopped directly in front of him. He didn't notice her at first, but when he glanced up, she saw a look of surprise on his face. He turned away. She didn't move, her eyes firmly fixed on him. He was in his thirties, she guessed, but in his black jeans, white T-shirt, and white running shoes he looked like a teenager.

"I'm told you're looking for Johnny Kung," she said.

His head swivelled towards her and she saw that she had flustered him. His eyes flickered briefly in her direction and then looked to the right, where the man Chew had identified as his partner was watching them.

"Are you looking for Kung?" she said.

"What's going on here?" the man's partner said.

He was short, only a few inches taller than Ava, but he was lean and wiry and looked as if he could take care of himself in a fight.

"I was asking if you two are looking for Johnny Kung," Ava said.

"What business is that of yours?" he said, moving closer, his eyes roaming over her body.

"Because I am as well."

"Is that a joke?"

"No, I'm completely serious."

"What is he, your father or something?"

"Of course not."

"You look young enough."

"My age is irrelevant," Ava said, looking at each of them in turn. "I just want to say that if you are looking for Kung, then we shouldn't get in each other's way."

"Who are you?"

"My name is Ava Lee."

"You use an English name?" the man on the sofa said.

"I'm Canadian."

"My English name is Andy, and he's Carlo. Now what the hell do you want with Kung?" he said.

"She has to be his girlfriend," Carlo said, switching from Mandarin to Cantonese.

"He owes money to one of my clients. I'm here to try to collect it," Ava said in Cantonese.

"Now you really are joking," Carlo said.

"I'm quite serious, and unless I'm mistaken I think you're trying to collect money from him as well. When I went to his office today, they mentioned that other people were after him. I assume it's you two."

"What outfit do you work for?" Andy said.

"What do you mean?"

"If you're in the business, you've got to be working for someone."

"I'm working alone. What outfit are you with?"

"Chow Tung's."

Ava's face registered no reaction.

"You've never heard of him?" Andy said.

"No."

"God, you are a rookie. There aren't many people in Hong Kong who haven't heard of him."

"Why is that?"

"There's no reason to get into all that," Carlo interrupted. "We work for him. That's all you need to know."

"And you're right that we've been hired to get money from Kung," Andy said.

"How much are you trying to collect?" Ava asked.

The two men stared at her.

"I'm after a million dollars," Ava said.

"Hong Kong?" Andy asked.

"U.S.," she said.

"Shit, that's twice what we're chasing him for," Andy said to Carlo.

"And like I said, I'm not working for anyone but myself and my client."

Carlo smiled at Ava. It was a complicated smile, she thought, part condescending, part protective, and certainly flirtatious.

"Okay, I believe you. But tell me how, exactly, you think you're going to get Kung to give back a million dollars," he said.

"Why don't you tell me about your plan first?" Ava asked.

"Listen, I'm really trying to be polite with you, and that's mainly because I think you're in way over your head and probably need someone to look after you, but we're on a job and we don't have time for this," Carlo said.

"On a job? All you're doing is sitting in the lobby, and from what I've heard, you've been here for days."

Andy rose from the couch, and she saw he was about the same height as his partner and even skinnier. "Ava, could you excuse Carlo and me for a minute? There's something I want to talk to him about in private."

"Sure, I'll stand over by the door," she said.

As she moved towards the hotel entrance, the two men

slid ten metres in the other direction. She watched as they spoke. Andy was quite animated, his hands moving up and down like an orchestra conductor's. Carlo occasionally nodded, and once he turned and looked in Ava's direction. Finally she saw Carlo shrug, and then both men walked towards her.

"We have an idea we'd like to talk to you about," Andy said.

"I'm listening."

"You wanna sit?" he said, motioning towards the couch.

"No thanks," Ava said, not wanting to be physically so close to either of them.

"Okay, here's the thing. Kung is staying in the hotel, but he's not alone."

"He has two goons with him."

"How'd you know that?"

"The bellboys told me."

"Yeah, he has two thugs with him, and they're the problem. He doesn't go anywhere without them."

"And they're probably armed," Carlo said. "It's too risky to make a play for him when they're around."

"We need to isolate him, to get him on his own," Andy said.

"And if you can do that?"

"We'll grab him. We've got an apartment about five blocks from here. We'll keep him there until he agrees to pay."

"Grab him?"

"The only way he'll ever pay is if he feels he has to. We'll hold him until he realizes he has no choice."

"How long will that take?"

"We have methods that tend to shorten the time frame."

"I bet you do," Ava said. "And that isn't meant to be critical."

"So what do you think?" Carlo said. "Do you want to work with us on this?"

"And how would I do that?"

The two men exchanged glances. "We've heard that Kung is a cunt-hound," Carlo said.

"What he means is that he has a reputation as a ladies' man," Andy said.

"Thanks for explaining that," Ava said.

"This is his fourth night at the hotel and so far it's just been him and the goons. He's got to be getting horny," Andy said. "We thought maybe you could help him get over that."

"I beg your pardon?"

"I don't mean sleep with him."

"I hope not."

"We just need you to get his attention so he invites you out for dinner or a drink."

"Without the goons?"

"You're quick—good. Yeah, without them. You'd have to insist that they not go," Andy said.

"You know, if you unbuttoned that shirt a bit, you could be a really hot-looking woman," Carlo said. "Hot enough that he'd tell those guys to take a hike if he thought he had a chance to get into your pants."

"I guess I should take that as a compliment," Ava said drily.

"You see where we're heading with this?" Andy asked.

"It's obvious enough, but tell me, what happens if he wants his guys to go along?"

"Then no dinner or drinks for you and we go back to our Plan A."

"Waiting in the lobby?"

"More or less."

"Okay, so what happens if there are no thugs?"

"Like I said, we grab him and take him to our apartment."

"I would want to go with you."

"You don't trust us?"

"Not especially," Ava said. "So what's the apartment address?"

"Why do you want to know?"

"Because if I agree to do this, I want to know where I can find you in case I need to."

"We have a place upstairs from the Jupiter Boutique on Winter Street," Andy said.

"Does this mean you're game?" Carlo asked.

"Not yet. I also need to know what happens about the money I'm owed. I'm not going to do any of this without your commitment that I'll get my fair share of what you can collect."

"What's a fair share, in your head?" Carlo said.

"Well, since my client is owed double what yours is, I should get a larger share. Not twice what you get, but something larger, like sixty percent."

"No way," Carlo said. "Fifty-fifty is the best we could do, and I'm going to have to phone our boss to get him to agree to even that."

"Go ahead, I'll wait."

Andy hesitated. "You know, I don't think we really have to call him."

"No, I insist," Ava said. "Let's have everything clear right at the beginning. I don't want to play my part and then have a problem with the split."

"Okay, you wait here," he said.

The two men huddled near the hotel entrance. Andy held his phone at a distance from his mouth and Ava assumed they had it on speaker mode. When they came back, she saw that Carlo had a smile tugging at the corners of his mouth.

"I think we have a deal," she said.

"We do."

"Good. Now I think I should get myself back to Kowloon."

"What?" Andy said.

"If I'm going to play the role, I'd like to put on some clothes that are more appropriate."

Carlo looked at his watch. "Try to be back here at six. Kung usually leaves the hotel in the early afternoon. He has an office that's about two blocks from here. Then he comes back around six and leaves again for dinner or whatever at seven. So our best bet is for you to bump into him on the way in, at six, or on the way out, at seven."

"What kind of office?"

"Just a hole in the wall."

"Does anyone else work there?"

"Not that we saw, and we did bang on the door when we knew he wasn't there. He probably uses it to make phone calls, check faxes, and the like."

"And store files?"

"I have no idea."

"Forget about the office. Let's concentrate on tonight," Andy said. "You'll need a story, you know. You can't just throw yourself at him. He's too smart for that."

"I'll be prepared," Ava said as she turned to leave.

(9)

***WHAT HAVE I GOTTEN MYSELF INTO?* AVA THOUGHT** as she left the hotel. *Nothing yet, until I'm sure Carlo and Andy are genuine.*

The two men weren't very bright, Ava thought. Neither did they seem to be particularly devious. She would have found Carlo's leering and his crude mouth offensive if it wasn't actually kind of funny. He wasn't the least bit attractive, but he threw himself around as if he was irresistible to women. Andy was gentler, at least on the surface, and she liked the way he showed some concern for her feelings. Still, she couldn't help but think that she had blundered her way into the beginning of a business relationship. She wasn't usually that impetuous, but right now she couldn't think of any other options for getting close to Kung and to Mr. Lo's money. She just hoped that jet lag wasn't wreaking havoc on her judgement.

It wasn't quite one o'clock, and now that she had her visa she could easily get to Mong Kok and back to Shenzhen before six. She also had time to visit the Jupiter Boutique. The taxi driver hadn't heard of it but he knew Winter Street, and on the first pass by they saw the store. Off to the right of the entrance was a plain wooden door that looked as if it would lead upstairs. Ava rang the doorbell. When no one answered, she went into the boutique and found herself surrounded by women's undergarments.

"Excuse me," she said to a heavily made-up middle-aged woman, "I'm looking for two friends of mine named Carlo and Andy. I thought they were renting the apartment upstairs, but I rang the doorbell and no one answered."

"They must be out."

"So I have the right place?"

"I'm not sure what you would want with them, but yes, it is the right place."

Ava took the same cab to Lo Wu station and within ten minutes was on the train to Mong Kok. Confirming the apartment had relieved one anxiety; now her mind focused on another—the lie she would need to spin to Johnny Kung.

What she didn't doubt was the look she could convey. With makeup and her hair pulled back, and in pumps, a tight black pencil skirt, and a pink shirt unbuttoned to reveal the swell of her breasts, she would be sexy. But Andy was right, that wasn't going to be enough. She needed a plausible reason for approaching him, and it wasn't until she was on the train heading back to Shenzhen that she had one that might work. And *might* was the operative word.

Her train got into Shenzhen at five thirty and she caught a cab to the hotel, again overpaying for it. When she walked through the front doors, Andy and Carlo were where she'd left them a couple of hours before, Andy on the couch and Carlo lingering by the door. Carlo's eyebrows rose when she passed him, but to her relief he said nothing.

Pang wasn't so passive. "Wow," he said when he saw her.

"Thanks."

"You look terrific."

"Let's hope my uncle thinks the same."

"What?"

"Nothing," she said.

Both Andy and Carlo were now sitting on the lobby couch. She walked over to the men she was now beginning to think of as partners. "Has he come back to the hotel?" she asked.

"No, your timing is really good," Andy said.

"So how do we do this?"

"Carlo is going to go outside so he can see Kung coming from a distance. When he does, he'll signal to me. I suggest you stand over by the elevators so it doesn't look like we're together. When Kung reaches the door, I'll raise my hand. Then you're on your own."

"I have to say I'm a little nervous."

"Do you have a strong story?"

"I have a story. Who knows how strong it is?"

"You look fantastic, so the story may not matter that much."

"Thanks," she said, pleased by the compliment and the non-lascivious way it was given.

"Now, Ava, the best thing for us is if he takes you to a restaurant for dinner. Don't agree to eat here in the hotel, or any hotel for that matter, because security could get involved."

"I'll do my best."

"And you have to insist that it's just him and you. You don't want his guys anywhere in the vicinity."

"I know."

He smiled and lowered his eyes. "Now I'm getting a bit nervous," he said.

"Are you worried about grabbing him?"

"No, we're old hands at this stuff. He'll come along easily enough if he knows he has no choice."

"You're that persuasive?"

"I have a gun and Carlo has a knife."

"Good grief!"

"Don't look so panicked. What did you think? That we'd say 'pretty please' and he'd co-operate?"

"No. I just didn't realize you'd need all those weapons."

"Well, we have them, but usually we don't need them. Besides, Kung is a pro. He knows the game."

"I sure hope so."

"And if you're really that worried about it and want to back out, it isn't too late."

Ava shook her head. "No, I've come this far."

"Good."

"Tell me, though, what happens if this doesn't work?"

"We go back to waiting. It's been four days now and I figure Kung can keep hanging around for weeks. It's making me crazy already, so I don't even want to think about failing."

She looked at her Citizen watch. "Well, it's almost six, so I should get into position."

"You're sure you know what he looks like?"

"Thick head of hair combed straight back, a round face with a small nose and mouth, and he's broad across the shoulders and chest."

"Right, and he's short, and when he left earlier today he was wearing a red shirt. His guys were in jeans and T-shirts. One of them always walks in front of him and the other is about two steps behind."

"Okay, I won't miss him."

Ava walked towards the elevators and then veered off to the left. She positioned herself next to a table that was against a wall. She had a clear view of the entrance and could see both Andy and Carlo.

Ten minutes passed, and Ava began to feel increasingly uncomfortable. Loitering in a hotel lobby, especially looking the way she did, wasn't a natural state for her. She suspected that she was beginning to draw the attention of a man in a black suit. He stood on the other side of the elevators, watching people come and go. She was sure he was security and would soon come over and ask her to move along and take her business elsewhere. She was contemplating this when she realized that Andy was waving his arms at her. She shook her head to clear it and then focused on the hotel entrance.

A huge man, at least six foot four and built like a truck, led the way. Just behind, she saw the flash of a red shirt.

They started across the lobby towards the elevators. A third man, as large as the first, trailed, his eyes darting in all directions.

Ava began to walk towards them. When the first man was almost parallel to her, she turned sideways and glanced at the man in the red shirt.

"Mr. Kung, what are you doing here?" she said.

He looked quickly in her direction, turned away, and then stopped walking and stared at her. Ava could see she had his interest. The bodyguards moved protectively closer to him, their eyes now taking in Ava and everything around her.

"Do I know you?" Kung said.

"Yes, of course you do. I've met you several times

at the import office in Mong Kok. My aunt, Fan Ying, introduced us."

"The receptionist?"

"Yes."

"I don't remember," he said, and then smiled. "And I have an excellent memory for pretty women."

"Well, the last time was about a year ago and I was probably wearing jeans and a sweater. I've graduated since then and found a job, so I'm dressing a bit better."

"Obviously," he said, taking advantage of the clothing reference to examine her more closely. "What brings you to Shenzhen?"

"I have a sales call early tomorrow morning, so I decided to take the train over today. So I wouldn't have to get up at dawn."

"You came alone?"

"Yes, I did, and I have to say I find it a bit overwhelming. I've never been to Shenzhen before and it isn't quite what I expected. It's so big, but not like Hong Kong big. There's all this construction and the dirt and the noise. It just feels so disorganized. It's nice to see a familiar face."

He smiled again. "You're staying here?"

"No, I'm at another hotel nearby, but my boss is supposed to be staying here and I just came by to see if he's checked in. He hasn't, so I was just heading out."

"Where to?"

"I thought I'd stop at one of the restaurants on the way back to my hotel."

"Eat by yourself?"

"Yes."

"I can't allow that," Kung said, moving closer. "Let me take you to dinner."

"I don't feel right imposing myself on you and your friends like that," she said.

"It's no imposition. And besides, your aunt has been very helpful to me and this is a way I can pay her back."

"Still," Ava said, glancing nervously at the bodyguards. "I don't think I would be comfortable with quite so many men."

"What if it was just you and me?"

She lowered her eyes. "I think that would be acceptable."

"Terrific. Do you have a restaurant in mind?"

"No, I was just going to walk around until I found a place that looked nice."

"There's a Szechuan place about two streets away that I really like."

"That sounds nice."

He looked around the lobby. "I have to go upstairs to shower and freshen myself. Why don't you sit over there and wait for me? I'll be ten minutes or so."

"Yes, Mr. Kung," she said.

"Call me Johnny."

"Yes, Johnny."

"And I didn't catch your name."

"Ava."

He smiled. "I'll see you in ten minutes, Ava."

As Kung went towards the elevators, Ava began to walk to the lobby couches. The bodyguards hadn't budged when he left and Ava could feel their eyes burning into her back. After she sat down, she avoided looking in their direction for a few minutes and then took a quick glance. They were gone.

Andy sidled close to her but kept his face turned away. "What happened?" he mumbled.

Ava put her hand to her mouth in case she was being watched. "We're having dinner, just him and me."

"We'll be nearby," he said, and then left.

(10)

KUNG'S TEN MINUTES STRETCHED INTO TWENTY, and again Ava found her anxiety building. Was Kung upstairs calling the office in Mong Kok? Where were the bodyguards? It had all been so easy — too easy. Surely he suspected something. Even if he didn't and they went to the restaurant, she wasn't convinced that Kung would go quietly with Andy and Carlo. It was all so random, and the more she thought about it, the looser and less likely to succeed the plan seemed. She was almost ready to go looking for her accomplices when she saw Kung cross the lobby towards her. He had changed into a dark blue silk shirt and a pair of grey slacks. There was no sign of the bodyguards.

She stood and smiled at him.

"Hello, little Ava, are you ready to go?" he said.

"Your friends really don't mind that it's just the two of us?" she asked, not detecting anything strange in his manner.

"Don't concern yourself with them. They do what they're told."

As they walked towards the entrance, Kung's hand reached out and clasped Ava's elbow. The move surprised her and she struggled not to wrench it free. *Relax*, she told herself. *This will be over soon enough.*

They made a right from the hotel. "This restaurant is very good," he said. "It has a specialty dish I love—cold noodles with chili sauce. Have you tried that?"

"No," she said, looking around quickly for signs of his men or of Carlo and Andy. She didn't see any of them.

"I think you'll enjoy it."

He continued to hold her elbow as they walked, but it was a light grip and she didn't feel constrained by it.

"What business do you have here?" he asked.

"I'm an accountant. We're trying to sign up a new client," she said. "How about you?"

"I'm an importer."

"I thought as much, since my aunt's office is full of traders and importers."

She waited for him to respond, to add something to his short reply. She was relieved when he didn't, and happy to lapse into her own silence.

The restaurant was as close as he had promised. When they walked through the front door, Ava was engulfed in the aromas of fried garlic, ginger, and chilis. Her appetite spiked. She hadn't eaten all day, she realized. The place was rather stylish, with carved wood-panelled walls and a wooden floor. Along one wall, massive shark fins were displayed in glass cases.

"This is lovely," she said.

The hostess guided them to a table set for four near the front. Ava took a chair, expecting that Kung would sit across from her. Instead he sat next to her, their knees touching. He faced the door, she noticed, and wondered if that was the reason for his seat choice.

"Do you drink?" he asked.

"Tea will be fine."

"I'm having beer. You sure you don't want something stronger?"

"Maybe a glass of white wine. But only one. I do have to work tomorrow."

Kung signalled for a waiter. As he did, Ava's eyes drifted towards the plate-glass window at the front of the restaurant. She saw Andy and Carlo walking by and felt a slight flush. Didn't they know that she and Kung were there?

"What are you looking at?" Kung asked.

"Nothing."

"My men aren't joining us, if that is what you're worried about."

"Not at all," Ava said, and then wondered why he felt it necessary to mention that.

The waiter arrived at the table. Kung ordered a Tsingtao beer and asked about the wine selection.

"All we have is house wine. The white is a Swiss Chardonnay."

Ava had never heard of Swiss wine. "That will be fine," she said.

"And I want a platter of cold noodles with special Szechuan sauce as a starter. We'll order the main meal after that."

As the waiter left, Kung's eyes glanced towards the window. Then his face froze, and Ava felt a rush of fear.

"What's the matter?" she said.

"Just a minute," he said, reaching into his shirt pocket for his cellphone. He hit the speed-dial button, his eyes locked onto the restaurant entrance. "Li, I'm at Yang's Restaurant. Those two jerks from the hotel lobby are outside. You and

Wong should get over here and clear them out."

Ava struggled to stay calm. It was an effort. The plan, such as it was, was already falling apart.

"Well, if you can't find Wong, come by yourself. You should be able to handle them," Kung said and closed his phone.

She started to stand.

"Where do you think you're going?" Kung asked, his hand gripping her wrist.

"I beg your pardon?" Ava said.

"Sorry," he said quickly, lifting his hand. "There's a couple of creeps outside who I think have been tailing me. It's sort of set my nerves on edge."

"Why would they do that?"

"A business dispute."

"Must be serious if they're following you."

"More annoying than serious. Now, why were you getting up?"

"I need to go to the washroom."

"Of course," he said, politely half-rising from his seat.

She didn't feel completely steady as she made her way to the bathroom. Jet lag, hunger, and panic were combining to take their toll. She just hoped she looked somewhat under control.

She went into an empty stall, locked the door, and sat with her elbows on her knees and her head in her hands. *What a mess*, she thought. The thug named Li would arrive before Carlo and Andy and she'd be stuck with Kung for dinner, or worse. Or all three men would get to the restaurant at the same time, and then what? She tried to think of something, anything positive and came up blank. She left the stall and went to the sink to wash her hands. She stared at herself in the mirror. *You fool*, she thought. *You flew all those thousands of kilometres to get Mr. Lo's money back and you don't have a clue what you're doing.*

"You fucking assholes!"

It was Kung's voice, and then she heard Carlo yell, "Come quietly with us and you won't get hurt. If you put up a fight, I'll put this knife right through your ribs and we'll carry you out."

Ava ran back into the restaurant and saw Carlo and Andy on either side of Kung. Carlo was holding a knife to Kung's ribs, and Andy's small handgun was in Kung's lower back.

"We've got him," Carlo shouted to Ava.

She quickly looked around. The waiters had retreated behind the bar. The other customers were trying to ignore the goings-on. Kung's head spun in her direction and she saw hatred cross his face.

"You fucking bitch," he spat.

Ava walked to the men. "What do we do now?" she asked.

"We have a taxi waiting outside. That's what took so long. Our regular guy didn't show, so we had to get his brother to transport this piece of shit."

"Then let's go," Ava said and started towards the door. The men followed, Andy pushing Kung with the gun barrel while Carlo kept the knife at his side.

They were almost at the entrance when the man who'd preceded Kung across the hotel lobby appeared in the window. He took a quick look inside and in three steps was at the door, with a knife visible in his right hand.

"Shit," Carlo said.

"Let him go," the man said.

"Don't do anything stupid or I'll cut him."

"Like fuck you will," the man shouted and lunged forward.

Ava sensed, rather than saw, Carlo and Andy recoil, and she knew the bigger man already had the upper hand.

He had to get past her to get to the other men, and he reached out with his left arm to throw her aside. As he did, she took a small step to her right so that she was directly in front of him. He swung his arm. She ducked and moved forward, her right arm extended with the knuckle of her index finger pointing at his chest. Then she lowered her hand and drove the knuckle into his gut. He staggered back, his head collapsing forward and his hands grabbing at his stomach. As he wavered, Ava took another step forward and two to the right. Before he could straighten, her knuckle shot into his head, just behind the ear. He fell sideways onto the floor as if he'd been hit by a steel beam.

"Let's get out of here," Ava said.

Andy and Carlo didn't move. Their mouths were open, as was Kung's.

"Stop gawking and let's go," she said.

(11)

THE THREE MEN CLIMBED INTO THE BACK SEAT of the taxi, with Kung in the middle. Ava sat in the front. The driver swung away from the curb as soon as the last door closed.

"You should know I'm being kidnapped," Kung yelled at the driver. "If you go to the nearest police station, I'll make it worth your while."

"Fuck off," the driver said without turning around.

The car went quiet. Then Andy said, "Ava, how did you do that stuff?"

"I don't want to talk about it."

"No, tell me. How did you drop that guy?"

She stared straight ahead.

Winter Street was quiet and the Jupiter Boutique was closed. They bundled out of the taxi and stood awkwardly on the sidewalk while Carlo unlocked the apartment door. Andy stood between Ava and Kung, but she could feel Kung's hatred towards her burn right through him.

Carlo led them upstairs. Andy was behind the importer, his gun in his back. Ava was the last to enter and closed and locked the door. The apartment was directly above the boutique and about twelve hundred square feet, large by Hong Kong standards. It was clean and neat and had the slightest smell of disinfectant. The living room was furnished with an orange velour couch and easy chair, a wooden coffee table, and a television. The kitchen was off to the left; it was large enough to contain a round glass-topped table and three wooden chairs. A fourth wooden chair was against the wall near the bathroom. Andy pushed Kung towards it and told him to sit. When he did, Carlo moved in behind, pulled back Kung's arms, and taped his wrists together.

"You don't need to do that," Kung said.

"It's procedure," Andy said, and then turned to Ava and smiled.

She didn't understand the need for the tape and was about to speak, when she was overtaken by an enormous yawn. Suddenly she felt completely exhausted, depleted of all energy, and her head felt as if it were filled with mush. It was seven a.m. in Toronto, and the adrenalin rush that had kept her going was spent. Total fatigue washed over her.

There were two doors leading off the living room. Both were closed.

"Are those bedrooms?" she asked.

"Yeah."

"Do you mind if I use one? I think I need a nap."

"Use either of them."

"How long will this take?" she asked.

"Depends on how stubborn Kung is," Andy said, glancing at him.

"I don't have any money left," Kung said.

"Ah, the negotiations start already," Andy said. "Somewhere between him saying, 'I don't have any money left,' and me saying, 'We want every dollar you've ever made,' we'll reach a deal. Sometimes it goes on for days, but not this time. Kung's pissed us off by making us wait around the hotel, and then by setting that thug of his on us. We'll make it happen fast. Don't worry, though, if anything happens we'll wake you."

Ava went into the farthest bedroom. It had a double bed and a plain wooden dresser with a sports bag sitting on it. She took off the chenille cover and pulled back the sheets. She thought about taking off her shirt and skirt and then discarded the idea. She went to the window and looked outside: dusk was setting in. She closed the curtains and the room was plunged into darkness. She fell onto the bed, her face burrowed deep in a pillow. She couldn't remember the last time she had been so tired. She heard raised voices; for a moment they held her attention, but then they faded and vanished as she lost consciousness.

As always, she dreamt. And, as always, her father dominated the dream. She couldn't remember when this nightly game of hide-and-seek-and-never-find had started, but it had been a recurrent dream for as long as she could remember. Sometimes they were in a hotel, other times in an office building or a huge mall. It was always just the two of them and they were always preparing to leave for some unknown destination. Her father would give her a chore, a simple thing like getting their suitcases from their hotel room. Off she'd go, eager to please him, only to run into an escalating series of misadventures. Ultimately she would go back to where he had been and find him gone. She would wake then, permeated by a feeling of loss.

This time they were in an airport. They had six suitcases and were trying to check them in and get to the gate for their flight. They had only twenty minutes before they had to board, and they were at the end of a long check-in line. Her father said he'd go ahead and hold the plane at the gate until she arrived. She didn't believe it was possible but said nothing. The line crawled forward, her anxiety increasing with every passing minute. When she finally reached the counter, she had five minutes left but still thought it was possible to make the flight. Then the counter clerk told her that she could check only four suitcases. As Ava debated between leaving two behind or repacking six cases into four, her time ran out. Then she heard her name being called and someone knocking on a door. Where was the door?

"Ava, it's Andy."

She opened her eyes to semi-darkness and struggled to remember where she was.

"It's Andy," he said, knocking more briskly.

"Yes," she said.

"You've been asleep for about twelve hours."

She took several deep breaths to gather herself. "Give me a minute. I'll be right out."

"We have good news," he said.

She slid from the bed and went over to the window. When she drew the curtains back, she saw that Winter Street was alive with early morning traffic. She returned to the bed and kneeled beside it, her hands clasped in front of her face. She said a whispered prayer to Saint Jude, the patron saint of lost causes, thanking him for having delivered her safely to Hong Kong and Shenzhen, and for protecting her the night before when the man had charged at her. Ava had been raised a Roman Catholic, but the Church's stance on homosexuality made her feel unwelcome. She had rid herself of any attachment but she still felt the tug of religion; only now she expressed it in her own way.

Ava stood, straightened her skirt, and tucked in her shirt. She opened her purse, took out a brush and ran it through her hair, fixing it back with a clasp. Feeling more presentable, she opened the door and walked into the living room.

Andy and Carlo sat at the kitchen table with mugs in front of them. Kung was still taped to the chair. His upper body was wet.

"I need to use the bathroom for a moment," Ava said.

"We're not going anywhere," Carlo said with a smile.

Five minutes later, washed and refreshed, she came back into the living room. "That smells like coffee," she said, pointing to their mugs.

"The jar is on the counter," Andy said.

It was Nescafé instant, the same brand she drank at home. She put a teaspoon and a half in a mug and filled it with hot water from a Thermos. She took a sip. "That's wonderful," she said.

"Come and join us," Andy said, sliding his chair sideways to make room for her at the table.

She looked at Kung as she passed him. He seemed to be sleeping, but his face was pinched and distorted. "He doesn't look so jolly."

"It was a long night for all of us," Carlo said.

"And if I heard Andy correctly, a night that ended well."

"Four hundred thousand," Andy said, and grinned.

Ava took another sip of coffee. "Is that American or Hong Kong dollars?"

"American."

She stared at the table and then glanced at Kung again.

"What's the matter? You don't seem especially happy," Andy said.

"I don't mean to sound ungrateful, but —"

"But what?" Carlo interrupted.

"My client is owed a million dollars and yours half a million. Did Kung understand what the total debt was?"

"Yeah, we told him."

"Four hundred thousand is a long way from those numbers."

"Look, we know what we're doing," Carlo said. "We've been at this business for three years and we've developed a good sense of who is bullshitting and who's not. It took us all night to get him to agree to four hundred thousand. We put his head in the toilet more times than I can count."

"So that would be two hundred thousand each?" Ava asked, realizing that she had provoked Carlo.

"Yeah."

"And how is that arranged?"

"What do you mean?"

"How do we get the money?"

"Kung will call his money guy and they'll arrange to get it in cash for us. When we get the cash, we turn Kung loose."

"How long will that take?"

"A day or two."

"And in the meantime, Kung's thugs are looking for us."

"Don't worry about that. He'll phone them and tell them to back off. Now that we have a deal, he'll see it through. He's too smart not to."

"Does it always work like this?" Ava asked.

"Work like how?"

"You negotiate with guys like Kung, knowing going in

that you're prepared to settle for so many cents on the dollar," Ava said.

"This is a cash business. We take what we can get right now. We don't have the time to wait for people to dispose of assets."

"But you don't how much cash he actually has, do you?"

"After what we put him through, I think we have a pretty good idea."

"Maybe he just outlasted you."

"He offered the four hundred thousand hours ago. We kept at him. He didn't budge. I think it's all he's got."

"You can't be sure."

"Like I said, we've been doing this a long time. We have experience that you don't."

"True enough, but why don't we at least make the effort to find out if he has more?"

"And how would we do that?"

Ava shrugged. "He has that office he's using here in Shenzhen. He must have some financial records there. I'd like to look at them. I'd also like to get into his computer and see what I can find."

"What makes you think you'd find anything?"

"I'm an accountant. I'm trained to poke around in people's accounts."

"We made a deal with him," Andy said.

"I didn't sign off on any deal," Ava said.

"And we called our boss and told him it was done."

"Then phone him again and tell him I don't want to go along with it until I have more information about Kung's real financial situation."

"That won't go over very well. He will already have called the client and told him how much money he's getting back."

"What if I can get more? Will the client object?"

Carlo shook his head. "You don't understand how this business works. We made the deal with Kung and it's been passed down the line. You should leave well enough alone."

Ava drained her coffee and walked around the table to make another. As she stood at the counter, she heard Carlo mumbling something to Andy. "Please don't talk behind my back," she said.

"I was just saying I thought you should be happy about getting two hundred thousand back. Without us, you had no chance of getting anything."

"You don't know that."

Carlo smiled. "Believe what you want."

"What did you say your boss's name was?" she asked when she sat down again.

"Chow Tung," Andy said.

"Then please call him for me. I'd like to speak to him."

Carlo and Andy exchanged nervous looks, and Ava felt a twinge of doubt. Had they actually spoken to their boss from the hotel lobby? Had he really signed off on a fifty-fifty split? Had they used her to get to Kung and were now getting ready to dump her and keep the four hundred thousand for themselves?

"What do you want to talk to him about?" Andy said.

"Getting more money out of Kung," she said. And then another reason for the men's being nervous popped into her head. "I'll tell him I think you two did a great job. I'm not going to be critical."

"What's the harm in that?" Andy asked Carlo.

"I still don't like it. We made a deal."

"We actually made two deals, and the first one was with Ava. She's right when she says she didn't sign off. Maybe we should give her a chance to get more out of Kung."

"I don't want to be the one to call Uncle," Carlo said.

"I'll do it," said Andy.

Carlo sighed. "Okay, but do it from the bedroom."

"Uncle and Chow Tung are the same man?" Ava asked as Andy left.

"Yeah, but nearly everyone calls him Uncle."

"And you've been with him for three years?"

"Longer than that for both of us, but three years in this business."

"What business were you in before?"

"A bit of this and a bit of that."

"That sounds mysterious."

"Better to leave it that way."

Kung groaned and they both looked at him. Ava had almost forgotten he was there.

"I'll untie him in a while so he can call his guys," Carlo said. "Then I'll probably leave him untied. He's no threat to us, and as long as Andy or I am here, he's not going anywhere."

"Do what you want with him, but don't let him make any phone calls until I've had a chance to get the information I want."

"Assuming Uncle goes along."

The bedroom door opened and Andy reappeared, holding the phone in his hand. "He wants to speak to you," he said, motioning for her to come over.

"Yes, Mr. Chow," she said, taking the phone and stepping inside the bedroom.

"Andy tells me that you are not particularly pleased with the arrangement that has been made," a soft voice said.

"No, sir, I'm not."

"He also says that you are an accountant."

"I am. Actually, I'm a forensic accountant."

"Trained in finding money that someone does not want found?"

"Exactly."

"When I spoke to Andy last night, he was rather vague about your affiliations. He suggested that you are working entirely on your own."

"I am."

"That is very unusual in Hong Kong, although I do have to say it speaks well for you if a client feels he can put that much trust in a young woman, however well trained she might be."

"I'm not from Hong Kong."

"Really, I would never have guessed. Your Cantonese is perfect."

"Thank you. My mother would be pleased to hear that. It is the only language we speak at home."

"And where is home?"

"Toronto... Canada."

"And your client?"

"Also from Toronto, although he is Chinese."

"Well, that is a surprise, but perhaps it should not be. The world is shrinking faster than most of us can grasp. But in any event, I assume that you too have Hong Kong or southern Chinese roots."

"My mother is from Shanghai but lived and worked in Hong Kong for many years. My father is a Hong Konger and still lives there."

"Ah. That sounds complicated."

"I've never thought of it that way."

"No, just as you evidently do not think it strange that

you travelled all that distance, by yourself, with the hope of convincing a man like Kung to return money he stole from your client."

"My client is a desperate man. I am his last resort."

"What kind of man asks a young woman with no experience of men like Kung or of this part of the world to undertake a job like that?"

"One who was enough of a fool to find himself a million dollars out of pocket to Kung."

Chow laughed. The sound was so much deeper than his speaking voice that she thought he had something caught in this throat, until she heard the humour in it. "No wonder Carlo and Andy were so anxious to work with you."

"That wasn't the impression I had. I thought I was just convenient bait, something to try to entice Kung with."

"Are you always this direct?"

"I try to be, although I don't like rudeness."

"Direct and polite—those are qualities that I share. So let me ask you, what made you think you could find a way to convince Kung to repay your client?"

"Mr. Chow, why does that even matter now? I met your men and we struck a deal. We were able to take Kung because of our collective efforts, and I contributed as much if not more than your men. Now all I'm saying is that if I can be given the chance to get more information out of him, maybe I can find more money for us both."

"What information?"

"I want to know where he does his banking, and by that I mean everywhere he does his banking. I already know what bank he paid my client from, but I'm sure there will be other banks, account numbers, and passwords. And then I want access to his office and his computer so I can confirm whatever he tells us — and find out what he neglected to tell us."

"Then what?"

"I will locate every dollar he has."

"You sound very confident."

"It's what I've been trained to do."

"I have to admit that it is always easier to strike an agreement when you know exactly what the other person's position is."

"So let me find out."

"If you can, then I presume you will want us to reopen negotiations with him. Assuming, of course, that he does have more than four hundred thousand dollars," Chow said slowly.

"Do you doubt that he has more money?"

"No, not at all. And if you can locate it... Well then, Ms. Lee, I will ask Carlo and Andy to persuade Kung to sweeten his offer."

"Thank you. But I'll need access to Kung's office and whatever records he has there."

"I will tell the boys to do whatever is necessary to accommodate that."

"Now, it would be helpful to know your client's name and what they were selling to Kung."

"Royal Meats, and they sold him pork ribs and sides."

"And they are owed half a million U.S. dollars."

"Thereabouts."

"And what bank did Kung use when he did business with them?"

"When he paid, which was not often, it was through the Guangzhou Chemical Engineering Bank. They shipped against purchase orders issued by Kung. He was recommended to them by a friend."

"Like my client."

"Friends who have poor memories, or just disappear when a problem emerges."

"Exactly. Well, hopefully I can find what I'm looking for. And let me say that I appreciate your giving me the chance."

"No thanks are necessary. Any success you have will benefit us all, Ms. Lee."

"My given name is Ava."

"Ava it is, and I would prefer that you call me Uncle."

(12)

CHOW TUNG WAS A SURPRISE TO AVA. SHE couldn't quite equate a man who was so polite and soft-spoken, his every word measured, with one who could run a business as rough as his seemed to be, with employees as casually violent as Carlo and Andy. Yet she had felt comfortable talking to him and liked the way he listened to her, waiting until she had made her case before giving his opinion.

Carlo and Andy were standing in the kitchen when she left the bedroom. Kung's head was slumped onto his chest and Ava figured he was still sleeping.

"Well?" Andy said.

She handed him the phone. "Uncle wants to talk to you."

Andy nodded as he listened to his boss. Then he put the phone into his pocket. "Uncle agrees with Ava. We need to get the banking information from Kung and we have to get into his office," he said to Carlo.

"Shit," Carlo said.

Andy shrugged. "I guess we should wake him."

"Kung won't like this," Carlo said.

"Who cares if he does or doesn't?" Ava said. "What is this,

honour among thieves? He owes my client a million dollars and I'm determined to get back as much of it as I can."

"We had a deal, that's all, and normally we don't go back on our word."

"Yes, you had a deal — one that I didn't agree with," Ava said.

"Uncle wants us to get the information and that's what we're going to do," Andy said, moving between them.

"I'm glad someone can remember which side he's on," she said.

"Goddamn it," Carlo said.

"Enough," Andy said and walked over to Kung. He shook him by the shoulders. "Wake up, we need to talk to you again."

Kung groaned. "I'm thirsty," he said.

"Get him a glass of water," Andy said to Carlo, and then turned back to Kung. "I'm going to untie your hands. You can have all the water you want, and if you need to go to the bathroom that's not a problem either."

"What time is it?"

"Just past eight."

"I can call my money guy now if you want."

"Not yet. We have a few more questions for you."

"Like what?" Kung said as Carlo came over to him with a glass of water.

Andy went behind him and peeled off the tape that held his wrists. "Drink first," he said.

Kung downed the water in four large gulps. "Can I have more?" he said.

Two glasses later, he said, "Now I have to pee."

"No problem, but do me a favour and empty your pockets onto the table over there before you do," Andy said.

"Why?"

"Because I asked."

It took an effort for Kung to get to his feet, and his initial step was a stagger. Ava flinched, thinking that he might make a run for the door. But he walked towards them and put a wad of bills, his wallet, and a set of keys on the table. "Satisfied?" he said.

"Thanks," Andy said.

When the bathroom door closed, Andy took a close look at the keys. "One of these should be for the office," he said.

"Can I look at his wallet?" Ava asked.

Andy tossed it to her. She opened it and then sighed. "No bank cards, though I guess that would have been too easy."

"I'll get his chair," Andy said. "We might as well sit him here at the table with us."

Kung came out of the bathroom, saw his chair at the table, and smiled. Andy had positioned it between him and Carlo, and directly across from Ava.

"Sit," Andy said.

"What else do you want to know?" Kung said.

"Which of these keys is for your office door?" Andy asked.

"Why?"

"Ava is going there."

"Why?" he said, his head pivoting between Carlo and Andy.

"Just a second, I don't want us to get ahead of ourselves," Ava said softly. "Mr. Kung, in case it hasn't been explained to you, I'm representing the interests of Hedrick Lo. You remember Mr. Lo, I assume."

"The chicken-feet guy."

"Yes, exactly, and the guy to whom you owe approximately a million dollars."

"These two didn't mention his name. All they said was you were after a million dollars."

"You have more than one debt that size?"

"Trading is a high-volume, low-margin business. Numbers can be deceiving. Lots of deals I do run into the millions, but that doesn't mean there's profit at the end of the day. Sometimes people have to wait to get paid."

"Well, we're not waiting any longer."

"I did the best I could when I settled on four hundred thousand. How you split it with them," he said, motioning to Carlo and Andy, "is your business."

"Let's put the four hundred thousand aside for now. What I want to know, Mr. Kung, is the names of the banks you use. You paid Mr. Lo — when you paid him — through the China Agricultural Bank. What other accounts do you have? For example, the account that Carlo and Andy are trying to settle, which bank is involved in that? You can tell me directly or we can call their boss and find out."

"Tell her," Andy said. "If I have to phone my boss, I'll be pissed."

"The Guangzhou Chemical Engineering Bank."

"Thank you," Ava said, pleased that the name matched the bank Uncle had mentioned. "Now, are those two banks the only ones you use?"

"Yeah."

"I'm not sure I believe you. You don't have a Hong Kong–based bank?"

"The Agricultural Bank has a Hong Kong office."

"Okay, now what I need from you are the account numbers for the two banks."

"What's this about? We already have a deal."

"Not with me, you don't."

Kung shot an angry glance at Carlo. "Do I have to listen to this crap?"

"You do," Andy said. "My boss decided that we want to know how much cash you have lying around. He wants Ava to look into your bank accounts."

"Why didn't you say that before? Why did you go through that fucking charade, with your yelling and threats?"

"There's been a change of plan. I don't want to say anything else," Andy said.

"Fuck you."

"I don't think that's a helpful attitude," Ava said.

"And fuck you too, you bitch."

"You need to calm down or I'll be forced to tie you to the chair again, and then we can start persuading you to be co-operative using a knife instead of a toilet," Andy shouted.

Kung sat back in the chair and closed his eyes. "I don't remember the account numbers," he said.

"But if I go through your files in the office I'll find them?" Ava said.

"Of course. Be my guest."

"Do you do online banking with both accounts?"

"Yeah."

"Passwords, please."

"TRADER22 for each of them. Capital letters and the number twenty-two."

"Do I need a password for the computer?"

"No."

"Thanks for being co-operative."

"When you look in the accounts, you'll see that I have just over four hundred thousand dollars."

"How much more?" she said.

"Ten thousand and change, and if you want the ten thousand you can have it."

"Shit," Carlo said.

"I told you, I'm giving you everything I have."

Andy glanced at Ava and she saw disappointment on his face. "Do you still want to go to the office?" he asked.

"Of course."

"Okay, I'll go with you. Carlo can stay here," Andy said, and then turned to Kung. "It's time for you to call your thugs. You don't have to tell them where we're going, but you do have to say that everything is under control and that if they see us they're to leave us entirely alone."

Kung nodded. "No problem. You and that bitch go and waste your time, but call me as soon as you see what's in those accounts. I want to get your cash organized so I can get the hell out of here."

(13)

ANDY WAS QUIET DURING THE TAXI RIDE. AVA could sense his doubt about the need to go to Kung's office. She thought about saying something and then decided to leave things as they were. She'd find more money or she wouldn't. Either way, she didn't feel the need to justify taking the time to confirm Kung's claim.

The three-storey red-brick office building was on a side street between the train station and the hotel. For a building that looked to be only ten years old, it was shabby. The windows were stained and dusty, the brick was chipped, and the blue paint on the front door had faded. The door also had hack marks that could have been made by a machete.

"Charming place," Ava said.

"Typical of the older part of Shenzhen," Andy said. "They threw up these places in what seemed like a few weeks. The original tenants were here to make a quick killing and weren't too interested in anything fancy."

There wasn't an elevator, but Kung's office was on the second floor, up one short flight of stairs. Its door was plain grey steel with one lock. Andy opened it and they stepped inside. The office had a metal desk, two one-drawer filing cabinets, a small table that held a fax machine, and four chairs. Ava went behind the desk and sat down.

"I could be a while," she said. "You don't have to stay."

"I think it's better that I do. If one of Kung's goons decides not to listen to him, you might need me."

Ava shrugged. "That's your decision, but thank you for being considerate."

"Can I help?"

Ava started opening the desk drawers. "I'll tell you in a minute." The middle drawer was empty. The right-side drawer had files marked WIRE TRANSFERS and LETTERS OF CREDIT. She took them out and stacked them on the desk. The left-side drawer was full of business directories and phone books. Ava got up and went to the nearest filing cabinet. She saw files fat with purchase orders, shipping documents, and invoices. Those also went onto the desk. The other cabinet gave up all kinds of files devoted to the banks Kung had named. She pulled them out. "I seem to have everything I need to start," she said.

"I feel kind of useless," Andy said.

"Well, you can sit and watch me look at paper or you can go and get us some lunch."

"Lunch sounds good."

"I'd love some fried noodles."

"I'll lock the door when I leave. Don't open it unless you hear three knocks."

"Don't rush," Ava said, opening the China Agricultural Bank file.

She restricted her search to the time when Lo and Kung were doing business. If she couldn't find what she was looking for, she'd go further back, but her feeling was that if Kung had been pulling the same scam for years, she'd find its roots in the Lo deals.

She worked quietly and steadily, matching letters of credit and purchase orders to shipping documents, and then found the wire transfers Kung had sent to Lo at the beginning of their relationship. Then she looked at the invoices that Kung had cut when he sold the goods, and she matched them against the inbound manifest. Every single kilo of chicken feet had been sold. She pulled out Kung's accounts receivable file. Not only did they appear to have been sold, but every invoice was stamped PAID and dated. Now she turned to the bank records. Some statements were missing for the months she was interested in, but in the ones she did find, it appeared that the money from the sales of the chicken feet had found its way to the China Agricultural Bank.

Ava had separated the Royal Meats paperwork from Lo's, and now she turned her attention to it. She had just confirmed that all that company's products had been sold when she heard three sharp knocks. She walked to the door and pressed her ear against it. "Is that you, Andy?"

"Yeah. My hands are full."

She thought his voice sounded slightly strained, and her nerves jumped. "Just a second," she said. She moved to the right of the door and pressed her back against the wall. If there was someone else with Andy on the other side, they would push the door as hard as they could, trying to ram her, and rush inside. Positioned to the right, she was clear of the door and would have an unobstructed view of anyone coming in. She turned the handle and then saw Andy's foot kick the door. She slid further along the wall, her right hand poised to strike.

"Hey, don't hit me," Andy said, stepping inside with his hands cradling a large brown paper bag.

"Sorry, I thought you had someone with you," Ava said, relaxing.

He had bought fried noodles with beef in XO sauce, steamed baby bok choy, and salt-and-pepper shrimp. He opened the bag and put the containers on a chair, then placed chairs on either side. "How's it going?" he asked.

"Not bad. There's a paper trail for the goods. Now all I have to do is get more fully into the bank records. It looks like he sold all the chicken feet and pork," Ava said as she plucked a long, thin slice of beef from its nest of noodles. It was so tender she hardly had to chew. "I wonder how they manage to get the beef so soft," she said.

"Magic water," Andy said.

"What?"

"That's what we call it. My wife and I have a noodle shop at the Kowloon MTR station. My father-in-law opened it years ago and we bought it from him last year. He had this concoction that he soaked pork, beef, and chicken in to soften it. My wife knows what's in it but I don't. She just says it's magic water and tells me not to worry about it."

"Oh, I wish I hadn't asked."

Andy shrugged. "Don't worry. She wouldn't let me eat it if she thought it would harm me," he said. "Now, you didn't finish telling me about the money. You said he sold everything, but did he make a profit?"

"It looks like it. Not huge amounts, but there was certainly enough margin that he seems to have covered his costs and pocketed some profit."

"So if we're owed a million and a half, there should be that much in those two accounts."

"You would think so, but there isn't. I took a quick look at the balances on the last statements from both banks, and they add up to just over four hundred thousand, like he said."

"So where is the money?"

"I don't know yet. It could have been spent, or tied up in new inventory, or just moved to another account somewhere. I'm missing a couple of paper bank records, but once I go online I should be able to at least find a starting point."

Andy reversed his chopsticks, picked up two shrimp from the tray, and put them on Ava's plate.

"Thanks," she said.

"Could you answer another question?"

"Sure."

"You brushed me off when I asked you, but Carlo and I were talking about it last night when you were sleeping, and it's really bugging us."

"Is this about me and that thug of Kung's?"

"Yeah. How in hell did you do that? He's twice your size but you floored him like he was a midget."

"There isn't any mystery to it," Ava said. "I practise a martial art that's called bak mei. It's a very old form and it's designed to cause damage. In this case I hit a pressure point at the base of his rib cage where there's a gathering of nerve endings. The person's size doesn't matter — a blow there with enough force is incapacitating."

"I've never heard of bak mei, and I thought I knew most of the martial arts."

"Well, bak mei is only taught one-on-one. It's passed down from father to son, or in my case, mentor to student. I just never imagined I would ever have to use it."

"Whatever it is, it works."

"I know. I guess I have my mother to thank."

"She taught you?"

"Good God, no, but when I was young, she insisted that my sister and I be fully developed young women. She put us into Chinese, abacus, and ballet classes, but I drew the line when it came to learning the violin, so my mother gave me a choice between gymnastics or kung fu. I took kung fu and that eventually led me to bak mei."

"I have two daughters, and my wife is pushing them into dance and music as well. Maybe I'll insist on a martial art."

"It can't hurt. How about Carlo? Does he have kids?"

"You gotta be joking. He's a lover, or so he thinks. Most of the action he gets he pays for, and there aren't many mama-sans in the Hong Kong clubs or over in Macau who don't know him."

"And what about Uncle?"

Andy shook his head. "There's no wife and no kids that anyone's ever heard about. He's a bit of a loner and not a talker. Keeps things close to his chest, but when he tells you something, it's always good to listen, because he's not wrong very often and he always tells the truth. Maybe you'll get to meet him when we've finished this job."

"And why would I want to do that?" Ava said.

Andy blinked as if surprised by her response. "No particular reason, other than I think the two of you might get along."

"What makes you think that?"

"You're both smart."

"That's not much of an answer."

Andy shrugged and looked down at his food.

"I told you a lot of things about me when you asked how

I took that guy out. Now it's your turn. Tell me a bit more about Uncle."

"Like what?"

"What business was he in before? Carlo wouldn't say anything when I asked him at the apartment."

"Uncle was a dragon head."

"A what?"

"That's what they call the guy who runs the organization. It's an inside term."

"What kind of organization calls its leader a dragon head?"

"It's an old Chinese society, a brotherhood."

"How big is it?"

"It has hundreds, maybe even thousands of members. I don't know the numbers."

"And what does this society do?"

"It looks after the brothers and their families, kind of like a union."

"How?"

He shook his head. "I couldn't give you any details. I was just a worker."

"Uncle isn't with the organization any longer?"

"No, he retired. He's got all the money he'll ever need, and besides, I think there was a lot of stress attached to the job."

"This money-collecting business seems stressful enough to me. What made him get into it?"

"People came to him."

"I don't understand."

"When he retired, I think his plan was to buy some horses and spend his days at the Happy Valley and Sha Tin racetracks. But people kept coming to him for help getting their money back from the scumbags who'd taken it. Some of them were friends and he couldn't say no to them. Word got around and, I think before he knew it, he was in the business. And Carlo and me and some other guys had new full-time jobs."

"Obviously he's good at it."

"He's the best."

"What makes him the best?"

Andy shrugged again, and Ava could see he was feeling uncomfortable.

"It's isn't my place to talk about Uncle," he said. "I think I've probably said too much already."

Ava placed her chopsticks on her empty plate. "And what I think is that I'd better get into those electronic bank records. Again, you don't have to hang around if you don't want to."

He shrugged. "There's a coffee shop a few doors down from this building. I'll go there and then check back with you in about an hour."

"That's sounds just fine, and if I'm finished before then I'll come and find you."

He left with the paper bag filled with the remains of their lunch. Ava made sure the door was locked behind him and then went back to the desk. She logged on to the China Agricultural Bank website, entered the account number and TRADER22, and "Kung Imports" appeared. She had separated and stacked the letters of credit, purchase orders, wire transfers, manifests, and invoices to one side of the computer. Now she matched invoices to deposits and wire transfers to outgoing funds. Within five minutes she was smiling.

Over the past twelve months, the money flowing into the China Agricultural Bank account had come from the sales of Lo's products and nothing else. His customer base was only a bit broader — five major customers and then a few smaller ones — so it didn't take long to see that the numbers fitted. She was able to confirm what the partial paper records had already told her: every pound that Lo had shipped had been received, sold, and paid for.

Now she switched over to the Guangzhou Chemical Engineering Bank and found the same pattern. That account was the depository for the money Kung made selling Royal Meats' products. There were no other suppliers, and again only a handful of customers.

At first Kung had paid both Lo and Royal promptly and in full, but then the delays started and finally non-payment became the norm. The only question was, where had he moved the money he'd received?

She scrolled through the Guangzhou statements. Money that had left the account was always sent by wire transfer. On the statements, every withdrawal was listed as a wire but showed only a date, an amount, and an account number for the recipient. Ava opened the wire transfer file on the desk and found the detailed instructions. From the Guangzhou bank, wires had been sent to two companies: Meridian Trading and Bai Trading. They shared an address, on Bute Street in Kowloon. According to the wires, the money sent was for the purchase of toys from Meridian Trading and shrimp from Bai Trading.

Ava turned to Kung's purchase order file and saw that he had issued POs to both companies and had been invoiced from the Bute address. It took her fifteen minutes to work her way through all the shipping documents, manifests, and inventory reports. When she was finished, she was convinced that either Kung had never taken possession of the goods or the goods had never existed.

She repeated the process with the China Agricultural Bank statements. Again Meridian and Bai had been paid for goods for which there were purchase orders and invoices but no other indication the goods existed.

Bute Street was where Ava had gone to find Kung in Kowloon. She knew it was no coincidence. The bank where both Meridian and Bai had accounts was the Kowloon Light and Power Bank. What were the odds that the two companies would share a bank?

He could have made more of an effort, she thought. *Unless he was just trying to evade taxes, and purchase orders and invoices were all the Chinese collectors wanted to see.*

Ava started to print the bank statements and put together the files she wanted to take, but then she thought of something else. She wrote down the account numbers for Meridian and Bai Trading and then logged on to the Kowloon Light and Power Bank website. She entered the account number for Meridian, and when the password prompt came up, she typed in TRADER22.

She hadn't actually expected to get access to the account, so it almost shocked her when she did. The American dollars that had been wired to the Kowloon bank had been converted into Hong Kong dollars at an exchange rate of HK$7.50 for every American dollar. There was close to HK$5.5 million in the Meridian account.

Ava logged out of that account and then tried Bai Trading, scarcely believing that TRADER22 would work again. It did. The account held HK$4 million.

She did a quick conversion from Hong Kong back to American dollars. Together, the two accounts in the Kowloon bank contained more than $1.2 million U.S.

(14)

AVA SAT AT THE DESK AND STARED AT THE COM-puter screen as she tried to figure out what to do.

Even before she had gained access to the accounts using Kung's password, she had been convinced that Meridian and Bai Trading were shell companies set up by Kung to hide money. There wasn't much doubt in her mind that the money in the Kowloon bank came from the sales of Mr. Lo's and Royal Meats' products. Kung could wave around his phony purchase orders and invoices, but without any shipping or inventory records they had zero substance. The only complete paper trail ran from the suppliers to Kung to his customers, back to Kung again, and then through the two banks to the Kowloon bank. As well, the dates showed that the money was sent to the supposed trading companies as soon as Kung was paid by third parties for the pork or chicken feet. That money should have been sent to Lo and Royal. Ava's conviction that Kung was stealing became 100 percent certain after she had gotten into the Meridian and Bai accounts.

Now what to do? She could call Mr. Chow, or Uncle, as she was beginning to think of him, and explain what she'd found. Then what? He'd tell Andy and Carlo to start negotiating with Kung again. How long would that take? How much more money would they be able to get out of him? It was they, not she, who had Kung under control. What could she do if they decided to cut a bargain-basement deal that satisfied their client and then turned Kung loose?

The only leverage she had was the money. Rather than just knowing where it was, if she could bring it under her control, then she would have the upper hand in terms of dictating the final settlement. The problem was, to get control of the money, she would have to transfer it from Kung's bank accounts to hers or someone else's. She would have to steal it.

Well, not really steal it, she told herself. Kung was the thief. All she was doing was trying to reclaim the money for her client. Still, she knew she was on shaky moral ground and probably even shakier legal ground. If she were at home in Canada, she would never consider what she was now contemplating. There were rules of law there, and a system that could be trusted to be fair. But what Chinese or Hong Kong laws had she already broken by looking into Kung's bank accounts, even though he'd given her the password?

Worse, what Hong Kong or Chinese laws would she be breaking by transferring money out of the Meridian and Bai accounts? And even if she wasn't breaking any laws, what kind of connections did Kung have? What kind of trouble could he cause? The idea of being detained at the Chinese border or at the airport in Hong Kong filled her with dread.

Maybe, she thought, *I should discuss it with Uncle*. Maybe she should try moving the money to his account and let him deal with the local authorities, with whom he must be more familiar than she was. *No!* she thought savagely. Mr. Lo was her client. She'd found his money and a possible way to get it back to him. Not to go ahead and do so would be irresponsible.

And then it occurred to her that she might not be able to transfer the money. She was looking at the Bai records. She clicked on the link that said MANAGING YOUR ACCOUNT. One of the options it offered was electronic transfer. Maybe Kung hadn't signed up for that service. And if he had, maybe there were limits on the amount that could be moved from the account at any given time. She chose the transfer option and a blank form opened up.

Ava looked at the information required about the recipient and quickly filled in her own company name, address, phone number, and contact person. She reached for her bag and took out a card from her Canadian bank manager. The bank's name, address, phone number, account number, and swift code were all on it.

The sender portion wasn't as straightforward, since she wasn't sure if the information Kung had provided to the bank was legitimate. *What the hell*, she thought, as she typed in BAI TRADING, the Bute street address, and the phone number on the invoice. Finally she added Johnny Kung's name as the contact and authorizing officer. She waited for the form to disappear or for asterisks to appear next to her entries or for any other indication that she was about to be rejected. But the website took her to the next page.

Now the question was, how much could she dare send to Canada? She didn't want to empty the bank account entirely but she also didn't want to send some minor amount on a test basis, in case transfers were restricted to one a day. She decided to try to send herself HK$3.6 million. Even though she knew it was highly unlikely there would be any negative backlash if she failed, she felt the slightest tremor in her fingers and a cold sweat on her brow as she typed in the numbers. She stared at the amount and then repeated the numbers aloud to make sure they were correct. Then she hit the SUBMIT button.

The web page disappeared. Ava's cold sweat turned hot. She closed her eyes, and when she opened them again, expecting the worst, she saw a line that read: Your transfer has been completed. We will send confirmation to your email address. You can print a copy from our website.

She pressed the PRINT button, closed the account, and switched over to Meridian's.

Five minutes later she had dispatched HK$5 million from Meridian to her Canadian bank account. She tried to imagine what her branch manager would think when he saw the overnight deposit reports. Since she'd opened the account, the largest amount she'd ever had in it was $8,000. When the Hong Kong dollars were converted to Canadian, her account would contain more than $1.2 million.

She pushed the chair back from the desk and took a deep breath. She had just stolen more than a million dollars. But any guilt or anxiety she had was quickly swamped by a rush of almost sheer joy as she contemplated Mr. Lo's reaction. He wouldn't care how she'd got the money. Why should he? And why should she? But there was still one more loop to close.

She headed out the door and was at the top of the stairs when she saw Andy at the bottom. "I need you," she said.

"You sound excited," he said, and began to run up.

"You have to call Carlo and get me Kung's email address. If he has more than one, I want them all. And obviously I'll need his passwords."

"Let me see what I can do."

"There is no 'let me see.' I have to have them. I don't care what Carlo has to do. Tell him to cut off Kung's balls if he has to."

"You are excited," Andy said.

"Sorry."

"*Momentai*," he said, taking his phone from his pocket as he walked into the office.

Ava went back behind the desk. "I'm waiting," she said.

Andy smiled as he called Carlo. "Hey, our new boss lady needs some information from Kung. Get us all of his email addresses, with passwords... Yeah, right now." He covered the mouthpiece with his hand. "Carlo's talking to him."

"What a ride this has been," Ava murmured, and then realized she had landed in Hong Kong less than thirty-six hours before. "What a day."

"Trader22@hktelco.com," Andy said to her.

"Capital letters?"

"All small."

"And is that the only email address he has?"

"According to Carlo it is."

"Kung has almost no imagination, and thank God for that," she said as she logged in to Kung's email. Again she felt a flicker of anticipation mixed with fear as she waited for the inbox to load. When it did, she saw two emails from the Kowloon Light and Power Bank at the top of the list. Ava opened them, read the confirmations, sent them to the printer, and then deleted them.

She took several deep breaths. "We're done here," she

said. "I think we should go back to your apartment and chat with Johnny Kung."

As they walked down the stairs, it suddenly occurred to her that $400,000 was still sitting in the Guangzhou and China Agricultural bank accounts that Kung had acknowledged were his. In all the excitement of raiding the Kowloon accounts, she had forgotten about them. For just a second she thought about going back to the office, but then dismissed the idea. She didn't want to press her luck. Besides, Carlo and Andy had already negotiated that amount to be paid. As long as they held Kung and he didn't find out about the Kowloon withdrawals, he'd pay that too. *Let the guys have that victory,* she thought.

It was midafternoon when they left the office building. There wasn't a cloud in the sky and the sun should have been visible. It was there, Ava could see, but looked like it was behind a veil of dust and floating debris.

Andy went to a vacant taxi stand and looked up and down the street as he tried to hail a cab. Then Ava saw Kung's men walking towards him. "Andy, be careful," she said.

He didn't have time to turn around before one of the men hit him from behind, driving his fist into the nape of his neck. Andy staggered forward, and the man kicked him in the back. Andy collapsed onto the street, directly in front of the oncoming traffic. The man reached down, grabbed him by the T-shirt, and dragged him onto the sidewalk. Then the man kicked him so hard in the ribs that his body seemed to jump in the air.

"Stop that," Ava yelled.

Both men turned to look at her.

"Now it's your turn," the man Ava knew as Li said.

"You're making a mistake," Ava said.

Li shook his head. "This time you won't surprise me."

"No, I mean we've reached a deal with Johnny Kung. There's no need for this."

"That's him. I'm me."

"He's not going to be happy."

"Who gives a fuck?"

"He's the one paying you."

"By the day. We're freelancers. No Kung, no money."

"So why are you bothering with us?"

"We changed the plan. We figure we'll trade you and the little asshole for Kung."

The two men were directly in front of her, about ten metres away. Ava glanced quickly to her right and left. A group of pedestrians had stopped to take in the confrontation. They seemed more curious than concerned.

"That won't work," she said.

"Maybe not, but while we're waiting for an answer, I'll at least have the satisfaction of beating the shit out of him and you."

"I'm not going anywhere with you," she said.

"I don't remember giving you a choice," Li said, taking a step forward.

She took a step back, studying the two men as she did. Li's partner had slid to one side, and Ava figured they would come at her from two directions. In the light of day, they looked even larger than they had when she saw them in the hotel and Li in the restaurant. But they also seemed bulkier, less agile and quick.

"Don't try to run," Li said.

"I'm not going anywhere without my partner," she said.

"That's true enough, so why don't you make it easy on everyone and come along quietly," Li said, and then waved his arm at the spectators. "We don't want to scare all these people, do we?"

"Fuck off," Ava said, not sure how the words had found their way out of her mouth, and surprised by their intensity.

Li's face contorted and then he forced a smile. "Take the bitch from the left," he said to his partner, as he took steps to the right.

They were still anticipating that she would run and were cutting off her escape routes. Li's partner, looking uninterested and bored, started towards her almost casually. When he was a couple of paces away, he reached out to grab her arm. Ava retreated until her back found a wall. He leaned forward, slightly off balance, and his right hand gripped her left arm. The instant she felt his touch, her right hand crossed her body and latched onto his elbow. She dug her thumb into the soft flesh on the underside of the elbow and found the nerve she was seeking. She pressed hard, and he screamed and pulled back, his arm dangling uselessly by his side. She thought about hitting him, but Li had already moved in. She swivelled to face him.

He ran at her as he had in the restaurant, and she wondered why he thought that strategy would work this time. But as he drew near, he twisted to one side, and the phoenix-eye fist that Ava had aimed at his stomach hit him in the ribs. He groaned but didn't stop. He threw a punch at her head. She ducked, only to have his fist smash into her shoulder and knock her against the wall. Li turned quickly to look at his partner. Beyond the two of them, Ava could see Andy trying to get to his feet and reaching into his pocket.

"Don't use your gun," she shouted at him.

Li flinched and took a quick look back at Andy. As he did, Ava drove her knuckle into his nose. She heard it pop, and was splattered with gushing blood. Li reeled, his left hand holding his nose, his right fist flailing at her. She leapt to her right and was about to bring him down with a kick to the back of his knee when her legs were swept from under her and she crashed onto the sidewalk. She looked up. Li's partner loomed over her, his arm still dangling, a maniacal look on his face. She rolled away from him and then saw Andy limping towards them, his gun pointed.

"No," she yelled.

Then a whistle screeched and she heard the sound of heavy boots on the sidewalk. Two policemen emerged through the ring of spectators.

Thank God, Ava thought.

"Sergeant Li, what's going on here?" one of them asked.

(15)

AVA HAD NEVER BEEN IN A JAIL CELL BEFORE. In fact, she'd never so much as seen a prison, from the outside or the inside.

The policemen who handcuffed her, put her in the back of their squad car, and drove her to what she assumed was their precinct office had been polite enough, if a bit firm. They weren't as restrained with Andy. His arms were yanked back and twisted before the cuffs went on, and they threw him into the back of the car, whacking his knee with a baton as they told him to stay quiet.

They removed the cuffs when she got to the office and turned her over to a short, stocky woman with a corporal's two stripes on the arm of her blue shirt. Ava was directed to a chair beside a desk, where she sat and watched the corporal empty her bag and list its contents on a sheet of paper.

"Sign here," the corporal said.

When she did, the corporal opened Ava's passport and compared the signatures.

"What now, fingerprints and a mug shot?" Ava asked.

The corporal raised an eyebrow. "You haven't been charged with anything yet."

"He attacked us," Ava blurted. "We were defending ourselves. I know he's a policeman, but that shouldn't make any difference."

"Listen to me, girl. The best thing you can do while you're here is not talk. Don't tell me too much. Don't talk to anyone else until you know the score. I have to put you in a holding cell with other women, who'll probably want to gab. Don't talk to them either."

"A cell?"

"We have to keep you somewhere until they decide what to do with you."

The corporal was completely matter-of-fact, but instead of calming Ava, her manner was unnerving. "Do I get to make a phone call?" Ava said, her mouth dry, a slight stutter to her speech.

"This isn't America."

"I'm Canadian."

"You still don't get to make a phone call."

"But I need to let people know what's going on, where I am."

"After they decide what to do with you, you can contact someone. Until then, like I said, keep your head down and your mouth shut."

"Okay."

"Just one thing — they told me you broke Li's nose."

"I might have."

"He's a pig with women. It's time someone taught him a lesson."

"That wasn't my intention."

The corporal shrugged. "I'll take you to the cell now."

The office was long and narrow, but with enough space between the two rows of desks for Ava and the corporal to walk side by side. Andy was at the desk closest to a large steel door. He was still handcuffed, and one of the arresting officers sat next to him while another, behind the desk, was asking questions.

The corporal punched in a security code. The door buzzed and opened into a large room that had three cages on either side. The cages had steel bars on all sides and across the top. They were about three metres high and maybe five metres square along the sides. A wooden bench ran along each side, and in one corner was a toilet without a seat, a roll of rough-looking toilet paper on the floor next to it. Ava recoiled.

She kept her eyes locked on the wall in front of her, trying to fight off her panic. Every eye in the room was locked on to her, with the exception of a female police officer sitting on a stool, her attention on a magazine.

"Open up," the corporal said.

The officer grunted as if she was annoyed at being disturbed. When she saw Ava, she closed the magazine and stood up.

"Well, she's different from our regular customer," she said. "What's she charged with?"

"Nothing yet."

The officer walked to the nearest cell, took a key from a set on a long chain strapped to her belt, and unlocked the door. "There you go, sweetheart. It's all yours," she said.

Ava walked into the cell. There were already two occupants: a woman in ragged jeans and a stained T-shirt who sat slumped on the bench with her head in her hands, and a young woman who was lying on the floor in a fetal position. One of her feet was touching a puddle of vomit.

Ava sat on one end of the bench, as far from her cellmates as possible. She rested the back of her head against a bar, closed her eyes, and tried to think of anything other than the situation she was in. Except she had no idea what her situation actually was, other than that she was sitting in a jail cell in China facing unknown charges and unknown penalties. What would they do to her for hitting a policeman? She had read about how arbitrary, speedy, and punitive Chinese law was. Now she wished she hadn't, because her imagination was running wild and filling her with fear.

They would have to let her get a lawyer, she told herself, but if they did, who would it be? She would have to call her father. As she thought about how that conversation would go, embarrassment and humiliation added to the emotions she was already experiencing. Strangely, she had no qualms about what her mother might think. Ava knew Jennie Lee would support and defend her no matter what she did with her life; any judgement Jennie passed would be silent. If Ava had been in Canada, her phone call would have been to Richmond Hill to unleash her mother. But there was no point in doing that here in China. The only person she could call was her father. *God, what a mess*, she thought.

The woman on the bench made a strange coughing noise and got to her feet. She glanced at Ava with glazed and distant eyes. For a second, Ava thought she was going to speak to her, but the woman turned and walked towards the toilet, stepping over the woman on the floor to get there. As she started to pull down her jeans, Ava turned her head.

She closed her eyes again and forced herself to think about bak mei exercises. At times when she couldn't sleep, she would go through them in her mind, imagining in slow motion the springing, sinking, and thrusting moves of the tiger. Now she used the exercise as a distraction, repeating the moves over and over, imagining that Grandmaster Tang was on the offensive while she parried and neutralized his attacks. She was deep into it when someone yelled in her ear. She jumped at the noise.

"Dinner," said a woman holding a small metal tray near the bars.

The woman on the floor didn't react, and Ava realized she hadn't noticed her move since she'd been in the cell. She was either sleeping or unconscious, or dead. Ava didn't want to find out which was true.

The other woman had returned to the bench. She waved her hand at the tray. "I don't want to eat your shit," she said.

Ava looked at the lump of white rice, a soggy green vegetable, and a couple of pieces of grey meat swimming in brown gravy. "I think I'll pass as well," she said.

When the meal trolley left, the woman next to her said, "What are you in for?"

"I'm not really sure. I think there's been a mistake," Ava said.

"Sure, a mistake," the woman said, and leaned in close, her foul breath filling the air.

Ava gagged and turned away. She stood and walked towards the cell door. There were no windows in the room and the overhead lights were dim, probably deliberately so. The other cells were full and most of the prisoners were eating. A feeling of despair washed over her.

The corporal had taken her watch, along with her other possessions, so Ava had no idea what time it was. It had to be five, or maybe even six, if dinner was being served. How long would it take them to decide what to charge her with? She hadn't been read her rights — surely they had to do that. Was there a time limit on how long a person could be held without being charged? *Slow down*, she thought. *Your mind is running off in all directions.*

She was still standing at the cell door when the dinner lady came back with her trolley and collected the empty trays. When the woman opened the door to leave, Ava caught a glimpse of the corporal walking towards it. The door closed and then almost immediately reopened, and the corporal walked in. She came directly to Ava's cell.

"Let the girl in the pink shirt out," she said to the woman on the stool.

"What's going on?" Ava said.

"Just come with me."

Ava followed her into the office, her heart beating so loudly she thought it had to be audible.

The woman stopped at her desk. Ava's bag sat on top of it. "Open the bag and go through it. Make sure everything is there," she said.

"What's going on?" Ava asked, trying not to be too hopeful.

"You're released."

"No charges?" Ava said.

"No."

"I don't understand."

"The word came down from above — that's all I know. And if I were you, I'd take my bag and get the hell out of here as fast as I could before someone changes their mind."

Ava felt light-headed and took several deep breaths to steady herself. She opened the bag and took a quick look at the contents. If anything was missing it wasn't apparent, and she wasn't about to waste time identifying every item.

She picked up her bag. "How do I get out of here?"

"That door leads to the reception area. The main entrance is there. Big double glass doors, you can't miss them."

She walked with urgency to the door, and when she reached it, she barrelled through, determined not to stop until she hit the street. Then she saw Andy standing by the glass exit doors. He smiled and waved as if he hadn't a care in the world.

"What the hell happened?" Ava asked loudly as she approached him.

"Uncle."

"What do you mean?"

"Uncle happened. He made some phone calls, called in some favours, and probably greased some palms."

Ava shook her head. "I've never been so frightened in my life."

"That's funny."

"Why?"

"I just finished telling Uncle that I've never met anyone, man or woman, as fearless as you."

"You shouldn't give him the wrong impression."

"Well, you can correct it when you meet with him. He wants you to call him. He mentioned something about taking you to dinner tonight — assuming you want to go back to Hong Kong."

"Try and stop me. I'm catching the first train I can get on."

"I can't say I blame you. It's been a hell of a day."

"But I'm not sure about dinner."

"Uncle is a gentleman, if that's what you're worried about. I think he just wants to repay you for saving my butt."

"I'm really not sure."

"Please, as a favour to me, call him."

"What about you and Carlo?"

"We're staying here one more night to clean up the Kung mess."

"Mess?"

"Uncle will explain."

"I don't have his number . . ." Ava said hesitantly.

Andy pulled his phone from his pocket and hit speed dial. He listened for a moment and then passed it to Ava.

"This is Ava Lee," she said.

"I am so happy you are safe," Uncle said.

"No more than I am."

"Are you still in Shenzhen?"

"Yes, but I'm heading for the train station as soon as I finish talking to you."

"Where are you staying in Hong Kong?"

"I'm in Kowloon, at the Oriental Crocus."

"I know it. My apartment is about ten minutes away from there. Did Andy mention to you that I would like to take you to dinner?"

"That isn't necessary."

"Perhaps not, but I would like to do it all the same. Do you like hotpot?"

"Yes."

"There is a very good place close to your hotel. I can send my driver to pick you up and you can meet me there."

"Mr. Chow — Uncle — I'm not sure I'm up to it."

"Look, it is only seven o'clock. You will be at your hotel by eight or so. Shower and change, get rid of the smell of Shenzhen. I will ask my driver to be at the hotel at nine. He will be driving a silver Mercedes. He will be wearing a black suit, white shirt, and black tie. His name is Sonny."

"Well, I am hungry."

"There is nothing better for hungry people than hotpot. This place has Kobe beef and shrimp the size of small lobsters, which the owner reserves for special customers. I am fortunate that he considers me to be one."

"Okay."

"Excellent. I will meet you there."

Ava closed the phone and handed it back to Andy. "I'm heading for the train station and I'm going to meet Uncle for dinner in Kowloon."

"You won't be sorry," Andy said. "Well, I guess we should say goodbye."

He held out his hand. Ava stepped forward and kissed him gently on the cheek. "Thanks for everything," she said. "Now tell me, in which direction is the train station and do I need to take a taxi? When we were in that squad car, I was so upset I didn't notice where we were going."

"Go two blocks straight down there and hang a left at the movie complex. The station will be visible from the corner."

"Great. Well, I'm off. Maybe I'll see you around," Ava said, waving goodbye.

She had a spring in her step and was at the station in just a few minutes. A train was scheduled to arrive in ten minutes, and it couldn't come fast enough. All she wanted was to put Shenzhen behind her. She walked into the passenger holding pen and was already contemplating the joy of a hot shower when two thoughts interceded.

She had forgotten to ask Uncle what Andy meant by the "Kung mess."

And—perhaps an even stronger indication of how distracted she was—she had somehow neglected to tell anyone that she had wired more than a million dollars to Toronto.

(16)

AT FIVE TO NINE, AVA WALKED OUT OF THE ELEVATOR and into the lobby of the Oriental Crocus Hotel.

She had no idea how long she had been in the shower. She'd scrubbed every square inch of her body over and over again, and then washed her hair twice. Even after she dried herself and was getting dressed, the smells of soap and shampoo were still powerful.

On the train going back to Kowloon she'd had second thoughts about accepting the dinner invitation from Uncle. Then she had realized that she didn't have his phone number, so had no way of cancelling except by telling his driver that she wasn't going with him, and she was too polite to do that. So dinner it would be, and as she showered and then dressed, the thought of Kobe beef slivers and huge shrimp simmering in a hotpot became more and more enticing. For a small woman she had a huge appetite, and more than once her mother had admonished her for eating like a glutton. She would have to show restraint at dinner, she told herself. And as she got dressed, she decided to be as restrained in the way she looked.

She put on a white shirt, which she buttoned almost all

the way to her neck, and a pair of roomy black linen slacks. The pumps she had worn to Shenzhen were replaced by flats. She pulled back her hair and fastened it with a plain white plastic clasp. She put on just a touch of red lipstick and black mascara, and then dabbed the Chanel perfume her mother had given her for Christmas on her wrists and collarbones. When she stood in front of the mirror, she was pleased to see a conservatively dressed young professional woman looking back at her.

She was ready to leave at a quarter to nine, but then she noticed the light on the hotel phone was blinking. She followed the automated directions and was told there were two voice messages in her box. Her mother had left the first.

"Ava, I just wanted to make sure you arrived safely. I have told your father that you're there, so you should expect a call from him. As well, I played mah-jong with Mrs. Lo last night. She is thrilled that you're helping her husband. I just hope her expectations are realistic. Anyway, call me when you can."

Her father was the next in line. "I hear you are in Hong Kong. Call me on my mobile so we can arrange a lunch."

She looked at her watch. It was too early to phone her mother and probably too late to reach her father on his mobile. Both calls would have to wait until tomorrow.

The hotel lobby was almost empty when she got there. As she walked towards the exit, a very large man dressed in a black suit, white shirt, and black tie dominated her line of vision. He stood just inside the door, his back leaning against the wall. Ava guessed he was six foot three and had to weigh 250 pounds. As she got closer to him, she saw that his brow was furrowed and he seemed to be scowling. His eyes were rather small, almost sinister, and that impression was heightened by the coarseness of his skin, which was pockmarked on both cheeks.

When he saw her, he straightened, and the scowl diminished as his face appeared to relax.

"Are you Sonny?" she asked.

"Yes, and you must be Ava Lee."

"I am."

"Uncle is waiting for you at the restaurant, so we can go there now."

"Wonderful."

He went to the door and held it open for her. As she passed through, almost brushing against him, his size was even more apparent. A silver Mercedes idled at the curb. The doorman stood next to it, as if standing guard. He made a move to open the front passenger door, but before he could, Sonny slipped past Ava and reached for the rear door handle. She stopped, surprised by his speed and agility. The doorman backed away from the car. Ava slid into the back seat and watched as Sonny passed an HK$50 note to the other man.

They rode in silence to the restaurant. Unlike her mother, who had a need to fill the air with idle chatter, Ava was comfortable with quiet. She gazed out the window. Mong Kok was alive with people shopping at the night street markets and coming and going from the numerous neon-lit restaurants. After a few minutes, Ava saw a sign for Tsim Sha Tsui and knew they were nearing Victoria Harbour. As she looked ahead, waiting for the harbour and the magnificent Hong Kong skyline to appear, she caught Sonny's eyes in the rear-view mirror. They weren't as sinister as they had first seemed, but they were watchful and cautious.

The car turned right before they reached the harbour and Ava found herself in a part of Tsim Sha Tsui she had never been to before. They drove past the back of the Peninsula Hotel and then onto a side street that had the same bustling fervour they'd just left behind in Mong Kok. Sonny parked the car directly in front of Ming's Hot Pot. Ava started to open her door, but Sonny was already out of the car, his hand reaching for the handle.

"Go right in," he said. "Just tell the host you're with Uncle."

The restaurant was packed, and she had to fight her way past a throng at the door to get to the host's stand. He looked at her and said, "An hour, maybe two hours before there's a table."

"I'm with Uncle — Mr. Chow Tung."

"Ah, okay, right this way," he said, turning and not so gently pushing aside the waiting customers.

They had to walk through the entire restaurant to get to the private room. Ava estimated there had to be sixty tables seating anywhere from four to twenty people. All of them were full, and the noise level was deafening. Even more distracting for her was the air quality. The restaurant's ventilation system wasn't working or was overburdened, because the steam rising from the pots was like an aromatic fog.

There was more than one private room at the rear. The host stopped at the first and then knocked loudly on the closed door. "Uncle, your guest is here."

Ava couldn't hear any noise from inside and was surprised when the door swung quickly and completely open. She found herself looking directly into the eyes of a small, thin man wearing a black suit and a white shirt buttoned to the neck. He was perhaps two inches taller than her, and he couldn't have weighed much more, either.

"You must be Ava," he said, extending his right hand and flashing a smile that exposed brilliant white teeth.

"Uncle," she said.

"Andy said you were a beautiful young woman. For once he did not exaggerate, although I have to say you are even younger than I expected."

"I don't know what to say."

"Nothing has to be said. Now you must be hungry. Come, let us sit."

Ava stepped inside, the restaurant host trailing.

"Uncle, do you want me to turn on the fire now?" the host asked. "And would you like another beer?"

"Wait just a moment, Ming. I need to find out if Ms. Lee is ready to eat and if she wants something to drink," he said as he pulled out her chair.

"I'm famished," Ava said. "And I would really like a glass of dry white wine."

"I have Italian, German, and Swiss wines," the host said.

"The Italian will do," Ava said, wondering how Swiss wine had conquered China.

"I ordered the Kobe beef, shrimp, oysters, mushrooms, and some green vegetables. Is there anything else you would like?" Uncle asked.

"No, that sounds just fine."

"Then light the fire and bring the food, the wine, and another beer," Uncle said to Ming.

"Yes, Uncle," the host said, bending down to fire up the gas fixture.

When he left, Ava found herself the subject of another penetrating stare. She started to turn away, but then she wondered why she should and looked directly at him. He was of an indeterminate age. His hair was black, flecked with traces of grey and cropped close to his scalp. There were fine lines under his eyes, and more around the edges of his mouth. *He could be fifty, sixty, or seventy*, she thought.

His gaze didn't waver and she tried to act as resolute. His eyes were incredibly dark, the irises a rich deep brown, and their depth was intensified by the pure whiteness of the sclera. Strangely, she didn't feel that he was trying to intimidate her. It was more as if he was searching, trying to see into her.

"I have to thank you for getting me out of Shenzhen," she said, finally lowering her eyes.

"After what you did for Carlo and Andy, it was my pleasure."

"Andy said you had to call in favours."

"Unfortunately, a cost was involved."

"I'm sorry it came to that."

"The favours do not matter. They are always there in the new China if you have *guanxi*. And I do."

"He mentioned there was a mess with Kung."

"He gave you none of the details?"

"No, he said you would fill me in."

"That surprises me but pleases me. Andy is quite taken with you, and I was sure he would not be able to resist telling you."

"He told me nothing at all, and I am obviously anxious to know."

Uncle leaned forward, his hands folded neatly in front of him. As he began to speak, the door opened and Ming walked in with the drinks. Directly behind him came two women carrying large trays.

"We will wait until Ming is done," Uncle said.

The drinks were served and the women put the trays on a side table. They set the main table with bowls, plates, chopsticks, small wire baskets, napkins, various sauces, and chilis. Ava looked at the array of food and her stomach almost ached. The beef was cut into long, thin slices that were almost transparent. The shrimp, their shells and heads still on, had to be six inches in length. The broth was already bubbling. Ming poured soy sauce into a small bowl for each of them. Then he said to Uncle, "Would you like me to make one of the pots spicy?"

"Ava, what do you prefer?" Uncle asked.

The large pot was divided into two by a strip of metal. "One side spicy is fine with me," she said.

"Go ahead, Ming," Uncle said.

When he finished, Ming stepped back from the table and hovered.

"This looks wonderful," Uncle said. "Check back on us every ten minutes or so. I have a feeling that the cold beer and cold white wine will be going down very easily."

Ming closed the door as he left.

Uncle lifted his bottle of Tsingtao. "*Gom bui*," he said.

Ava stretched across the table and tapped the rim of her glass against his bottle. "*Gom bui*."

Uncle picked up a set of chopsticks and began to put the raw food into the pots. He left the beef for last. "It will take only a few seconds for the meat," he said, handing her one of the small wire baskets, which he had layered with slices of beef.

She dipped it into the spicy broth and after no more than five seconds took it out. She emptied it onto her plate and then picked up a piece. It melted in her mouth.

For the next few minutes they busied themselves with the pots, taking out food and putting more in, until her hunger began to abate. He ate as eagerly as she did, and more rapidly. In fact she couldn't remember seeing anyone eat quite so quickly. It surprised her. This was a man whose outward demeanour was so calm.

The shrimp were plucked from the pot last. Uncle put two on his plate, peeled the shell from one, leaving the head on, and passed it to Ava. She dipped the shrimp into the bowl that held a mixture of soy sauce and chilis and savoured the first bite. The flesh was perfect, delicate but firm all the way through. When she was done, she saw Uncle eyeing the head.

"I don't eat these. Would you like it?" she asked.

He nodded with a smile and she passed it to him. He put it in his mouth and sucked. Ava had tried it once at the urging of her mother, and though the head meat had incredible flavour, the consistency put her off.

"I need another beer. More wine for you?" he asked.

"Please."

He walked to the door, opened it, and waved a hand. He had hardly resumed sitting before Ming was there with their drinks and an ice bucket, in which he left extra beer and a half-empty bottle of Pinot Grigio.

"How do you find the food?" Uncle asked her.

"Couldn't you tell?"

"I come here often. Ming spoils me."

Ava sipped her wine and began to feel the stress of the day ebb. "You were going to tell me about Kung," she said.

"We had to let him go," Uncle said quietly. "That was part of the deal to get you and Andy released."

"Oh."

"I know you must be disappointed, after everything you have gone through, but it was either that or have Li press charges against you for assault and against Andy for attempted murder."

"Andy didn't try to kill anyone."

"No, but he was silly enough to wave around a gun in public."

"You said letting Kung go was just part of the deal."

"Well, it was more involved than that, but we need not get into it."

"No, please, I'd really like to know. You know I am new to all this, and I would like to understand how things work in China."

Uncle shrugged. "The first thing you should know is that there is no one China. Each province and each major city has its own peculiarities, and there are many subtle differences among them that take time to understand. Shenzhen is so new, so raw, that it is still finding its way. I like to think of it as the Chinese equivalent of the American Wild West. Anything goes."

"Andy implied that you had to pay off some officials."

"That is normal enough."

"And when you say we had to let Kung go, does that mean we didn't collect any money from him?"

"It does."

"So you are out of pocket on top of that."

"It is not a concern."

"I want to repay you that money."

"That is not necessary."

"But —"

"Please do not go on about the money. Things happen for a reason. And in this case it brought you to my attention, so good has come of it."

"I don't understand."

"I would like you to come and work for me."

(17)

AVA REACHED FOR HER WINEGLASS AND IN TWO large sips almost drained it. She refilled it from the bottle in the ice bucket.

"I wasn't sure what you were going to say to me, but offering me a job wasn't anywhere in the mix," she said.

He pushed his chair back from the table. "Do you mind if I smoke?"

"Not at all."

He took a package of Double Happiness White Label cigarettes from his jacket pocket, lit one, inhaled deeply, and then blew the smoke away from the table. "I have more business than I can handle, but some of it — some of the most interesting and potentially lucrative jobs — I have to turn away because I do not have the right kind of people for it."

"Excuse me, Uncle, I'm not a hundred percent sure just what your business is. I understand that you collect debts, but is that the extent of it?"

"It is."

"And you are Hong Kong–based?"

"I am, although I have a client base that goes beyond."

"And you use Hong Kong collection methods, or at least the approach I saw Andy and Carlo take?"

"Do you mean threats, intimidation, embarrassment, kidnapping, and ransom, in all their variations?"

"Yes," Ava said. "Uncle, I could never work like that."

"You misunderstand me," he said. "It is true that right now we do practise traditional collection tactics, but that is mainly because of the rather limited talents of the people I have working for me. But as well, it has been my experience that the thieves we chase are not usually inclined to be responsive to gentle persuasion or empty threats. When I was a young man, starting my business, I soon learned that most people do the right thing for the wrong reason. I have drummed that lesson into the men who work for me, and some have become adept at finding those wrong reasons.

"That said, the clients I mentioned earlier — the ones I have had to turn away — they have problems that demand a far more sophisticated approach in terms of detection and recovery. The sums of money involved are, I assure you, far more substantial than what we were trying to pry out of Kung. Someone with your talents would be invaluable."

"I'm not really looking for a job," Ava said.

"And I was not looking for someone to hire. We seem to have stumbled into each other."

"And Uncle, I'm not sure what talents you're referring to. I'm an accountant."

"Exactly, and one who happens to speak Cantonese, Mandarin, and English fluently."

"There must be others who are in Hong Kong already."

"There are. But I have not met any with the imagination and flair you displayed in getting Kung to rise to the bait."

"I was jet-lagged and not thinking clearly."

"You are modest as well."

She had to smile. "Actually, my mother is always taking me to task for being a know-it-all."

"There is nothing wrong with having confidence. There is also nothing wrong with having the ability to look after yourself. In this business there are always physical challenges. Andy said he could not believe that you took Kung's man down once, let alone twice."

Ava shook her head. "It wasn't anything I enjoyed or would want to repeat. The fact of the matter is I have my own business in Toronto. I also don't think I could live in Hong Kong, with all the ties I have in Canada."

"When we first spoke, you mentioned that your father lives in Hong Kong. So you have ties here as well, no?"

She drank some more wine, even though she knew it was getting to her. She looked at Uncle. He was smoking another cigarette, and he did it with the same urgency with which he ate. *There are strong currents running beneath that calm surface*, she thought. "My mother is a second wife and we are a second family. After we were shipped off to Canada, my father took a third wife and now there's a third family. My roots are in Canada," she said.

"Are you always so plain-spoken?"

"I try to be."

"What is your father's name?"

"Marcus Lee."

Uncle paused. "I believe he and I know each other. Not well, but in Hong Kong, when a man has business of a certain size, it is difficult for it to be otherwise."

"Well, as I said, my father may be here," Ava said, having no wish to pursue the subject, "but my roots are in Canada."

He nodded. "So, if you won't come to Hong Kong for family, will you come for money? Whatever you are earning now, I will double."

"I just can't," she said. "I've tried working for other people and it didn't work. In fact, it was a disaster. I may be young, but I'm not so young that I'm prepared to start repeating mistakes."

"I understand." He sighed. "I too was anxious to be independent when I was your age. So then, we will finish dinner and part as new friends."

"Yes, as new friends."

"Tell me, have you informed your client yet about our collective failure? That is always the hardest part of this job."

Ava gasped and felt the blood rush to her face.

"Did he react that badly?" Uncle asked.

"No, it isn't that at all."

"Then why do you look so distressed?"

"Uncle, suppose I had managed to get my hands on some of Kung's money. Would the deal you struck with him compel us to give any of it back?"

He became still, his face expressionless as he stared at her across the table. Then his lips tightened and formed a small smile. "Andy said you seemed excited at some point in the day. He did not know why. I think I do."

"Yes. I'm so sorry and I feel so silly. You completely distracted me with your talk about a job."

"You found some of Kung's money?"

"I did, and I accessed the account and transferred it to my bank account in Toronto."

"How much?" he asked.

"Just over a million dollars."

"Hong Kong?"

"Canadian."

He closed his eyes. When he opened them, she saw a gleam.

"You are an amazing young woman, Ava Lee," he said as he reached for some shrimp and put them in the pot. Then he added oysters and mushrooms. "Would you like more beef?" he asked.

"Please."

They ate the beef quickly. Uncle opened another beer and Ava poured herself more wine, until the bottle was almost empty. When the mushrooms and oysters popped to the surface of the broth, Uncle served them both.

"Thanks," she said. "Uncle, I have to say, I find it strange that you haven't mentioned the million dollars."

"I am still digesting the information. It was not expected."

"It's a lot of money, and we have to decide how to split it."

"How much are you charging your client?"

"Ten percent of what I recover, but he's paying my expenses."

"We charge thirty and pay our own way. My experience is that paying your own expenses works better in the long run."

"I don't have any experience."

He laughed. "You are learning quickly enough. Now as for the split, given the extraordinary circumstances involved, I suggest that we take the two hundred thousand that we were going to get from our deal with Kung, and you take the balance."

She blinked in surprise. "That's not fair. We had agreed on fifty-fifty, and you paid off the police. We should split that cost as well."

"We cannot take that much. We did not earn it."

"We had an agreement. I don't feel right going back on it."

"You are not. I am the one making the changes."

"Uncle, I want you to take your half."

"No," he said quietly, but forcefully all the same. "I only insisted on fifty-fifty because I thought my men would be doing all the heavy work and you were just along for the ride. That is not how it worked out. As it turns out, without you we would have nothing. Our shares must more accurately reflect our contributions. The figure of two hundred thousand is entirely fair and satisfactory."

"What about the bribes you paid?"

"They were minor. Shenzhen is still so new that the scale has not reached Shanghai proportions."

Ava sighed. "I really don't know what to say."

"Yes will be sufficient."

"Then yes. Yes and thank you."

"And thank you for not arguing too much about it," he said.

She nodded and reached for her wineglass. It was almost empty. She took the bottle out of the ice bucket and poured the last dregs into her glass. "I can't remember the last time I drank a bottle of wine by myself," she said.

"And I cannot remember the last time I offered someone a job and they turned me down and then gave me two hundred thousand dollars," he said with a smile.

(18)

THEY LEFT THE RESTAURANT TOGETHER, BOTH OF them tipsy. It was close to eleven o'clock but the restaurant was still packed, with people jostling at the front for the next available table. Sonny was waiting for them just inside the door. He was leaning against the wall, scowling, his eyes darting around the room. Ava wondered if he had been there the entire time. When he saw them, he gave a slight nod and turned towards the exit, clearing a path as he went. That drew Ming's attention, and he left his stand to run towards Uncle and Ava.

"Thank you for another wonderful meal," Uncle said, passing him what Ava saw were several Hong Kong thousand-dollar notes.

"No money from you," Ming said.

"If you want me to come back, you will take my money," Uncle said.

Ming lowered his head. "It was an honour, as always," he said, letting Uncle press the money into his palm.

The night air was chilly and Ava shivered when they reached the street. Luckily the car was parked exactly where Sonny had left it, in front of the restaurant. She saw a policeman standing next to it, and assumed it was about to be or had just been ticketed.

Sonny opened the back door of the Mercedes. Uncle stepped back so that Ava could slide in, and then he followed. As Uncle was getting in, she heard Sonny say to the policeman, "Thanks for looking after the car," and saw some hundred-dollar notes exchange hands.

The drive to the Oriental Crocus seemed faster than the drive to Ming's, and again there was no conversation in the car. Sonny was focused on his driving and Uncle seemed lost in his own thoughts.

When they got to the hotel, Ava reached into her bag. "Uncle, here is my email address and fax number. Please send me your banking information as soon as you can and I'll arrange to wire the money we agreed upon."

"I will do it tomorrow," he said.

"I'm not sure when the money will actually clear and go into my account, or how long a return will take, but I'll advise you once I know."

"I have no worries about any of that."

"Then goodnight, and thank you for a great meal," she said as Sonny opened the door.

"It was my pleasure."

Ava started to leave the car but then hesitated, stopped, and turned back. She leaned in and gently kissed Uncle on the cheek.

As she walked through the lobby of the hotel, it began to dawn on her that the most remarkable two days in her life were ending. Given everything she had gone through, she could scarcely believe that she had landed in Hong Kong only forty hours before. It had been a whirlwind. What surprised her was how comfortable and in control she had felt in most of the situations.

When she got to her room, she undressed, washed, and threw on a black T-shirt. It was almost noon in Toronto, and she debated who to call first, Mr. Lo or her mother. She sat on the side of the bed as she dialled.

"*Wei*," the familiar voice said.

"Mummy, it's Ava."

"I'm so glad you finally called. I've been worried."

"Everything is fine."

"So you got in okay and the hotel is passable?"

"The flight was okay and the hotel is clean."

"And the jet lag?"

"Not an issue."

"When do you start working on Mr. Lo's problem?"

"Mummy!"

"I don't mean to be pushy, but I'm playing mah-jong with his wife tonight and I know she's going to ask questions."

"Well, you can tell her that I have been busy," Ava said, hearing the excitement in her own voice. "In fact, I haven't stopped working since I arrived."

"Have you made any progress?"

"I think you can call it that."

"Ava, don't be coy with me."

"Mummy, I got back all of his money," she said.

Her mother fell uncharacteristically silent. "Don't tease," Jennie finally said.

"He was out of pocket around a million dollars. I have managed to recover it all. By the time I deduct my commission and expenses, he'll have about nine hundred thousand back in his account."

"How is this possible? His wife told me he used every means imaginable."

"Don't sound so shocked," Ava said. "You know me better than anyone. You know that when I think I'm right, I can't take no for an answer."

"And you're not teasing?"

"Mummy, as if I would about something this serious."

Ava could hear her mother breathing heavily. It was usually a prelude to tears. And the tears flowed most often when her pride in her daughters overcame her.

"I can hardly wait to see Mrs. Lo," Jennie gasped.

"Well, before then I have to talk to Mr. Lo. I'm going to do that when I hang up with you."

"Yes, go and do that," she said. "And Ava, have you heard from your father?"

"He left me a message. I'll call him in the morning."

"When do you plan to leave Hong Kong?"

"Maybe as soon as tomorrow."

"Why don't you take an extra day or two? Spend some time with him."

"I'll see," Ava said. "Now let me call Mr. Lo."

His office phone rang five times and went to voicemail. Ava was disappointed and wondered how much information she should leave. "This is Ava Lee," she said, and then she heard the phone picked up.

"Yes, this is Lo," he said.

"I'm calling in to report."

"What took you so long? It's been three days since you left. I was just about to phone the hotel to make sure you'd checked in."

"Don't speak so rudely to me," Ava said, annoyed at his tone.

"I didn't know what you were doing. What was I supposed to think?"

"Well, I wasn't taking a holiday, if that's what's on your mind."

"I'm sorry if I was rude. It's gotten worse here since you left. My wife's brother is now sticking his nose in my business and asking questions about the money he put into it. I can't bluff him and I can't lie to him. All I can do is try to avoid him, and I can't do that much longer. Once he finds out, he'll ruin me with the whole family."

"Calm down," Ava said.

"I can't sleep and I'm not thinking straight. This is as calm as I can be."

"Mr. Lo, I have managed to get back some of your money," Ava said quietly.

"What!"

"I have managed to get back some of your money."

"How much?" he said, his voice starting to crack.

"By the time I deduct my commission, you will have about nine hundred thousand dollars back."

"Aaahhhhhhhh!" he shouted. He began to talk, but Ava couldn't understand a word he was saying. She realized he was crying; his words were being drowned in deep, heavy sobs.

She waited, not sure what to do or say. A minute passed and the sobbing began to ebb, but he still didn't seem capable of speech.

"Mr. Lo, I think I can have the money in your account within the next day or two. So if you're talking to your brother-in-law, keep that in mind."

"I prayed," he said.

"Yes, Mr. Lo, I'm sure you did."

"I haven't prayed in years, but I got down on my knees and prayed. My wife saw me and said, 'Is it that bad?' and I couldn't answer her. Now I can."

"I'm glad your prayers were answered, Mr. Lo."

"I have to call my wife," he said.

"Yes, you do that," Ava said as his line went dead.

She sat on the side of the bed for a minute. *Lo didn't even say thank you*, she thought bitterly, and then the memory of him huddled and weeping on the floor outside her office came back to her. For him, this was as much about maintaining the respect of his wife and his family as it was about the money. It was natural enough for him to want to reach out to them.

Ava yawned. Like the night before in the apartment in Shenzhen, the adrenalin that had kept her going was spent. She leaned towards the pillow and then keeled sideways, sleep enveloping her.

(19)

AVA SLEPT WHAT HER MOTHER CALLED THE SLEEP of the dead, with no dreams, and oblivious to the external world. When she woke, light was pouring in through the bedroom window. She stretched her arms above her head, yawned, and felt energy coursing through her body. She swung her legs over the side of the bed and was about to head for the bathroom when her room phone rang. She glanced at the bedside clock and saw that it was eight thirty. *Daddy,* she thought.

"Hello," she said.

"Ava, good morning, this is Uncle."

"Yes?"

"Were you sleeping?"

"No, I just woke up."

"And did you sleep well?"

"Yes."

"So you have not had breakfast?"

"No."

"Good, because I am calling to invite you to breakfast. There is a congee restaurant in Tsim Sha Tsui, near the Pacific Mall and across from the Star Ferry terminal, called Morning Blessings. Could you meet me there in about an hour?"

"I don't understand."

"I was thinking about our conversation last night, and there are some things I would like to go over again."

Ava closed her eyes. She felt butterflies in her stomach. Did he want to rework the money arrangement?

"I thought everything was settled."

"Not quite, from my side, so I would appreciate it if you could come."

"Okay, in about an hour," she said.

She drank two instant coffees, showered, brushed her teeth and hair, and then put on a black T-shirt and her Adidas jacket and training pants. She didn't bother with makeup and tied her hair back with a rubber band. All the while, her mind was turning over thoughts about the money. She was angry with herself for not having insisted he tell her over the phone why he wanted to meet, but she hadn't been fully alert when the call came. She also knew she could have refused to go, but there was something about him — the careful, polite, almost concerned way he spoke — that she found hard to resist.

She got a taxi outside the hotel, and within ten minutes it was navigating the traffic circle at the Star Ferry terminal and heading towards the Pacific Mall. Victoria Harbour was on her left; across the water the Hong Kong skyline was glittering in the morning sun. The brilliantly coloured skyscrapers, sheathed in steel, glass, aluminum, bronze, and copper, soared dramatically over the water.

Morning Blessings was in a row of stores and restaurants that faced the terminal with the mall behind them. When the taxi stopped in front, Ava looked for the Mercedes and then for Sonny. There was no sign of either.

The restaurant had two rows of booths running from front to back, towards the kitchen. The booth walls were high and Ava couldn't see Uncle from the doorway. She was halfway to the kitchen when she heard him say her name.

He sat by himself, his feet barely touching the ground, a pot of tea and a Chinese newspaper in front of him. He was wearing a black suit and white shirt, but as she slid into the booth and faced him, she saw that both looked freshly ironed; there was no lingering trace of the aromas of Ming's Hot Pot. There was no trace of the night before in his face, either, as she looked into those clear, gleaming eyes. She diverted her attention to his newspaper.

"A racing form," he said. "Horse racing is my hobby. Or, more properly stated, betting on racehorses is."

"I hear it's very popular here."

"It borders on mania."

"I've never experienced it."

"Perhaps one day I can introduce you to it," he said. "Now, forgive me for being impolite and not offering you tea."

"I would prefer coffee if they have it."

"Only instant."

"Perfect."

He raised a hand in the air and a server appeared as if out of nowhere. Ava had never before encountered anyone who commanded such immediate attention. "Coffee for my guest," he said, and then turned back to Ava. "The congee here is not quite as watery as is typical. Is that okay?"

"Yes."

"I like mine rather plain, with mushrooms, some chopped spring onions on top, and salted duck eggs on the side."

"I'll pass on the mushrooms and duck eggs. I wouldn't mind some chicken in it, though, and I like *you tiao*."

"That is what we will have, then," he said to the server. When she left, Uncle smiled at Ava across the table. She found his smile slightly tentative, and felt uneasy.

"I hope I did not call too early," he said. "I did not sleep well. I was up by six and waited until what I thought was a reasonable hour."

"I was awake, after a very good night's sleep."

"Well, as I said, I did not sleep well. When I got home last night, I received a phone call from an old friend in Guangzhou. After speaking to him, my mind kept going back to our conversation, and I realized I needed to talk to you again."

"Uncle, I can't revisit our money agreement," she said quickly. "I have already called my client in Toronto and told him what I've recovered. It would cause him enormous grief if things changed. I can't do that to him."

"What made you think that is what I wanted to discuss?"

She shook her head. "I just assumed it had to be that."

"It is not," he said, as the server arrived with two bowls of congee.

Jennie Lee made congee several times a month, but her boiled rice concoction was more like gruel than porridge. The Morning Blessings version looked thick enough to support a vertical chopstick. Ava sprinkled white pepper over the top and dipped the tip of her *you tiao*, a fried breadstick, into it. She nibbled the bread while Uncle covered his bowl with pepper.

He tasted his congee and then put his spoon aside. "My friend from Guangzhou has a problem. He thinks that one of his employees, a bookkeeper, has embezzled millions.

He wants to find him, find out how he did it, locate the money, and get it back. He asked me to take on the job. I told him I did not think I could, because I do not have the right people to undertake a problem of that size and complexity. He told me he would wait for me to give him a more definite answer. He is quite distressed. That is when I started to think about you."

"Uncle, we went over this last night."

"I know, and it is not my intention to repeat myself," he said. "Tell me, what kind of business do you have in Toronto?"

"I have a small accounting firm."

"One person?"

"Yes, just me."

"And what type of customers do you have?"

"Individuals and some small businesses."

"Do you find it stimulating and challenging?"

She was holding a spoonful of congee with shredded chicken in front of her mouth. She paused, wondering where he was going.

"I ask that question because, when you were just now talking about your client in Toronto, you used the word *grief*," Uncle said. "I have no doubt, given that description, that your ability to recover at least part of his money has spared him a lot of grief."

"That is true."

"The people who come to me, like your client who came to you, are desperate. They have exhausted all their legal means. Most of them are clinging onto their businesses, their families, and their lives by their fingernails. We are their lifeline. If we fail them, what is left? The destruction of everything they have worked for? Personal humiliation?

No future for their families?"

Ava thought of Mr. Lo crying on the telephone. "I think I have some understanding of how traumatic it could be," she said.

"Now let me rephrase my question. What has given you the best sense of doing something meaningful since you started your small business?"

"The question is redundant."

"I know it is, and I apologize for being obvious. My point is, you have special talents that you need to use. I can give you the opportunity."

"Uncle, I don't mean to be impolite," Ava said quietly. "But despite all your talk about saving lives, you still charge thirty percent as a recovery fee."

He nodded and smiled. "This is Asia, and the standard rate is thirty percent. If I charged less, there would be an assumption that we did inferior work, and I doubt that we could attract clients of quality. And as I told you, I pay all of the expenses associated with any job, including bribes. We are not always successful, and so those costs have to be absorbed somehow. Finally, I assure you I have never had clients complain about our fee when we return money to them. Seventy percent of something is far superior to one hundred percent of nothing."

"But you are still making a healthy profit."

"Of course the business is profitable. But the talents of people like Carlos and Andy are best suited to more mundane jobs, and those do not normally have large dollars at risk. I would like to be able to expand our customer base to include jobs involving more money and with greater challenges attached to them. It is not that those types of clients do not come to me. It is that in good conscience I do not think I could give them proper service, and so I have had to turn them away."

"And if I worked for you, that would change?"

"Yes. Would you disagree that your training qualifies you? My friend in Guangzhou needs expertise, not muscle."

"No, but I've already told you that I don't want to leave Toronto and I don't want to work for anyone else."

"You do not have to leave Toronto," he said. "I was thinking about this last night. What does it matter where your home base is? Our clients are all over Asia, and we have even had some enquiries from North America. Do you object to travelling from Toronto?"

"No."

"And the travel might not be that strenuous. There are often time lapses between jobs, and my understanding of your profession is that much of it can be done by computer anyway. What do I care if you spend your down time in Toronto, or whether your computer is in Toronto or Hong Kong?"

"Even if all that is true, I don't want to work for anyone."

"What if you became my partner?"

He said it so casually that at first Ava wasn't sure she had heard him correctly. Now he looked across the table at her with an almost amused expression in his eyes.

"How would that be possible? I have no money to put into a business," she said, pushing aside the other, less obvious objections that were crowding into her head.

"It is hardly a business in the normal sense of the word. I have no office. My staff, including Carlo and Andy, come and go as the work demands. I have no need for your money, or for anyone else's."

"So what kind of partnership would it be?"

"The simplest kind. We shake hands and then we share risks and rewards on an even basis. I will provide all the initial financing at no cost to you, but after we accrue profits we can set some aside as our joint investment. And from the start, I will advance whatever money you need to live until our venture is self-sustaining."

"Uncle, we hardly know each other," she said.

"I learned a long time ago to rely on my intuition when it comes to trust. My first instinct has always been the strongest and best, and it is telling me that you are someone worth knowing and someone I can trust. Now, you may not feel the same way about me, but I think you must have some sense of how I work from the events of the past few days."

She shook her head. "This is crazy."

"Ava, I was born in a village outside Wuhan, in Hubei province. The Communists came to power when I was a young man, and I had to decide if I was going to live my life as I thought fit or to allow other people and other factors to live it for me. When Mao's policies resulted in the deaths of those around me, I decided to leave. With some friends, I found my way to the coast. We swam to Hong Kong, where I knew no one and no one knew me. Still, I made my way in unfamiliar surroundings and created a life that some think has been successful."

"And your family in Wuhan?"

He closed his eyes. "They are dead. All of them. My mother and father and brother all died within a year of my leaving. I was told they were reduced to eating grass. I have no other relatives that I am aware of. I have never forgiven the Communists."

"I'm sorry."

He stared at her. "Thank you, but I have never had a large capacity for grief. I prefer looking ahead to looking back. Swimming to Hong Kong limited my soul as well as my body. So trying new things, even at my age, holds no fear for me. I suspect you have the same spirit of independence and adventure."

"I have to admit that I felt completely engaged and energized when I was in Shenzhen. But I have trouble accepting that I can or should do something like that for a living."

"What pressing obligations do you have in Toronto right now?" Uncle said.

"Nothing special."

"Then why not take one small step and see where it leads?"

"One step?"

"Guangzhou. Let us take on that job. If we are unsuccessful, I will pay you a decent fee anyway. If we can get some money back, I will split it with you. Give it a try. When you are done, if you do not think the work is for you, you can go back to Toronto and your business. If you want to continue working with me, you can do so with the understanding that you may terminate our agreement on a day's notice."

"You are being incredibly flexible, and generous."

"As I said, I trust my instincts."

"What the hell," Ava said, and then looked at the man across from her. "Okay, I'll give Guangzhou a try, but no commitments beyond that."

He smiled and held out his hand. "If I am right, I suspect it will be the last time we ever have to shake on anything."

(20)

AVA LEFT MORNING BLESSINGS WITH A BOUNCE in her step and a feeling of anticipation rippling through her. Despite her hesitation about working with Uncle, there was something in his quiet, understated manner that encouraged confidence and fuelled her enthusiasm. She was already looking forward to tackling the job in Guangzhou. And it was a trial, she reminded herself. If it didn't work out, all she was risking was a few days of her time.

They had agreed that Uncle would arrive at her hotel at noon. He would call the client to tell him they were taking the job, get more information, and start making arrangements for the trip to Guangzhou. It was only a two-hour car ride, and Uncle said Sonny would drive them.

Ava started walking towards Mong Kok. She was outside a jewellery store near the Peninsula Hotel when her phone rang.

"Hello."

"Ava, it's Daddy."

"I'm so happy to hear from you."

"Is everything okay? I've been waiting for you to call me. I knew you were here on that business we talked about and

I didn't want to disturb you, but I was beginning to get worried. Then I spoke to Mummy this morning and she told me about your grand success. She's so proud of you. We both are," he said.

"Daddy, things couldn't have gone any better. I got back from Shenzhen just last night. I was going to call you, but Mummy said it was easier to reach you in the morning. I was going to phone in a few minutes."

"So you're in Hong Kong?"

"I'm in Kowloon."

"Then I want you to grab the Star Ferry and come over to this side at noon for dim sum. I'll take you to Man Wah, at the Mandarin Oriental."

"Oh, Daddy, I can't. I'm leaving for Guangzhou then."

"Guangzhou?"

Ava took a deep breath. "I've taken on another collection job."

"Another client of yours with the same kind of problem?" he said, his tone disbelieving.

"No, it's a client of a man who runs a collection business here in Hong Kong. He's asked me to help him. They need someone who has accounting skills."

Her father was quiet.

"Daddy, I am an accountant, and I am trained to do forensic work. It's a waste for me not to use whatever talents I have. I won't say I enjoyed all my time in Shenzhen, but the end result gave me a greater sense of satisfaction than I can describe."

"Ava, you have to be careful."

"Daddy, I'm an accountant. What could possibly happen?" she said, thankful she hadn't been forced to call him from the jail in Shenzhen.

"Some of the people in that business are completely unsavoury. Who is it you're working with?"

"A man named Chow Tung, although most people call him Uncle. He said you and he might know each other."

"The name is vaguely familiar, and nothing horribly negative comes to mind, so that's a good thing. I just don't like the idea of your doing that kind of work. I don't care who it's with."

"I managed to take care of myself in Shenzhen," Ava said, wondering if anyone would ever believe what had really happened there.

"I know, and I'm sure you'll probably do as well in Guangzhou. But remember, I'm only a phone call away. And even if you don't need me, make sure you let me know as soon as you're back in Hong Kong."

"It's just one job. It should be a matter of a few days," she said.

"Be careful," he said.

"I promise," she said, and closed her phone.

She was turning to resume her walk when she noticed a display case in the window of the jewellery store. It was filled with bracelets and necklaces made from white and green jade and encrusted with diamonds, rubies, and sapphires. They looked incredibly expensive. Each had a small card next to it; there was no price, only information about the piece. To Ava's surprise, most of them were more than a hundred years old, and several were older than that. She was about to turn away when she spied a small item tucked into a corner of the display.

It was a long white pin. She thought at first it was made from white jade, but as she leaned in closer she saw that it was ivory. The card read: IVORY CHIGNON PIN, QING DYNASTY, CIRCA 1680.

Rather hesitantly, Ava opened the shop door and walked in. She was the only customer, but she was forced to stand awkwardly near the door while a middle-aged man and woman chatted behind the counter. The woman, her hair arranged in a helmet-like coif and her face layered with makeup, finally acknowledged Ava with a nod of her head.

Ava was accustomed to the peculiarities of service in Hong Kong, or at least Jennie Lee's views of service in Hong Kong. Jennie believed that store personnel treated customers in direct relation to the amount of money they were perceived to have, and that judgement came from an assessment of the clothes, purse, watch, and jewellery worn by the shopper. When Jennie shopped in Hong Kong, she dressed as if she were meeting the Queen. In her Adidas jacket and training pants and with her Citizen watch on her wrist, Ava knew she wasn't creating the same impression.

"Can I help you?" the woman said, not moving.

"There's a piece in the window I'm interested in looking at."

"You understand that everything we sell is antique and rare?"

"I read the cards," Ava said. "I'd like to see the ivory chignon pin."

"The only one we have is from the Qing Dynasty."

"That's the one."

The woman started to say something, but before she could, her companion moved from behind the counter and walked towards Ava. He was short and round and looked almost comical in his grey suit, white shirt, and large floral bow tie. "I'll get it for you," he said.

He reached into the window and removed the pin. "Come over here, where we have mirrors," he said.

Ava followed him to an alcove near the back of the store. He turned on some overhead lights and held the pin in his palm so she could see it glisten.

"For ivory this old, it's amazing that it's retained its lustre and hardness. Many pieces of this age are scarred and yellowed. This was made from a beautiful piece of material for someone very important, and you can tell it has been prized and looked after all these years."

"I don't mean to be rude, but how do you know its actual age?"

He smiled. "I'm actually glad you asked, because I went to great trouble to verify it. I sent the ivory to a museum laboratory in Milan, Italy, for spectrographic analysis," he said. "The mount, of course, is platinum and it's new. I put it on after I got the report back from Italy. Would you like to try it on?"

"Could I?"

"Of course. You have beautiful hair that's just the right length for a piece like this. Would you like to do it yourself?"

"Please."

Ava's hand trembled very slightly as she took it. She had never held anything so beautiful and delicate. She removed the rubber band, ran her fingers through her hair as she pulled it back and twisted it, and fixed the pin. "I wish I had a brush," she said.

"It still looks wonderful," he said. "Turn your head to the right and you can see it."

She did as he asked and almost gasped. In contrast with her black, silky hair, the ivory shone like a long white streak of brilliant light.

"It looks so beautiful, almost like it was made for you," the man said.

"I think so too."

"I would like to be able to tell you that a Chinese empress wore it, but it could easily have belonged to the favourite concubine of a wealthy man."

"Whoever had it made had exquisite taste."

"So let's say it was an empress, shall we?" he said with a smile.

"As long as that doesn't increase the cost."

He hesitated, and Ava sensed he was uncomfortable.

"How much is it?" she said.

"Ninety thousand."

"Hong Kong?"

"Of course."

That was more than twelve thousand Canadian dollars. Four days ago there had been less than one thousand dollars in Ava's checking account. Now she had $1.1 million, and more than a hundred thousand of it was hers.

"I will need the spectrographic analysis and whatever other documentation you have to verify its age."

"Of course."

"In that case, I'm taking it home with me."

"Shall I box it?"

"No, I'm going to wear it."

He smiled. "I am sure it will bring you luck."

"Why do you say that?"

"At the time this piece was made, women wore ivory as a way to fend off evil. I've always preferred to think of it the opposite way—as a good-luck charm. This pin has more than three hundred years of good luck attached to it. When you wear it, you should think of that, and of all the women who accumulated that luck."

"I've never felt particularly lucky or believed in things like fate," Ava said softly. "But I think maybe it's time that I started."

THE WATER RAT OF WANCHAI

(1)

WHEN THE PHONE RANG, AVA WOKE WITH A START. SHE looked at the bedside clock. It was just past 3 a.m. "Shit," she said softly. She checked the incoming number. It was blocked. Hong Kong? Shenzhen? Shanghai? Or maybe even Manila or Jakarta, where the Chinese hid behind local names and were often all the more Chinese because of it. Wherever the call originated, Ava was sure it was somewhere in Asia, the caller ignorant about the time difference or just too desperate to care.

"*Wei,* Ava Lee," a male voice said in Cantonese. It was a voice she didn't recognize.

"Who is calling?" she said in his dialect.

"Andrew Tam."

It took a second for the name to register. "Can you speak English?"

"Yes, I can," he said, switching. "I went to school in Canada."

"Then you should know what time it is here," she said.

"I'm sorry. Mr. Chow gave your name and number to my uncle and told him I could call you anytime. He also said you speak Mandarin and Cantonese."

Ava rolled onto her back. "I do, but when it comes to business, I prefer English. There's less chance of confusion, of misunderstanding from my end."

"We have a job for you," Tam said abruptly.

"We?"

"My company. Mr. Chow told my uncle he was going to discuss it with you." Tam paused. "You are a forensic accountant, I'm told."

"I am."

"According to what Mr. Chow told my uncle, you have an amazing talent for finding people and money. Well, my money is missing and the person who took it has disappeared."

"That is rarely a coincidence," Ava said, letting the compliment slide.

"Ms. Lee, I really need your help," Tam said, his voice breaking.

"I need more information before I can say yes. I don't even know where or what the job is."

"It's a bit of a moving target. We're based in Hong Kong and we were financing a company owned by a Chinese, which has offices in Hong Kong and Seattle and was doing production in Thailand for a U.S. food retailer."

"That isn't very helpful."

"Sorry, I don't mean to be so vague. I'm actually better organized than I sound; it's just that the stress right now is —"

"I understand about the stress," Ava said.

Tam drew a deep breath. "After talking to my uncle about your company yesterday, I forwarded a complete package of information to a family member who lives in Toronto. Could you free yourself later today to meet?"

"In Toronto?" It was an oddity for her work to involve her home country, let alone city.

"Of course."

"When?"

"How about dinner in Chinatown?"

"I would prefer something earlier. Dim sum, maybe."

"All right, I'm sure dim sum will be fine."

"And not in the old Chinatown downtown. I'd rather go to Richmond Hill. There's a restaurant, Lucky Season, in the Times Square Mall, just west of Leslie Street on Highway 7. Do you know the area?"

"Yes, I do, generally speaking."

"Tell them to meet me there at one."

"How will they recognize you?"

"I will recognize them. Tell them to wear something red — a shirt or sweater — and to carry a copy of *Sing Tao*."

"Okay."

"Man or woman?"

"A woman, actually."

"That's unusual."

He hesitated. She sensed that he was about to launch into another explanation, and she was about to cut him off when he said, "My uncle tells me that Mr. Chow is your uncle."

"We're not blood relatives," Ava said. "I was raised traditionally. My mother insisted that we respect our elders, so it's natural for me to call our older family friends Uncle and Auntie. Uncle isn't a family friend, but from the very first time I met him it seemed appropriate. Even as my business partner he is still Uncle."

"He's a man whom very many people call Uncle."

Ava knew where Tam was headed and decided to cut him off. "Look, I'll meet with your contact later today. If I'm happy with the information she brings and I think the job is doable, then I'll call my uncle and we'll confirm that we're taking the job. If I'm not happy, then you won't hear from me again. *Bai, bai*," she said, putting down the phone.

She struggled to find sleep again as Tam's voice, with its too familiar sound of desperation, lingered in her ears. She pushed it aside. Until she took possession of his problem, that's all it was: his problem.

(2)

AVA WOKE AT SEVEN, SAID HER PRAYERS, STRETCHED for ten minutes, and then went to the kitchen to make a cup of instant coffee, using hot water from the Thermos. She considered herself to be Canadian, but she still clung to habits engrained by her mother, such as an always full rice steamer and a hot-water Thermos in the kitchen. Her friends made fun of her taste in coffee. She didn't care. She didn't have the patience to wait for it to brew and she hated waste; anyway, her taste buds were strictly attuned to instant.

She emptied a sachet of Starbucks VIA Ready Brew into her cup, poured in the water, and went to fetch the *Globe and Mail* at the door. She brought it in and settled onto the couch, turning on the television to a local Chinese channel, WOW TV, that had a current affairs show in Cantonese. There were two hosts: a former Hong Kong comedian who was trying to extend his best-before date in the boondocks, and a pretty young woman without any showbiz pedigree. She was low-key and seemed intelligent and classy — not a usual combination for women on Chinese television. Ava had developed a slight crush on her.

When the show broke at eight for a news summary, Ava dialled Uncle's cellphone number. It was early evening in Hong Kong. He would have left the office by now, maybe had had a massage, and would be sitting down to dinner at one of the high-end hotpot restaurants in Kowloon, probably the one near the Peninsula Hotel.

He answered on the second ring. "Uncle," she said.

"Ava, you caught me at a good time."

"Andrew Tam called me."

"How did you find him?"

"He speaks English very well. He was polite."

"How did you leave it?"

"I'm meeting with someone today who has details about the lost funds. I told Tam I'd talk to you after I had the information and then we'd decide what to do."

Uncle hesitated. "It isn't so straightforward from my end. I'd like you to make the decision about whether or not we take on the job."

Ava tried to think of some other time when she'd been the sole decision maker on a job. She couldn't. "Why leave this up to me?" she asked.

"Tam is the nephew of a friend, an old and very close friend. We grew up together near Wuhan, and he was one of the men who swam here from China with me."

She had heard the tale of the swim many times. Over the years the danger that Uncle and his friends encountered during those eight hours in the South China Sea, escaping the Communist regime, had become a distant memory, but the brotherhood they had forged remained all-important. "So it is that personal?"

"Yes. I knew it would be hard for me to be objective, so I thought it would be best for the nephew to tell you what happened, and then you can decide if the job is worth taking on its own merits. And Ava — don't agree to do it if it doesn't have merit."

"What about our rate?" she asked. It was usually thirty percent of what they recovered, split evenly between them.

"For you, yes, but for me . . . I can't take my share. He's too close."

She wished he hadn't said that. It made it even more personal, and they tried to keep the personal out of their business.

"Call me when the meeting is over," Uncle said.

Ava hung up and puttered around the apartment, answering emails, catching up with bills, looking into winter holiday packages. She debated what to wear to the meeting. Since she didn't need to impress anyone, she decided on a black Giordano T-shirt and black Adidas training pants. No makeup, no jewellery.

She looked at herself in the mirror. She was five foot three and her weight hovered around 115 pounds. She was slim but not skinny, and her running and bak mei workouts had given her legs and butt nice definition. She had large breasts for a Chinese woman, large enough that she didn't need a padded bra for them to get noticed. In the T-shirt and training pants her shape got lost; the outfit made her look smaller and younger. There were times when looking young worked to her advantage. There were also times when a different look was needed, so she had a wardrobe of black form-fitting linen and cotton slacks, knee-length pencil skirts, and an array of Brooks Brothers shirts in various colours and styles that showed off her chest. The slacks and shirts, worn with makeup and jewellery, were her professional look: attractive, classy, capable.

At eleven she called downstairs and asked to have her car brought up from the garage.

Ava's condo was in Yorkville, in the heart of downtown Toronto. Like the properties around Central Park in New York, Belgravia in London, and Victoria Peak in Hong Kong, it boasted the city's most expensive real estate. She had paid more than a million dollars for the condo — in cash. Her mother, Jennie Lee, had been pleased by her choice of location, and was even prouder that her daughter wasn't carrying a mortgage. The condo came with a parking spot in which she had deposited an Audi A6. It was a waste of money, that car. Most everything she needed was within walking distance or, at worst, a five-minute subway ride. The only time she used the car was to visit her mother in Richmond Hill.

At ten after eleven the concierge called to say that her car was available. As Ava drove east along Bloor Street, she passed five-star hotels, innumerable restaurants, antique dealers and art galleries, and high-end retailers such as Chanel, Tiffany, Holt Renfrew, and Louis Vuitton — stores she rarely ventured into. She knew that if she did, any mention of her mother's name would set off a serious round of kowtowing.

She took the Don Valley Parkway north towards Richmond Hill, and for once the traffic was flowing smoothly. She got to Times Square half an hour early. The mall was named and modelled after one in Hong Kong; its main building, fronting Highway 7, was three storeys high. The parking lot in the back was encircled by stores selling Chinese herbs, DVDs, and baked goods, and by restaurants serving every type of Asian cuisine.

Toronto has a huge Chinese population — half a million or more — and Richmond Hill is its epicentre. About twenty kilometres north of downtown, Richmond Hill is a sprawling expanse of suburban tract housing and malls. East and west along Highway 7, the malls are almost exclusively Chinese. Once a traditional European-Canadian suburb, Richmond Hill is a place where English isn't needed anymore. There isn't a service or commodity that can't be acquired in Cantonese.

It wasn't always this way. Ava could remember when there was only the old Chinatown downtown on Dundas Street, just south of where she lived now. In those days her mother had been a bit of a pioneer, one of the first Chinese people to settle in Richmond Hill. Every Saturday she still had to drive Ava and her sister, Marian, into Toronto for their Mandarin and abacus lessons. While the girls studied, she shopped for the Chinese vegetables, fruit, fish, sauces, spices, and ten-kilo bags of fragrant Thai rice that made up their diet.

All of that had changed when Hong Kong began to prepare for the end of British colonial rule in 1997. The uncertainty of life under Communist China hadn't exactly caused panic, but many felt it would be prudent to have other options, and Canada made it easy for those with money to establish a second home. Toronto's downtown area couldn't accommodate the influx of new Chinese immigrants, so Richmond Hill became the next best landing spot — and why it was chosen was simple.

For years, Vancouver, British Columbia — more specifically, the nearby suburban city of Richmond — had been the most desired location for Chinese immigrants coming to Canada. Its name evoked wealth and was therefore considered auspicious. Ava's mother was no exception; she had lived in Richmond during her first two years in the country. When Toronto began to supplant Vancouver as the economic hub of Canada, western Chinese-Canadians migrated to Richmond Hill because they assumed it would be like Richmond, B.C. — that is, Chinese. Eventually, as always with the Chinese, more begot more, until you could walk into nearby Markham's Pacific Mall and believe you were in Hong Kong.

Ava had to circle the Times Square parking lot twice before she found a spot. The Lucky Season was full, and she had to wait ten minutes before getting a table. Her mother had introduced her to the restaurant, which on weekdays offered every dim sum dish for $2.20. A party of four could drink all the tea they wanted, stuff themselves for an hour, and still spend less than thirty dollars on a meal. It was remarkable, Ava thought, and all the more remarkable because the food was excellent and the portions traditional dim sum size.

Her mother ate there two or three times a week, but this was Tuesday, and Ava knew she had an appointment with her herbalist, followed by her weekly session with the manicurist. Still, she did a quick scan of the room just in case.

Ava sat at a table facing the front door. There was a steady stream of people, none of them too rich or too poor to pass up two-dollar dim sum. It amazed her to what lengths the Chinese would go to for perceived value. You could put four restaurants serving almost identical food beside each other, and for reasons that seemed beyond logic, one of them would develop a reputation for being the best. That restaurant would be besieged by long lines, creating endless waits, while the others would be almost blissfully empty. Her mother epitomized that mentality.

Jennie Lee was a constant presence in Ava's life. It was something she had grown to accept, although her sister had problems with it, mainly because she was married to a *gweilo* — a Caucasian with British roots — and he couldn't understand their mother's need to maintain such close contact with her daughters. He didn't have any concept of family Chinese-style: the constant intrusions, being joined at the hip for life, the obligations children had to their parents. He also couldn't fathom the life that had brought their mother and them to Canada.

Their mother had been born in Shanghai and, though raised in Hong Kong, considered herself to be a true Shanghainese — which is to say strong-willed, opinionated, and loud when required, but never rude, never tacky, and never pushy, like Hong Kongers. She had met their father, Marcus Lee, when she worked in the office of a company he owned. He was from Shanghai too. She became his second wife in the old style, which is to say he never left or divorced the first. Ava and Marian became his second family, acknowledged and cared for but with no hope of inheriting anything more than their names and whatever their mother could put aside for them.

When Ava was two and Marian four, their mother and father had become embroiled in a dispute, and Jennie's presence in Hong Kong became too much of a burden. Ava learned later that a third wife had emerged, and though her mother accepted subservience to wife number one, she wasn't about to play second fiddle to a newcomer. In any event, their father decided that the farther away they were, the happier his life would be. He relocated them initially in Vancouver, a direct flight from Hong Kong if he wanted to visit but far enough away for them not to be a nuisance. But her mother hated Vancouver; it was too wet, too dreary, too much a reminder of Hong Kong. She moved the girls to Toronto, and there were no objections from the Hong Kong side.

They saw their father maybe once or twice a year, and always in Toronto. He had bought their mother a house, had given her a generous allowance, and looked after any special needs. When he did come to visit, the girls called him Daddy. Their mother referred to him as her husband. For one or two weeks they would lead a "normal" family life. Then he was gone, and the couple's contact would be reduced to a daily phone call.

It was, Ava realized later, a businesslike relationship. Their father had got what he wanted when he wanted it, and her mother had the two girls and a notional husband. He would never deny her or the family, and her mother knew that; so she deliberately set about squeezing him for every dollar's worth of security she could get. He must have known what she was doing, but as long as she played by the rules, he was okay with it. So she had the house, she had a new car every two years, and she was the beneficiary of a life insurance policy that would replace her monthly allowance (and then some) if anything happened to him. He paid all the school fees, and she made sure the girls went to the most expensive and prestigious schools she could get them into. He paid separately for family vacations, dental work, summer camps, and special tutoring. He bought each of the girls their first car.

Marcus Lee had four children by his first wife, two with Jennie, and another two with wife number three. His third wife and their two children lived in Australia now, and Ava was sure that he loved and looked after them as much as he did the other children and wives. It was — at least to Westerners — a rather strange way to live. But in Chinese eyes it was traditional and acceptable, and Marcus Lee was respected for the manner in which he discharged his responsibilities. It wasn't a lifestyle for a man without wealth. Marcus had been fortunate in that regard, making his first serious money in textiles before manufacturing went offshore to places such as Indonesia and Thailand. He made a successful transition into toys and again showed foresight by exiting before Vietnam and China became major players. Now most of the family's capital was tied up in real estate in the New Territories and in the Shenzhen economic zone; by all accounts it was delivering a steady revenue stream and building value.

Jennie never worked again after Marian was born. Her life was devoted to being a second wife and to raising her two girls. Given her husband's absence, her life's focus had narrowed down to the girls. Not that their mother didn't have other interests. She played mah-jong a couple of times a week, and once a week she took the Taipan bus north to Casino Rama for a day of baccarat. She had also made a semi-career out of shopping. Everything she bought had to be the best. She had a complete aversion to knockoffs; if she wanted a Gucci bag, it had to be a real Gucci bag.

Jennie Lee was well past fifty, but she didn't look it and didn't want to acknowledge it. She loved nothing better than being mistaken for her daughters' older sister. And she spent money on maintaining that look: creams, lotions, herbs, hairstyling, clothes. Marian had two children of her own, but since they were being raised in Ottawa with their *gweilo* father, their Chinese was scant. They knew that *gweilo* means "grey ghost" in Cantonese. The other word they knew was *langlei*, which means "beautiful one." That was how they referred to their grandmother. Calling her anything else — such as Grandma — was a no-no.

In many ways Ava's mother was a princess, spoiled and self-indulgent. But then again, so many Chinese women were. They made the "Jewish princesses" Ava had known in university look like amateurs. And that thought crossed her mind once more, when she saw a woman in a red silk blouse with a copy of *Sing Tao* tucked under her arm walk into Lucky Season and survey the room.

She was tall for a Chinese woman, and made taller still by stiletto heels that looked as if they were made from the finest, most supple red leather. The silk blouse was worn with a pair of black linen slacks and a gold belt with the Chanel logo on the buckle. Her eyebrows were plucked into two thin lines and her face was caked with makeup. And even from a distance Ava could see the jewellery: enormous diamond stud earrings, two rings — one looked like a three-carat diamond, the other was carved green jade surrounded by rubies — and a crucifix encrusted with diamonds and emeralds. The only thing that marred the picture of a perfect Hong Kong princess was her hair, which was pulled back and secured demurely at the nape of her neck with a plain black elastic.

Ava stood and waved in her direction. The woman's eyes settled on her, and in them Ava read — what? Disappointment? Recognition? Maybe she hadn't been expecting a woman. Maybe she hadn't been expecting one dressed in a black Giordano T-shirt and Adidas track pants.

They greeted each other in Cantonese, and then Ava said, "I do prefer English."

"Me too," she said. "My name is Alice."

"Ava."

"I know."

They perused the dim sum menu, finally ticking off six boxes. When the waiter took their sheet away, Ava said, "I know this place seems ridiculously cheap, but the food is very good."

"I've eaten here before," Alice said.

"So, Alice, how do you know Andrew?"

"He's my brother."

"Ah."

"That's why I'm here. Andrew's trying to keep this problem quiet. He doesn't want to unnecessarily alarm other members of the family."

"Someone else already knows — your relative in Hong Kong who went to my uncle."

"He is my mother's brother, our oldest uncle, and he is very discreet. But even then he doesn't know that much, only that Andrew needs help collecting some money that is owed."

"Three million dollars."

"Actually, a bit more than that. Maybe closer to five million when all is said and done."

"Is this one of those Chinese deals?" Ava asked.

Alice looked confused.

"You know," Ava continued, "one of those deals where someone needs some money and can't get it from a bank or other normal sources, so they go to their family, but if the family can't come up with enough money they go to a friend of the family, or maybe he has a friend, an uncle, and the money finds its way to the person who needs it and there are handshakes all around — not a shred of paper — and everyone in the chain, all the family members and friends, has a share in the responsibility for making sure the money is repaid."

"No, it wasn't like that at all," Alice said. She pulled a fat manila envelope from inside the *Sing Tao*. "Everything is in here. There's a letter from my brother explaining how the deal was structured and how it progressed until it went off the rails. There's all kinds of backup documentation: the original lending contract, purchase orders, letters of credit, invoices, emails. My brother is quite thorough."

"That's a welcome change," Ava said.

The first of the dim sum arrived: chicken feet in *chu hon* sauce and crescent-shaped chive-and-shrimp dumplings. They both reached for the chicken feet, and the conversation waned as they sucked skin and meat from bone. Then came har gow, spicy salted squid, shrimp and meat wrapped in steamed bean curd, and radish cake. Alice kept Ava's teacup full, and Ava tapped her finger on the table in a silent thank-you each time the other poured.

"Are you involved in the business?" Ava asked.

"No, I have nothing to do with it, but my brother and I are very close."

"What kind of business is it?"

"It's a company that specializes in financing purchase orders and letters of credit. You know how it is these days. Companies get big orders and may not have the money to finance production. Even if they have letters of credit, the banks can be very sticky. And even if the banks do help, it's never for the whole amount. So my brother's company fills in the gaps. It advances the company money for production — at very high interest rates, of course, but the companies know that upfront and build it into their margins."

"How high?"

"Minimum two percent a month, normally three."

"Nice."

"They're filling a gap."

"I wasn't being critical."

"Anyway, once in a while they have a problem. Normally, because of the amount of due diligence they do — and because they don't finance anything that seems risky and the purchase orders and letters of credit are typically from blue-chip companies — those problems have been small and infrequent."

"Until now."

"Yes."

"What was the blue-chip company, or is this an exception?"

"Major Supermarkets."

Ava was caught off guard. "That's the largest food retailer in North America."

"Yes."

"So what went wrong?"

Alice started to reply and then caught herself. "I think

it's better if you read the contents of the envelope. If you need more information or any clarification, you should call my brother directly. His cellphone number and private home number are in the envelope. He doesn't want you to email him or call him at the office. He also said you could call him anytime, night or day. He hasn't been sleeping much."

"All right, I'll read the documents."

"This is very difficult for him," she said slowly. "He prides himself on being cautious and always acting with integrity. He's having trouble accepting that this is actually happening to him."

"Stuff happens," Ava said.

Alice fingered the crucifix around her neck, her eyes taking in the simpler one that Ava wore. "You're Catholic?" Ava asked.

"Yes."

"Me too."

"You live here in Toronto?"

"Yes, I'm the only one. The rest of the family is in Hong Kong."

"What do you do?"

"We're in the clothing business, my husband and I. He is Chinese too — mainland — and we have factories there and in Malaysia and Indonesia."

"Tough business. My father was in it for a while," Ava said.

"We've been lucky. My husband decided years ago that the only way to survive was to move into private-label lines. So that's all we do now."

"Are you involved in the day-to-day activities?"

The woman looked across the table, her eyes suddenly

curious. Ava wondered if her question had hit a sore spot. "I don't mean to pry," she said quickly.

"*Momentai*," Alice said. "I have two sons now, so I spend most of my time raising them and looking after our home. My husband keeps me up to date on most things, and I still have to suck up to the wives of the buyers, but no, I'm not that involved."

Ava reached for the dim sum list but Alice beat her to it. "I'll pay," she said.

"Thanks."

Ava's Adidas jacket was draped over the back of her chair. As she turned to get it, she saw Alice's eyes lock onto her again. "Have I said or done something wrong?" she asked.

"No, not at all. It's just that you look familiar to me. Where did you go to school?"

"York University here, and then Babson College, near Boston."

"No, before that. I mean high school."

"I went to Havergal College."

"I'm an Old Girl, too," Alice said.

"I don't remember you."

"Do you have an older sister named Marian?"

"Yes."

"I was in the same class as her. We were part of the first big wave of Chinese students and we hung around together. You would have been, what, two or three years behind us?"

"Two."

"I remember seeing you with Marian."

Ava searched her memory and came up dry, but then Marian had hung out with a gaggle of Chinese girls that reached double figures. "She's married now and has two daughters and a husband who is a rising star in the Canadian public service."

"Is he Chinese?"

"No, Canadian."

"That's Havergal Old girls for you: they know how to marry well," Alice said, and then glanced at Ava's ring hand. "You aren't married?"

"No," Ava said.

"A working girl."

Alice held up the dim sum list for a server to collect and take to the cashier. When it was gone, she folded her hands neatly in front of her, and again looked intently at Ava. "How did you get into this kind of work? I mean, it is a bit unusual. My brother told me what it is your company does, and when I was told I was meeting a woman, my imagination certainly didn't envision you. In fact, I assumed the woman would be more of a go-between than an active participant in the business. You are active, aren't you?"

"I am."

"I thought so . . . I wasn't being condescending. My husband has had to employ companies like yours in the past, so I know something about how they operate and the kind of people who work in them. That's why I didn't expect to meet someone quite so young."

"And on top of that, I'm a woman," Ava said with a little smile.

"Yes, that too."

"So how did you get into this?"

The question caught Ava off guard. She was more used to asking questions than being asked, and she hesitated. "It's boring," she said.

"Please," Alice insisted.

Ava poured tea for them both, Alice tapping her finger on the table in thanks. "It really is boring."

"I'm not sure I believe you."

Ava shrugged. "When I got out of school, I went to work for one of the big accounting firms in Toronto, and I quickly found out it wasn't for me. I was a crummy employee, really. I found it difficult being part of a big bureaucracy, doing what you're told without being able to question the effectiveness or efficiency of it. Looking back, I was probably quite arrogant, a bit of a know-it-all, always ready to argue with my bosses. I lasted six months before packing it in. I think they were as glad to see me go as I was to leave.

"I decided to open my own little firm, so I took an office up here — two buildings over, actually — and began doing basic accounting for friends of my mother and some small businesses and the like. One of them, a clothing importer, believe it or not, ran into a problem with a supplier in Shenzhen. When he couldn't collect his money, I asked him to let me try, for a percentage of whatever I could recover."

"What made you think you could do that?"

"I've always been persuasive."

"And you actually went to Shenzhen to do this?"

"Yes, but when I got there, I found that the supplier had been screwing over more than one customer, and there was a line-up waiting to go after him. Except, of course, he was nowhere to be found. He'd taken off with whatever money he had left. In the course of nosing about, I discovered there was another company trying to do what I was doing. I figured it would be counterproductive to compete against them, so I suggested we join forces. That's when I met Uncle."

"Yes," Alice said, her eyes averted. "Andrew mentioned Mr. Chow. He has his reputation, of course, and who knows really what's true or not . . . So he's not a blood relative, then?"

The same question her brother had asked. "No, he's a Chinese uncle in the best sense of the word," Ava said.

"I see."

She wants to ask me about him, Ava thought, and then quickly moved on. "I didn't deal with him directly at first. He had some people working for him who were, frankly, a bit rough around the edges — the kind you'd expect to encounter in a business like that. They agreed to work with me, although I think, looking back, they were probably humouring me, or maybe they thought it was a way to get me into bed. Anyway, Uncle had a great network of contacts and we tracked down the guy in no time. But when it came to collecting, Uncle's people had no finesse whatsoever. The guy would have talked his way out of returning about two-thirds of the money he owed if I hadn't gotten involved and done a little forensic accounting work.

"Word got back to Uncle about what I had done, and he asked me to come and work with him. I said I wasn't thrilled about his other employees. He told me he'd phase them out, that he thought my style and his were compatible. That was ten years ago, and the business has been just Uncle and me for most of that time."

"And you've obviously been successful."

"We've done well enough."

The bill came to the table and Alice put twenty

dollars on the tray. "Ava, did my brother sound desperate to you?"

Ava slipped on her jacket. "Not any more than most of our clients do."

"Well, let me tell you, he is desperate. That five million dollars represents nearly all the capital our family has accumulated over the past two generations." She reached across the table, grabbing Ava's hand and squeezing. "Please do everything you can to help."

(3)

IT WAS ALMOST FOUR O'CLOCK WHEN AVA PULLED UP in front of her condo, tossed her car keys to the concierge, and went upstairs, the manila envelope, still unopened, tucked under her arm.

She opened a bag of sour candy, made herself a coffee, and sat at the kitchen table. Her mind wandered. It had been a long time since she had thought about, let alone discussed, how she and Uncle had gotten together and built their business. She had told Alice Tam the truth, but it was the barebones truth. When she thought about how naive she had been when she started and what she was now able to handle, it was as if she were looking at two different people.

In the beginning she'd been adept enough at the financial side of things, her curiosity, imagination, and training helping her track and find money in places where the thieves had thought it untraceable. And at first that was her main focus. Only gradually did she take on the collection role. She began by working on targets as the soft opener — she had a knack for getting people to talk, especially men, who saw her as a soft-spoken, polite, exotic young thing who needn't be taken too seriously. By the time they realized the opposite was true, it was usually too late.

Ava didn't start closing accounts until she saw the muscle Uncle was using botch projects by going too far. There's a fine line between instilling enough fear to get someone to do what you want and applying so much pressure that the target figures he's toast no matter what he does, so he might as well try to hang on to the money. Ava had a talent for finding the tipping point. Uncle would say, "People always do the right thing for the wrong reason." Ava made that her mantra, striving to pinpoint the core self-interest in her targets, the one thing that was more important to them than hanging on to stolen money.

Uncle also said, "Once they have the money they forget where it came from, how they acquired it. In their minds, it is theirs. You need to remind them that it has a rightful owner and that the only thing open for discussion is how they are going to return it."

Not that they didn't try to hang on to it anyway. Being yelled at, cursed, and threatened was just part of the job. Knives, guns, and fists weren't uncommon either, and that's why Uncle said he used muscle. If there was going to be intimidation and violence, he wanted to have the most firepower. The problem, in Ava's mind, was that the muscle invited a negative reaction. One look at Uncle's original crew and the targets would gear up for the inevitable conflict. The violence clouded the process, made the money almost a secondary objective.

Ava urged Uncle to let the enforcers go, using them only on a must-need basis. His only concern was the potential for physical danger the targets posed. "I can look after myself," Ava said. And the truth was, she could.

She had started taking martial arts when she was twelve and had almost immediately shown ability. She was quick, agile, and fearless. In a matter of months she was so far ahead of everyone else in her class that the teacher moved her up to train with the teens; a year later he moved her again, to work out with the adults. By the time she was fifteen, Ava's skill paralleled his. That was when he took her aside and asked if she was interested in learning bak mei. It was an ancient form, he explained, reserved for the most gifted. It was taught only one-on-one, traditionally passed down from father to son but now also from mentor to student. There was one teacher in Toronto, Grandmaster Tang. Ava met with him several times before he agreed to accept her as a student. She was his second pupil; another teenager, Derek Liang, was the first, and though he and Ava never learned or practised together, over the years they had become friends.

From time to time Ava had called upon Derek to help her with collection. It was something they never discussed with their other friends, none of whom knew about her job. They had simply come to accept that once in a while Ava would leave the city on business for a few days or even weeks. She doubted they even noticed she was gone.

Ava thought that bak mei was the perfect martial art for a woman. The hand movements were quick, light, and short; they snapped with tension to their fullest extent, where the energy was released. It didn't take a lot of physical strength to be effective. Bak mei attacks were meant to cause damage, directed as they were at the most sensitive parts of the body, such as the ears, eyes, throat, underarms, sides, stomach, and, of course, groin. Kicks were hardly ever aimed above the waist. Bak mei hadn't come naturally to Ava. She had to learn to overcome her lack of power — at least, compared to Derek and Master Tang — and to exploit her strengths: her lightning-quick reflexes and her uncanny accuracy.

And learn she did. "I can look after myself," she had told Uncle. And in all the years they'd been working together, she'd never given him any reason to doubt her.

They had been profitable years, with Ava earning enough money for the condo and the car and an impressive investment portfolio. But the best thing about the jobs she and Uncle did was that when they were successful, the income was only part of the satisfaction. First there was the ride getting to the money — it was never the same twice, and though it taxed her emotionally, it also forced her to expand her senses and her thought processes. Then there were the clients. Although she complained about them sometimes, especially those who in utter desperation were far too clinging and demanding, she also accepted Uncle's conviction that they were simply lost souls looking for redemption. "When we get them their money back, what we are really doing is saving their lives," he would say. Ava believed that too.

Ava reached for a black Moleskine notebook resting on the corner of the table, opened it to the first page, and wrote *Andrew Tam* across the top of the lined page. Every job she had ever done had its own notebook, a meticulous day-by-day record of everything she deemed relevant. The completed notebooks sat in a safety deposit box at the Toronto-Dominion Bank two blocks from her condo.

The manila envelope was stuffed with paper, and she quietly groaned at the prospect of wading through it all. However, a quick scan soon brought a smile to her face. The paperwork was beautifully organized, a complete chronological record of Andrew Tam's dealings with a company called Seafood Partners, starting with a letter from him summarizing the events from start to finish. The letter even referred to appendices that were attached and neatly numbered. Ava admired his thoroughness. Then she wondered what moment of madness had caused him to go into business with a seafood company.

Of all the characters she had dealt with in the past, the seafood guys were the worst. It was as if they were programmed to steal, and once they had your money, getting it back was harder than pulling teeth with your fingers. One of her clients in Vancouver had bought two forty-foot containers of Chinese scallops; when the product arrived in Canada, he found that the boxes — clearly marked SCALLOPS — were filled with freezer-burned mackerel. It had taken her close to two weeks' trekking around seafood plants in dusty, dirty Dalian in northeast China, on the Yellow Sea near the Korean border, before she caught up with the packer. It took another week before she got the money back. Even then the job wouldn't have wrapped up so quickly if Uncle hadn't put her in touch with a high-ranking general. They had to split their recovery fee with him (and probably the rest of his unit), but without his influence she might have been there for several weeks more.

Tam's company was called Dynamic Financial Services. It was on Des Voeux Road, almost next door to the headquarters of the Hong Kong Shanghai Bank, on Queen's Road in Central, the very heart of Hong Kong's financial district. About a year before, Seafood Partners had come to Dynamic Financial Services with a master purchase order from Major Supermarkets for six million pounds of Thai shrimp, cooked, peeled, and deveined, with the tail on.

Ava made her first note: *Who introduced Dynamic to Seafood Partners?*

The purchase order was of twelve months' duration, and the selling price was locked in for the entire period.

Note 2: *Isn't shrimp a commodity? Don't prices fluctuate? How could Seafood Partners commit to Major Supermarkets for a year?*

The product was to be packed under Major Supermarkets' own label, and Tam had affixed a copy of their specifications. They didn't seem particularly onerous. There had to be an average of thirty-seven to thirty-nine shrimp in every bag. Each bag had to have a true net weight of one pound, true net weight being the weight after the shrimp had thawed. The tails were to be a uniform red colour, with no black tails allowed. Tripolyphosphates and/or salt were permitted up to a residual level of two percent. The shrimp had to be processed from fresh and frozen only once. On the specification sheet Tam had highlighted in yellow the net weight requirement and the tripolyphosphates level.

It was anticipated that Major Supermarkets would need about 500,000 pounds of shrimp a month. In order to manage that level of business, Seafood Partners would need to have 1.5 million pounds of shrimp in their system at any one time — an on-hand inventory of 500,000 pounds, another 500,000 pounds in transit to the U.S. from Thailand, and another 500,000 pounds being processed. Seafood Partners was buying the shrimp at $4.10 a pound and selling to Major Supermarkets at $4.80 a pound.

Note 3: *Given what was essentially 90 days' financing at 2 to 3 percent a month, and given customs, storage, trucking, and distribution charges, how the hell did Seafood Partners expect to make money?*

The master purchase order was from Major Supermarkets to Seafood Partners. Seafood Partners assigned the purchase order to Dynamic Financial Services, and Dynamic issued letters of credit to the Thai packer and imported the product into the U.S. Major Supermarkets had six distributors that drew up weekly purchase orders for shrimp; Seafood Partners and Dynamic Financial Services were copied on those purchase orders. Seafood Partners released the product from inventory and Dynamic Financial Services sent an invoice for the product directly to Major Supermarkets. The cheques went to Dynamic, which took its money and interest off the top and then sent the balance of the funds to Seafood Partners.

Note 4: *Why didn't Dynamic retain complete control of the inventory? Why did they allow Seafood Partners to release product?*

After five months, relations between Major Supermarkets and Seafood Partners began to go sour. Shrimp sales were not meeting expectations, and the buyer at Major Supermarkets was having second thoughts about the length and volume of his commitment. The documentation included copies of emails that had gone back and forth, and in many of them the buyer was looking for price relief. He claimed that the market had tanked and that he could buy the same shrimp more cheaply almost anywhere. He needed help to remain competitive.

At first Seafood Partners refused. A deal was a deal, they repeated. The buyer kept at them to reduce their prices, making (not very subtle) threats to go elsewhere to average down the cost of Seafood Partners' product. Finally Seafood Partners relented and dropped their selling price to $4.40.

Note 5: *Didn't Dynamic Financial Services ask if dropping the selling price of the shrimp was even remotely possible?*

As Ava read on, she could see the train wreck coming. She didn't know what form it was going to take, but Tam's yellow highlighting of the net weights and chemical levels offered a clue.

There are several ways to make more money on a basic food commodity than the market warrants. Cheating on weights is perhaps the simplest. Put a label weight of one pound on a bag and then put 15 ounces of product in it, and you can increase your profit by seven percent. If someone actually weighs the bag, the packer has a problem. But the weight of shrimp is easier to manipulate than most other seafood products, since you have to add an ice glaze to protect the flesh. Under normal circumstances a five percent glaze is added, meaning that a one-pound bag's gross weight becomes 16.8 ounces. If Seafood Partners put a twelve percent glaze on the shrimp, the bag would still have a gross weight of 16.8 ounces, but 1.8 ounces would be ice, leaving only 15 ounces of shrimp. The product would pass any rudimentary inspection.

Another common trick is to "pump" the product, to add moisture to it. Ava didn't know who had discovered this technique, but she knew that just about every protein sector — including beef and chicken producers — does it. With shrimp it's very simple: all you have to do is soak them in a chemical solution, typically a tri-polyphosphate. The longer you soak the shrimp and the more potent the solution, the more moisture the shrimp absorbs. The moisture adds weight — artificial weight.

The economic impact of adding weight goes beyond the extra weight itself. Shrimp are sold by size: the larger the size, the higher the price. Shrimp that come to between 31 and 40 pieces per pound sell for more than smaller shrimp that count between 41 and 50 pieces per pound. So if Seafood Partners added enough weight chemically to change a 41–50 count into a 31–40 count, they would make more on a per pound basis.

How many stunts had Seafood Partners tried? As it turned out, all of them. Ava could hardly believe it. Cheating using one method was risky enough. Trying two was begging for trouble. Doing all three? Craziness — or complete desperation.

And Major Supermarkets had caught them out. Actually, the U.S. Food and Drug Administration caught them first, in a random inspection, which was when the weight discrepancy was identified. The FDA turned the problem over to Major Supermarkets' in-house quality-control team, which bored in and exposed the whole mess. It was the excuse the buyer needed to get out of the twelve-month contract. The day after the internal inspection results, Seafood Partners were informed that they had been delisted. The product already in stores was to be picked up, the master purchase order was cancelled, inventory in the U.S. and on the water was now their problem, and none of the outstanding invoices would be paid.

Seafood Partners did not tell Dynamic Financial Services about the fiasco. It was not until Dynamic called Major Supermarkets about the outstanding invoices that they were told what was up. In the meantime, Seafood Partners had moved the inventory and Dynamic had no idea where it was. More than a million pounds of shrimp had gone missing. Add close to a million dollars in unpaid invoices, and Dynamic was out of pocket at least five million dollars.

Andrew Tam had done a good job of piecing it all together. There were copies of the financing agreement, the master purchase order, the letters of credit Dynamic had issued, and examples of Major Supermarkets' purchase orders. He had also attached the FDA inspection report and Major Supermarkets' quality-control team reports, and he had somehow accessed a series of emails from Seafood Partners to the packer that outlined, in bold terms, what they wanted him to do.

Note 6: *Has Tam spoken to the packer? Does the packer have any liability?*

Ava checked her watch; it was 4 a.m. in Hong Kong. She dialled Tam's cellphone number. To her surprise he answered. "I was hoping you'd call," he said.

"I've just finished going through your paperwork. What a mess."

There was silence from the other end, and Ava wondered if she had insulted him. Then he said, "Tell me about it."

She looked at her notes. “I see two signatures on the financing agreement on behalf of Seafood Partners. How many partners are there?”

“Those are them: George Antonelli and Jackson Seto. Antonelli lives in Bangkok. He handles production and the technical side of things.”

“Like short weights?”

“I guess. Seto kind of floats between Seattle and Hong Kong. He seems to have residences in both places. He is the marketer and the money guy.”

“I take it you’ve spoken to them about this problem?”

“I’ve tried to.”

“And?”

“They initially tried to pin it on the buyer for Major Supermarkets, saying that he was just looking for a way to get rid of them and buy some cheaper product. But after I got hold of the FDA's and Major’s inspection reports, they switched gears and told me I should be going after the packer, that he had screwed up the specifications and was liable for any loss. The packer was the one who supplied me with the emails from Antonelli instructing him to change the specs. The emails were very specific.”

“And then what?”

He paused. “And then they stopped answering my emails and taking my phone calls,” he said.

“Where is the company registered?”

“Hong Kong.”

“Bank account?”

“Also in Hong Kong, and it has nothing in it.”

“Is that the account you sent money to?”

“Yes.”

“Always to Hong Kong?”

"Yes."

"They could have an offshore account."

"I wouldn't know."

She chewed on a sour candy. "Tell me, Andrew, who made the introduction? Who brought you together?"

"An old schoolmate of mine. He met Seto in Hong Kong through another friend of his. Seto mentioned that he was looking for purchase-order financing and the schoolmate put him on to me. I don't think he knew Seto very well."

"I've looked at the numbers, and the profit margins look thin. That didn't concern you?"

"Seto told me they're standard for the industry, and then he implied — actually, more than implied — that they were getting back-ended by the packer."

"How about when the selling price to Major Supermarkets was reduced — still no concern?"

"Quite a bit, really. But I still had all my costs and interest covered, and Seto told me they would get what they needed from the packer."

"You did the invoicing?"

"Yes, it wasn't onerous. Usually about six invoices a week, and with net thirty-day payment terms, we had only twenty-four to thirty invoices outstanding at any time."

"Why didn't you retain ownership of the inventory?"

"We did."

"Then how come your inventory disappeared on you?"

"Seafood Partners was authorized to do releases. We aren't equipped to deal with warehouses and truckers and the like. I mean, there's a twelve-hour time difference between here and most of Major Supermarkets' distribution centres, and sometimes they wanted product on very short notice. I don't have the staff to handle logistics."

Ava walked over to her window. It was late afternoon and winter's darkness was settling in. Below her the traffic crawled bumper to bumper up Avenue Road. It would be that way till past six o'clock. "Do you have any idea where the inventory is?"

"No. I talked to the warehouse and they gave me the name of the trucking firm that did most of the pickups. They wouldn't give me any information. They said their customer was Seafood Partners, and unless Partners authorized it they weren't in a position to release any information to me."

"Are their names in the file Alice gave me?"

"Not all of them."

"Can you email them to me?" she said.

"I'll do it when I get to the office."

"What else have you done to recover your money and your shrimp?"

"I hired collection agencies."

"Agencies?"

"One in Bangkok, one in Seattle, and one in Hong Kong."

"Regular firms?"

"What do you mean?"

"I mean they don't use machetes."

"Ms. Lee, we are a reputable financing firm."

"That doesn't answer my question."

"I used collection agencies that were recommended to me by various friends. They are — were — very professional. They just weren't effective."

"So you went to your uncle."

"I had to talk to someone, and he has been through a hell of a lot."

"Including swimming from China."

"Yes, that's true. With your uncle."

"That is the story," she said.

"And now they've brought us together," he replied.

She picked up the sheaf of documents he had provided and leafed through them, looking for personal information on Seto and Antonelli. When she couldn't find any, she asked Tam what he had.

"I have phone numbers and some addresses."

"No passport copies, Hong Kong ID card, driver's licences, photos?"

"No."

"Email me what you do have. Also, send me the name and phone number of the guy who hooked you up with Seto."

He paused again. In her mind's eye she could see him sitting in the dark in some apartment in Hong Kong, the mid-levels probably, a nice middle-class 110-square-metre apartment that would have cost more than a million dollars and still didn't offer a view of the waterfront beyond the wall of skyscrapers that lined Victoria Harbour. You had to be higher — in the upper levels, on the Peak — and have a net worth of a lot more than five million dollars to be able to afford that view. The Peak was the top of Victoria Mountain, the highest elevation in Hong Kong. The mountain ran straight up from the harbour, through the financial district, and past a host of five-star hotels, shops, and restaurants, the land costs rising with every yard.

"Ms. Lee," he asked quietly, "does this mean you're taking the job?"

"Yes, we're taking the case," she said.

"How long do you think it's going to take?"

"I have no idea, and please call me Ava."

"Ava —"

"Really, I have no idea, and not just about the time. I also have no idea if I'm going to be successful or not. And I mean that — we make no promises. We do the best we can and sometimes it's good enough. I'm sure my uncle explained that to your uncle."

"He said you're remarkably good at what you do."

"That doesn't mean it always works."

"Do we need to talk about your fee?" he asked.

"Did your uncle explain how it operates?"

"He said you keep one-third of everything you collect."

"We do. It seems like a lot, but we don't ask for anything upfront, we pay all our own expenses, and if we don't collect, then not only do we not get paid, we are also out of pocket for the money we've spent."

"Yes, he said that too."

"Good."

"Andrew, send me the information I requested, and be available if I need to talk to you. If you don't hear from me for a while, don't sweat it. I'm not going to call you with regular updates."

She hung up and walked back to the window. It was snowing, and the long-range forecast called for more of the same. A week or two in Hong Kong and Bangkok didn't seem like such a bad idea.

(4)

AVA SLEPT WELL AND WOKE WITH A SENSE OF purpose, but she didn't hurry her morning routine of prayer, stretching, coffee, *Globe and Mail*, and TV. It was nine o'clock before she called Uncle. From the background noise she could tell he was in a restaurant. She explained to him in detail what had happened to Tam.

"Stupid," Uncle said.

"We've seen worse."

"He is supposed to a professional."

"He finances purchase orders. Who is more creditworthy than Major Supermarkets?"

"True. What will you do?"

"I'll start off by finding the shrimp and/or the money."

"Will that be hard?"

"No, I should get it done this morning."

"And then?"

"I'll have to find Seto and Antonelli."

"That's an unusual combination for partners: a Chinese and an Italian. They usually like to stick to their own."

Ava hadn't thought about it, but it was true. "I might

have to come to Hong Kong and I'll probably have to go to Bangkok."

"When?"

"In a day or two."

"Let me know your schedule. I'll meet you at Chek Lap Kok."

"Uncle, I may need some help in Bangkok."

"I'll call our friends."

"If I go, I'd like a car and a driver who can speak English and handle himself, and I'll need some of the usual odds and ends."

"It will be a cop. That is who we are connected to. It has to be either the police or the army, and since we don't smuggle drugs or sell rocket launchers, the cops are the best choice."

"That's fine. As soon as my schedule is set, I'll send it to you."

She had called Uncle from her land line. She put down that phone and pulled out her cell, opened the back, and took out her local SIM card. From a drawer in her desk she pulled out a business card organizer, but there were no business cards in the clear plastic sleeves. Instead there were about forty SIM cards, each neatly identified by city and country; in the back were prepaid phone cards. She found the SIM card she wanted and slid it into her cell. When the phone was turned on, it read WELCOME TO AT&T 202-818-6666 — a Washington, D.C. number.

The Andrew Tam file was open in front of her. She found the phone number for the trucking firm that moved most of the shrimp and punched it in.

"Collins Transport," a woman said.

"This is Carla Robertson from the Food and Drug

Administration," Ava said. "I need to speak to the person who runs this business."

There was a pause. Any mention of the FDA always caused a pause. "That would be Mr. Collins."

"Then put me through."

Another pause. "I'm afraid he's in a meeting."

"Ma'am, I don't care if he's in a meeting. It's imperative that I speak to him. Please interrupt whatever he's doing and put him on the line."

"Let me see what I can do."

"Thank you."

It was a few minutes before Collins picked up the line. Ava guessed that he really had been in a meeting. "Hello," he said, "this is Bob Collins."

"Mr. Collins, good morning. My name is Carla Robertson and I'm a senior inspector with the FDA here in Washington."

"Yes, Ms. Robertson, what can I do for you?"

"Mr. Collins, about eight weeks ago your firm picked up multiple truckloads of shrimp from the Evans Cold Storage Warehouse in Landover, Maryland."

"We did."

"That shrimp, Mr. Collins, had been inspected by us and found to violate several FDA regulations. It was our intent to put it on formal hold, but before the paperwork could be processed the product was moved by your trucking firm."

"Ms. Robertson, we had no idea about any FDA involvement," he said quickly. "We were given the business and treated it like we would any other. The cold storage facility would never have released the order if it was on hold."

"As I said, we were slow to act, but the product should not have been moved. Who authorized it?"

"A company called Seafood Partners."

"Have you done business with them before?"

"Actually, no. We got the business through a freight broker. We never talked to them."

"Where did the product go?"

"Biloxi, Mississippi," he said.

"Where in Biloxi?"

"The Garcia Shrimp Company."

"I would like an address, phone number, and contact name for that firm."

"I don't have it at my fingertips. Can I email it to you later?"

"No, I'll wait."

She heard him mutter and then put the phone down. The next voice she heard was that of the receptionist, who gave Ava the information she wanted. Their contact at the Garcia Shrimp Company was a man named Barry Ho. What was a Chinese guy doing running a shrimp company with a Mexican name in Mississippi?

She dialled the Biloxi number Collins's receptionist had given her. The phone went directly to voicemail. She debated about leaving a message, but in the end she did, emphasizing how important it was for someone to get back to her.

Twenty minutes later her cellphone rang. "Carla Robertson, FDA."

"This is Barry Ho."

"Thanks for returning my call so promptly."

"When it comes to the FDA, we take things very seriously," he said, with a slight trace of a Chinese accent and a stronger trace of stress.

"We appreciate that. It makes our job a lot easier when we get cooperation."

"So what can I do for you? Your message said it was important."

"Do you do business with a company called Seafood Partners?"

Ho hesitated, and Ava swore she could hear him wondering whether he should try to bullshit her or not. "Yeah, I do. Not that often."

"According to our sources, they trucked a substantial amount of shrimp to your plant about eight weeks ago."

"That's right."

"Why did they ship it to you?"

"They needed it repacked. That's our specialty — repacking."

"Repacked how?"

"They had a couple of problems."

"Such as?"

"Ms. Robertson, I'm not sure I should be talking to you without their permission."

"Mr. Ho, we inspected this product just before they moved it. We were about to put it all on hold, but they beat us to the punch. Now, there's no way you could have known that, and we're not going to hold you responsible for acting as if everything was above board. But let me assure you, it would be beneficial for you to tell me what you know."

Ho sighed. There was no upside to refusing her. "Well, the product was packed in retail bags for sale at Major Supermarkets, and it was short weight. We repacked a lot of it for another retail chain, and the rest we put up in a Seafood Partners bag."

"With the correct weights?"

"Of course, and it wasn't easy. Usually we need to overpack by about five percent to make up for glaze. This time we were at ten percent and more."

"Who was the retailer?"

"G. B. Flatt."

"In their bags?"

"Yeah."

"How much product?"

"Twenty truckloads."

"Do you still have any of the product?"

"No, no, we shipped it out as soon it was repacked."

"Where did the G. B. Flatt product go?"

"To their central distribution centre in Houston."

"And the balance?"

"To a warehouse in Seattle."

"Which one?"

"Continental. They only have the one freezer."

"Care of?"

"Seafood Partners."

"Have you been paid?"

"We wouldn't let product leave our warehouse unless we were paid."

"By cheque?"

"Yeah."

"From Seafood Partners?"

"Yeah."

"You wouldn't have a copy of that cheque handy, would you?"

"Sure."

"Please get it for me."

She heard a filing cabinet opening and closing, paper rustling.

"I have copy in front of me," he said.

"Give me the particulars," she said.

It was from Northwest Bank, a major financial institution headquartered in Seattle. Seafood Partners had an account at a branch near Sea-Tac Airport. Ho provided the address, phone number, and account number.

"Who did you deal with at Seafood Partners?"

"Jackson Seto."

"Just him?"

"No one else."

"Did you ever meet his partner, George Antonelli?"

"No, and I never really met Seto. We did business over the phone."

"When was the last time you heard from him?"

"I called him about four or five weeks ago, when the last of the product was repacked."

"What phone number did you call?"

He gave her the same cellphone number that Andrew Tam had provided.

"Tell me, Mr. Ho, how did Jackson Seto find you?"

He laughed. "In this business, sooner or later everyone in the U.S. needs to find me. That's all I do — fix other people's problems."

"Well, this is one problem I would appreciate your not discussing any further with Seto. There is no reason for you to call him, and if by chance he calls you, I would not mention this conversation."

"He's all yours."

"Thanks."

"But I'd be happy if you could make a note in the report you're going to write that I was cooperative."

"Consider it done, Mr. Ho," she said.

Ava did a search on the Internet to find G. B. Flatt. It was the largest retail food chain in Texas, with more than three hundred stores. She trolled through the various departments until she found the seafood director in a sub-listing in the perishables department. The name was J. K. Tran — Vietnamese for sure. Man or woman? Not so certain.

She debated whether or not to maintain the FDA persona. *It's working well enough*, she thought. Carla was on a roll.

J. K. Tran wasn't happy to hear from her. "We've done nothing wrong," he said the instant she mentioned the FDA and Seafood Partners.

Why is he so defensive? she wondered. *Is he on the take? Did Seto pay him off to take in the product?*

"Mr. Tran," she said slowly, "our interest is solely in Seafood Partners. We have already talked to Barry Ho at Garcia Shrimp, and he swears that the product is now entirely within regulations. My problem is that we told Mr. Seto the product was not to be moved. I just need to confirm that you have that product. We have no, I repeat, no axe to grind with G. B. Flatt. You can keep the product. I just need you to confirm who you bought it from."

"Seafood Partners."

"Jackson Seto?"

"Yes."

"How much did you pay?"

"Why do you need to know that?"

Tran's not slow, she thought. "There's going to be a fine. It will be based on the value of the goods sold."

That must have sounded plausible, because Tran said, "I paid four dollars a pound."

"For how many pounds?"

"Just over 900,000."

"And how were they paid?"

"We sent them a wire."

"Is that usual?"

"It was a one-of-a-kind deal. The price was exceptional, so we didn't mind the terms."

"Where was the wire sent?"

"I don't know."

"Who does know?"

"Accounts payable."

"Who should I speak to there?"

"Rosemary Shields."

"Mr. Tran, could you do me a favour? Put me on hold, call Rosemary, and tell her to give me the wire information. I will make sure that you, she, and G. B. Flatt are kept out of this mess as we go forward."

"Wait," he said.

The line went dead for close to five minutes, and Ava began to think she had been cut off. She was just about to hang up and redial when Tran came back to the phone. "The wire was sent two weeks ago. It went to Dallas First National Bank, 486 Sam Rayburn Drive, Dallas, Texas."

"Whose bank account?"

"Seafood Partners, who else?"

"Do you have a contact at the bank?"

"No."

"Phone number?"

"None."

"Well, thanks for this. I'll follow up with the bank."

Ava hung up and went back to her computer. Dallas First National was a two-branch bank, and the main branch, on Sam Rayburn Drive, was located in a strip mall. Jeff Goldman was the chairman, president, and CEO. *Busy man*, she thought.

The FDA cover wasn't necessarily going to have an impact on Goldman. It was time to bring Rebecca Cohen out of the drawer.

She called the general phone number provided on the website. For close to a minute she listened to a Texas drawl extolling the virtues of hometown banking and personal service, and then she was transferred to voicemail. Again she debated about leaving a message. In the end she felt she had no choice, and added that the number she was giving was her direct personal line.

Goldman didn't call her back until mid-afternoon. In the meantime Ava had convinced herself that he had checked her out and was never going to call, so it was with some relief that she saw the 214 area code appear on her screen.

"This is the Treasury Department, Rebecca Cohen," she said.

"Ms. Cohen, I'm Jeff Goldman, Dallas First National Bank. You called me earlier today."

The accent was hardly Texan; he sounded more like a New Yorker. "Yes, I did, and thank you for returning my call."

"Ms. Cohen, exactly what part of the Treasury Department are you with?"

"Internal Revenue."

"That's still pretty vague."

"My section specializes in money laundering," she said.

"So why in hell are you calling me? We're a local bank, a mom-and-pop shop."

She waited for him to consider some possibilities, then asked, “Do you have a customer called Seafood Partners?”

She heard his fist banging on the desk. “Shit,” he said.

“How long have they been a customer?”

“Shit, shit, shit.”

“Mr. Goldman,” she prodded, “how long have they been a customer? Not very long, I would wager.”

“About three weeks,” he said, his voice pinched.

“Who opened the account?”

“A Chinese guy named Seto.”

“How much did he put in the account?”

“A thousand dollars.”

“Did he do it in person? Did he come into your branch?”

“That’s the only way we do business.”

“So you met him?”

“No, one of my account officers handled it. I mean, it was a business account with a thousand-dollar deposit. I saw the guy, though. Tall, real skinny, scrawny moustache.”

“And then about two weeks ago the account received a wire transfer from G. B. Flatt in Houston for close to four million dollars. You saw that, I bet.”

“I sure did.”

“You didn’t find that a bit strange?”

“No, why would I? We’re a small bank, but this is Texas, this is Dallas, and million-dollar transactions are common enough.”

“Still, one of your staff brought it to your attention.”

“We had to make sure it was legit.”

“How did you do that?”

"We called the issuing bank, and then to make doubly sure, we called the accounts department at G. B. Flatt."

"And?"

"Flatt said they had bought a lot of shrimp from them. It made sense."

It was time to back up, she thought, not to press too hard too quickly. "This Seto — what kind of information did he provide on his company?"

"They're registered in Washington state, with a Seattle address."

"So why use a Dallas bank?"

"He told my girl they were thinking of relocating to Texas. Looking at the deal they did with Flatt and knowing how big the shrimp business is in places like Brownsville, it was kind of logical."

"So they didn't have a Dallas address or phone number?"

"No, everything was Seattle."

"Can you give me that information, please?"

"It'll take a minute."

"I'll wait."

The address and phone numbers were the same ones she had gotten from Andrew Tam and Barry Ho.

"Now, Mr. Goldman, that money from G. B. Flatt, is it still in their account at your bank?"

"Some of it is," he said carefully.

"How much?"

"About ten thousand."

"Are you joking?"

"No, and the way this conversation is going, I wish I was."

"Mr. Goldman, don't fret," she said. "This happens all the time. A bank, a good honest bank, opens an account for a customer who seems entirely above board, takes in deposits for genuine commercial transactions, and then at the customer's request transfers that money elsewhere for what are thought to be other real commercial transactions. That's just about what happened, isn't it?"

"You got it."

"So where did the money go?"

"The British Virgin Islands," he said.

"I could have guessed," she said.

"How's that?"

"Mr. Goldman, the BVI are the world's tax haven. There are more than half a million offshore companies registered there — that's about half the world total."

"I run a small local bank, that's all," he said.

"I understand, I understand. Now, to which company was the money sent?"

"S&A Investments."

"Address?"

"I have a copy of our wire in front of me. It was sent six days ago to S&A Investments, P.O. Box 718, Simon House, Road Town, Tortola, British Virgin Islands."

"Care of which bank?"

"Barrett's"

"Account?"

"Account number 055-439-4656."

"Great," she said. "You've been just great."

"We don't like to get mixed up in things like this," he said.

"I know, but sometimes it's difficult to avoid people like Seto."

"Never again. I'm closing his account as soon as I get off the phone with you."

"Oh no, don't do that," she said quickly. "Please leave it alone. I need you to call me at once if Seto comes back to the bank or contacts you in any way."

"Ms. Cohen, you do know there was a second wire as well?"

Ava couldn't help being surprised. "No, I didn't."

"Yeah, for just over a million dollars, from Safeguard, a retail food chain in Portland, Oregon. We sent it to the same account in the British Virgin Islands."

"When?"

"Two days ago."

It looked as if Seto had cleared out the inventory. That was a good thing. Money was easier to repossess than goods, and she wouldn't have to worry about selling it if she got her hands on it.

"You've been terrific, Mr. Goldman. Let's hope I don't have talk to you again."

It was just past two o'clock and Ava hadn't eaten anything all day except a bowl of congee for breakfast. There was a Chinese restaurant on Bloor Street that served dim sum till three. She looked out her window at the street below. It wasn't snowing but it was cold and blustery, and the few pedestrians who had ventured out were wrapped up tightly and walking as quickly as they could, chins buried in their chests. She called the Italian restaurant where she had eaten the night before and ordered a pizza for delivery.

Then she called the travel agent she always used to book her trips. Most of her friends booked online, but she preferred having a buffer between herself and the airlines in case she had to make schedule changes, which she often did. She told the agent to book her on a flight to Seattle and to reserve a seat from there to Hong Kong and then on to Thailand.

Ava called her mother and her best friend, Mimi, to let them know she was getting out of town. The winter was wearing her down, she said, and she was heading to Thailand for ten days or so of fun and sun.

"Are you going through Hong Kong?" her mother asked.

"Yes."

"Will you call your father?"

"No."

She heard disappointment in her mother's voice. "So, you are just seeing Uncle?"

"Mum, I'll be in transit in Hong Kong. I probably won't see anyone."

Ava travelled light. It took her less than half an hour to pack her Louis Vuitton monogrammed suitcase and her Shanghai Tang "Double Happiness" bag. The suitcase was where she packed her business look: black linen slacks, a pencil skirt, Cole Hahn black leather pumps, two sets of black bras and panties, and three Brooks Brothers shirts in powder blue, pink, and white — one with a button-down collar, the other two with modified Italian collars, and all of them with French cuffs. She chose a small jewellery case to hold her Cartier Tank Française watch, a set of green jade cufflinks, and a simple gold crucifix. She then went through the leather pouch that held her collection of clasps, pins, barrettes, headbands, and combs and took out an ivory chignon pin she especially loved, adding it to the jewellery case. Ava wore her hair up nearly all the time and liked to accentuate it. Nothing did so better than the chignon pin.

Her toilet kit was always packed and ready to go: toothbrush, toothpaste, hairbrush, deodorant, shampoo, Annick Goutal perfume, one lipstick, and mascara. The shampoo was in a hundred-millilitre bottle, as required by airport security. She had four such bottles neatly packed in the plastic bag that was also required. Only one of the bottles held shampoo; the other three contained chloral hydrate.

The contents of the Shanghai Tang bag were more eclectic: the Moleskine notebook, two fountain pens, her computer, running shoes and shorts, a sports bra, socks, three Giordano T-shirts, a Chanel purse to take to meetings, and two rolls of duct tape. Ava went to the kitchen, took thirty Starbucks coffee sachets from a container, and tossed them into the bag.

At eight she called Uncle.

"*Wei*," he answered.

"I found the money," she said.

"The shrimp?"

"No, the shrimp have been sold already. I've located the money."

"How much?"

"About five million."

"Where is it?"

"British Virgin Islands."

"That's not a surprise," he said. "Half of Hong Kong has bank accounts there."

"I'm heading for Seattle tomorrow morning to see if I can find Jackson Seto and persuade him to give the money to Andrew Tam."

"What do you think?"

"I have no expectations. I get into Seattle tomorrow

morning around eleven. Both his office address and supposed home address are downtown, within a couple of blocks of each other. Who knows, I might get lucky."

"If you don't?"

"I'm booked on Cathay Pacific tomorrow night into Hong Kong."

"Are you staying?"

"Maybe a day or two. I want to check out Seto's Hong Kong address in Wanchai, and I might meet with Tam. I also want to talk to the guy who introduced Seto to Dynamic Financial Services."

"Let me know how it goes in Seattle. I don't care what time you call. If you come to Hong Kong, where do you want to stay?"

"The Mandarin."

"I'll book it for you just in case."

"Thanks, Uncle."

"And I'll meet you at the airport."

"You don't have to."

"I know, but I want to."

She usually slept well. Her sleep mechanism was bak mei, the basic moves played and replayed in slow motion. That night was a little different. The core form was the panther, but this time she had a target: a tall, skinny Chinese man with a scrawny moustache and five million dollars in a bank account in the British Virgin Islands.

(5)

SEATTLE WAS A BUST. THE OFFICE WAS CLOSED, EMPTY. Seto had moved out of the apartment the month before.

Ava was back at Sea-Tac Airport four hours before her flight was scheduled to leave, so she killed some time getting a full body massage in the Cathay Pacific business lounge. She called Uncle just before boarding. He again insisted he'd meet her at the airport and she again told him he didn't have to. She knew how much he hated the new Hong Kong International Airport at Chek Lap Kok. He lived in Kowloon, no more than ten minutes by car from the old airport, Kai Tak.

Kai Tak had been theatre and drama, the planes approaching Hong Kong precariously through mountains and skyscrapers, crossing Kowloon Bay, their wing tips almost touching the lines of laundry on the balconies of the apartment buildings that pressed in on the airport. Then there was the bus ride from the tarmac to the tired old terminal, which had been built for 1950s levels of air traffic, and the long lines at Customs before one emerged into a small, cramped Arrivals hall where hundreds, if not thousands, of people lined the corridor, waving and yelling at the incoming passengers.

Ava wasn't as nostalgic about Kai Tak as Uncle. To her mind, the Arrivals hall at Chek Lap Kok might be huge and sterile, reducing people to ants scurrying under its soaring roof, but its almost brutal efficiency made up for any deficiencies in its character.

"I'll sit in the Kit Kat Koffee House," Uncle said.

The business-class section of the airplane was more than half empty, and the window seat next to her was vacant. That was good; Ava wasn't one for casual conversation with strangers, and now she didn't have to find an excuse to avoid it.

It would be a thirteen-hour flight, leaving Seattle at 7 p.m. (10 p.m. Toronto time) and getting into Hong Kong at 11 p.m. the following day, factoring in the International Date Line. Ava hated that, because jet lag was almost inevitable. The only way she could avoid it was not to sleep at all on the plane, and for her that just wasn't possible. For reasons she couldn't understand, the moment a flight took off her eyes began to close. On a one-hour flight to New York in the middle of the day, she could sleep for forty-five minutes. During one seventeen-hour flight from Toronto to Hong Kong, she figured she had slept for fifteen hours.

The Seattle–Hong Kong flight turned out to be not that extreme. Ava managed to stay awake long enough to eat dinner and to watch a Hong Kong action film starring Tony Leung and Andy Lau. Then she fell asleep until the flight attendant woke her two hours before landing, to serve her breakfast.

When the plane landed, Ava found HKIA its usual

ruthlessly efficient self. She was off the plane and through Immigration, Baggage Claim, and Customs within twenty minutes of landing. She spotted Uncle at the back of the Kit Kat, a plain, square box with round glass tables, metal chairs, and posters of coffee beans on the walls. He had a Chinese newspaper open in front of him and an unlit cigarette dangling from his mouth. Even in Hong Kong there were places where you couldn't smoke now.

He was tiny, not much taller than Ava, and thin. He was always dressed the same way: black lace-up shoes, black slacks, a white long-sleeved shirt buttoned to the neck. The monochromatic image was part convenience, part camouflage. It made him easy to overlook — just another boring old man not worth a second glance, except to those who knew.

Ava thought Uncle was somewhere between seventy and eighty, but that was as close as she could come to determining his age. Many people meeting him for the first time guessed that he was younger, and not from politeness. His face was fine-boned, with a small, straight nose and a sharply defined chin with a hint of a point; his skin had not begun to sag, and he had only the faintest of wrinkles around his eyes and on his forehead. His hair was cropped close to the scalp; Ava could see streaks of gray, but it was still predominantly black.

"Uncle," she said.

He looked up from his paper, a smile cracking his face as his eyes fell upon her. She loved his eyes: pitch black pupils and dark chocolate brown irises set in a sea of white that seemed immune to lack of sleep or too much alcohol. They were eyes whose age was indeterminable:

lively, curious, probing. Ava had learned rapidly that Uncle's world was defined through those eyes, not through his words. They could embrace you, mistrust you, detest you, adore you, question you, or not give a damn whether you lived or died. And she knew how to read them in all their subtlety. Ava had seen their many moods, although their darkest intent had never been directed at her. She was part of his unofficial family, after all, the only kind of family he had ever had.

She leaned down to kiss him on the forehead. "You didn't have to come," she said.

"I was eager to see you," he said. "You're as beautiful as ever."

"And you look as young as always."

He looked around. "I don't like this place. We'll go to Central for noodles. Let me call Sonny. I'll have him bring the car down from the garage."

They walked through the cavernous Arrivals hall, Uncle's hand resting lightly on her elbow. Two Hong Kong policemen watched them as they neared the exit. The older of the two nudged the younger and they nodded their heads in Uncle's direction. Ava saw the movement, looked sideways, and caught Uncle nodding in return.

Sonny was leaning against the front fender of the car. It was new, a Mercedes S-Class.

"What happened to the Bentley?" Ava asked.

"I sold it. Sonny said it was time to move into this decade."

Ava had never known Uncle to be without Sonny, and she'd never met anyone who had. He was technically Uncle's driver, a monochromatic match to his boss in his black suit, white shirt, and plain black tie. He was tall for Chinese, a couple of inches over six feet, and heavy-set. For someone that large he was quick — deadly quick — and he could be vicious when the circumstances required. He was one of the few people in the world whom Ava feared physically. And he wasn't talkative. If you asked him a question, you got a simple answer with no embellishments. Beyond that he didn't seem to have any opinions he needed to share.

When they approached the car, Sonny gave Ava a small smile and reached for her bags. She and Uncle climbed into the back seat as he put them in the trunk.

It was a quick ride to the city centre. Their route took them over the Tsing Ma Bridge, six lanes of traffic on the upper deck, rail lines beneath. The bridge always took Ava's breath away. It was close to a kilometre and half long and soared two hundred metres above the water. The Ma Wan Channel, part of the South China Sea, glittered below in the early morning sun as sampans and fishing boats skirted the armada of huge ocean freighters waiting to be escorted into Hong Kong's massive container port.

They slowed when they reached the city proper, caught in the last of the morning rush hour. Hong Kong isn't a city filled with private cars. Finding a place to park isn't easy or cheap in a place where office and retail space is rented by the square inch, but there are red taxis everywhere, scurrying like beetles. Sonny drove carefully — too carefully for Ava, but he was a cautious man, maybe even deliberately cautious. It was as if he were restraining his true nature. She had seen this trait in him when he attended meetings with Uncle. He didn't do that often, but when he did, he remained standing off to one side, his eyes flickering back and forth as he followed the flow of conversation. Ava realized that his body language changed along with the tone of the meeting. If Uncle was having his way, Sonny was placid. Any opposition to Uncle's position caused him to tense, his eyes growing dark.

The financial and commercial heart of the Hong Kong Territory is divided into two main areas: Hong Kong Island and Kowloon, two dense urban settings connected by the Cross-Harbour Tunnel and the Star Ferry. Ava's hotel was on the Hong Kong side, in the Central district, set just back from Victoria Harbour and a short walk to the financial sector.

They reached the Mandarin within forty minutes of leaving the airport. Uncle walked into the hotel with her and sat patiently in the lobby while she checked in. She sent her bags to the room.

"There is a noodle shop a block from here," Uncle said when Ava joined him. "We'll walk."

It always took her a day or two to adjust to Central foot traffic — the jostling, the pushing, everyone eager to get to the next corner, where they could wait in a throng before shuffling along to the next intersection, their pace dictated entirely by the mob around them. Ava and Uncle were hemmed in on all sides by a crush of people. Central streets weren't a place for the claustrophobic.

The noodle shop was a hole in the wall, ten tables with pink plastic stools. The place was full, but a man in an apron came from behind the counter to tell two young men sitting by themselves to move to another table that was occupied but had vacant seats. He then waved Uncle and Ava to the empty table and bowed as Uncle walked past.

She ordered har gow — shrimp dumplings — and soup with soft noodles. Uncle ordered beef lo mein and a plate of gai lin, steamed Chinese broccoli slathered in oyster sauce, to share.

"How is your mother?" he asked while they waited for their food.

"As lively as ever."

"A crazy woman."

Ava's mother was highly sociable and made friends as easily as other people changed clothes. Marian and Ava's friends weren't immune from her attention. It bothered Marian but never Ava; she saw it as just a natural extension of her mother's all-consuming interest in their lives. So it had come as no surprise when her mother, in Hong Kong to visit her own friends, called Uncle and said she'd like to meet him, to find out what kind of man her daughter was working for. If Ava had been working in Toronto for a North American firm, she would have been mortified, not because of what her mother had done but more because they wouldn't understand why she was doing it. But Uncle understood Chinese mothers; they met and got along well enough that from time to time Jennie Lee felt free to pick up the phone and call Kowloon. Just keeping in touch, she called it.

"She sends her love," Ava said.

Uncle shrugged off the lie. "Will you call your father while you are here?"

"I don't think so."

The two men had never met but they knew of each other, as the wealthy and powerful of Hong Kong tend to do. "Maybe just as well. I hear that the wife in Australia is causing him problems."

Ava hadn't heard that news and the surprise registered on her face.

"It is smart of him, keeping them all separated. I don't know, though, where he finds the energy or the time to keep them satisfied."

Their food came. She poured tea for both of them. The restaurant was full, a steady flow of people coming and going.

Uncle ate quickly, hardly bothering to chew his food. For a man who was otherwise outwardly serene and calm almost to an extreme, it was an unusual characteristic. She wondered sometimes if this might be truer to his nature than the bland, confident face he liked the world to see.

"There isn't any point in going to the Wanchai address you were given for Jackson Seto," he said, pushing his empty plate aside. "I sent someone there today. He hasn't lived there for at least six months."

"Do you have another address for him?"

"No."

"Hong Kong phone number?"

"No, but you might get better information from Henry Cheng. He is the one who connected Seto to Andrew Tam. You have an appointment with him tomorrow in his office at 11 a.m. He doesn't know why you want to talk to him, but he should be cooperative enough. One of my friends called him and made the arrangement."

"Where is the office?"

He passed her a slip of paper. "Kowloon side, Nathan Road."

"I was thinking of going to see Andrew."

"Why don't you wait until you see Henry Cheng?" Uncle said. "And even then it may not be a great idea. What can you tell him? That you've found out where his money is? What good does that do him? You might create false expectations."

"I'll think about it."

"You know, Andrew's uncle, my friend, used to call me every three weeks. Now he calls me twice a day. He is nervous for the nephew. The family does not have the kind of money where they can afford to lose thirty million Hong Kong. The repercussions would be massive. When he calls, I tell him I know absolutely nothing. And I'll keep telling him that until you tell me it is over, one way or another."

"I need to find Seto."

"Maybe Cheng can help."

"And I need to find George Antonelli, the Bangkok partner."

"Our friends in Bangkok have already been working on that. By the time you get there they should have all the information you need."

"I don't think Antonelli has access to the money. From what I can gather, Seto has those controls."

"But Antonelli can give you access to Seto."

"Exactly."

They walked slowly back to the hotel together, his arm looped through hers. The Mercedes was parked near the hotel entrance. Sonny stood near the car's front door, watching them as they approached. He opened the back door for Uncle and helped him into the car. Ava said goodbye and turned to walk into the Mandarin.

"Call me after you meet with Cheng," Uncle said to her back.

(6)

AVA LOVED THE MANDARIN ORIENTAL HOTEL. THE very first in the chain had been built on the Chao Phraya River in Bangkok in 1887. She had first discovered it when she was dating a banker and had travelled there with her for a four-day conference. They had splurged on their accommodations, booking the Somerset Maugham Suite in the Author's Wing. After the banker left for her meetings in the mornings, Ava took the hotel's private ferry across the river to its spa and indulged.

Her afternoons had been split between the wing's lounge, where she introduced herself to the works of Joseph Conrad and Graham Greene, and the restaurant terrace on the Chao Phraya. She was hardly a literary historian, but the fact that Conrad, Greene, Maugham, Noel Coward, and James Michener had all stayed and supposedly written there fascinated her. And the river was alluring in its own way. It was broad, brown, and sluggish, and as busy as a North American highway with ships, tugs, and barges working their way north from the Gulf of Thailand into the interior, while water taxis and ferries worked their way from east to west, dodging the bigger vessels as they went.

Most evenings her friend had an official function to attend, so Ava ate at the hotel by herself. There was a Chinese restaurant — the China House — on the hotel property next to the main building. It served perhaps the best Chinese food she had ever eaten up till then: abalone that had been gently braised for twelve hours, stir-fried black chicken, soy-braised pomfret.

The thing that had struck her most about the hotel was its level of service. It wasn't just that it offered good service — that was routine for every five-star hotel in Asia — it was more that the staff seemed to anticipate everything she did or wanted to do. In the four days she had never pressed an elevator button. On her first day there she ordered ice at exactly four o'clock. The ice was there again the next day, the day after, and the day after that, always at exactly four o'clock. And every staff member in the hotel seemed to know her name.

The only negative was the hotel's location, which was outside the city core. If you wanted to go anywhere else in Bangkok, you had to contend with traffic that was perpetually paralyzed. The hotel wasn't a place for someone who needed to get about quickly.

The Mandarin in Hong Kong did not have a location problem. After a quick shower and a change into her business attire, Ava walked out the front door and got to the Star Ferry in ten minutes. After a five-minute wait she was crossing Victoria Harbour to her meeting with Henry Cheng in Kowloon.

It was a pleasant day for Hong Kong, about room temperature, slightly overcast, with a light breeze. She sat at the back of the ferry, taking in the sun and looking at the skyline. There was nothing like it in the world — a solid wall of skyscrapers lining the harbour like some medieval fortress. The Hong Kong and Shanghai Bank. Central Plaza. Two international finance centres. The Hopewell Centre. The Bank of China building, designed by I. M. Pei. More than forty buildings over sixty-five storeys high. New York couldn't even come close.

The ferry docked in Timshashui on the Kowloon side. She thought about taking a taxi but had time to spare, so she walked instead. When she got to Henry Cheng's office on Nathan Road it was five minutes to eleven.

Kowloon isn't as aggressively modern as Hong Kong Island. The building on Nathan Road was only five storeys high, its brick exterior faded and chipped. She rode its single elevator to the top floor and found that Cheng's company occupied half of it — about three thousand square metres — a large office by Hong Kong standards. A hundred or so employees were working in an open-concept area. A handful of closed offices was at the far end, and a boardroom with its door open that Ava could see was empty. The receptionist noted her name and said in Cantonese that Mr. Cheng was expecting her; would she please follow her to the boardroom.

Ava sat there and waited. The office tea lady stuck her head in the door and asked if she wanted anything.

"I'll have some green tea," Ava said.

Henry Cheng was carrying a bottle of water when he arrived. He looked at Ava in her linen slacks and pink Brooks Brothers shirt with green jade cufflinks and said, "You're not what I was expecting."

"I'm not sure how to take that," she said.

"It doesn't matter. Never mind," he said, offering his hand. "I'm Henry Cheng."

"Ava Lee."

He sat a couple of chairs away from her, tapping his fingers impatiently on the table. "What can I do for you?"

He was short and chunky, and Ava guessed he was in his mid-forties. His hair was parted in the middle and swept over his ears in a style that might have suited someone twenty years younger, six inches taller, and forty pounds lighter. *He's still Hong Kong slick*, she thought, eyeing his Gucci loafers, tailor-made dress shirt with monogrammed cuffs, and D&G belt around a thirty-eight-inch waist. "I need to know about Jackson Seto."

"I know next to nothing."

"You introduced him to Andrew Tam."

"I mentioned Andrew Tam to Seto, and I called Andrew to tell him I was referring Seto to him. But I was never part of any meeting between them, and I had nothing to do with the business they did."

"How did you meet Seto?"

"I met him through his brother, whom I do know very well."

"What's his name?"

"Frank."

"How did it come about that you met?"

"I was having lunch with Frank when Jackson came into the restaurant. He joined us and we started to have, you know, the normal kind of conversation businessmen have. Sometime during lunch Jackson mentioned that he was looking for some purchase-order financing and I brought up Dynamic Financial. Andrew — if he hasn't told you — and I went to school together."

"That's it? Nothing more than that?"

"That's all."

"You never saw Seto again?"

"Never saw him, didn't talk to him."

"Andrew suggested that you might have received a finder's fee."

"No," Cheng said forcibly. "At the time the only reason I even mentioned Dynamic was that I thought if I helped Jackson, it might help me in my relationship with Frank. Little did I know."

"What do you mean?"

"Frank is embarrassed by his brother. He wants nothing to do with him and is quite determined to keep him away from his social circle."

"When did you find that out?"

"When I had lunch with Frank a few months after that first meeting."

"Who is this Frank Seto?"

"He is married to Patty Chan, Carter Chan's only child."

"Ah, the all-powerful Mr. Chan. Is he still the wealthiest man in Hong Kong?"

"Maybe in all of Asia."

"Nice catch."

Cheng shrugged. "Patty is ugly and fat, but she's going to be the richest woman in Hong Kong when Carter dies."

"What does Frank do?"

"He tries to keep her happy."

"No, I mean his job."

"He tries to keep her happy," Cheng said and laughed. "Officially, though, he's the president of a real estate operation they own, Admiralty Properties. The office is on the Hong Kong side, Gloucester Road, overlooking the harbour. He wanders in there a few times a week."

"Where does he live?"

"The family — the entire Chan family, including Carter, lives — where else? — at the top of the Peak. Security is very tight at the house. Actually, I should say houses, because it's more of a compound."

"I get the picture," Ava said. "Still, I'd like to talk to him."

"Good luck."

"Would you —"

"No, I wouldn't," Cheng interrupted. "If you want to speak to Frank, contact him yourself. I've told you all I know. I understand that Andrew may have problems as a result of dealing with Jackson. I'm sorry about that, but none of it was my doing. Andrew had an obligation to do his own due diligence." Cheng stood up. "Now I have another appointment."

Ava rode the elevator to the ground floor but waited until she was back on Nathan Road to call Uncle. She gave him a summary of her meeting with Cheng, then said, "Can you arrange for me to sit with Frank Seto?"

"I don't know Frank Seto. I do know Carter Chan, but if I was face down on the street bleeding, Carter would probably kick me for good measure," he said. "I'll tell you who does know Carter, though, and probably Frank Seto too."

"Who?"

"Your father."

(7)

MARCUS LEE DIDN'T SEEM SURPRISED TO BE HEARING from his daughter, but then he never did. Whether it was six days, six weeks, or six months since their last contact, he always acted as if they had just had breakfast together.

"Hi, sweetheart," he said, "are you in Hong Kong?"

When she had phoned his office the receptionist had said he was in a meeting and wasn't to be disturbed. "Could you tell him that his daughter Ava called?" she said.

"Ah, wait," the woman said. "For you, I can disturb him."

For some reason it made her feel good to hear that, and then to hear him "sweetheart" her when he came on the line.

"I am."

"That's funny. I talked to Mummy this morning and she didn't mention that you'd be here."

"A last-minute change of plan. I'm really heading to Bangkok, but I need to do something here first."

"Where are you now?"

"I just got off the Star Ferry on the Hong Kong side."

"You know, it's almost lunchtime. Do you want to join me?"

"Why not?"

"They have very good dim sum at the Shangri-La Hotel. Why don't you grab a taxi and meet me there in about ten minutes."

When Ava arrived at the hotel, her father was already standing by the restaurant host, waiting for her. He was just under six feet and slender, with no hint of middle-age spread. His hair was still jet black and fashionably long at the back. *God, he's handsome*, she thought. He wore a charcoal grey suit with a white dress shirt and a red silk tie — the very picture of conservatism.

Her mother swore that Ava bore the closest physical resemblance to him of any of the children, even though she'd only seen pictures of the four sons from the first wife and knew nothing of those from the third. It wasn't just that Ava was lean and easy on the eyes. Her entire appearance was striking: a combination of good looks, the ability to carry herself well, and an aura of self-confidence.

Marcus Lee saw her and waved, then walked across the lobby to meet her halfway. He threw his arms around her and they hugged. She could feel a hundred eyes on them.

"You look gorgeous, sweetheart," he said.

"Thanks, Daddy. You look great too."

"I'm still running, still watching what I eat."

"It shows."

The restaurant was jammed but a table had been held for them. He ordered from the dim sum menu without asking her what she wanted. Her mother loved that about him, that he always took charge.

"I told Mummy this morning that I'm planning to come over to Toronto in May, when the weather improves. I'll stay maybe for the whole month. I hope you'll be there," he said.

"It's a long way out, and with my work —"

"Anyway, I'm giving you notice. I told Mummy that maybe we could have a family holiday. You know, take your sister and her kids and you and go on a cruise, or down to the Bahamas."

"How is everyone here?" Ava asked as if she hadn't heard him.

"Good, really good. Jamie and Michael are in business here. Neither of them is married yet, although Michael is now living with a girl for the first time. David is in Australia finishing up a Ph.D. and trying to find himself. Peter has just joined Barclay's Bank."

It always amazed her that he could talk about the children from his first marriage with such ease in front of her. What was as surprising was that her mother spoke about them and took pride in them as well, as if they were part of her extended family. Ava wondered if it cut both ways. Did they even know she existed?

"Yes, Mummy keeps me posted," she said.

The waiter put a small tureen of hot and sour soup on the table. Her father filled her bowl.

"So, what brings you east again?"

"Business," she said.

"Are you still working with Chow?"

"Yes, of course I am."

"I can't help but wish you weren't."

"But I am."

"Be careful," he said. It was the same thing he said every time Uncle's name was mentioned.

"Daddy, I'm an accountant," she said.

His eyes flickered in her direction. She felt a nervous flutter in her stomach, her face flushed, and she found herself confronting the fact that this man was nobody's fool. He knew what she did for a living, and though she never discussed her work in detail, he'd been in business long enough and knew Hong Kong and China well enough to know what it could entail.

"So what is this business?"

"The usual. Someone took off with someone else's money, and I'm trying to track it down and have it returned to its rightful owner."

"You make it sound so simple."

"It is."

"Do I know any of the principals?"

"I don't think so, and even if you did I couldn't acknowledge it."

"So why did you call me, then?"

The question was asked gently but the point was direct; she couldn't lie to him. "I need to speak to a man named Frank Seto. He is Carter Chan's son-in-law. I'm quite sure that if I approach him on my own I'll be put off. I was hoping you could help me."

"I don't know Frank very well," he said. "Still, I can't imagine him getting himself immersed in anything untoward."

"It isn't him. He has a brother who I'm trying to locate, and so far there's nothing but dead ends. I'm hoping that Frank can help me."

Their food arrived: shu mai, fried turnip cake, scallops fried with salt, and steamed duck feet with mushrooms.

"I'm not sure my calling Frank will do any good. He might not remember me," he said. "On the other hand, Carter and I have had a long and uneventful relationship. In his own strange way, he may even consider me a friend. I'll call him and see what he can set up. You want to meet with Frank, correct?"

"Yes, thank you, Daddy."

"Would you find it upsetting if I came along?"

She glanced up at him.

"It might make things easier all around," he said.

"What would you tell him? I mean, what would you tell him about me?"

"That you are my daughter, of course. What did you think I would say?"

"I don't know. I mean, Mummy and me and Marian are in another world. This is your world here. I don't know who knows what about what."

"You aren't a secret, if that's what you think."

"I don't think I need a complete explanation," she said.

"Well, anytime you do, just ask," he said. "I know it seems to Westerners that some of us Chinese have very complicated lives. Actually, the opposite is true. There are rules to this tradition of ours, and as long as everyone — and that includes the wives — plays by the rules, the family remains harmonious. What are the other options? Divorce? Secret mistresses? Messy and hurtful."

She sat mute, a shu mai between her chopsticks.

"I know it's old-fashioned, but I was raised that way, and it can't be helped," he said.

"No, I guess not," she said.

They finished lunch and went into the hotel lobby. He turned on his cellphone. "This could take a while," he said to her. "I have to get past a receptionist and then at least two personal assistants." He was sitting directly under a harsh overhead light and still looked ten to fifteen years younger than he was. Ava saw several women close to her own age glancing at him as they walked past.

"Marcus Lee calling for Carter Chan," he said. It took less than a minute. "Hello, Carter, this is Marcus . . . I'm well, thank you. And you and the family? . . . Actually it's a family matter I'm calling about. I need a personal favour. My daughter Ava needs to speak with your son-in-law. It's about a matter that does not involve him directly, or you or any of your interests. She's a forensic accountant, and the issue concerns Frank's brother. I don't know much more than that . . . He is? Can you give me a number where she can reach him?" He took a small notepad and pen from his inside jacket pocket and wrote down two phone numbers. "And Carter, could you contact Frank yourself and ask him to speak with her? If she calls directly, well, you know . . . Thanks, Carter."

"Frank is in the U.K.," he said to Ava. "This is his Hong Kong cell number, and Carter says he normally has it on. The other is his hotel number. Carter will have someone call him and tell him to be cooperative. You should wait until that happens." He checked his watch. "It's about six in the morning there. Give it a few hours."

He walked her out to the taxi stand. They hugged, his intensity catching her off guard. "I am really happy you called me," he said. "I love you, you know, and I'm very proud of you. Just be careful, huh?"

"Thanks for making that call. I love you too."

"Try to join us in May, will you?"

"I'll try."

(8)

AVA PHONED UNCLE WHEN SHE GOT BACK TO THE Mandarin. She told him about her meeting with her father and about her possible access to Frank Seto. "I'm leaving tonight for Bangkok," she said. "My flight leaves here at six on Thai Air. I've decided to take your advice and not see Andrew Tam."

"I think that's best. I'll pick you up at the hotel at three thirty."

"That's perfect. See you then," Ava said.

She checked her watch. Not enough time to change and go for a run. She went online and searched Frank Seto. Ninety percent of the references were about his relationship to the Chan family, and the balance were reports about Admiralty Property deals. Seto didn't seem to exist outside of the Chans. There were photos of his wedding from multiple sources. He was as skinny as Jackson; the bride was twice his size. Some men like fat women, but all men love money. She wondered if Frank Seto had found the perfect combination.

The Mercedes was in front of the hotel entrance right on schedule. Sonny opened the back door for her and she slipped into the seat next to Uncle. He had a file folder resting on his lap. He waited until they were on the highway before he passed it to her.

"This came through this afternoon. Our friends worked quickly. Antonelli will be easy enough to contact. He is a creature of habit; he stays at the Water Hotel. I know you like the Mandarin, but it is miles from the Water and against traffic. They suggested the Grand Hyatt Erawan. You can walk to the other hotel from there."

She knew the Hyatt, or rather she knew Spasso, the hotel's nightclub — one of the classiest pick-up joints in Bangkok.

Ava opened the file. There was a photo of Antonelli clipped to a page of data. He was short, fat, and bald and had a black mole on his right cheek. "Not pretty, is he?" she said.

In the photo he was standing next to a gorgeous Thai girl. "It is Thailand. He does not have to be," Uncle said.

She scanned the documentation. "He's American, Atlanta-born and -raised, and evidently still married. He has three sons in their teens. The family lives in Georgia. He wires money to them every month and seems to visit three or four times a year."

"He and Seto have been in business together for close to ten years," Uncle said.

"And in trouble before."

"It seems to come around every two years."

"And they get away with it."

"So far, but then the people they scammed before were mainly Indian and Indonesian. Some of them tried to get their money back, but it is almost impossible to do it legally when so many jurisdictions are involved."

"How much money?"

He shook his head. "They started small and worked their way up. Andrew Tam is the biggest by far."

She closed the file. She would read the rest on the plane.

"You'll be met at the airport."

"I'd rather take a taxi," she said.

He knew she preferred working alone unless she needed a specific kind of help. "I made the arrangements," he said.

"Cancel them, please. I still have to figure out how I'm going to handle things, and I don't want the pressure of worrying about someone waiting around for me. Just give me a name and contact information. I'll call when I'm ready."

"They have the logistical material you requested."

"I'll call if I need it. Hopefully I won't."

(9)

IT WAS A TWO-AND-A-HALF-HOUR FLIGHT FROM HONG KONG to Bangkok. Ava slept for most of it. She had been to Thailand at least six times and it was by far her favourite place to crash. Whether she stayed in Bangkok, Phuket, Ko Sumoi, or Chang Mai, Thailand was always an oasis.

This was, however, her first time at the new airport, Suvarnabhumi. The old airport had always been the worst part of the trip, coming or going. Huge lineups at Immigration, slow baggage claim, waits of maybe half an hour for a taxi, and if it was raining you could be there for hours. Then a ride into the city that sapped whatever energy you had left.

So it was a bit of a shock for Ava when she breezed through the new complex. Like HKIA, Suvarnabhumi had been built and staffed to get you into the country as fast as possible. When she walked into the Arrivals hall, she almost ran straight into a sign that read UNCLE CHOW. She nodded at the young man holding it.

"*Sa wat dee kap*," he said. He wore blue jeans and a black T-shirt that showed off his muscular frame. He was about five foot nine, and his hair was so close-cropped that the stubble on his chin was almost as long. He looked tired, his eyes tinged with red and swollen underneath, making them appear smaller than those of most Thais. Still, he gave her a quick and easy smile. Despite his casual dress, Ava knew he was a cop.

"I'm Ava," she said. "But I told Uncle that I was going to take a cab."

"Arthon, and I never got that message." He reached for her bags.

"No, I'll handle it," she said.

"Do you want the ride?"

"Why not?"

He led her outside the terminal. His car was parked in a zone clearly marked NO STOPPING / NO PARKING. On the dash was an official-looking sign with a logo and the words DTAM-RUAT — she knew that meant "Police." Just behind the car, a man in uniform was putting a Denver boot on a silver Lexus. He and Arthon exchanged waves.

He seemed hesitant about which door to open. She went to the front passenger side and tossed her bag in the back. "What a difference from the old airport," she said.

"It wasn't so much fun when it opened. There were many birthing problems," he said. Ava noticed a slight British inflection in his speech.

"You went to school in the U.K.?" she asked.

"Four years at Liverpool U."

This is not your average cop, she thought. To go to university overseas meant at the very least that he came from money. He's probably Chinese Thai, she thought. None of Uncle's friends with whom she had worked didn't have Chinese roots.

"Are you by any chance Chinese?" Ava asked.

"I'm Chaozhou."

"Do you still speak Chinese?"

"No, we're assimilated. Fourth generation now."

Arthon pulled the car out of the airport almost directly onto an expressway. They sped into Bangkok, but then traffic slowed when they got into the city. It was always bad in the city. Seven-days-a-week bad. Twenty-four-hours-a-day bad. This despite an extensive infrastructure of expressways, sky trains, and subways.

Arthon was quiet, his eyes on the road. The only sound was a Neil Diamond CD playing on the car stereo. She was the first to speak. "What have they told you about me?" she asked.

"All I was told was to give you whatever help you needed," Arthon said. "I read the file on your man Antonelli. He's a bit of a pig."

"He sure looks like one."

"The file says he lives at the Water Hotel. You can walk there from the Hyatt Erawan. The Hyatt is on Rajdamri Road. When you come out the front door, turn right and walk about a kilometre past CentralWorld to Petchburi and go left there. The Water Hotel is only a couple of hundred metres from the intersection."

"I think I've been there," she said. "Is there a large market on the corner?"

"About four thousand booths selling every knockoff known to man. We raid it every month. Of course, we give them twenty-four hours' notice before we do."

"And another market where you can buy bootleg DVDs and all kinds of computer software?"

"That's the Pantip Plaza, further down Petchburi."

"Okay, I know the area. Now, does Antonelli have a routine?"

"According to our sources, on weekdays he comes down to the lobby lounge around 7:30 a.m.; has coffee and a biscuit, sometimes toast; works on his laptop; sometimes has a meeting. His driver and car show up around 8:30 a.m. He goes to Mahachai — that's northwest of Bangkok, about sixty kilometres. He has an office in a seafood plant there. He works there till three or four and then heads back to Bangkok to beat the traffic. He'll get back to the hotel by five, just in time for happy hour in Barry Bean's Bar, which is one level below the lobby. He'll drink margaritas until seven and then eat in the Italian restaurant upstairs."

"So I can count on meeting him in the lobby?"

"That's what we're told. He's there every morning."

"You said that he's a pig. What exactly did you mean?"

"So you haven't read the file?"

"Not yet."

He looked sideways at her as if trying to gauge her appetite for steaminess. "A short, fat, ugly American comes to Thailand and finds out that with enough money in his pocket he can be George fucking Clooney. That's Antonelli. He thinks he's George Clooney — George Clooney with some ugly twists. He started out with bar girls; some of those evenings ended badly because after fucking them he took to beating them. Charges were filed twice and then withdrawn when the Mama-Sans were paid enough. The fat man then switched over to boys for a while, and that was even worse. He hit one so hard he almost killed him. It must have cost a ton of money to get those charges dropped."

The Grand Hyatt came into view. Arthon put on his turn signal. "Read the report — it's all in there," he said.

A ramp from the street led up to the Hyatt entrance. Arthon had to get in line. Security was tight. All the cars were being searched and their underbellies examined using mirrors on long poles.

"We had some terrorist scares last week," Arthon said. "They mainly stick to the south, but the word was that they were targeting Bangkok. Five-star hotels are always popular."

As they approached the security checkpoint he rolled down his window and yelled something in Thai at a man in a black suit. They were waved through. He parked in front of the hotel and made a move to exit the car.

"No, that isn't necessary," Ava said. "I'm just going to check in and head for bed."

He shrugged. "Tomorrow?"

"Let's just play it by ear. I have to figure out how to handle Antonelli. I'll probably walk over to the Water Hotel in the morning as a starter. How about I phone you if I need you?"

"I live more than an hour away from this area," he said.

"I'll keep that in mind."

He passed her a business card. "My office number is on the front, my mobile is on the back. Mobile is best."

She took a quick glance at the card. He was a lieutenant. Ava was impressed.

(10)

HER ROOM HAD ALL THE ASIAN FIVE-STAR BELLS AND whistles: teak floors, Chinese black lacquer console and dresser, stylish modern beige leather chairs with expansive footrests, a desk with a leather captain's chair, and a king-size bed with a brilliant white duvet so plush it looked as if it could swallow her whole. The bathroom was all mirror and glass and marble, the walk-in shower large enough for six people. All the room lacked was the quiet dignity of the Mandarin.

Ava showered and climbed into bed in a T-shirt and panties. She extracted from her wallet the paper with Frank Seto's U.K. phone numbers and called his cellphone. It was late afternoon in London.

"Frank Seto," he said on the second ring.

"Ava Lee."

"I was told to expect a call from you."

"Thanks for taking it."

"My father-in-law and your father have been friends for many years."

"So I'm told. I'm calling about your brother."

"I have three brothers."

"Jackson."

"He is one of them."

Ava knew then that whatever cooperation she got would be grudging. "I'm trying to locate him," she said.

"Why?"

"I have a client who has a business relationship with Jackson. There are some outstanding issues that need to be resolved and he hasn't been able to reach him. He hired me to help."

"And what makes you think I would have any interest in Jackson's business dealings?"

"I haven't made that assumption."

"And what makes you think I would have any idea how to reach him?"

"He is your brother."

"In name only," he said sharply. "We have nothing in common. He's been a problem for our family for many years."

"Yet you introduced him to Andrew Tam?"

"Shit, that was completely incidental. Andrew and I were having lunch when Jackson came into the same restaurant. Believe me, I'm not in the habit of hooking up Jackson with my friends or business associates."

"He's burned some of them?"

"He burns everyone, sooner or later. He can't help himself."

"I'm really sorry to hear that," she said. "It must be difficult for someone in your position." He didn't respond, and she knew she had gone off mark. "Anyway, Frank, I would be grateful if you could help me find him."

"Weren't you listening? I have no idea where he is or how to get in touch with him."

"Would your brothers?"

"No, and neither would my mother, so your enquiries should end with me."

"I had a Seattle address for him, but the place is vacant," she said.

"The last address I had for him was in Boston, not Seattle."

"How many years ago was that?"

"At least five."

"I also had a Hong Kong address for him, in the Wanchai district. Again it came up empty."

"We were all born and raised in Wanchai, but the rest of us escaped. He keeps going back. He likes grunge, I guess. But I've only known him to stay in hotels there."

"Any particular one?"

"No. He's strictly a two- or three-star-hotel kind of guy, and you know how many of them there are in Wanchai."

"Do you have a phone number for him?"

"This is the number I have," he said, and gave her the same cellphone number she had been trying to reach for days.

"Well, I guess I've run into another dead end," she said.

"There isn't much I can do about that."

"Evidently not. Well, anyway, thanks for taking my call."

"Make sure you tell your father that I did," he said.

"Are you always this rude?" she shot back.

"My brother brings out the worst out in me," he said, and cut off the connection.

Ava turned her attention to the Antonelli file and

began to read it in detail. He was now her primary interest. She had hoped she would be able to work her way around him, to avoid alerting Seto that they were coming after him and the money. Now she would have to go after him directly.

The file was quite detailed. Given the short notice, Uncle's Thai friends had done a remarkable job of using his passport to track his movements. The first official sighting of Antonelli in Thailand had been six years before. He had landed at the old Bangkok airport, got a six-month tourist visa, and then gone to southern Thailand, to the city of Hat Yai, in Songkhla Province near the Malaysian border, and checked into the Novotel Hotel. The visa was renewed six months later in Malaysia. A note in the file said that Antonelli probably drove there from Hat Yai — about an hour away — crossed the border, and then re-entered Thailand. It was all legal. Over the next eighteen months he renewed the visa three more times, flying back to Atlanta each time. On each trip to the U.S. he didn't stay more than a week.

The Novotel had his passport on file for two years. It appeared that he had been involved in business with a fish processing plant in Hat Yai, but when the Muslim terrorists in southern Thailand targeted the city — the largest in the area, with a population of about a million people — and began blowing up hotels and shopping malls, Antonelli moved north to Bangkok. He stayed at an apartment hotel on Petchburi Road for the first three months and then moved three blocks to the Water Hotel. He had been there ever since.

After five months in Bangkok, his name showed up on two official documents. The first was a work visa through

Seafood Partners. The second was a document registering him as a minority shareholder in the company; its majority shareholder was, as required by law, a Thai. The Thai owned a separate shrimp and fish processing plant, Siam Union and Trading. Ava assumed that the Thai's shares in Seafood Partners were a sham, declared simply to enable Antonelli and Seto to do business in the country. Over the next two years, Seafood Partners shipped multiple containers of shrimp to the U.S. and became embroiled in dispute after dispute about short weights, mixed grades, and excess glaze.

The company also became an importer, buying whole grouper and snapper from India, the Philippines, and Indonesia, processing the fish, and exporting it to the U.S. The only problem was that it bought according to terms and paid well for only about six months. Then the company stopped paying invoices and started making complaints about every quality issue imaginable. Eventually the lawsuits were flying. Seafood Partners fought every claim, confident that time, cost, and the complications involved in cross-border legal action would discourage the exporters. They were right. One by one, the lawsuits disappeared.

But the Thai Department of Fisheries did not go away. All the quality issues related to the shrimp exports caught its attention. After a cursory examination, the department cancelled the licence of the processor, Siam Union and Trading, leaving Seafood Partners, even though it was the exporter of record, untouched.

Next Antonelli flew to Atlanta for what looked like six months. He seemed to have returned when they landed the Major Supermarkets business. Ava couldn't believe that Major Supermarkets had actually given them that business. Where was their due diligence?

She read on. Antonelli maintained a Thai bank account with a balance that rarely exceeded a hundred thousand baht, about three thousand dollars. His hotel bills were paid with a Visa credit card issued by a U.S. bank. His car and driver had been paid for by Siam Union, and when that company left the scene, by the same Visa card used to pay the hotel bill.

There was no mention of Seto in the file, not in reference to the formation of Seafood Partners or in the lawsuits. She now wished she had asked the Thai police to run a casual check on him. At the very least she would have found out how often he came and went, and where he stayed when he was in Bangkok.

One thing that caught her eye was Antonelli's cellphone number, which had a Thai area code. She made a mental note to ask Arthon the next day if he had any way to access calls made to and from that number.

At the back of the folder were copies of the assault complaints filed with the police against Antonelli. None of them had remained active for very long. Ava leafed through them and stopped before the end. It was like reading sadomasochistic pornography. She wondered what the wife in Atlanta would think about his habit of beating up defenceless women and boys. Then again, maybe she knew.

The bedside clock said it was almost midnight. Ava tried to convince herself that she was tired and slipped under the covers. Fifteen minutes later she got up, put on her linen slacks and a clean shirt, and went downstairs to Spasso, which was one level below the hotel lobby.

During the day and into the early evening, Spasso was the Hyatt's Italian restaurant. After 9 p.m. it began its transition to nightclub. Tables were cleared, the bandstand was set up, the bar was fully staffed, and security manned the door. It was one of the most popular high-end clubs in Bangkok, and Ava knew it would be going full blast until at least 2 a.m.

When she walked in, the place was jammed with the usual mix of young *farang* professionals — residents and tourists — and Thai girls on the make. This wasn't a place for backpackers. It also wasn't a place for bar girls from Soi Cowboy, Nana Plaza, or Patpong, the three most popular downmarket night spots in a city that advertised in-your-face sex clubs, night markets, lurid shows, and cheap by-the-hour hotel rooms for *farangs* who were squeamish about taking the bar girls back to their own hotel. The Thai girls at Spasso were amateurs, part-timers, teachers and students and the like, trying to make a few extra dollars and hoping, just hoping, to hit the jackpot — a *farang* boyfriend who would send monthly financial support when he got back home to North America or Europe, and who might give her the blue-eyed baby that had become a status symbol among these girls.

The foreigners in the club weren't all from the West. Ava saw some Japanese, a few Koreans, and a cluster of what looked like wealthy, hip Arabs. None of them were a natural attraction for the girls; they homed in on the Westerners. The Japanese and Koreans wouldn't get any action until the girls had explored all their Western options and found them wanting. The Arabs would have to wait as well, and they weren't being patient about it. One of them had ordered a large tub filled with ice and about forty shooters in test tubes. He held a shooter in each hand and waved at the girls to come and take what they wanted. He was getting the odd nibble but was having trouble getting the girls to stay.

Ava found a small table at the back of the club as far as possible from the stage, which had a set of drums and two guitars on it. To one side, propped on an easel, was a sign that read MANILA MAGIC. She groaned. Filipino cover bands were an Asian cliché. There wasn't a five-star hotel anywhere in Asia that didn't have one playing. The noise level in the room was already deafening; she could hardly imagine what the band would add to it.

She ordered a glass of white wine and sat back, content to dissect the action, trying to figure out who was going to get lucky. She could feel eyes turn in her direction. She ignored them, discouraging attention.

The band came onstage — three guys on the instruments and two female singers — and broke into a pretty horrid rendition of "Proud Mary." As she watched, a blonde crossed her line of sight. From the distance she looked about thirty. She wore black silk pants and a green silk blouse.

The blonde worked her way through the crowd towards Ava, and the closer she got the faster Ava's interest waned. She was closer to forty than thirty, and she had heavy thighs and a big ass.

"Hi, I'm Deborah," she said. "Can I join you?"

Ava hesitated and then realized she wouldn't mind the companionship. "Sure, but I've got to tell you right off the top that you're not my type."

The woman looked flustered. "I'm sorry, I thought you were —"

"I am, but you're still not my type. Sit down anyway."

"This is a tough place for girls like us," Deborah said, holding her own glass of white wine.

"Where are you from?"

"Washington, D.C. You?"

"Toronto."

"Here on business?"

"Yes, and you?"

"Same."

"Where are you staying?"

"Here."

"Me too. This is my first trip to Bangkok, and I can't fucking believe how great these hotels are, how great the service is."

"How long are you staying?"

"Another five days."

"Well, Spasso is not where you should be. These girls are focused on *farang* cock. They're all very entrepreneurial, and they know that's where the money is."

"So where should I go?"

"Over on Royal City Avenue — RCA — there are a couple of bars you might enjoy. One is called Nine Bar; the newest one is Zeta. I liked Zeta last time I was here. Most of the girls are young — you know, early twenties — and some of them are just figuring things out, still experimenting, enthusiastic and eager as hell but lacking technique. They would take to a woman like you."

"Are they bar girls?"

"No, not really. They don't expect to get paid. Mind you, if you slipped them twenty or thirty dollars they would appreciate it. But it isn't necessary."

"Would I have any problems if I went by myself? I

mean, at home I'm quite circumspect. Dyke bars aren't my thing."

"No problems."

"Is it close?"

"Ten minutes by taxi. But then in Bangkok everywhere is ten minutes by taxi, according to the drivers, unless of course there's traffic," Ava said and smiled.

"Thanks. I have to work early tomorrow morning, so I'm going to head out," Deborah said.

"The girls will still be there tomorrow night," Ava said.

"Can I buy you a drink before I go?"

Ava shook her head. "No, I think I'm finally getting tired enough to go to bed. And besides, if I have to listen to another Filipino cover band murder Shania Twain, I think I'll go crazy."

(11)

AVA POPPED A COUPLE OF MELATONIN TABLETS before going to bed and slept through until 6 a.m. It was too early to call Arthon, so she phoned her mother. She would be at home, since it was still too early for dinner and mah-jong. Ava told Jennie about having dim sum with her father. As always, Jennie overreacted. Nothing pleased her mother more than her daughters' contact with their father. She pretended that she was happy for their sakes, but Ava knew it was just as much about reaffirmation of her status as wife number two.

Ava boiled some water and made a cup of instant coffee. She turned on BBC World, but after five minutes she gave up and reached for her running gear and a rubber band to tie her hair back. She was always of two minds about running in Bangkok. There was the safety, security, and clean air of the hotel gym, while her other option was to run outside and fight the smog, the smothering humidity, and the carnival of people. But she knew that the Hyatt was only about a kilometre from Lumpini Park, and she loved running there. When she stayed at the Mandarin Hotel, sometimes she would even take a taxi there and back. Lumpini it would be.

At six thirty the sun was visible but not yet oppressive. The streets were already lined with traffic but the smog hadn't had time to build to its midday thickness. She turned left from the hotel and headed to the park, dodging dogs and sidewalk cracks and rises.

In a city with virtually no greenery and few public recreational facilities, the park was a magnet for all kinds of athletes. Thousands of people were there, nearly all of them Thais. She joined the throng circling the park on a three-kilometre track, which was thoughtfully marked every two hundred metres in white paint. It was a catholic group, with no apparently dominant gender or age. The only people who stood out in the running group were the businessmen, who held their shirts and jackets in their hands so as not to get them sweaty.

The track was on the outer perimeter of the park. In the interior it was just as busy, with pockets of activities that made the place so interesting to her. There were tai chi practitioners, several groups of them, silently performing their rituals. Old men and women waving swords and fans in precise slow-motion patterns. Bird-lovers with their cages. People playing badminton, tennis, and a Thai form of lawn bowling or bocce. All this took her mind off the running. In the gym she was usually good for five kilometres; at Lumpini she did three full laps before heading back to the hotel.

She showered, dressed in her business suit, put her slacks and shirts in a laundry bag and requested same-day service, and then went down to the lobby with the Antonelli file and her notebook. She reread the file as she sipped some ice water. How to approach him? How to get him to open the door to Seto? She had Antonelli's cellphone number. If Arthon could patch into his phone and trace calls to and from it, that could save her some time. She called Arthon and told him what she wanted.

"It won't be easy," he said. She could hear street noises in the background. "You can buy a SIM card anywhere here, and there are tons of pay-as-you-go phone-card companies. It isn't like the U.K. or North America, where you have only a handful of carriers. It could take me a while to find his carrier, and then I have to see if we've penetrated them already."

"Please try," she said.

"What are your plans for today?" he asked.

"I'm heading over to the Water Hotel in a few minutes. I'll see if I can engage Antonelli in conversation."

"Using what pretext?"

"Feminine charm," she said.

He didn't respond, and for a moment she thought he was mocking her. Then he said slowly, "When you read the data on Antonelli, did you take note of the section that mentioned what he likes to do now on weekends?"

"I don't remember it particularly, but I assume he hits the bars."

"More precisely, he goes to Nana Plaza."

"And how is that different from Soi Cowboy or Patpong?"

"On the first two floors it's the same old bar-girl shit, but when you get to the third floor — that's another thing altogether. When we were in the car, I didn't get a chance to finish my story about him. Antonelli has graduated from women and boys and gotten into *katoeys* — ladyboys. The third floor at Nana Plaza is all katoey. The violence seems to have toned down since he switched. Maybe he's found what he was looking for."

"Oh."

"Like I said, he's a pig."

It took longer than she had planned to walk to the hotel. Ava had to cross a couple of intersections, and the traffic lights were programmed to change about every five minutes. So you waited; if you tried to jaywalk you would meet inevitable death, because Bangkok traffic stopped for no one.

It was just after eight when she finally walked into the Water Hotel. It was supposed to be a five-star establishment, but she could tell from the lobby that it fell short. The furniture looked worn, and the staff uniforms showed frayed edges.

She spotted Antonelli right away. There was a lounge to the right of the lobby where they were serving coffee and tea. He sat on a sofa, his computer open on his lap, a cup and saucer and a plate of toast sitting on a small table beside him. He wore a *barong*, the loose Filipino shirt that is the fat man's friend.

His head was virtually bald, apart from a few straggly strands of hair stretched from ear to ear. He was even bigger than he had looked in the picture. His jowls swallowed up his neck, and the *barong* was stretched so tightly across his gut that she could see his white T-shirt between the buttons, which were threatening to pull apart. When he sat back on the sofa, his feet barely touched the ground. But as he typed, Ava noticed that his pudgy fingers moved quite deftly.

The lounge was busy, which gave her an excuse to sit almost directly across from him. She ordered coffee and waited for a chance to attract his attention. But Antonelli was focused on his computer, lifting his head only to look at his watch. When her coffee came, she took a sip and said, "My God, is the coffee here always this bad?"

He took a quick glance at her but said nothing. Then he closed his computer, slipped it into a wheeled briefcase, stood up, and rolled out of the lounge. She watched him exit through the giant glass doors at the entrance. An elderly Thai man stood at the curb. He took the briefcase and put it in the back of a black Toyota SUV. Antonelli, with some difficulty, climbed into the back seat. Then the car drove off.

Well, wasn't that successful, Ava thought.

She phoned Arthon and told him what had happened. She could almost hear him smile. "I'll give it another go in the bar tonight," she said. "In the meantime I'm going to go shopping, try to catch a nap, and wait for you to call me back with the cellphone information I need."

"I told you that won't be easy."

"One other thing," she said. "We asked you about Antonelli, but we are also trying to locate a guy named Jackson Seto. Antonelli is our primary source, but it would be useful to know what you can dig up on Seto and his movements both to and from and in and around Thailand. I've been assuming he's still in the U.S., which is why we didn't ask about him initially. That may have been a mistake on my part."

"Jackson is an English name. Does he have a Chinese

name — a proper name? Because if he does, his passport will likely be in that one."

"I don't know."

"We'll look under Jackson and see if anything comes up. Where will you be?"

"On this phone or at the Hyatt."

It was too early to shop at Pantip Plaza, the techie mall almost directly across the street from the Water Hotel, so Ava walked back to the Hyatt. She got *wai*'d at the door, *wai*'d in the lobby, and *wai*'d at the elevator. *Wai* is the most basic form of respectful greeting among Thais, palms held together in prayer fashion and accompanied by a bow. The closer the hands are to the face and the lower the bow, the greater the respect being shown. As a woman in business attire, Ava seemed to generate a considerable amount of deference — *from everyone except George Antonelli*, she thought.

When she got to her room, she stripped down to bra and panties and hung up her clothes. Then she napped for a couple of hours. When she woke, she saw no reason to dress up, so she slipped on her track pants and a T-shirt. There weren't any *wai*s this time when she left the hotel.

At Pantip she ordered all five seasons of *The Wire* — fifteen DVDs — for forty dollars, and then she bought three film-editing software programs for one of her friends. The software cost three dollars for each program; her friend would save a couple of thousand dollars. While she waited for the DVDs to be burned, she went across the street and had a bowl of tom yam kung.

After Chinese hot and sour soup, which ranked as her uncontested favourite, tom yam kung was at the head of the second-tier list. Like a good hot and sour seafood soup, it is made with a chicken stock base and a generous amount of shrimp. Cilantro, straw mushrooms, scallions, fish sauce, lime juice, lemongrass stalks, and kaffir lime leaves are added to produce a flavoursome broth, its surface dotted with a crimson oil slick from the final ingredient, red chili peppers. The soup had a clean, clear aroma, like pure oxygen with just a hint of citrus.

After lunch she went back to Pantip to collect her DVDs. As she was paying for them, Arthon called. He had had no luck with Antonelli's phone, but they had compiled some information on Seto.

"Can I drop it off at the Hyatt?" he asked.

"Fifteen minutes," she said.

"More like an hour," he countered.

"I'll meet you in the lobby."

(12)

AVA WAITED FOR ARTHON FOR CLOSE TO TWO HOURS. She drank several glasses of fruit juice and read all the newspapers in the lobby: the two English-language papers — *The Nation* and the *Bangkok Post* — a Chinese paper, the *International Herald Tribune*, and the Asian edition of the *Wall Street Journal*. The news was all the same: the economy was in tatters. This usually made for good business for Ava. Desperate times called for desperate measures.

Arthon came through the front door, leaving his car running right outside. He had clout, no doubt about that. He was better dressed than he had been the night before, in tight blue slacks and a form-fitting red Lacoste golf shirt, with sunglasses perched on his head. If she hadn't known him, she might have figured him for a dealer.

Arthon didn't apologize for being late — given the traffic, it is understood in Bangkok that meeting times are an estimate at best. "I can't stay," he said quickly as he handed her two sheets of paper.

"That's it?"

"Seto's comings and goings. That and his hotel stays

are all we have on record. He's been here three or four times a year for the past six years, at first going to Hat Yai and then to Bangkok. He stayed at the Novotel with Antonelli when he was in the south, and at the Water Hotel when Antonelli moved north."

"Seafood Partners?"

"If he was a partner, he was a discreet one."

"When was he last here?"

"About five months ago."

When he was organizing the Major Supermarkets scam, she thought.

"I have one more thing for you," he said, passing her what looked like a passport photo. "I didn't know if you had one."

She looked at her target. Thick black hair streaked with grey and combed straight back with no part. Long, thin face with a small mouth, looking even smaller under a moustache that drooped on the right. His eyes were almost hidden by hooded lids. He stared right into the camera with a look of defiance.

"Now I have to go," Arthon said. "It's payday and I still have some collections to make. What are your plans for tonight?"

"Barry Bean's for happy hour. Maybe I can get Antonelli to talk to me if he has a few drinks in him."

"Call me if you need me. I should be free by about seven."

Ava got to the bar by six, figuring that happy hour would be in full swing. Barry Bean's was packed but there was no sign of Antonelli. She mentioned his name to her waitress and was told that "Kuhn George" would be along eventually — he hardly ever missed happy hour. She chatted with a German bathtub manufacturer who was thinking about relocating his business to Thailand but was trying to do it without bringing his wife and kids. The problem was that his wife wasn't an idiot.

At seven the bar staff gathered in one spot, a bell was rung, and they yelled, "Happy hour is over, happy hour is over." Still no sign of Antonelli.

Ava called Arthon.

"Oh shit, I forgot this was Friday," he said.

"What do you mean?" she groaned.

"On Fridays he goes to an Italian restaurant near Soi Cowboy. It's owned by actual Italians and is one of the trendiest spots in town. After dinner he shows up at Nana Plaza for his weekly romp with a katoey."

"Does he bring her back to the hotel?" Ava asked.

"No. Security checks all the guests brought back to the rooms and holds their ID until they leave. Antonelli wouldn't want the staff to know he's into ladyboys. He uses a hotel attached to Nana that rents rooms by the hour."

That might even be better, she thought. "Arthon, it might be useful if we had proof of his little habit."

"What do you mean?"

"Pictures," she said.

He didn't hesitate. "It's worth a try, but I'd have to pay someone, and maybe more than one person."

"How much are we talking about?"

"Five thousand baht at least, maybe even ten."

Two to three hundred dollars, Ava calculated. "That

sounds reasonable, but only if we actually get the pictures."

"Let me see what I can arrange."

"Call me later?"

"Whether I'm successful or not?"

"I need to know either way."

Ava closed her phone and went upstairs to the Water Hotel's Italian restaurant that Antonelli frequented. It was deserted. The hostess was happy to have someone to talk to and was very forthcoming about Antonelli, or "Khun George" — a verbal sign of respect, the equivalent of "Mister" in English. It turned out that Khun George ate a lot, was very demanding, and tipped badly. Ava was finding it easy to work up a big dislike for him.

After dinner she walked back to the Hyatt. The streets were even more difficult to negotiate than earlier in the day because the night markets and restaurants — appearing as if by magic on the sidewalks — were in full swing. She shuddered when she saw the level of sanitation. There was no running water, and plates and cutlery were being washed and rewashed in the same tub. Ava had eaten street food once, and it had taken her two days to get over the food poisoning.

She thought about going down to Spasso, and then about going to Zeta. She ended up in her room watching HBO. At around eleven she fell asleep.

Although she felt like she had been asleep for a while, it was only eleven-thirty when the phone rang.

"Bingo," Arthon said. "And with one who hasn't completed the surgery — she has tits and a cock. Our guy burst into the room when they were in the middle of their fun, both of them completely naked and Antonelli staring right into the camera. He is one very ugly *farang* with no clothes on. His tits are almost bigger than hers."

"When can I get the photos?"

"Tomorrow morning. I'll drop them off first thing."

(13)

ARTHON CALLED AVA AT EIGHT THE NEXT MORNING to say he was on his way. She had already been up for two hours and had gone for another run in Lumpini Park. Saturday morning was even busier than Friday, and after two laps she walked the third so she could take in more of the sights and sounds. She hadn't known there were so many variations of tai chi.

When she got back to the hotel, she showered and changed and then camped out in the lobby to wait for Arthon. She was reading the *Bangkok Post*, which had an article in the lifestyle section about a katoey rock band. From the photo she couldn't have guessed that it wasn't just another gorgeous all-girl band.

Aside from his nasty violent streak, Ava had no issue with Antonelli's sexual tastes. She also knew Thailand well enough to be sure that the Thais wouldn't care either. Katoeys were a part of everyday life, an accepted third sex. Ava had been in public buildings that actually had three washrooms: for men, women, and katoeys.

A small cottage industry had developed around the katoey, and partly because of them the plastic surgeons in Thailand were some of the world's best. They had been lucky to catch Antonelli with one who hadn't yet completed the surgery. If she had, no one would have believed she was transgender. *Then again*, Ava thought, *maybe we weren't lucky. Maybe Antonelli likes them half and half.*

Arthon arrived on time, wearing the same clothes as the night before. He looked tired, and Ava guessed he hadn't slept. He slumped onto the couch next to her and groaned.

"Rough night of police work?"

"I wish," he said. "It's month-end and I had to make my collections. I'm responsible for the gambling joints, and some of them don't open till midnight."

"How much time do you spend on actual police work as opposed to running all these side businesses?"

"It's about fifty-fifty, although at month-end it gets crazy."

"And I didn't think gambling was legal in Thailand," she said.

"It isn't," he said as he passed her a large brown envelope.

There were five photos. She winced as she looked at them. Antonelli was even more repulsive with his clothes off than she had imagined, and even though she already knew about his partner, it was still a bit of a shock for Ava to actually see her.

"Wonderful," she said.

"Do you want me to be with you when you drop this on him? He might not be too pleased."

"It should be okay. What you can do for me is find out his room number at the Water Hotel. I'll slip a picture under his door and then arrange to meet him somewhere public where he can't go off on me."

"He's in room 3235."

"Thank you."

"I'm going home to get some sleep. If you need me, just call."

"Here, I owe you this," she said, giving him a roll of baht.

"Forget it. I talked to my boss and he said he'd kill me if I took anything from Uncle."

She shrugged. "Give it to a temple or something."

"I can't do that," he said. He stood up and stretched wearily. She noticed some of the female staff eyeing him. He noted them too and smiled and *wai*'d. *Wai*s all round ensued, and one of women, who looked about sixteen, drifted towards him. A few words were spoken in Thai and then she laughed, took his card, and walked with him to the front door. Ava could only admire how aggressive these women were.

She went back to her room and changed her clothes; the linen slacks and pink Brooks Brothers shirt would create the right impression. She went outside, intending to walk to the hotel, but the sky was clear and the sun was brutal. She didn't want to get there covered in sweat so she took a taxi, even though the ride would take longer than the walk.

She caught the elevator to the thirty-second floor. The corridor was empty save for the room maid's cart. Ava stood outside Antonelli's room for a moment, her ear pressed against the door. She heard faint noises coming from what sounded like a television. She had left one picture in the envelope, on which she had written: *Meet me in the lobby downstairs. I'm Chinese, a woman, and I'm wearing a pink shirt.*

Ava slid the envelope under the door, rang the doorbell, and then used the nearby exit to run down the stairs. She got out on the thirty-first floor and pushed the elevator button, hoping she'd get to the lobby before him, and hoping even more that he wouldn't get into the same elevator car as her. It took less than a minute to arrive.

She walked into a lobby that was nearly deserted and chose a chair in the middle of the lounge. Across from it was a couch, with a broad coffee table in between. She ordered an espresso and waited. A few minutes later the elevator doors opened and Antonelli charged into the lobby. He was wearing a Georgia Tech tank top, baggy shorts, and a pair of blue Crocs. His legs were pale and surprisingly smooth. He hadn't brushed his hair, and the few strands he had left were sticking up in the air. He looked around the lobby; she could see a mixture of anger, urgency, and desperation on his face.

Ava waved at Antonelli and smiled. He headed towards her, the envelope clasped tightly in his hand.

"You, you bitch! You Chinese bitch! You fucking Chinese bitch!" he yelled when he was still ten metres away.

"Have a seat," she said, pointing to the sofa.

He ploughed towards her, his face contorted, and for a second she thought he was going to try something physical with her. She shifted her feet, bracing herself for a countermove. He stopped when he was still a short distance away from her. "You fucking bitch," he spat.

Even from that distance she could smell breath that was foul from beer and God knows what else. His bared teeth were stained and coated with a yellow film. She guessed he hadn't taken the time to brush.

He brandished the envelope in front of him. "You fucking Chinese bitch."

"You're getting repetitive, and not accomplishing anything. I suggest you sit," she said.

"You were the one who was here yesterday. I remember you, you bitch. I thought there was something funny about you."

"Obviously there was."

He waved the envelope again. "What is this about? What the fuck is this about? I don't know you. There is no fucking reason for this."

The server hovered nearby with Ava's coffee, afraid to come any closer. "You can bring it over now," Ava said to her, and then turned to Antonelli. "Do you want something?" she asked. "I'm buying."

"Fuck off."

"Later. Right now we need to talk."

"What do you think you're going to do with this?"

"You are George Antonelli, correct? And you have a partner named Jackson Seto, and the two of you have been stealing money from a client of mine. That's why I'm here."

"I have no fucking idea what you're talking about."

"Yes, you do, but really it doesn't matter one way or another. I have very little interest in you or your hobbies. What I need to do is find Jackson Seto. I want you to help me."

"I still have no idea what the fuck you're talking about."

She pulled the file Arthon had given her from her purse and placed it on the table. "I know all about you.

I know how long you've been here, who you've worked with, how many scams you and Seto have pulled. I also know about the wife and kids back in Atlanta. Their address and phone numbers are in the file."

Antonelli sat down and reached for the folder. He opened it and started to read. She waited, watching his face for reaction. His jaw tightened, and he licked spittle from the side of his mouth.

"What the fuck are you trying to do?" he said finally.

"It's very simple — I need to locate Seto. You know where he is, or at the very least you know how I can contact him. You have two options. You tell me what I want to know, or I'm going to make a hundred copies of that photo — and the five others that I have — and send them to your wife, your kids, your Atlanta neighbours, your parents, any siblings you have, your in-laws, and anyone you're doing or have ever done business with. My experience is that Americans, particularly Americans in the South, and Baptists at that, are slightly less liberal about matters like this than Thais are."

He closed his eyes. *A good sign*, she thought. He was imagining the worst. He was calculating the odds. "How do I know —"

"You don't," she interrupted. "But I am in the habit of keeping my word. Just help me find Seto and the photos will be burned."

"Fuck."

"I'm sorry it had to be like this, I really am. If I could have found him any other way this wouldn't have been necessary," she said.

"What will you do if you locate him?"

"Get the money back."

"What if I direct you to him and you can't get the money back? What will happen to the photos?"

"Just get me to him. Do that and you're completely off the hook, I promise."

He chewed a fingernail while he thought. "You got a pen?"

She took out her notebook and Mont Blanc. "Go ahead."

"I'll give you his email address. He rarely checks it and normally doesn't answer directly. I email him and tell him I need to talk, and he phones me. But you can try. You never know."

"All right."

"Right now he doesn't have a North American or Asian phone number that works. You'll have to call 592-223-7878."

"What area code is that?"

"Guyana."

"He's in Guyana?"

"Obviously."

"Why Guyana?"

"We used to buy bangamary and sea trout there. We'd ship it to Atlanta, tray-pack, and sell it to the black and Hispanic markets. It was a good business for a while. Jackson has a house there, and a kind of wife, and he knows enough of the right people that he feels safe there. Whenever things get tight, he always fucks off to Guyana."

"You're sure I'll find him there?"

"He was there yesterday."

"Why does he feel safe there?"

Antonelli smiled. "Guyana is a shithole, filled with people who either helped make it a shithole or people who thrive in shitholes. Even for me — and I've seen a lot of shitholes — it's more shithole than I can stand. And Jackson has surrounded himself with the nastiest bunch of shitholes he could find. As long as he pays them, they'll do what he wants."

"What about the police?"

"Most of the people he's paying *are* the fucking police."

"Do you have an address for him?"

"Malvern Gardens. I don't know the number but there are only about ten houses in the subdivision. It's fucking grand by Georgetown standards, and he's the only Chinese there."

"Georgetown is the main city?"

"Yep. A shithole."

"I get the picture," she said.

"You think you do," he said. "Wait till you get there. However bad you think it is, it will be that much worse."

"If I get there and it turns out that Seto knows I'm coming —"

"I won't tell him."

"I mean it. If he has any clue —"

"Look, I don't want those photos in the wrong hands. You know that. You are a hundred percent fucking sure about that, aren't you? So I'm trusting that you will honour your word. That's all. Do I think you're going to be able to ambush Seto and get him to fork over the money? No, I don't. I don't think you've got a fucking chance in hell. So with that thought in my mind, why would I risk screwing you over? I'll not say a word to him. Nothing. You go and do whatever the hell you want. You just can't blame me if it doesn't work out."

"Give me your phone."

"Why?"

"Just do it, please."

He tossed his cellphone to her. She caught it and flipped it open. "I'm going to call the Guyana number you gave me," she said. "I'm also going to put the phone in speaker mode." She checked her watch. "It isn't too late there. Hopefully he'll answer. If he doesn't, then what? Voicemail?"

"Yeah."

"Either way, just tell him you're going away for a long weekend and that you'll be out of touch until the middle of next week. Is that plausible? Would you do that under normal circumstances?"

"I have."

She hit the numbers, put the phone in speaker mode, and placed it on the table between them. It rang four times before a muffled voice answered, "What the hell do you want, George?"

"Jack, just wanted you to know I'm heading down to Phuket for some R and R. I'm not taking my laptop, so you won't hear from me till next week."

"Whatever. Have fun." The phone went dead.

She was surprised to hear that Seto still had a trace of Chinese accent. His brother spoke flawless English and she had expected the same of him.

"Okay, you happy?" Antonelli said.

"One last thing," she said slowly. "Money. Do you have access to the money?"

"No," he said. "That's all Jackson."

"Has he sent you money?"

"He sends me money every month, but just enough to cover my overheads, my expenses."

"You don't profit-share?"

"We have a seventy-thirty split, and you don't have to guess who gets the seventy. Normally we wait till year-end, around Christmas, before we dip into it. By then we know how much we actually have. You know, there are a lot of fucking ups and downs in our business."

"So it seems."

"And you could be one big fucking down."

"Let's hope," she said, standing. She put the notebook and the envelope back in her purse. "Thanks for your help."

"What I hope is that I never hear your fucking voice again," he said.

"The feeling is mutual."

(14)

ANTONELLI'S DESCRIPTION OF GUYANA BEGAN TO FADE the moment Ava went online to find a flight to Georgetown. The most obvious carrier, she thought, would be a national airline. Every country has one. Except Guyana — theirs had gone bankrupt in 2001. And then there had been another, quasi-national one that went broke as well.

The predominant carrier that flew to Guyana was Caribbean Airlines, and all its inbound flights originated in Port of Spain, Trinidad. The best way to get to Port of Spain was through New York or Miami. She knew that Thai Air had a direct flight from Bangkok to New York. It left at midnight and got into New York in the late afternoon. There was a flight to Port of Spain at 7 p.m. She would have to overnight in Port of Spain and catch a morning flight to Guyana.

She checked the seating availability in business class; all the flights were wide open. She emailed her travel agent to arrange the flights and book her into the best hotels she could find.

Checkout time at the Hyatt was noon. She called

downstairs and negotiated a late checkout for half the normal daily rack rate.

Ava had missed two phone calls while working online, one from Arthon and the other from Uncle. She phoned Arthon. He was pleased, if a bit surprised, that things had gone so well. She told him to keep a set of the photos in case they were needed. He said he had been going to anyway, and she wondered what that implied for Antonelli.

When she called Uncle, he asked her how it had gone with Antonelli. That was his way of letting her know he was always in the loop, and that indeed it was his loop.

She described her meeting in detail.

"Where is this Guyana?" he asked.

"What, you don't have friends there?"

"I won't know that until I know where the place is."

"It's in South America. On the northeast coast, surrounded by Suriname, Brazil, and Venezuela, and a stone's throw from Trinidad. And I know that only because I looked it up."

"This is encouraging," he said, meaning that she had located Seto. Geography was lost on him.

"Do you want to say anything to Tam's uncle?"

"No, not until you have the money," Uncle said. "Ava, where you are at the Hyatt, the Erawan Shrine is right next to you."

"It is."

"Go there, will you? Light some incense, leave some flowers, make a donation, and pray for us all."

"I didn't know you were a Buddhist."

"I'm not, but neither is the shrine. It is actually Hindu, and it is devoted to the Thai version of Brahma

— I can never remember his Thai name — and his elephant, whose name I do remember, but only because of the hotel. It's Erawan."

"I'll go."

"Good. It's a lucky shrine. I've been there twice, and both times the results were more than I could have hoped for."

The shrine was on the corner of Ratchadamri Road, one of the busiest corners in one of the busiest cities in the world. The area was large, about twenty metres square, and was fenced, so Ava had to squeeze in through a gate. Even at one in the afternoon, with the sun at its peak, the shrine was filled almost to overflowing with concentric circles of worshippers standing around the statues of the six-armed Brahma and his elephant.

Ava bought a garland of flowers, an orange, and three incense sticks. She placed the flowers and the orange at Brahma's feet, where hundreds of gifts already lay. She lit the incense, held it in between her palms in the *wai* position, and began to pray, rocking gently back and forth, her lips moving, her words gentle.

It was mainly Thais who were praying. The tourists stood on the outskirts, taking photos of the worshippers and the troupe of Thai dancers who performed there every day, dancing to please Brahma so that he in turn would be kind to the supplicants.

Ava prayed for more than five minutes, naming all the members of her family and her closest friends. She asked for health and happiness, repeating the words like a mantra. When she had finished, she felt at peace. She put a hundred-baht note in the dancers' collection urn and returned to the hotel.

Since it was a Saturday the hotel had a couple of weddings booked. She couldn't move through the lobby without bumping into someone wearing a uniform or a gown. She figured that only people affiliated with the police or the military could afford to get married at the Hyatt. Their base pay was meagre, but the perks and kickbacks made up for it. Uncle said he had never met a retired police officer who wasn't a millionaire. She assumed that the same applied to the military.

If she had been feeling more sociable she could have quizzed Arthon about how it all worked. He had been pretty blasé about picking up contributions from casinos that weren't supposed to exist. She had heard that the street beggars worked like franchises, being assigned a specific spot to work their pathos and kicking back half their proceeds to the police. There wasn't a bar in the city that didn't contribute to the police pension fund. Every stolen car ended up being either sold or cannibalized by a special cop squad. The money moved upstream in an established and fully controlled pattern.

Still, she loved Thailand. Organized corruption was always superior to corruption with no rules. Uncle avoided doing business in places such as the Philippines and India and parts of China for that very reason.

Back in her room Ava switched on her computer and began a search on Guyana. This was new territory: a place in the world where Uncle's extensive network did not reach. Very quickly she deduced that George Antonelli hadn't been exaggerating all that much, if at all. The country — officially the Cooperative Republic of Guyana — had a population of about 800,000 people, most of them huddled along a sixty-kilometre strip of coastline, and a per capita income of less than $1,200. That ranked it 155th in the world, and she hadn't even heard of many of the countries that came in lower.

The country had one airport, with only a handful of airlines flying into it. It had no passenger railway. It did have more than eight thousand kilometres of road, but only about six hundred kilometres were actually paved, and on those it seemed that potholes were as prevalent as tarmac. A diesel-generated power grid provided about sixty percent of the country's actual needs; blackouts were a scheduled daily occurrence. She made a note to buy a flashlight. The water quality was also iffy. She made a note to buy water purification pills.

The population was predominantly East Indian, the descendants of indentured servants. But there was also a very large black population, the descendants of slaves. The two groups had a long history of antagonism. The rest were remnants of the original Carib Indians, a tiny group identified as European, and a small group of Chinese. The country had a remarkably high crime rate but also boasted one of the world's tallest wooden structures, an Anglican cathedral.

All in all, it didn't sound like a holiday destination.

Ava called downstairs to the concierge and told him she needed to buy a flashlight and some water purification pills. He told her she would find everything she needed at CentralWorld.

The shopping complex is on Ratchadamri Road almost kitty-corner from the Erawan Shrine, a five-minute walk from the hotel. CentralWorld is eight storeys high, and with more than half a million square metres of shopping space, it is the world's third-largest shopping complex. Ava found what she wanted, but only after a half-hour hunt.

Her shopping done, she settled in at the mall for her first full Thai meal since her arrival. She had just ordered when her cellphone rang. The caller was using a number blocker. She answered, since not many people had her number — only those she actually wanted to have it.

"Ava, this is Andrew Tam." He sounded nervous. "My uncle hasn't been able to get hold of your uncle. He is concerned about how things are proceeding."

"Andrew, please tell your uncle that when I'm on a case, I don't give my uncle daily updates. It's like I told you: when I have something to report, I'll call."

"It's getting quite tense around here. I'm under tremendous pressure from my family. I also have a meeting with my bank next week, and they're going to be asking some awkward questions. I'm not a very good liar."

"So this is about you, not your uncle."

"I am worried."

"Andrew, I have located the money. I know where it is. Now I have to go and get it. That sounds easier than it might turn out to be, which is why I haven't called you. Until I actually have the money, I have nothing and you have nothing."

"You've found it!" he said, grasping at the good news and ignoring the caveats.

"I have."

"Fantastic."

"Not until I get it."

"This is a great start, though, isn't it? I mean —"

"Andrew, stop," she said. "Look, you can tell the bank and your uncle whatever you want. If you need to buy some time, do it. I have found the money and I'm going after it. That doesn't mean anything until I get it. You do understand that? I'm not going to make any promises, I'm not going to give you timelines."

"Well, all I can say is that we believe in you."

She sighed. "What you mean is that you have no choice but to believe in me. That's a different thing. You don't know me, you don't know me at all. I don't like dealing in blind faith, which is why you haven't heard from me, and which is why, Andrew, you will not hear from me again until I can tell you either that I have the money or that I can't get the money. And when I say you won't hear from me again, it also means that under no circumstances are you to call me again. Are we agreed?"

"Yes," he said.

"Now, there is one thing I do need from you. I was going to relay it through Uncle but — since we're talking already — I need your bank information. On the chance that I can get to the money, the best way to move it will be a wire transfer. So email me all the particulars from your bank. I'll need the bank name and address, the account name and address, and the bank's IBN number and its SWIFT."

"I'll send it today."

"Tomorrow will be fine."

"Do you mind if I ask where the money actually is?"

"I'll call you when I have some hard information. Until then, try to relax." She closed the phone.

There were times when Ava disliked the way she had to act. Tam was a nice enough guy; he was just looking for any comforting news he could get. She had learned the hard way that clients who were desperate — and hers were nearly always desperate — heard what they wanted to hear. A glimmer of hope would become a done deal. And if by chance she didn't deliver, all of a sudden she was the villain, the heartbreaker, the liar.

When Ava got back to the hotel, she packed her bag and got ready to go to the airport. The travel agent had already booked and confirmed the flights by email. She had also put her into the Hilton Hotel in Port of Spain and the Phoenix in Georgetown, and had arranged for hotel limos to meet her when she landed.

Ava smiled when she read the agent's comment about the Phoenix: It has three stars, but every other hotel is one or two. What kind of place is this? But she didn't smile when she read what followed: Every travel guide says to exercise extreme caution in Georgetown. Going out alone, even during the day, is not recommended.

(15)

AVA LANDED IN PORT OF SPAIN RIGHT ON SCHEDULE at 7 p.m. It was already dark. Trinidad is in the southernmost reaches of the Caribbean, and fifty-two weeks a year, the sun falls like a stone behind the western mountain range at 6 p.m. From the air and all lit up, the city looked bigger than she had imagined. She guessed it was also a hell of a lot prettier from where she sat than it was on the ground.

She coasted through Immigration, Customs, and baggage claim, stepping out into air that was Thailand humid but filled with unfamiliar odours. Rotting leaves. Dead birds. Dog shit. Gas fumes. She couldn't put a fix on it, but she nearly gagged. When Ava walked through the Arrivals gate, she saw a large black man standing at the curb in front of a Lincoln Continental. He was holding a sign with her name on it. She signalled to him, he opened the back door, and she climbed in.

"That's some smell," she said.

"Mainly dead vegetation," he said.

She didn't need more detail. "How far to the hotel?"

"About half an hour."

For once she hadn't overslept on the plane. She had caught about eight hours en route to New York and that had been it. She was sleepy, which was good, because she wanted to be fresh the next day.

"Are you here on vacation or business?" he asked.

"Business."

"Staying long?"

"Just overnight. Tomorrow I head for Guyana. My business is there."

"Guyana. That is . . . one . . . crazy . . . place," he said.

"Have you been?"

"Don't have to go to know. We hear the stories — there are always stories. Nothing works. Can't trust no one. Can't go out at night with even a ten-dollar watch on your wrist. We get some of them here, Guyanese. They come with suitcases filled with shrimp and go from hotel to hotel and restaurant to restaurant trying to sell it. As if the chef at the Hilton is going to buy shrimp from some guy selling it out of a suitcase."

"Someone must be buying it or they wouldn't keep coming," she said.

He looked at her in his rear-view mirror to see if she was making fun of him. Ava wasn't laughing.

"The only good thing about Guyana is that it makes the rest of us in the Caribbean look good. No matter what kind of stunts our politicians pull or how many drug dealers we have or how bad our crime is, it's always worse in Guyana."

She knew that Port of Spain sat on the Caribbean Sea, but as they began to work their way along the highway into the city she could see no sign of it. She rolled down her window and listened. Nothing. "Where's the sea?" she asked.

The driver pointed left to a row of what looked like warehouses and abandoned factories. "It's there, behind those buildings."

On her right house lights glimmered weakly above a large brick wall that flanked the highway for at least two kilometres. "That's the wall of shame," the driver said, noting her interest.

"It isn't a sound barrier?"

"More like a sight barrier. That's Beetham Estate behind the wall, our biggest slum. You'll find squatters, shacks, people who live on scraps. Not a place to wander into. The government built the wall just before the Summit of the Americas was held here so the foreign dignitaries wouldn't have to look at Beetham on the way into the city. Building the wall was cheaper and quicker than doing anything about the slum. Hide it, pretend it isn't there. Mind you, not many taxi drivers are complaining. It used to be that if your car broke down on this part of the road the animals from Beetham would be on you in two minutes. Now with the wall it takes them a bit longer."

As they drove into the city, office towers, hotels, and small shopping complexes emerged from the night. Most of them were to the right of the highway, away from the sea. *What kind of place is this?* Ava thought. In Hong Kong, any kind of waterfront view, no matter how slight, drove up the real estate prices. Here it was as if they had decided they needed to distance themselves from the Caribbean.

The driver left the highway, turned right, and cut uphill through a series of narrow streets lined with houses and shops only a sidewalk away. It was a bumpy ride. Many of the streets were cobblestoned, and the driver had to come almost to a complete halt to navigate deep V-shaped trenches cut across the roadway.

At the top of the hill the road opened onto a broad expanse and the driver began to circle what was obviously a park. There was only a half-moon and not all the street lights were working, but as they drove along Ava was taken aback by the scale and variety of architecture they passed. "This is the Savannah, the Queen's Park Savannah," he said, meaning the park. "Used to play cricket here every Sunday, but now I just come for Carnival."

"What about these buildings?" Ava asked.

"That's All Saints' Church, and over there is the American embassy."

"No, I mean those," Ava said, pointing to a row of mansions that looked as if they belonged in a Victorian-era London neighbourhood.

"The Magnificent Seven, we call them. They were built over a hundred years ago by European businessmen who were all trying to outdo each other. That one there is now the president's house, and the rest I really don't know," the driver said.

They continued around the circle to get to the Hilton, which was adjacent to the Savannah and close to the Royal Botanic Gardens. The hotel's curious hillside structure was reflected in the interior. The lobby at the front of the hotel was on the ground floor, and Ava's room at the rear, which still had a view of the lights encircling the Savannah, was two floors below. Aside from the architectural eccentricity, when she opened the door to her room she found herself in a classic Hilton hotel room: clean, middle-class, dependable.

She ordered a Carib beer and a club sandwich from room service and then called Hong Kong. It was just past ten in the morning there, and Uncle, as usual, was at breakfast. "I'm in Trinidad. I leave for Guyana tomorrow."

"We don't have anyone there," he said.

"I didn't think we would."

"The closest we have someone is in Venezuela."

"I'll handle it myself."

"Ava, if you think you need help I'll call Venezuela."

"I don't need help," she said. "I'm staying at the Phoenix Hotel in Georgetown. I don't know if my cellphone is going to work there, so if you can't reach me that way, call the hotel. I don't know how long this is going to take, so don't get worried if you don't hear from me for a few days."

"You are sure he is there?"

"As sure as I can be."

"My friend saw me last night. We were at massage and I couldn't avoid him. He said you talked to Tam."

"He caught me by surprise."

"Well, nothing we can do but finish this project."

"How many haven't I finished?"

"A few . . . but then they were usually dead by the time we got to them."

On a previous case the client had assigned more than one group the job of recovering their money. Twice she had been in meetings with targets, easing them towards repayment, when the competitors intruded, blood in their eyes. She convinced one set to leave by promising to share part of the commission with them. The other had to be neutralized more forcefully.

"Do they have anyone else working this job?"

"No, no, no, it is just us. I am very careful about that now."

"All right, then I'm off to bed. I have an early start tomorrow."

Ava showered and then shampooed the smell of airplane out of her hair. She pulled on clean panties and a T-shirt and then sat on the bed to watch the local news. The lead story was about how Trinidad had become a major part of the South American drug pipeline to the U.S., which was reported with a mixture of shock and pride. The opposition leader, who was black, came on the screen to charge four cabinet ministers, who were all East Indian, with corruption. Lifelong politicians who had never made more than thirty thousand dollars a year, they had each somehow amassed a personal net worth in excess of ten million dollars. One of the cabinet ministers was interviewed in front of what appeared to be a local school. He looked directly into the camera and claimed to have gotten lucky in the stock market. *It's amazing*, Ava thought, *just how many politicians get lucky in the stock market.*

She turned off the television and crawled into bed, her mind randomly flitting ahead to Guyana. She had no idea what to expect when she got there, in terms of either the country or Seto. She knew well enough from trips to hinterlands in India, China, and the Philippines that her life's usual amenities might be in short supply, but it would be another thing entirely to experience deprivation of clean water and food she could actually identify. Guyana, from what she'd read, certainly held that potential. She could only hope she was wrong.

Then there was Seto. All he was right now was a passport picture, a fragment of a voice, and an address in a neighbourhood she didn't know in a city and country in which she had no connections. She could land tomorrow and find him gone. Maybe Antonelli had figured that keeping $2.5 million was worth a little — no, a lot of — humiliation. Or maybe when she got there she wouldn't be able to find a way to get to Seto. *But when has that ever happened?* she thought. *Not often. Actually, never.*

There was always a way; it just depended on what level of risk was warranted by the money at the other end. The risk and the reward weren't always in balance, and Ava liked to think she was pragmatic enough to recognize when that was the case and to make the appropriate decision. Five million dollars, though . . . her commission share of $750,000 was an awful lot of money, an awful lot of reward.

(16)

AVA'S WAKEUP CALL CAME AT SIX. SHE BRUSHED HER hair and teeth and put on her Adidas training pants, a clean bra, and a T-shirt. She pulled a copy of the *Trinidad Tribune* from underneath her door and left it on a table near the window. There was a kettle in the room; she turned it on and then sat down to read the paper while the water boiled.

There was a rehash of the television story from the night before, with pictures of all of the accused cabinet ministers. They looked like half a cricket team gone to fat. Ava skipped that story and read about the government's concern over the rising crime rate and their search for a new police chief. A Canadian from Calgary was one of the candidates. Ava thought that had to be a bad idea. How could a Canadian understand the social dynamics and financial imperatives of a place such as Trinidad?

She poured hot water into a mug and made herself some instant. She had drunk one coffee and was halfway through the second when the room phone rang to tell her the car had arrived. She took the elevator to the lobby and was greeted by a different driver, who looked East Indian. As he drove away from the hotel and onto the road that circled the Savannah, she asked him what he thought about the corruption charges against the cabinet ministers.

"The blacks," he said, as if that explained everything.

She asked about the drug trade.

"As long as the drugs don't stay here, who cares? It could be good for the economy."

Ava turned her attention to the passing city. The Magnificent Seven looked almost decrepit in the daylight, the bright morning sun exposing faded paint, chipped bricks, and raised roof shingles. The Savannah had lost some of its allure as well. She noticed that there was less actual grass than patches of bare ground pocked with clumps of crabgrass and weeds. Ava thought about something Uncle had said about older women in the morning light without makeup, then pushed it aside.

They rode quietly along the main highway. The factories and warehouses looked less oppressive now, and Beetham Estate seemed even more shabby. When they got to the intersection that took them to the airport, the car stopped for a red light. As it sat idling, a scrawny woman, her naked body streaked with mud and dirt, her hair matted, her breasts lying flat against her torso, jumped out and began pounding her fists on the hood. Her face pressed against the glass of Ava's window as she screamed obscenities. Ava recoiled.

"No worries," the driver said. "She's here every day. Just a mad woman."

"She needs help," she said, still alarmed.

"No money, no help," he said. "This is Trinidad. Go

downtown at night, there are a lot more people like her. Maybe not so crazy, but crazy enough."

"Shit," she said.

"So where are you going?" he asked as the car pulled away from the intersection, leaving the screaming woman behind.

"Guyana."

"Why?"

"Business."

"The only business in Guyana is monkey business."

"That's not my business."

"Just don't drink the Kool-Aid," he said, and laughed.

"What?"

"Kool-Aid — don't drink it. You don't remember Jim Jones?"

"Vaguely."

"An American preacher. He brought his entire church to Guyana and set up a commune. It didn't work out well."

"How so?"

"They had troubles. The entire group drank Kool-Aid laced with poison. They all died. There were nine hundred of them, as I remember, maybe more. The joke around here is that if you had to choose between Kool-Aid and living in Guyana, Kool-Aid would win out most times."

(17)

AVA WALKED OUT OF CHEDDI JAGAN AIRPORT INTO an atmosphere that even in the morning was fetid. She looked for a sign with her name on it. She noticed the person holding it before she actually saw the sign: a lone white man with blond hair, towering above a sea of black and brown faces.

She waved at him and he burst through the waiting group. He was wearing a red polo shirt with PHOENIX sewn over the heart, brown cargo shorts, and white socks pulled up to his knees. He walked awkwardly, with his knees almost locked, and his upper body was also stiff, biceps pushing out his sleeves, broad chest, thick neck. *Weightlifter*, she thought. *Steroids.*

"Welcome to Guyana," he said, reaching for her bags. He had a big, loopy smile on his face, and bright blue eyes that were nothing but friendly.

He led her through the crowd with his elbows stuck out to help clear her path. He threw the bags into the rear seat of a black Jeep with a gold phoenix stencilled on all four doors. Ava guessed she was expected to ride up front.

The car was running and the air conditioning was going full throttle. She shivered and sneezed. Some of the worst colds she'd had in her life had been the result of going from heat and humidity into freezers posing as retail stores. When she asked him to turn the air conditioning down, he looked at her as if she were demented but did what she asked anyway.

"I'm Jeff," he said.

"Hi, Jeff. How far is it to the hotel?"

"About forty-five kilometres," he said.

"Half an hour?"

"You haven't been here before, have you?" he said. She detected a New England accent.

"No."

"Didn't think so. We'll be an hour, maybe longer."

"That much traffic?"

He laughed. "Yeah, sort of."

They hadn't travelled more than a kilometre when they ran into a line of cars slowly bobbing and weaving from one side of the two-lane road to the other. Jeff joined the conga line. "They're trying to avoid the potholes," he said. "There are a few stretches of road between here and Georgetown that aren't riddled with them, but not many. So we're going to go as fast as the slowest car ahead of us. That's the way it is. Sorry."

"I'm glad you have a Jeep."

"There are some potholes even the Jeep couldn't get out of, especially in town."

Some of the holes cut across both lanes, and that caused extra delays as the incoming and outgoing traffic sorted out who had the right of way. Ava tried not to feel nauseated, focusing her attention on the scenery. It was mainly country, low-lying land dotted here and there with what looked like rice paddies. In the distance was the familiar sight of a sugarcane field. Sugar and rice — the agricultural staples of the poorest countries in the world.

The monotony of the landscape was punctuated every couple of kilometres by a village or, more often, a group of ten to twelve shacks. They were built almost right up against the edge of the road. There wasn't a brick in any of them. Most of them had some kind of wooden frame, the walls an interlaced mixture of planks of different woods, tarpaper, and corrugated tin. The windows were covered with strips of cloth.

Some residents stood leaning against the houses, watching the cars slalom past. Others sat outside on stools, goats tied to pegs bumping against them, children and chickens running around freely. Ava jumped a few times when she saw a child come too close to the road, but Jeff didn't flinch or slow down his twenty- to thirty-kilometre-an-hour crawl.

The area reminded Ava of parts of the rural Philippines where no one worked and each day was spent watching life drive by. She wondered how many of the people living in these shacks had travelled more than ten kilometres from where they lived.

The road began to improve a little after an hour, and Ava guessed they were getting close to Georgetown. Jeff had been quiet and intense during the drive, and Ava hadn't wanted to disturb his concentration. Now she said, "I don't mean to be nosy, but I thought I detected a bit of a New England accent."

He didn't take his eyes from the road. "That's smart of you."

"I went to school in Massachusetts for two years."

"I'm from Gloucester."

"How did someone from Gloucester find their way down here?"

Now he looked towards her, hesitated, then said, "I'm — I was — a fisherman. I came down here on a shrimper out of Florida. We were buying our catch at sea, paying cash to Guyanese boats. What the skipper didn't tell us was that those boats were financed by local gangsters, and they weren't too thrilled about our little black market, about us stealing from them. We were in the middle of a deal when two speedboats came out of nowhere and put us out of business."

"How did they do that?"

He glanced at her again. "They shot the captain and the other two men on the Guyanese boat and threw their bodies into the sea. They took our boat, scuttled it, and set us adrift in a lifeboat."

"Shit."

"Big-time shit. We somehow found our way to Georgetown. The skipper went to the cops and they acted as if what had happened was the most natural thing in the world. They told us we were fucking lucky to have made it to shore and maybe we ought to let it go at that. The skipper and the rest of the crew flew back to Miami, but I decided to stay here a while. That was five years ago. It ain't Miami but the work is steady, the beer is cheap, and the women are slutty."

"Those sound like great reasons to stay."

Jeff shrugged. "I didn't mean to sound like an asshole. It's just the way it is here."

"I didn't take any offence," Ava said. She noticed they were driving through larger concentrations of housing.

"Georgetown," he said.

The driving began to occupy him again as the potholes expanded in number and size. As they manoeuvred their way into the city, Ava was immediately taken by the fact that nearly every building was made of wood. A lot of the houses were ramshackle affairs two or three storeys high, with three or four apparently boxed together and some on stilts. Most of the wood was grey, bleached, weather-beaten, not unlike houses she'd seen on Cape Cod, except the houses on Cape Cod had glass windows, not wooden shutters or strips of cloth. In New England there had been flashes of colour as well, something Georgetown was almost devoid of, aside from a wall that had been painted in red with GOD IS IN CHARGE. ALL IS WELL.

The storefronts were a bit more colourful, their wooden exteriors decorated with hand-painted signs advertising a variety of wares and services. Their windows and doors were protected by thick metal screens, and inside it looked as if the service counters and cash registers were separated from customers by a metal fence that extended from countertop to ceiling. People were passing money through one slot in the screen and getting goods back through another.

"If they didn't do that," Jeff said, motioning to a string of storefronts, "they would be getting robbed every other day."

They were driving through the middle of the city now. Large white edifices began to appear, and they passed a building that housed various courts of law. From afar it looked elegant, but as they came closer Ava saw that paint was peeling off its exterior and some of the window shutters were broken and hanging at odd angles. There was a patch of dry, cracked earth between the sidewalk and the building, with a statue of Queen Victoria sitting on it. Both of the hands had been cut off and the torso was covered in graffiti. Ava looked away. There was something particularly depressing about public institutions — symbols of a nation — that were allowed to fall into such disrepair. It said as much about the people they represented as the structures themselves.

Ava next saw a wooden church spire soaring above the city's skyline.

"St. George's Anglican," said Jeff. "It's forty metres high at the peak of the spire, the tallest wooden cathedral in the world."

"And what is that?" she asked, her attention now caught by a clock tower in the other direction.

"Stabroek Market, the bizarre bazaar. You name it, you can buy it there — everything from pineapple to shoes to furniture, jewellery, and even a whole pig."

"The clock tower, what is it made of?"

"Corrugated iron. The whole building is made of iron, some corrugated, some cast. What would you expect when it was designed by an engineer and built by an iron company?"

"Interesting," Ava said.

"Interest wears off soon enough."

They reached the end of High Street. Jeff turned right and then did a quick left. "The hotel is straight ahead," he said.

The Phoenix Hotel was framed on either side by nothing but sky. It was a big white wooden box, six storeys high and four times as wide. A line of palm trees dotted the front of the property and marched around the outer edge of the circular driveway. A water fountain stood in the middle of the driveway: six dolphins spewing a cloudy-looking liquid.

Jeff pulled into the driveway and stopped in front of the hotel. The front doors had been thrown open and Ava could see directly into the cavernous lobby, which had a second set of open doors at the far end that offered an impressive view of the Atlantic Ocean.

She climbed out of the car and faced the hotel. To the left she could see a muddy brown river moving sluggishly towards the ocean.

"That's the mouth of the Demerara," Jeff said.

"Like the rum?"

"One and the same. The distillery is upriver."

She looked again at the colour of the river and made a note to avoid the rum. Near the river and slightly back towards town, she saw some familiar flags flying. "And over there?" she asked, pointing.

"Foreign embassies."

The American embassy was closest to the hotel and the Canadian was next in line.

Jeff carried her bags into the lobby. There was a breeze flowing from the ocean side, and huge fans churned overhead. Ava still felt hot, and she could only imagine how sticky it would get if the breeze subsided.

To her left was a café and a registration desk that was nine metres long and had one clerk standing behind it. To her right was a large sitting area filled with wicker furniture, the cushions rumpled and faded. Farther down was a bar with bamboo chairs and tables that were in better, if not pristine, condition.

As they crossed the lobby towards Registration, a large cockroach scurried across the hardwood floor almost directly in front of her. It startled her and she jumped. "Did you see that?" she said.

"No, I didn't see anything," Jeff said.

"It was a cockroach."

"We don't have cockroaches," he said.

"It had to be three inches long, with a gold body, black spots, and a black head."

"Son of a gun, that does sound like a cockroach," he said as he dropped her bags at the front desk.

She tipped him twenty dollars. He looked uncertainly at the bill in his hand. "This is way more than the normal rate around here."

"I insist. I appreciated the way you drove."

"Thanks."

"Jeff, tell me, do you ever make yourself and the Jeep available to guests for non-airport runs?"

"What do you have in mind?"

"Nothing too far out of the way, I would imagine. I may need a ride to a place called Malvern Gardens. Heard of it?"

"Yeah, I know it."

"And I may need you to wait with me a while when I'm there."

He shrugged. "I don't think that's much of a problem. The usual rate is ten dollars an hour."

"For you and the Jeep?"

"Yeah, but you have to pay for any gas I use, and I have to tell you, gas is expensive."

"What are we talking about?"

"Five dollars a gallon."

"No problem."

"Do you have any idea when you might need me? I've

got another airport run to make today and I've actually got to get going."

"There's no rush. How about I let the doorman know after I figure things out? Check in with him when you get back."

"That'll work."

Ava turned to the registration clerk and gave her name. For almost two hundred dollars a night — almost the same as the Grand Hyatt in Bangkok — she got an ocean view, a single bed, and a television, but no cable. There was Internet access in the business centre on the ground floor, but none in the room. If she wanted to make a long-distance call she would have to let the switchboard know so they could activate the service for her. There was no mini-bar or fridge in her room, and if she wanted ice she had to call down to the bar. She did get coffee and toast in the morning. When she asked about mobile phone service, she was told that if she had Bluetooth she could use her phone in Georgetown.

Ava rode the elevator to the fourth floor, unhappy with the hotel's concept of "three star." Anywhere in Asia, every service she'd asked about at the registration desk would have been provided. When she opened the door to her room, the Phoenix's rating tumbled to one star.

There were two single beds covered in pink chenille spreads, and the floor was covered with white tile. It reminded Ava of a hospital. The dresser and bedside table were tattooed with cigarette burns, and the bedside lampshade was slightly frayed, as was the shade on the single overhead light.

Ava went into the bathroom. No bathrobe, no slippers. Two thin towels and one facecloth. There was one bar of soap, wrapped in paper, and no shampoo. She checked the shower. No mould. She flushed the toilet. It worked.

Back in the room she gazed resignedly at the room's only feature that she liked: a rattan chair by the window. She sat in it and looked out at the Atlantic Ocean. The water was choppy, crashing against a seawall that extended over to the Demerara on the left and as far as she could see on the right.

It could be worse, she thought. At least it was clean, and she wasn't there for the hotel anyway. Somewhere out there Jackson Seto was waiting to be found.

(18)

SINCE HER MEETING WITH ANTONELLI, AVA HAD BEEN debating how to approach Seto. She had thought of phoning him first, maybe pretending to be a seafood buyer and setting up a meeting on that basis. There were a couple of problems with that idea. First, she didn't really know enough about the business to survive any rigorous questioning. And second, why would anyone come to Guyana to buy seafood without making preliminary arrangements?

No, her first contact had to be incidental. It hadn't worked with Antonelli, but he was into ladyboys. Not many heterosexual men could resist showing interest in Ava, so she had to find a way to get next to Seto and take it from there.

She walked down to the lobby and looked for the concierge or the doorman, neither of whom was on duty. She asked the front desk clerk where they were. "They're on break. Be back around one," the woman said.

"I need to buy a few things. Is there a mall around here?"

"The best place would be the Stabroek Market. It's just down the street to the right. You can't miss it — look for the tall clock tower."

"Yes, I've seen it."

"I wouldn't go dressed like that," the woman said.

Ava was wearing her running shoes and a T-shirt and track pants. "Why not?"

"I mean the jewellery. You should leave it here."

Ava had on her gold crucifix, her Cartier watch, and a green jade bracelet. "It's the middle of the day," she said.

"Don't matter. That watch — it's real?"

"Yes."

"I thought so. It's a magnet. You'll get all kinds of unwanted attention, and if they go for the watch they'll take the necklace and bracelet too."

Ava took them off and put them in a pocket that zipped closed. "Better?"

"Just be careful."

Outside the front entrance the heat was brutal and oppressive, and Ava thought about using the hotel Jeep, but she could see the clock tower and figured that Stabroek Market wasn't much more than a ten-minute walk. She was fine until she had gone about a hundred metres and the ocean breeze had dissipated. The sky was cloudless and the sun beat directly down, radiating off the tarmac; the heat seemed to penetrate through the soles of her shoes. She began to sweat, her eyes burning, beads dripping from the end of her nose, her panties absorbing what they could and then sending the excess down her legs. It was hotter than Bangkok, more humid than a Hong Kong summer. And then there was the smell. She held her breath as she walked past the decaying garbage and dog shit on the sidewalk.

When Ava was about twenty paces from her destination, she heard a buzz in the air, a mixed symphony of voices haggling and car horns blaring. It wasn't until she stepped onto Water Street that she had a full view of Stabroek Market. The building encompassed a large area of about sixty to eighty thousand square metres; it was, as advertised, completely encased, including the roof, in red iron. To Ava it looked less like a shopping centre than a steel foundry.

The noises she'd heard came from outside the building, where people were hawking goods from tables and stands shaded with tarps to fend off the sun. It was crowded, the stands were jammed close together, and people were milling about as they tried to avoid the bicycles and buses that circled the perimeter. Ava pushed her way past mounds of pineapples, plantain, bananas, coconut, okra, sweet potatoes, long beans, and spinach, sides of pigs and goats, and chickens clucking in cages. They were selling clothing outside as well, but not the knockoffs found in most Asian markets. These looked like second-hand garments that had been collected by a charity in the developed world and sold by the pound to some trader. Apparently there was a market for old Toronto Maple Leafs jerseys.

Ava went inside the market building to search for food and air conditioning. There were pockets of cold air here and there, and she lingered while she decided what to eat. She toured the stalls, trying to choose between chicken curry, duck curry, lamb and goat curry, rice and beans, and roti. She was about to give a curry a try when saw a vegetarian stand. She ordered three fried lentil patties with hot sauce and washed them down with mauby, a local soft drink made from tree bark.

After she finished eating, Ava wandered through the

market. It was eclectic, to say the least. Most of the fruit, vegetables, and meat available outside were also for sale inside, along with more second-hand clothing, shoes, furniture, dishes, household utensils, fish, shrimp, and a surprising amount of gold. She had read that Guyana had deposits of the metal. And here it was, mined, refined, and then fashioned into some of the crudest jewellery she had ever seen. It was super-bling — large, chunky necklaces and bracelets moulded into zodiac signs and commercial logos for brands such as Nike, Calvin Klein, and Chanel. But crude or not, the jewellery looked to be made from twenty- or even twenty-two-karat gold.

Ava didn't find what she wanted until she got to the very end of the market. It was dark there; the stalls were pressed closer together and there was no overhead light. She had to work her way around a throng of local shoppers, and as she did, she could feel eyes following her progress. The desk clerk hadn't been wrong.

She wandered into one of the stalls and was greeted by an East Indian woman wearing a sari, rolls of flesh cascading over her waistband. She seemed surprised to see Ava, and turned away as if she expected her to leave again. When Ava didn't go, the woman finally acknowledged her with a raised eyebrow.

"I want one of those," Ava said, pointing to a selection of knives locked in a glass case.

"Which one?"

"I can't tell. Could you open the case for me?"

The woman struggled to her feet and took a key from a drawer. She looked around suspiciously as she unlocked the case. When it was open, she motioned for Ava to come closer.

They were nearly all automatic switchblades, and it was a surprisingly good collection. She recognized Heckler and Koch, Blackwater, Schrade, Buck, and Smith and Wesson. Ava took her time appraising them and then asked the woman to pass her a Schrade. The blade was bit too short. "I prefer stilettos," she said.

The woman lifted the felt-lined tray; underneath was a row of Italian stilettos. "Everything from six inches to fifteen inches," the woman said.

"I think eleven inches will do just fine."

The woman passed her the knife. It was lightweight and fitted easily into her palm. She touched the button and the beautifully crafted blade hissed into view in a microsecond. "How much?"

"One hundred and fifty American."

"One hundred."

"One twenty-five."

"One hundred."

"One twenty, final."

"Done," Ava said.

It was hotter than ever when she exited Stabroek. A taxi with its windows open sat at the curb. She got in and told the driver to turn on the air conditioning and take her to the Phoenix.

"I don't have air conditioning," he said.

"Drive anyway."

"It is too close. You should walk."

She passed him ten dollars. "Drive."

At the hotel the doorman was back on duty. He was leaning against a wall, looking out at the empty lobby. She hadn't seen any other guests coming or going and was beginning to wonder if she was the only one staying there. He acknowledged her arrival with a nod. She nodded back and walked over.

"Is Jeff back from the airport yet?"

"No, but he should be here soon enough."

"When he does get back, could you please ask him to call my room? Tell him I'd like to use the Jeep this afternoon."

She stripped off her clothes when she got to the room. There was a full-length mirror on the back of the closet door, and she caught her image in it. She was proud of her body and worked hard at maintaining it, but not to excess. No powerlifting for her; she liked her leanness. She liked even more her proportions, which were just about perfect. She had a thing about girls with thick ankles or long torsos — they weren't for her.

Ava's sense of well-being disappeared when she stepped into the shower. The water spewing from the showerhead was a light chocolate brown. She waited for it clear. It didn't. She sniffed the water and detected a chemical odour. She waited for another minute, and when the colour still didn't change, she left the bathroom and phoned the front desk. "The water in my shower is brown," she said.

"Yes?"

"Did you hear what I said?"

"The water is always brown. We get it from the Demerara. We have our own purification system — the water is perfectly safe, but we can't do anything about the colour."

Ava hung up and climbed back into the shower. She closed her eyes, shut her mouth, and tried not to breathe through her nose, soaping and rinsing herself as quickly as she could. Getting to Jackson Seto was becoming more urgent.

When she got out of the shower, she put on a fresh T-shirt and track pants and waited for Jeff in the rattan chair. She passed the time reading a copy of the *Guyana Times*, which had been at her door when she came back from the market. The lead article was about some club owners who were complaining about police raids. The clubs were indeed illegal, but the owners maintained that the police were being too heavy-handed during raids and were driving away tourists. What made it even stranger was that the minister of culture and tourism was quoted as saying that the club owners had a point. The next page was one giant police blotter: a list of crimes committed over the past twenty-four hours. Arrests for drug dealing, robbery, mugging, and physical assault were pretty common.

Ava heard a knock at the door. She opened it to see Jeff standing there. He had changed his clothes and was now wearing jeans and a tank top. On his right shoulder was a tattoo of a lightning bolt.

"I called but no one answered," he said.

"I guess I was in the shower."

"You want to go somewhere?"

"Yes. I mentioned Malvern Gardens earlier and you said you know where it is."

"I do."

"That's where I want to go."

"It's a housing estate."

"I know."

"Do you have an address?"

"No, we need to find that out. The guy who lives there is named Jackson Seto."

"Wait a minute," he said, and squeezed past her into the room. He opened the bottom drawer of her dresser and pulled out a phone book. "He lives at number eight."

As they rode the elevator to the ground floor Ava said, "Before we go, there are a few things we need to make clear. For starters, I'm probably going to be sitting in the car with you for a while, and I have no idea how long. I'm looking for this guy Seto, and all I know is that he lives at 8 Malvern Gardens. When he does appear, we're going to follow him and see what happens. Are you okay with that?"

"What if you don't see him?"

"Then we'll go back tomorrow and do it all over again."

"Is this legal? I mean, are you a cop or something?"

"It's perfectly legal and I'm not a cop."

"Can I ask why?"

"No."

He gazed down at her. "Well, I can't say you look like much of a threat to anyone."

The Jeep had been left idling at the hotel entrance. Jeff started up High Street and then cut left. The road was littered with potholes, and one was so big it could have swallowed the front end of the vehicle. "Don't they ever fix those things?" Ava asked.

"No."

"Do they try?"

"Not so you'd notice."

When they reached the end of the street, they were confronted by a structure about six or seven storeys high made entirely of corrugated iron. Ava could see rows of razor wire along the top. The building had no windows, just a door barricaded by a semicircle of concrete pillars. Standing to the left of the door with their backs pressed against the wall was a line of women.

"What's that?" she asked.

"Camp Street Prison," he said.

"It must be an oven in there."

"No one much cares."

"And the women?"

"Waiting for visiting hours."

As they moved away from the city centre, the mix of retail stores gave way to rows of stucco, stone, and even brick houses, most protected by tall concrete walls with rolls of razor wire glinting fiendishly across the top. "I've never seen so much razor wire," she said.

"It's the choice of the budget-conscious middle class, who can't afford a personal guard or a security service. Ever come in contact with it?"

"No, of course not."

"It'll rip you to shreds."

They had left the city proper and were driving through countryside when a housing development, as isolated as an oasis in the desert, appeared on the right. From a distance all Ava could see was a brick wall and red tile roofs; she thought, *Gated community.* But as they drew closer she saw that the road leading into Malvern Gardens wasn't barred. Jeff stopped the Jeep between two stone pillars at the entrance to a cul-de-sac. There were five houses down each side and two at the end. The two-storey brick-and-stone homes were enormous, reminding Ava of high-end suburban developments in Toronto. Each sat on a one-acre lot surrounded by a stone wall about 2.5 metres high that was crowned with large shards of glass and razor wire. The only way into each compound was through heavy metal gates with sharp points at the top and more razor wire strung through them.

"This is Millionaires' Row," said Jeff.

The house numbers went up by fours. Seto's house was the second on the left. It had a latticed gate, and as they drove past Ava saw an old Mercedes and a Land Rover parked in the driveway. Someone was home.

She pointed back towards where they had turned off the main road. "If we park behind one of those pillars we can see everyone coming and going from the house," she said. "And if they turn left to go to the city, we'll have a clear view."

Jeff turned the Jeep around and parked behind the pillar. From that angle they could see Seto's gate and the end of his driveway.

"Now what?" he asked.

"We wait."

"Do you mind if I sleep?"

"Go ahead."

Jeff got out and climbed into the back seat to lie down. "I sleep lightly, so don't worry about having to wake me if we need to move."

She had kept her watch in the zippered pocket of her pants. She pulled it out and put it on. It was 3:30 p.m.

Jeff slept until just past five, when he woke with a start.

"Nothing yet," she said.

"I need to piss."

"Be my guest."

He went behind the car, his back turned to the Jeep.

"What time does it get dark?" she asked when he climbed back in.

"Six."

At five thirty Seto's gate swung open. Ava drew a deep breath. The Mercedes backed out onto the road and then crept towards them. Ava saw that the driver was a young East Indian woman, heavily made up, with lots of jewellery on both wrists and at least three gold chains around her neck.

"That's a disappointment," she said.

The gate remained open. *Somebody else is going to leave*, she thought. After a couple of minutes a wiry Asian man in jeans and a black T-shirt ambled out onto the road. He took a quick look around and then motioned towards the house. *He looks Vietnamese*, she thought.

"Get out of the car," she said to Jeff. "Go around back and pretend you're still peeing."

He went without question.

The Land Rover emerged from the driveway. It stopped and the Vietnamese man climbed in. As it turned the corner both passengers took a hard look at Jeff. Ava was slumped down in her seat but was able to get a clear view of them. Jackson Seto was driving.

Jeff waited until the Rover was well down the road before getting back in the Jeep.

"Now what? Do you want to follow them?" he asked.

"I'm not sure. Where do you think they're going?"

"A hundred to one they're headed for the city."

"It's just about dinner time. Is there a restaurant district?"

"Nearly all the decent places are in a four-square-block area."

"Any of them Chinese?"

"A couple."

"Let's give it fifteen minutes and then we'll head into town. We'll cover that area and see if we can find their cars."

"And if we can't?"

"That's my problem for tomorrow."

The sun was setting as they were driving back to Georgetown. Jeff hit a couple of potholes, and Ava was sure they were going to lose a tire.

Georgetown had taken on a different look. It took Ava a minute to realize that it was because only part of the city was lit while the rest was blanketed in almost total darkness. "Is there a power outage?" she asked.

"I guess you could call it that, except it happens every night. They only have enough power for half the city. So they alternate between east and west on a nightly basis. Tonight the east end gets electricity and the west end has to make do with candles. Most of the businesses have their own backup generators."

"What a place."

"Yep."

"The area we're going to, will it have power tonight?"

"Yeah, we're lucky," he said, and then turned towards her. "I hope you don't mind me asking, but I've been curious all afternoon. Just what is it we're doing, following this guy?"

"It's just business."

"What kind of business?"

Ava stared at the road. "I think it's better if I don't share that with you."

"Better for who?"

"Me."

Jeff shrugged. "We're getting close to the restaurant district. I'll circle."

It took less than five minutes to find both cars, which were parked outside a restaurant called China World. "The Chinese are so predictable," she said. "You could drop them in Paris on a street lined with three-star French restaurants and they'd still go looking for something Chinese, even if it was a hole in the wall."

"Are you going in?"

"No, we'll wait for them to come out."

They waited for an hour. The girl exited first. She was big, about five ten, and was wearing jeans that showed off muscular thighs and a high, firm ass. A tank top accentuated her large, round breasts, and Ava could see that she didn't need a bra. She blew a kiss towards the restaurant door, got into her car, and drove off. "That's a body," Jeff said.

The Vietnamese man came out next, with Seto a few steps behind. *He's Seto's bodyguard*, she thought, *or some kind of bumboy who doubles as a bodyguard*. He was small, but she knew that didn't mean anything. His type could be tough, vicious, and fearless to the point of stupidity. He was a complication she didn't need.

Seto too was a thin, reedy shadow. He was maybe six feet tall, but he slouched when he walked, making him look shorter than he was. He was wearing a pair of high-waisted black slacks secured by a belt that was on its last notch. Ava thought he looked almost emaciated; she could see that his chest was concave beneath his white dress shirt. His face was alive, though, his dark brown eyes darting here and there like a rat's, his mouth drawing hard on a cigarette.

They climbed into the Land Rover and drove away. "Let's follow them for a bit," she said.

They had barely gotten the Jeep in motion when she saw the Land Rover pull into a parking spot no more than two blocks away. The neon sign over the door read ECKIE'S ONE AND ONLY CLUB. Seto got out by himself, walked past the bouncer, and disappeared through the door.

"You know this place?" she asked Jeff.

"Everyone knows Eckie's. It's the best club in Georgetown, one of the few places that doesn't need cheap beer and sluts. They import some good DJs, and it's where the high-priced girls — amateurs and pros — go. Tourists and locals with money are the target."

"Who owns it?"

"I have no idea."

"Who is Eckie?"

"Don't know. I've been there a few times and I never met anyone called Eckie."

She sat quietly, weighing her options while watching the Vietnamese bodyguard smoke. The few approaches she could think of were flawed. Confronting him in the bar wasn't much of an option. No one knew her, and if there a fuss they would likely support the local — and that was without his bodyguard jumping in. If she tried to talk to Seto outside, Vietnamese involvement was a certainty, and it was too soon for her to trigger that kind of response without knowing more about to whom and how Seto was connected. Antonelli had said that Seto had strong ties with the police in Georgetown; she needed to find out how far up the chain those ties went. Still, doing nothing wasn't an option.

"Could you get me a local SIM card?"

"Yeah. Tomorrow morning okay?"

"That's fine."

"You're not going into Eckie's?"

"No, there's nothing for me to do tonight."

"So now what?"

"I'm going back to the hotel."

When they got to the Phoenix, Ava climbed out of the Jeep and turned to Jeff. "Call me when you have the SIM card. I assume you're free tomorrow if I need you."

"The day is clear so far."

She passed seventy dollars through the window.

"Thanks."

"Jeff, I don't want you to discuss any of this with anyone. Not a word. The name Jackson Seto doesn't exist for you."

"You didn't have to say that."

"It's always better to make things clear," she said, and threw another twenty-dollar bill onto the passenger seat.

(19)

AVA WOKE UP EARLY AND WAS DOWNSTAIRS BY SIX. The coffee shop wasn't open, so she drifted over to the business centre. It wasn't open either. She went to the front desk. "Can you open the business centre for me?" she said.

"It don't open till seven." A young man in a sports jacket two sizes too large was manning the desk.

"Do you have a key?"

"Yeah."

She put ten dollars on the counter. "Open it for me now, please."

There were forty emails in her main account. She worked her way through them in ascending order. Tam had sent her his bank information and overly enthusiastic good wishes. Her mother wanted her to know that she had had a big night at mah-jong. Uncle hoped she was safe. Her best friend, Mimi, was going to break up with the guy she'd been seeing for the past few weeks.

She logged onto Yahoo and, using her mother's home address, opened an email account under the name Eatfish12. She then sent an email to Jackson Seto. It said that she worked for a trading company in Toronto that was interested in importing cheap fish, and that she had been told Guyana was a good source. She was currently in Trinidad doing some sourcing but could get over to Georgetown on short notice if he thought there was an opportunity. She added that she had been referred to him by a friend of a friend who knew George Antonelli. She didn't think there was much chance he would answer. Still, it was worth a shot.

She wandered back into the deserted lobby. The coffee shop was still shuttered. The desk clerk held up ten fingers, so Ava flopped into one of chairs and turned on her cellphone. Uncle had called. She hit the redial button.

"I'm just making sure you are okay," he said. She knew he was with other people; he never used her name when he was.

"I've found him. I mean, I've seen him. Now I just have to figure out how to get to him."

"Difficult?"

"I don't know yet. I don't know enough about him or his habits. He has a Vietnamese bodyguard, which is not good. His house is like a mini fortress. And if he is as connected here as Antonelli claims, I can't count on the authorities — whoever they are — staying out of our business if it gets aggressive."

"Do you want me to send help?"

"No, let me find out more."

"Call me every day, then. I'll worry otherwise."

When Ava hung up, she noticed that an overweight middle-aged man had joined her. His large gut was accentuated by the tight T-shirt tucked into his jeans. The shirt read, GUYANA SUCKS. He had tattoos on both arms: RED DEVILS down one and MANCHESTER U down the other. He walked over to the coffee shop and rattled the closed grate. A young East Indian woman stuck her head out, saw him, and swung it open. Ava followed him in.

The coffee shop was small, but she tried to find a table as far away from him as possible. It didn't do much good.

"So what in hell are you doing here?" he called over to her.

She wasn't adept at identifying English accents, but even without the tattoos she could have figured out that he was from northern England and definitely working class. "I'm here on business," she said, wishing she had a book or a newspaper to hide behind.

To her surprise he got up, walked over to her table, and sat down. "I'm Tom Benson," he said.

"Ava Lee."

"So what are you doing in this hellhole?"

"Some business — financial. In and out."

"I should be so fucking lucky," he said, pronouncing it more like *fooking*.

"Really."

"Been here six fucking months and probably good for another six."

"And how is that?"

"The power. I'm here to fix it, if it can be fixed."

"You don't seem to be having much success, if last night is any indication."

The waitress came to the table. "Coffee and toast," he said, "and make sure you use bottled water for the coffee." He looked at Ava. "Don't order the eggs or any of the meat. It's given me at least two bouts of food poisoning. And you have to insist on bottled water or they use that shite from the river. They tried to sneak it by me once, but I went to the fucking kitchen and caught them. Now I pop in and out of the kitchen every so often to keep them honest."

"I'll have what he's having," Ava said to the waitress.

"I work for Rolls-Royce. They used to be in the diesel generator business, like about a hundred fucking years ago. This city has the last of those generators that are still working. They should have been replaced years ago but no one gives a shite, and even if they did they probably don't have the money. So the Guyana government went to the U.K. government and said, 'We have this problem. Could you arrange to send someone over to fix it?' The U.K. guys went to Rolls-Royce and said, 'Send someone over. We'll pay for him.' So here I am."

"Six months?"

"Right. The second week I was here, I figured out one of the major problems and told the Power Authority — what a joke they are — they needed to order some parts. They have to be custom made, see. They told me they ordered them from an outfit in the U.S., some high-end tool-and-die operation. I'm still waiting for those fucking parts."

"So what do you do? I mean, how do you fill your days?"

"At eight thirty they'll send a car and driver for me. I'll go to the office, make my long-distance calls back home, fuck around on the Internet, and then around eleven drag my arse into the boss's office and ask him if the parts have arrived. He'll say no and I'll have the driver bring me back to the hotel. I usually sit by the pool drinking beer all afternoon, and then I head into town for dinner. I didn't have this belly when I got here. I also had a girlfriend back home, and she's packed me in."

"So why do you stay?"

"The money mainly. I'm living here for virtually fucking free. All I have to pay for is my beer. Then, of course, there are the girls," he said, looking to gauge her reaction. When she registered none, he went on. "I mean, for a bloke like me this is heaven when it comes to the girls. At home you practically have to beg before you can get laid. Here I flash a few dollars and, voila, I have my pick of the lot — every night if I want."

"Sounds like fun."

"Not always. Sometimes it can get dicey."

"Meaning?"

"This is a rough place, even for someone like me. Have to be careful. I was robbed twice before I figured out it was smart to leave my watch, wallet, room key, and everything but the money I needed for the night here in the hotel. If you're going out anywhere, you should do the same thing. They'll fucking come at you for a plastic Timex, never mind a Cartier," he said, pointing at hers.

"Thanks."

"No bother."

Breakfast arrived. He didn't let the waitress leave until he had sniffed and tasted the coffee.

Ava took a sip of hers. It was instant coffee, Nescafé, she thought. She wondered whether, if she brought her VIA instant in, they'd make that for her.

"Tom, do you know a club called Eckie's?"

"Sure, it's my favourite. Better class of girls. Imported beer."

"Who owns it?"

"I wouldn't know."

"Have you ever seen a Chinese man hanging around the club?"

"A few."

"This one is tall and skinny, really skinny. His hair is streaked with grey and he's got a moustache that's a bit off balance and a pointy, thin face like a rat."

"Oh fuck, he's a madman, that one. Drinks like a fucking fish and treats the girls like shite. He tosses money around like crazy too, which gets the girls all excited, but I've never seen him actually leave with one or nip into one of Eckie's back rooms."

"I thought you said it's dangerous to have too much money on you."

"For me, for you, for any other fucking tourist. He's a local, that lad. I've seen the cops come into the club and give us all the fucking evil eye except for him. He has connections, he does."

"The police are, what, corrupt?"

Benson started laughing, slivers of wet toast spilling from his mouth. "Jesus, what do you think?"

"That's why I asked."

"Look, the army, the police, the security people — it's all one big happy gang here. You can't tell one from the other."

"So the Chinese guy is paying them off?"

"One way or another, but that's true for anyone in this country who has money. You don't get money and you sure as fuck don't keep money unless you're looking after the powers that be."

"And who are they, the powers that be?"

"I don't fucking know and I don't fucking care. As

long as I'm left alone, the cops and the army and the rest of them can fiddle away."

"That seems sensible," she said.

They walked to the elevator together. She sensed that he was going to come on to her and wasn't surprised when he said, "Would you like to go out tonight? You know, hit some clubs?"

"Tom, I'm not really your type," Ava said gently. "Believe me, I'm not."

(20)

AT TEN O'CLOCK AVA SLIPPED HER NOTEBOOK AND her Canadian passport into the Chanel bag and went downstairs. Dressed in a black knee-length skirt, black pumps, and a white shirt, she looked every inch a conservative, serious businesswoman.

She went straight out of the hotel up to Young Street, turned right, and walked two and a half blocks to a white wooden house the size of a small apartment building that flew the Canadian flag. She assumed that the embassy offices were on the ground floor and the residences above. She had expected to meet security at the double doors, but there was none. In the small air-conditioned vestibule, a young black woman sat at a reception desk behind a plastic shield that was perforated at mouth level.

Ava walked towards her, the woman eyeing her as if she were a thief. "Hello, my name is Ava Lee. I'm Canadian and I'm here on business. I've run into a bit of trouble and I need to speak to the ambassador," she said, flashing her passport.

"There is no ambassador. We have a high commissioner, and he sees no one without an appointment."

"This is an emergency. If he isn't available, is there anyone else who can help me?"

"I'm not sure —" she began, and then was interrupted by the appearance of a man who didn't look to Ava much like a diplomat.

He stared at her from behind the shield, his hand resting on the woman's shoulder. Ava smiled and held up her passport. "I'm having some problems and I hope you can help."

There was a slit at the bottom of the shield. He pointed to it. "Slide your passport through there, please." She did. He took it and examined her picture and all her visas and entry stamps; then he spread it apart to check the binding.

"What's the problem?" he said.

"Do I have to stand out here?"

He thought about it. "No, I guess not." He reached down and hit a button. The door to the offices buzzed and swung open.

She walked through and held out her hand. "I'm Ava Lee."

"Marc Lafontaine."

He was a hulk of a man, layered with muscle. "You're not the high commissioner, are you?" she said.

"I'm with the RCMP."

"Ah."

"I'm the security around here."

"You may be exactly the person I need to talk to."

"No one ever wants to talk to me."

"Don't be so sure."

"What is it you want to discuss?"

"Out here? You don't have an office?"

"Pushy, aren't you?"

"Desperate is more like it."

That caught his attention. "Follow me," he said. "We normally don't let people back here, but you don't look like a threat."

His office was modest, containing a metal desk, a wooden swivel chair, and two four-drawer metal filing cabinets. On a coat rack in one corner, his uniform hung inside a plastic dry-cleaning bag. She noticed there were three stripes on the sleeve. Two photographs of three young girls sat on top of one of the filing cabinets. "Are those your daughters, Sergeant?"

"Yes, and call me Marc."

"Are they here with you?"

"They're in Ottawa with their mother."

"I see." She looked at the pictures and then at him. He had short auburn hair cropped close to his scalp, thin eyebrows, a long nose, and a chin that was distinctively pointed. All the girls shared that chin. "They look like you," she said.

"We don't get many Canadians walking in off the street the way you just did. Tell me why you're so desperate. That is the word you used, right?"

"That may have been a bit of an exaggeration. It's a bit too soon to tell."

"Are you going to make me guess what this is about?"

She had dealt with Mounties several times before. They had not been very imaginative but they had been rigorously honest, and she knew they valued the same in return. She had no intention of lying to him; she just needed to gauge how much she could tell him. "As security, I imagine you have to deal with the local police and the like."

He nodded.

"Well, I need to know how the system works here."

"You are going to tell me why, aren't you?"

"I represent a Canadian company that was bilked out of a substantial amount of money by someone currently residing in Guyana," she said carefully. "I'm here to try to collect some or all of that money."

His face didn't register any emotion; he had probably heard this story before. "That's why there are lawyers. I can recommend a couple if you want," he said.

"This has gone beyond lawyers," she said. "Besides, the scam took place in the U.S., the money is probably in an offshore account, and the culprit is here. You can imagine how complicated any legal action would be, involving four separate jurisdictions."

"I can. Now you haven't told me just what you do. Are you a lawyer?"

"I'm an accountant, a forensic accountant."

"So you tracked the money."

"I did."

"And you know who took it and where he or she is?"

"His name is Jackson Seto. He has a house in Malvern Gardens, on the outskirts of Georgetown, and he's there right now."

"I know Malvern Gardens. Him I've never heard of."

"Why would you?"

He shrugged. "You'd be surprised."

"Anyway, I need to tackle Seto head-on."

"What's stopping you?"

"I've been told by several sources that he's connected to the people who run things in Guyana, that he probably has some measure of protection."

"If he lives in Malvern Gardens it wouldn't surprise me to know he's connected."

"To whom?"

"What do you mean?"

"How do things work here? You just can't land at the airport, pay off a few cops, and all is well. There has to be some kind of established system, yes?"

"Very established."

She waited. "Is it my turn to guess?" she finally said.

He looked troubled.

"You know, if we need to be off the record, that works for me. Both ways, of course," she said.

"Do you want to start?"

"Are you serious?"

"Yes, I am."

With anyone else she might have asked for more assurance of discretion, but she knew from experience that he would take offence. Mountie honour is a prickly thing.

"As I said," she began, "I'm here to try to collect money that was stolen from a client. To do that, I need to meet with Seto to try to persuade him that it would be in everyone's best interest if the money were returned."

"And how exactly would you do that?"

"Well, I would try to reason with him initially, and if that failed . . ." Time to take a little leap of faith. "Then I would pressure him in any way I could, and that might include some physical interaction."

"Physical interaction?"

"I'm not as gentle as I look," she said.

"How extreme might this physical interaction get?"

"He's no use to me dead, crippled, maimed, or otherwise unable to function."

"You're serious?"

"Absolutely."

He shook his head, a tiny smile tugging at the corners of his mouth. "I am so glad I came to work today."

"I don't actually find this amusing."

"I'm sorry," he said, still shaking his head. "It's just that I'm sitting across from a young, beautiful woman who can't weigh much more than a hundred and ten pounds, who tells me she's an accountant and then tells me she's here to rip this Seto guy a new asshole."

"That's the way it is," she said. "My problem — my potential problem — is that if I have to go beyond reasoning with him I'm going to run into his friends, and my experience in the developing world is that I won't stand a chance. They'll run me right out of the country, or worse."

"Here it would probably be *or worse*."

"So I need to know who they are."

"Why?"

"So I can make them my friends, or at least disentangle them from Seto."

"Just how much money does this guy owe?"

"About five million."

"Wow."

"So who do I need to talk to?"

He pushed himself to his feet, walked to the door, and closed it. "This is off the record — we are agreed on that?"

"I wouldn't have told you what I just did if that wasn't the case."

He sat down, leaned back, and looked at the ceiling. "It's called the Guyana Defence League. During the 1960s the communists were active here and Cheddi Jagan was prime minister for a while. At the time that made Guyana only the second communist government in the Americas, after Cuba, and the U.S. sort of went ballistic. They pushed — and financed —Jagan's former political partner, Forbes Burnham, into going up against his old colleague; they had been allies in forcing the U.K. to surrender their colonial power. There were strikes, riots, boycotts, and a lot of random violence against Jagan and his people. The fact that he was East Indian and Burnham was black only made it worse.

"Anyway, Jagan ended up in jail and Burnham became prime minister, supported by the Americans. At the time there was only a small police force in Guyana. The Americans needed assurance that the communists wouldn't be coming back, so they invested heavily in building an army and creating a clandestine special forces unit. Because the country is so small, they came up with the idea of grouping all these security forces together, creating the Guyana Defence League.

"The communists came and went. Burnham was in and out of office. Even Jagan — who was now a social democrat — got a chance to be the leader again. Through it all, the Guyana Defence League remained intact and developed methods of operation that are still in play today. Basically, the person who heads up the special forces is the top man. The military report to him, the police report to him. He moves officers back and forth at will among the various services. So when you're dealing with the police, you aren't really. Everything flows upstream."

"Including money?"

"Especially money."

"I've just left Thailand, but it feels like I haven't."

"I'm sure the scale is different," Lafontaine said. "This is a small, poor country. There's only so much graft to go around, and the politicians feed at the same trough."

"Who heads up the Defence League?"

"Commissioner Thomas for the police, and General Choudray heads up the military. One's black, the other East Indian, and that's the way it always is: one of each. The strange thing is, they report to a white guy, the infamous Captain Robbins."

"A white guy — that's curious."

"Isn't it. When I arrived here, I met him at a High Commission function. He has two daughters at school in Toronto — Havergal College — and Canada is his country of choice in terms of making investments. I thought he was just a fat, jolly businessman until the High Commissioner pulled me aside and told me to be careful, very careful.

"He's had the same job for twenty years. There isn't a man in any of the forces who is not beholden to him for his job, and in this country, with unemployment at around thirty percent, that's no small thing. He also knows where all the bodies are buried, and he's probably responsible for a number of them himself. There isn't a politician whom he doesn't know inside out, and I can't imagine there's one who would defy him. It has been tried, though. Last year there was an East Indian minister of mines who decided the royalties that were going to the Defence League should end. His house was broken into and he, his wife, and his mother-in-law were shot dead. They never found the perpetrators.

"So, Ms. Lee, if Seto has protection, it emanates from Captain Robbins, directly or indirectly."

"How do I meet Captain Robbins?" she asked.

Lafontaine smiled again. "You're serious, aren't you? I mean, really serious. I keep looking at you and thinking you're pulling a practical joke on me."

"Do you have a phone number for him?"

He opened a Day-Timer that sat on his desk. "Write this down, though I don't think it will do you any good. He doesn't take calls and he never returns calls unless he wants to talk to you, not vice versa."

"Thanks for all this," she said after writing down the number in her notebook.

"We're here to serve."

"That's always been my experience with the Mounties. You're a very professional group."

He nodded in acknowledgement. "Where are you staying?"

"The Phoenix Hotel."

"Neighbours."

"Sort of."

"Tell me, would you like to have dinner with me while you're here? You could keep me up to date on your progress."

She looked over at the pictures of his children.

"I'm divorced," he said.

Two propositions in one day, Ava thought, and unless she was wrong, Jeff was a potential third. For reasons she didn't understand, *gweilos* found her attractive. In Hong Kong she could stand on a street corner holding a sign reading PLEASE TAKE ME OUT TO DINNER and not get this much action.

"I wouldn't mind having dinner with you, but in keeping with our honesty policy I have to tell you I'm gay."

"I did say dinner; I wasn't assuming anything else," he said, but the flush that crept up his cheeks told her differently.

"How about I keep in touch with you? Can I get your cell number?"

He handed her a business card. His title read ASSISTANT TRADE COMMISSIONER.

"I'll let you know how it goes with Captain Robbins."

(21)

JEFF WAS STANDING AT THE ENTRANCE OF THE PHOENIX wearing slacks and a Polo golf shirt. He looked happy to see her, and she knew she was going to end up saying no to him as well.

"I have your SIM card," he said.

"How much do I owe you?" she said as she took it.

"Twenty."

She gave him thirty.

"Will you need me today? I have to make a run to the airport around one. After that I'm free."

"I'm not sure. Call me when you get back."

The room was way hotter than when she had left. The maid had turned off the air conditioning. She turned it back on and for good measure jacked it way down.

She undressed; her clothes were damp even though it was no more than a three-minute walk from the High Commission. She put on her running gear. It was really too hot to run but she needed to think, and running freed her mind. Before leaving the hotel she checked her emails at the business centre. Nothing from Seto. That was no surprise.

From the literature in the room she knew there was a walkway along the seawall. The path was grass, and running on grass was easy on her legs. Add the sea breeze to that and she thought maybe it wouldn't be too tough, despite the heat.

The Georgetown seawall had been built during the nineteenth century by the Dutch, the original colonists, before the British ousted them. Georgetown, and in fact most of the northern coastline, was below sea level. The Dutch were experts at keeping the sea at bay, and they had constructed an impressive bulwark of stone about two metres wide and a metre high.

Ava began jogging towards the Atlantic. It was close to low tide, and between the wall and the ocean was a large expanse of sandy beach. On her right was Seawall Road, which was lined with embassies and consulates. There was hardly any traffic on the road and virtually no one on the path. Ava could see maybe two or three kilometres ahead. A woman was on the beach tossing sticks to a dog, and farther down she could see two figures sitting on the seawall.

She had run about a kilometre before the seated figures became distinct. They were two East Indian men, sitting maybe twenty metres apart. As she drew near she noticed she had attracted their attention. She thought about stopping and turning back, then told herself she was being silly. It was the middle of the day, and they were in a wide open area.

When she was five metres from the first man she saw him stiffen, and her senses prickled. She sped up to get past him. Just as she did, the second man jumped off the wall onto the path. She was trapped between them.

One of the men was about five foot ten and had to weigh at least two hundred pounds. He wore ragged blue shorts and a T-shirt that read DRINK COORS. The other, who was a bit taller and not much thinner, was wearing soiled jeans and a singlet that exposed his chest and armpits. Ava noticed he had only one eye. It was fixed on her, and it wasn't conveying kind intent.

She stopped and turned so that she was facing the wall and had a clear view of the two of them.

"This can be easy or hard — your choice," the one to her left said, a knife now visible in his right hand.

Ava saw no reason to respond; the outcome would be the same. The other man didn't seem to be armed, so she decided to take on the one with the knife first.

They inched towards her, trying to maintain equal distance. Ava moved left to bring her closer to the one with the knife. He waved it in the air until he was about half a metre from her. Then he reached down to grab her hair with his left hand, the knife held back, poised to strike.

She retreated backwards about half a step. When he tried to close the distance, she stepped forward. Her right arm rocketed towards him with the force of a piston. The extended knuckle of her index finger crashed into the bridge of his nose. She wasn't sure which she noticed first, the crack of cartilage or the gush of blood. He sagged to the ground, dropping the knife as both hands moved to cradle his nose. She picked up the weapon and threw it over the wall.

The other man hadn't moved as she put his friend out of action. Now he edged towards her, his fists balled. He didn't move very well; his hips seemed to propel his legs.

She knew she could avoid his swings but she wasn't about to give him the chance. When he was within striking range, her right arm shot out again. This time she used the base of her palm to strike at the centre of his forehead. He reeled back and she leapt after him, her left fist driving into his Adam's apple. He collapsed, his eyes rolled back, and his hands clutched his throat as he gasped for air. She had known people to die from that blow.

The whole incident had taken no more than thirty seconds. She looked around. There was no one in view, no cars on the road. She turned and began to jog back to the hotel, past the woman throwing sticks to her dog.

(22)

"HOW WAS YOUR RUN?" THE DOORMAN ASKED WHEN Ava arrived back at the Phoenix.

"Okay," she said.

She had bought two bottles of water to take to her room. She didn't recognize the brand and then saw it had been bottled in Georgetown. She added a water purification pill to each of them. When the pills had done their work, she sat in the rattan chair and looked out at the ocean. She was ready to phone Captain Robbins. She didn't expect him to take her call, but she did expect him to return it. That was when she would be challenged to capture his interest and get him to meet with her, or at the very least to send someone who had his trust.

She punched in the number and waited. Just when she thought it was going to flip into voicemail, a woman's rich, cultured voice said, "The office."

"I would like to speak to Captain Robbins, please," she said.

There was a long pause, and Ava wondered if Lafontaine had given her the correct number.

"I'm afraid that Captain Robbins is not available."

"Well, could you have him return my call, please? My name is Ava Lee and I'm affiliated with Havergal College. Do you need me to spell Havergal?"

"No, I know Havergal," she said. "Is there anything I can help you with, or is there a specific message you would like me to pass to the Captain?"

"No, I need to speak to him directly."

"He has the number for the college. He can call you there."

"No, I'm at a conference and I'm using my mobile. Let me give you my contact information," Ava said, and gave her Toronto cellphone number.

"Is this about either of his daughters?"

"I'm not at liberty to say. Please have him call me when he can."

"I will pass on the message."

Then Ava phoned downstairs to ask about laundry service. The front desk told her it could be back in her room by that evening. She left the bag outside the door for pickup and climbed into the shower. The water seemed less thick, less brown, and she stayed in longer than usual.

Her cellphone beeped when she emerged from the bathroom — a message. *Already*, she thought.

It was Captain Robbins's receptionist, asking her to call back.

She dried her hair and dressed while reviewing her pitch in her head, deciding just how much she should or shouldn't say. That was always difficult to determine when you were dealing with someone you didn't know, and in this case, knew nothing about except that he just might be the most powerful man in Guyana.

"The office."

"This is Ava Lee."

"Just one second, Ms. Lee."

Robbins was on the line almost instantly. "This is Robbins. What can I do for you?" He had an accent that sounded familiar but wasn't like anything she had heard in Guyana.

"My name is Ava Lee and I'm afraid I've called you under some mildly misleading pretences. But I really need to speak to you and I was told that you're a difficult man to get hold of."

There was silence from his end.

"I am a Havergal Old Girl, by the way, and I'm in Georgetown on business, not Toronto, though that is my home. I apologize for taking this approach." She waited for the sound of the phone being disconnected.

"Ms. Lee, who gave you this number?"

"The Canadian High Commission. I went to them for help and they said you were the man I should speak to."

"That's highly unusual. What kind of problem can you have that the Commission can't help with?"

His voice was plummy, even richer than his secretary's. His speech was slow, even, and full of confidence, in control.

"It's a business problem with a considerable amount of money involved," she said, invoking the magic word.

"And you think I can help?"

"I've been told that if anyone can, it's you."

"Someone thinks too highly of me. Still, it would be churlish not to try to assist a Canadian visitor recommended to me by the High Commission, and a visitor who happens to be a Havergal graduate at that. Where are you staying in Georgetown?"

"At the Phoenix."

"This is obviously a discussion that we shouldn't continue over the telephone. Are you going to be at the hotel this evening?"

"Certainly."

"I'll send someone there to meet with you. His name is Patrick West. I'm not sure when exactly he will be free, so try to leave the entire evening open if you can. I'll give him your mobile number, and I know he has the Phoenix's number, so if there's any change in plans he can contact you."

"Thank you so much."

"No promises, mind you, but Patrick is a good man and quite resourceful. He has my confidence, so make sure you're completely open with him."

You clever girl, she thought as the line went dead.

The afternoon was going to drag, so Ava set out to fill it with as much activity as she could. She took a taxi back to Stabroek and wandered aimlessly for an hour. In an area close to the market she found a bookstore. Most of the offerings were second-hand but she found a copy of *Tai-Pan*, James Clavell's historical novel about the early days of Hong Kong.

She was hungry but reluctant to experiment again with the local cuisine. The bookseller recommended the Kentucky Fried Chicken outlet just around the corner. She couldn't remember the last time she had eaten fried chicken of any kind. Still, there weren't many funny things they could do to it, so she decided to eat there.

Jeff was sitting in the lobby when she got back to the hotel. He waved to her. He was on the verge of becoming a nuisance.

"Are we in business today?" he asked.

"I have some things I need to do here," she said. "You can help out, though."

"How is that?"

"Go back to Malvern Gardens and keep tabs on Jackson Seto. You'll have to park somewhere else this time or they'll get suspicious. I think you should drive past the entrance and then turn the car around and park it in the direction of Georgetown. Stay about a hundred metres away. They shouldn't notice you if they leave."

"If they leave, I follow?"

"Only if you're sure it's okay. Keep well back. There aren't that many places he can go anyway."

"You want me to call you if anything happens?"

"Sure. Use the Guyana number you have for me."

She checked her emails again before going upstairs. Still nothing from Seto.

Her backup cellphone was fully charged. She slipped the Guyanese SIM card into it and turned on the phone. She placed it and her regular mobile on the small table next to the rattan chair. She still had some hours to kill. Hopefully James Clavell would help.

(23)

IT WAS DARK WHEN AVA WAS WOKEN BY A RINGING phone. The Clavell book was open on her lap to page thirty. She looked at both her mobiles before she realized it was the hotel phone.

"Yes?" she said.

"Ava, this is Marc Lafontaine. I'm just finishing work and I'm still wondering if you would like to have dinner with me."

She was still groggy from her nap and his name didn't register at first. Then it clicked and she almost groaned. Half of her wanted to hang up and the other half realized she might need him again before this project was finished. "I can't leave the hotel," she said. "I have a meeting here tonight and I'm not sure of the time."

"We can eat at the hotel. It's not that bad."

"All right, but if my appointment arrives while we're eating I'll have to leave."

"I understand. I'll see you in the lobby in, say, fifteen minutes?"

"Okay."

She brushed her teeth using bottled water and then

splashed some on her face. Her linen slacks were still presentable and she had a white cotton shirt she hadn't worn yet. She thought about putting on makeup for her meeting with Patrick West, and then decided against it. The more innocent she looked, the better.

There was a bar and lounge beside the lobby. Marc Lafontaine was sitting at a table with a Carib beer and a bowl of peanuts in front of him. "Glad you could join me," he said. "We don't get many Canadians coming through here, and truthfully it gets pretty lonely. I'm grateful for the company."

She knew he meant it, and she felt a twinge of guilt for having thought about blowing him off.

He looked at the two cellphones as she placed them on the table. "Busy girl, eh?"

"I'm trying to be. I managed to get in touch with Captain Robbins and I'm scheduled to meet one of his people here tonight at some time or another."

"You've got to be kidding! You actually got through to Robbins?"

"I did."

"That's amazing."

She smiled. "Well, that's the easy part."

"Do you want a drink?"

"White wine would be fine."

"I'll have to go to the bar to get it. There's no table service here."

He returned with her wine and another beer for himself. "They have a restaurant on the second floor. It's Georgetown's version of fine dining. I've eaten there three or four times and not gotten ill. The only thing is, they normally have only a quarter of the menu available, so I ask them what they do have rather than wait to be told they don't have something."

"Sounds good. I just want to tell the front desk where I am before we go upstairs, in case the Captain's man comes asking for me."

The restaurant was empty except for them. A sign by the entrance said PLEASE WAIT TO BE SEATED. Ava wondered who had thought that was necessary.

They were taken to a seat by a window. The lights from the part of Georgetown that had electricity sparkled in the night. "It looks almost attractive," he said.

She told him about meeting the Englishman Tom Benson that morning, and about his daily trek to the power company. Lafontaine laughed and told her that Benson's attitude was the only way to deal with Guyana and still stay sane. If you expected things to change, you were a fool.

She talked about Asia and about how North Americans in particular often went with preconceived notions of how hard life must be there, only to find themselves in Hong Kong or Singapore or Bangkok or Shanghai. The lifestyle in those places was more refined and luxurious than what they would find in just about any city in North America.

The waiter appeared with menus. "Just tell us what you have," Lafontaine said.

They had a choice of grilled snapper, broiled chicken, baked pork chops, and roast beef. There was only the one fish, and Ava chose it. Lafontaine ordered the chicken.

She asked him about his children in Ottawa. As Lafontaine began to talk about them, he suddenly caught himself. "There's something I really need to talk to you about," he said. "I hope you won't think I'm being rude."

"What is it about?"

"This morning when you told me that you were gay, you were being serious, yes? Not just keeping me at arm's length?"

"Marc, I could not have been more serious."

"I believe you," he said. "The thing is, homosexuality is illegal in Guyana. In fact, it's punishable by life imprisonment. Now, I haven't heard about anyone being prosecuted, but the law is on the books. And they really frown on any display of affection between two people of the same sex." He stopped, clearly uncomfortable. "I'm not trying to pry into your life or anything, but you need to be careful here, circumspect."

"I wasn't planning on going to gay bars," she said.

"That's good, because there aren't any."

"Thanks. Enough said."

Ava directed the conversation back towards his children. They were all teenagers and drifting away from him. She listened to him lament the fact and realized he knew absolutely nothing about girls. She was about to give him some suggestions when her Guyanese phone rang.

"Hi, Jeff," she said.

"He left the house about an hour and a half ago and went out to eat — guess where — and then went to drink and party — guess where."

"Same as last night."

"He's a creature of habit."

"Good. Pack it in. There's no reason to hang around there anymore tonight."

"What are you up to?" he asked, his voice cracking ever so slightly.

"I'm having dinner with a friend from the Canadian

High Commission, and then I have a meeting with a Guyanese government official. I'll see you tomorrow and settle our accounts."

Out of the corner of her eye she saw the restaurant host hovering. The moment she ended her phone call he walked to the table. "There are some people downstairs waiting to see you," he said.

"Call downstairs and tell them I'll be right there," she said. "And bring me the bill."

"I'm paying," Lafontaine said.

"No, you're not," she said. "You've done quite enough for me today as it is."

While they waited for the bill to arrive, Lafontaine said, "People? I thought you were meeting one person."

"Me too."

"Would you mind if I walk down with you?"

"Not at all."

There were three people sitting in the lounge: two large black men who looked as if they had come directly from the gym to an *Esquire* photo shoot, and a very pale, rotund man with a sly smile and a glint in his deep blue eyes.

"Christ, that's Robbins," Lafontaine said.

The three stood as Ava and Lafontaine approached, and she was shocked by how physically imposing Robbins was. His men were both over six feet tall, but Robbins was a shaved head taller. His belly mounded under a black satin shirt draped over black jeans; his face was round and jowly. His heaviness made him look, if anything, more dangerous. And then there was his skin — it was the colour of paper. In a country where everyone was some variation of brown, he was a ghost.

His eyes found her and didn't let go.

"Ah, Sergeant Lafontaine," Robbins said, his eyes still on Ava. "So it was you who gave Ms. Lee my phone number."

"Captain."

"What shall I say to you for unleashing this young woman on us?"

"I don't know what you mean."

"And why would you? Look at her — a Havergal graduate, tiny, well-mannered, a Chinese doll. And then . . . Ah, I'm not being polite. This is Patrick and this is Robert," he said, motioning to his men. "I thought you should meet them," he said to Ava, "and truthfully, they wanted to meet you.

"My plan, Mr. Lafontaine, was to send Patrick to meet with Ms. Lee, but after what happened today I couldn't resist the opportunity to meet her myself. Robert, why don't you explain?"

"I was called by the police today after they picked up two men at the seawall," Robert said.

Robbins interrupted. "It seems that a young Chinese woman was jogging there when she encountered these men. They are known to us, and not as particularly good citizens. Some minor theft charges, some more serious rape allegations, though never proven . . . Still, they told an interesting story. They claim they were sitting on the seawall, minding their own business, when this young woman ran by. They do admit they ogled her, and maybe made some inappropriate comments, but certainly did nothing to warrant the attack that ensued. One of them had his nose destroyed. The other had his windpipe crushed and is lucky to be alive. These are not small men, Mr. Lafontaine. I daresay even you or I would have found it a challenge to take on the two of them at the same time. You do jog, don't you, Ms. Lee?"

"Once in a while."

"The victims, or villains — call them what you will — said the woman in question came from this hotel. And as far as we can ascertain, Ms. Lee is the only Chinese woman in residence." Robbins stared at her, his expression not the least unkind. "So tell me, how do you explain the damage you inflicted on these men?"

"I restrained myself," Ava said.

Robbins exploded with laughter. Patrick and Robert followed suit. Marc Lafontaine looked as if he had wandered into the wrong wedding reception.

"Marc, I have business to discuss with Captain Robbins, and I don't think you should be here," she said softly.

"Ms. Lee is quite right. We do have business to discuss, Mr. Lafontaine," Robbins said, wiping tears from eyes. "This is no place for you."

Lafontaine started to say something but Ava cut him off. "I'll call you if I need you."

They watched him leave, the three men still chuckling. Robbins said, "When I heard this story, how could I send Patrick to meet you alone? What if he offended you?"

"Don't make fun of me or the situation I was in. They were going to rape me. I dealt with them, that's all."

"Apologies," Robbins said. "Sit, please." Robbins sat down as well; his two men stood on either side of his chair. "I have daughters, as you know, and I am sensitive to the situation you found yourself in this afternoon. I'd like to think that anyone who tried that with my girls would be equally indisposed. Except I can't imagine my girls inflicting that kind of damage. You are an amazing young woman, Ms. Lee. That's why I wanted to meet you in person. I thought you would be built like a shot putter, yet here you are, not much more than a hundred pounds soaking wet."

"I appreciate that you came," she said.

"I'm drinking beer. What can I get you?"

"Nothing, thank you. I'm quite sated."

"You speak like a Havergal graduate."

"I am one."

"I believe you. So what is this business you're involved in? It doesn't sound like something a Havergal grad would pursue."

"I'm a forensic accountant. I find money that has been misappropriated and try to return it to its rightful owner."

"And there's misappropriated money in Guyana?"

"No, the money is in the British Virgin Islands, but the thief is here."

"Name?"

"Jackson Seto."

Robbins's eyes showed no sign of recognition, and she felt a surge of optimism. If he didn't know the name, Seto couldn't be all that high in the food chain.

"Boys, do you have any information for me?" Robbins asked.

Patrick leaned forward and whispered in Robbins's ear.

The Captain looked at her and said, "Could you excuse us for a moment, Ms. Lee? We need to chat amongst ourselves."

She left the lounge and sat in the lobby, her back deliberately turned to them. In what seemed like less than a minute there was a gentle tap on her shoulder. Patrick was looking down at her. "The Captain will talk to you now."

Now it was just the two of them; the men had moved to the lobby.

"Seto is a friend of a friend," Robbins said.

"I want to be a better friend."

The Captain put his fingertips together, placing them against his nose. "To whom?"

"That's your decision."

"Tell me what your plans are for this Seto."

"I have to convince him to give the money back."

"Using logic?"

"Yes."

"And if that fails?"

She shrugged.

"And what would we be expected to do?"

"Stay out of it. Keep everyone out of it."

"That sounds simple enough."

"That isn't to say that I might not need active assistance at some point."

His eyes glittered, and she wondered why he seemed so amused.

"There is a substantial difference between turning a blind eye and becoming actively involved in whatever it is you have in mind," Robbins said.

"Everything has a price."

"You are a mercenary, Ms. Lee."

"I am an accountant," she said.

"Exactly."

"Obviously I can't be sure what kind of help I might need until I can actually get to Seto and spend some time alone with him."

"Give me an idea, though, will you?"

"I'd like all the information you have on him. You must have a dossier somewhere."

"That's not difficult."

"He has a Vietnamese bodyguard. I would like to have him put out of circulation for forty-eight to seventy-two hours."

"Go on."

"Seto seems to go to Eckie's Club every night. I'll try to talk to him there. If he isn't cooperative I'll need a place to take him. I can't very well bring him back to the hotel. His house would be ideal but I'm not sure that will be doable, so I want to have a backup plan."

"This is getting more expensive. You know that, yes?"

"If I do need to start moving him around I'll need some physical assistance, so you might have to assign someone to me."

"Is there more?"

"Not for now."

"Those are a lot of ifs."

"I always think it's better to plan for the worst."

"You do know that he pays a fee to some friends to look out for his interests?"

"I'll pay more."

"But you'll only pay once. He pays annually. Then there are all those ifs. How do we factor those into the equation?"

"I want you to assume that I'll need all the help I've outlined here and to give me a figure that accommodates them and makes everyone happy about upgrading friends."

He put the beer bottle to his lips and drank delicately. "I'm not good at numbers," he said.

Ava was not going to be the one to put the first offer on the table. It was Uncle's primary rule of negotiation: let the other party start. Not that she needed that advice. Her mother had practised that her entire life, in every transaction, big or small, that she had ever made. Even at the Chanel store in Toronto, her mother regarded the sticker price as merely an opening bid in the negotiation process. Ava had absorbed that life lesson. She turned her palms upward, as if helpless to know where to start, caught his eye, and let him know she was waiting for him.

He breathed deeply, a sigh of exasperation. She could almost see him calculating. How much money was she here to get? How much could Seto have gotten away with? He was in Guyana, after all, not the Cayman Islands, so it couldn't be a fortune. What percentage of it could he claim?

"Two hundred thousand will get you all the assistance you need," he said.

She had expected a larger sum. "That's too much, Captain. My clients would never agree to pay that amount."

"Then . . . ?"

She couldn't insult him. They had paid for help before, sometimes up to ten percent of the amount owed. But that had been based on a successful recovery. This was a payment with no guarantees attached. All she knew was that without the Captain she probably had zero chance of success.

"One hundred thousand — U.S. dollars of course," she said.

"Cash?"

"We prefer wire transfers."

"Upfront."

Uncle hated paying upfront. The most he had ever agreed to was half upfront and half at the conclusion. But the Captain hadn't been making a request — those were his terms. She sensed that trying to negotiate those terms would put a crimp in what had so far been a relatively painless exercise. Uncle was going to have to put up with it.

"Yes, upfront."

The Captain's face broke into a smile. "Okay, let me speak with my friends. If they're happy with the arrangement I'll let you know and give you the details of how the money should be transferred." He nodded in the direction of Robert and Patrick. "You've met the boys. If we go ahead I'll lend one of them to you as a . . . liaison. Do you have a preference?"

"Who is senior?"

"Patrick."

"He's the one I'll take."

"Assuming we do business," the Captain said.

"Assuming."

(24)

AVA CALLED THE NUMBER LAFONTAINE HAD GIVEN HER and got his voicemail. She left a message apologizing for the way their dinner had ended. Nothing else. If things went as planned, she wouldn't have to speak to him again.

Uncle answered her call on the first ring. "Ava, when will you be finished with this project?"

Ava was caught off guard. Uncle never rushed a job. "I'm not sure. Two days, maybe three. I made progress today . . . Has something happened?"

"We have landed a huge client. Have you heard of Tommy Ordonez?"

"The Filipino billionaire?"

"That's him. He is ethnic Chinese; the family name is actually Chew but he changed it to fit in with the Filipinos. He has a brother here in Hong Kong, David Chew, and another in Vancouver, Philip Chew. Tommy is the eldest, so all of the family money flows through and around him. He called me today through a friend."

"Tommy Ordonez got screwed in a deal and needs us to chase money for him?" she asked.

"Don't be foolish — he never gets screwed," Uncle said. "The brother in Vancouver is the one who was unwise. Someone, who obviously doesn't know he is Tommy's brother, took the family for more than fifty million in a land swindle. If it were the Philippines or China or anywhere else in Asia, Tommy would look after it himself. Canada is another world. So a friend referred him to me. We have the contract. I had to cut our rate, but not that much."

"I need at least three days, and that's not a promise," she said.

"If Tam weren't the nephew of my friend... You think three days?"

"Minimum."

"Where are we?"

"I've found him. I think I've bought off the local muscle. Now I need to get my hands on Seto and get the money back to Tam."

"How much to buy off the locals?"

"One hundred thousand, upfront, all of it by wire."

"You know —"

"I know," Ava said, louder than she intended. "It can't be done any other way, and without them I'm nowhere. This is like a Chinese provincial backwater where one guy controls everything and nothing happens unless he says so. In this case, the main guy won't give the green light unless the money is sent to him upfront."

"He is that powerful? He is that insistent?"

"Yes and yes."

"Okay, Ava, I understand. Where do I send it?"

"I won't know until tomorrow."

"As soon as you know —"

"Uncle, I want to get out of here more than you want to make Tommy Ordonez the happiest man in the Philippines."

"Sorry," he said.

She wasn't used to getting apologies from Uncle. Normally if he made an error — and that was seldom enough — he'd correct it and tell her about the change in the situation without acknowledging a mistake had been made in the first place. And she, of course, would accept the change as a given and never mention the events that had preceded it. It was enough that they both knew; there was no reason for her to be disrespectful by remarking on it and no reason for him to explain himself. She guessed that he was feeling guilty about pushing Tommy Ordonez at her when the Tam job was still on the boil.

"Let me finish here," she said, "and then we'll make the Chews one big happy family."

Ava crawled into bed with the James Clavell novel. She slept amazingly well and didn't wake till just past eight. Skipping breakfast and Tom Benson, she went for a completely uneventful run. When she got back to the hotel, Patrick was asleep in the lobby, his head on the back of the chair, his mouth half open.

She tapped his arm. He snorted and his eyes flicked open, immediately alert.

"I was on a run," she said.

"Yeah, they told me," he said. "Here, the Captain wanted me to give this to you. It's what we could come up with on Seto last night." He handed her an envelope. "He's been coming here on and off for years, mainly to do fish business, but recently just to hang. He's never been a problem."

"Is that because someone decided to leave him alone or because he was saintly?"

"Who knows, but if he was left alone it was because he never went over the line."

"Who's the woman?"

"Anna Choudray. They've been together for about six years. She was a bar girl when they met. They aren't married but he must like her a lot 'cause she's the legal owner of the house in Malvern Gardens, lucky her. The Vietnamese is Joey Ng. He travels under an American passport, the same as Seto. He isn't new; he's been here with Seto quite a few times."

"I was told this is where Seto comes when things get too hot elsewhere."

"Could be. Like I said, he's trouble-free here."

She wiped sweat from her brow. "I need to shower and change. It will take me about half an hour. Will you stay and have breakfast with me?"

"Of course."

"This means that the Captain has accepted our arrangement?"

"I wouldn't be here otherwise."

"And you are my . . . liaison?"

"That isn't the word he used but the meaning is the same, I guess."

"Banking information?"

"In the envelope."

The shower could wait. Ava went directly to the business centre, opened the envelope, and sent an email with Robbins's bank particulars to Uncle and the Hong Kong accountant who handled their wire transfers. It was mid-evening there and nothing would move until the next morning, which meant that, given a twenty-four-hour transit time, the wire wouldn't get to Robbins until two full days from now. She didn't fancy spending two days doing nothing, so she asked the accountant to scan and email her a copy of the wire transmittal. It was being sent from the Kowloon Light and Power Bank, which was owned by some friends of Uncle, to the Cayman Islands branch of a Canadian chartered bank. Kowloon Light and Power was substantial enough that she was sure the Canadian bank wouldn't have any issues with the amount. In that case, maybe Robbins would accept the copy of the transmittal as confirmation and let her get started before he actually had the money.

It took her close to an hour to get things sorted out. That didn't seem to bother Patrick, who had fallen asleep again. A slight nudge wakened him. "Do you want some coffee?" she said.

"Sure, but not here. The coffee here is horrible."

They climbed into a Toyota truck sitting in the no-parking zone in front of the hotel. He weaved through the now all-too-familiar downtown terrain.

"I've already sent the bank directions. The wire should be done within the next twelve hours. I'll get you a copy of the confirmation once it's gone," she said.

"I don't need to know any of this, so it's best not to talk to me about it anymore. Just put the information in a sealed envelope. The Captain likes to keep details like that between himself and people like you. My directions are more basic."

"Such as?"

"Take Ng out and do what I can to help you with Seto." He looked hard at her. "The Captain says you're a debt collector. He says you must be a very special kind to come here by yourself and be able to wire $100,000 as if it were nothing."

"That's what I do for a living," she said. "Now, taking Ng out — how hard will that be?"

"Not a problem for us. How about Seto for you?"

She liked Patrick already. He was direct without being rude or aggressive, and he was confident and assertive.

"I'll meet him at Eckie's and try to convince him that it's in his best interests to cooperate with me," she said.

"What will you say? 'Pretty please, give me back whatever gazillions of dollars you scammed'?"

"Something like that," she laughed.

"Does it ever work?"

"You'd be surprised. Once they know I've found them and once they know I've located the money, most of them understand that I'm the best chance they have to give it back and maintain — how shall I say it? — their physical well-being. Mind you, this is me dealing with the Chinese — and all our clients are Chinese — in Hong Kong or New York or Toronto or Vancouver. They always assume that I've been sent by the triads, and that if they don't cut a deal with me they'll have four guys with machetes sitting beside their beds."

"The Captain thinks you are triad."

"I have no guys with machetes sitting back at the hotel," she said, smiling. "And I have no tattoos. Everyone knows that triads have tattoos."

"Do you think Seto will be as cooperative as your Chinese in Hong Kong?"

"Actually no, I don't. He thinks he's protected here. So I think I'm at Plan B already."

"So not much chit-chat?"

"No."

"What will you do?"

"Tell me first, how will you handle Ng?"

"Under our national security law we can detain anyone we suspect of anti-government activity for up to a week without laying charges and without providing a lawyer. They don't even get to make a phone call. We'll use that law to put Ng on ice for as long as you need. Now tell me about Seto."

"He seems to go to Eckie's every night. We'll confront him there. He's a scrawny little piece of shit — you shouldn't have any problem putting handcuffs on him and getting him out the door. We'll take him to his house. If the woman is in the club, she'll go with us. If she isn't, we'll deal with her at the house."

He didn't speak again until he stopped the truck at Donald's Doughnut Shop. She looked around; the neighbourhood was even more rundown than central Georgetown.

"I live over there," he said, pointing to a small red bungalow at the end of the street. "It's my mother's house."

They got out of the truck and entered the shop, sitting in the booth farthest from the door. The coffee wasn't instant but she didn't complain. Her doughnut was virtually oozing fat. She ate it silently.

"Seto owns a piece of Eckie's," Patrick said between bites. "That's how our people got to know him at first. Eckie's is not completely legal. By that I mean clubs in general aren't exactly legal, so if you want to operate one you have to make arrangements with the right people."

"Are there bouncers at the club, or might any of his partners choose to interfere with us?"

"If they know we're involved, everyone will stay out of the way. No see, no hear, no nothing."

"Then let's hope he goes to Eckie's."

"If we weren't involved, how would you — I mean, what do you do in other cases when people aren't co-operating?"

"There are always options," she said. "The most important thing is figuring out ahead of time what will work. If I think a direct approach will succeed, then I become direct. If I think there's going to be resistance, then I'm more discreet, less visible. In a case like Seto's, if I were acting alone I would use something like chloral hydrate to strengthen my position."

He raised an eyebrow. "Jesus, I haven't heard that mentioned in a while."

"I know, it's a little old-fashioned. But it's effective. There's something about waking up with your hands and feet bound, your eyes masked and mouth covered, that makes people want to be cooperative. It brings an unknown quality; it lets me create a bit of fantasy. Since I have you, that won't be necessary, but I'll still tape his eyes and mouth until we get to the house."

"No problem," he said.

"Where are you from?" she asked suddenly. "You and the Captain have a similar accent. I can't place it but I know it isn't from here."

"Barbados — we're both Bajans. My grandmother was his nanny, if you can believe that. He moved here more than thirty years ago and made his name, made his fortune. I was a boy in trouble back home when Gran called the Captain and asked him to take me on. So I came with my mother and my sister. It isn't Barbados, but we're doing okay."

"The Captain is an impressive man," she said.

"The Captain runs this poor excuse for a country," he said. "He keeps the animals in check."

She fought back an urge to comment on the potholes, brown water, and irregular power. "Thank goodness," she said.

"What are you going to do today?" he asked.

"I have a little shopping to do. Other than that I can't do very much until the Captain gives me the green light."

"I know." Patrick yawned. "I had a late night. I think I'll go to the gym and get myself revved. You want to come?"

"No, I ran this morning. I'm good."

"We were talking last night, Bobby and me, about the way you handled those two creeps. They're handy, both of them, so we couldn't figure out how you did it. I thought maybe you could show me at the gym."

"I practise bak mei," she said. "It isn't something you teach someone at a gym."

"Never heard of it."

"It's a Chinese martial art."

"Like karate, kung fu?"

"Like kung fu but not kung fu. No one makes movies about bak mei."

"What is it, then?"

"It's very old, very Chinese — Taoist in fact. It has never caught on in the Western world because it isn't pretty and it can't be made into a sport. It's purely functional, designed to inflict damage. And it can be lethal when applied to the extreme. I went relatively easy on those two."

"Do you use kicks?"

"Only below the waist."

"Nice," he said. "How did you learn this stuff?"

"I was already into martial arts and I was good, good enough that one of the teachers pulled me aside and asked if I had heard of bak mei. I hadn't. He explained that it was a secret art — in the old days, a forbidden art — and that it was only taught one-on-one: father to son, teacher to student. He asked me if I wanted to learn. When I said I did, he sent me to see Grandmaster Tang. I haven't stopped learning since."

"Show me some moves."

"It isn't something to be demonstrated."

"No juking and jiving?"

"Afraid not."

Patrick, thinking Ava was joking, waited, expecting her to get up and move into a fighting position. When she didn't, he said, "You aren't any fun."

"That's true enough."

"What do you want me to do?" he asked.

"I think I'd just like to go back to the hotel."

"You aren't any fun at all."

"That's still true."

An hour later, Ava was in her rattan chair with the James Clavell on her lap. Time would not move fast enough. She read for two hours and then was so restless she couldn't stay put anymore. She went down to the business centre, signed on, and then thought about Tommy Ordonez. It was one of her rules never to start thinking about the next case before the one she was working on was completed. She had done it twice and both times it had brought bad luck. She hesitated and then thought, *What the hell.* She was at least as curious as she was superstitious.

She googled Tommy Ordonez. He seemed to own half the Philippines. This job was enticing both in size and in terms of the participants. But why had Ordonez gone to Uncle? On any number of levels it didn't make any sense. Ava wondered what kind of deal Uncle had cut with him, or rather them. The older she got, the more inflexible she found herself becoming. If their rate was thirty percent, what did it matter if they were collecting ten million or a hundred million? The client was out the larger amount, and if she was their last hope, thirty percent was nothing. She loved Uncle and had enormous respect for him, but there were times when he was too accommodating with people who were above him in the power scheme. At some point she would have to talk to him about that. Not now, though.

For maybe the tenth time since she had been given Seto's account number at Barrett's Bank, she logged onto the Barrett's website. She hit the ACCESS YOUR ACCOUNT button and punched in the S&A account number. The program asked for the password. As before, she didn't even attempt to guess at one. She was leery of bank websites. They were sensitive in the extreme; if she entered the wrong password she was afraid it would trigger a reaction, and any reaction would not be to her benefit. She just wanted to confirm that the account was still active, and it was.

She figured the wire would be sent that evening and she would be able to get confirmation to the Captain the next morning. The money might even land in his account that day if she was lucky. If not, she would try to sweet-talk him into letting Patrick and her and whomever else they wanted to involve go after Seto tomorrow night.

Things had gone very well with this project. The money had been almost ridiculously easy to find, and Seto had become a sitting duck once she had located him. The only wrinkle had been the Captain and his crew. But if everything went according to plan, Tam would have most of his money back within twenty-four hours, and she would be on a plane back to Toronto the morning after.

(25)

THE WIRE HAD BEEN SENT THE NIGHT BEFORE, AND AVA had printed two copies of the confirmation. She called the Captain's office and was put directly through to Robbins.

"Ava, do you have some good news for me?"

"The wire went through last night. I have a copy of the confirmation. Can I bring it to you?"

"Is Patrick there?"

"I don't know. I haven't been downstairs yet."

"He should be there. Give it to him and ask him to bring it over to the office."

"I can bring it there myself."

"No, my dear, please just give it to Patrick."

"The money might be deposited into the account today," she said.

"That would be nice."

"If it isn't, I'm hoping you might take the copy of the confirmation at face value and let us deal with Seto tonight."

"That's possible," he said. "I don't like dragging things out unnecessarily. Let me see the wire and I'll tell Patrick how we are to proceed."

"Thank you."

Patrick was in the lobby reading a newspaper. He smiled when he saw her and held the paper out for her to see. There was a picture of the man whose nose she had crushed. "He claims he was walking along the seawall when he was viciously attacked by a woman with a cricket bat. The paper is urging people to be cautious until the police find the suspect."

"How stupid is that, to draw attention to himself that way?"

"He has a little life. For this morning at least he is in the spotlight. It happens all the time here. Something atrocious happens and instead of keeping quiet, the victims feel compelled to tell the world, or at least to tell Georgetown."

"Here," she said, handing him a hotel envelope. "Could you take this over to the Captain? He's waiting for it."

Ava was in the coffee shop working on her second cup of instant, which the waitress had agreed to make, when Patrick returned. The office, she figured, had to be in the neighbourhood.

He sat down, a contented look on his face. "The Captain sends his regards. We have the go-ahead for tonight."

She beamed. Good dim sum wasn't much more than a day away.

"How about Seto's friends? What have they been told?"

"The Captain has already had a chat with the one who counts. He'll make another courtesy call today to let him know it's going down tonight. The word will get out."

"Not prematurely?"

"You don't know the Captain," said Patrick. "Things get done the way he wants, when he wants — always. You have his word, and I'm here as proof of that. No one is going to warn Seto. No one would dare. The wrath of Captain Robbins is a terrible thing to experience."

"So how do we proceed?" she asked.

"My people are keeping an eye on Seto. The moment he leaves Malvern Gardens we'll know."

"If he doesn't follow the usual routine?"

"We'll work something out."

His casual manner took her aback. She was accustomed to working alone, to sweating every detail, to being thorough to the point of obsessive. Now she had to work with a team over which she had no control, and she had to accept that her plan was subject to the whims of not just Seto.

Patrick sensed her discomfort. "Ava, this is Guyana. At the end of the day, one way or another, you'll get Seto, because the Captain has said that's what will happen. If it's at Eckie's, great. If it's somewhere else, what does it matter?"

"What do you want me to do this afternoon?"

"Whatever you want. Go for a swim, go for a run, beat up some locals. I'll pick you up here at six and we'll go downtown, park near the restaurant, and wait for Seto."

Ava decided to go for another run. When she got back to the hotel, she showered and then went downstairs. She had toast and jam in the restaurant and killed some time on the computer, but it was still only four o'clock when she got back to her room. She turned on the television for the first time and watched old reruns of *M*A*S*H* and the *Bob Newhart Show*.

Six o'clock came and went without a word from Patrick. She checked and double-checked the kitbag she had packed with the odds and ends she would need for Seto. She also started getting her luggage organized for the trip home.

At six thirty she thought about calling Patrick and then held off, fearful of looking too anxious, like an amateur.

It was almost seven when her cellphone buzzed.

"Yes?"

"He's on the move, headed for downtown. I'll pick you up in five minutes. Be outside."

Patrick was at the entrance by the time she had worked her way downstairs. He looked at the kitbag in her hand and said nothing.

"Ng is with him, and the woman," he said as they left the hotel.

"The woman is good," Ava said.

They parked half a block from the restaurant and slumped down in the red Toyota truck. They didn't have to wait long. The Land Rover rumbled into the street and Ng parked it directly in front of the restaurant and jumped out. Seto took a bit longer and then stood by the back door, holding his hand out for the woman as she descended.

"How can they eat here every night?" Patrick asked.

"It's a Hong Kong thing," she said. "People there have incredibly small apartments, and getting outside is part of daily life. The fact that they also love to eat gives them the perfect excuse. There must be more restaurants per capita in Hong Kong than any other place on earth. And when they find a restaurant they like, they keep going to it."

"I should try this place sometime," he said.

"There will be two menus: one for Chinese, the other for . . . well, for non-Chinese."

"In that case I'll pass." Patrick looked around. "We can get out of the truck now if you want; they can't see us from inside. There's a roti shop over there that isn't bad. From the window we have a good view of the restaurant."

As they were about to get out of the truck a black Nissan sedan pulled alongside. The tinted window on the passenger's side slid down slowly and a black man with grey hair eased his head out towards them.

"Park near Eckie's," Patrick said to him. "They should be about an hour in the restaurant. Wait until Seto goes into the club before making a move on Ng. There's a woman with them. If she goes into the club we'll look after her. If she doesn't, you'll have to get her. Separate her from Ng. We'll need her with us."

The man nodded and rolled the window back up.

"They're a good team — experienced," he said to her as the Nissan left to position itself near Eckie's. "The Captain has given you some quality."

For what I'm paying, I should hope so, she thought.

The roti shack had three tables, all of them empty. They sat by the window, keeping the China World entrance in their line of sight. He ordered chicken curry and roti. She asked for plain fried rice and a ginger beer.

"Tell me," Ava said, "how does a man like Captain Robbins get into a position of such power in a country like this?"

"Do you mean how does a white man get into a position of such power in a country where ninety-five percent of the population is either black or Indian?"

"Yes, that's precisely what I mean."

Patrick bit his lower lip. It was question he could answer if he chose; he just had to decide whether he wanted to or not.

"The Captain was a policeman in Barbados. He came here as part of a Caribbean exchange program. That's one thing people don't understand about Guyana. Geographically it's in South America and we've got Venezuela and Brazil as neighbours, but culturally, socially, linguistically, we're part of the Caribbean. I mean, there are always Guyanese on the West Indies cricket team.

"At that time the Brits had already left, the blacks and East Indians were jockeying for power, transferring their hatred for the Brits to one another, and the Americans were sticking their noses — and putting their money — into the politics here. It was quite a mess. The Americans were looking for someone neutral, someone they could trust to be a pipeline for straight information, someone who could act as an honest broker between the blacks and Indians. There weren't many candidates. According to the Captain, he was about it. That's how it started."

"But to make it last as long as he has . . ."

"He did that himself. He didn't need the Americans to support him. You have to understand, he's about the only person in Guyana whom all the groups can support — because he's neutral, because colour doesn't matter to him. They trust him."

"And fear him?"

He ignored her question. "Those politicians — black and brown — they like to hear themselves talk. The Captain is always the quietest person in the room. He tells me, 'Patrick, listen, just listen. You'll be surprised how much you can learn.' Then there are the generals in our so-called army and the inspector general of the police, all of them with titles and uniforms and medals. You saw how the Captain dresses: blue jeans and plain shirts. That's his way. He doesn't need to play dress-up, he doesn't need to impress anyone. He's been in charge for more than twenty years; he doesn't need a fancy title. But you know, when he walks into a room with all those generals wearing all their medals, they're the ones who stand at attention. And they stay that way until he sits. I'm biased, I know that. He's like family to me. But I'm man enough to recognize a bigger man."

"I was told that he knows everyone's secrets, that he knows where all the bodies are buried, that the politicians are completely beholden to him," said Ava.

"Would you expect anything less?" Patrick said. "The politicians are window dressing, no more than that. The Captain keeps them on a leash. I don't ask how he does it; no one in Guyana does. We're just happy that he's here, keeping them under control. If it means he has to put a bit of fear into them, we're the better off for it."

"I wasn't being critical, just curious," she said.

Their food arrived. She picked at the rice. Patrick ate his chicken, dabbing the roti into the curry. When it was gone, he ordered another. "One more thing about the Captain," he said between bites, "is that he is really smart. I don't mean book-smart — though he is that too

— I mean people-smart. He can figure out anyone in ten minutes."

"What did he say about me?" she prodded.

"That you aren't what you appear to be, but by the time most people figure that out it's too late for them."

She shifted her attention from the plate to look at Patrick. His eyes were locked on the front entrance of China World. She didn't ask any more questions.

(26)

IT HAD BEEN DARK WHEN THEY'D ARRIVED, THEIR SIDE of the town being designated powerless for the evening. However, most of the stores and restaurants on the block were lit up. She could only imagine what it would be like walking the side streets on a moonless night. No wonder the crime rate was through the roof.

The name CHINA WORLD flickered in the window of the restaurant. The Chinese characters below the English lettering translated as "heavenly food." She couldn't remember ever seeing a Chinese restaurant whose English and Chinese names meant the same thing. Before she could file that thought away, Seto stood framed in the window. He was talking to a short Chinese man in an apron.

"I think he's about to leave," she said.

Patrick called a number from his cellphone. "Wake up, boys," he said.

"See the small guy in the apron?" he said to Ava. "He's one of our leading drug dealers; does most of the imports. He's also a friend of a friend. Until now it didn't occur to me that he might be involved with Seto and Ng. After all this is over I'll have to ask."

The trio exited the restaurant and climbed back into the Land Rover. Ava held her breath.

They followed the car as it lumbered two blocks and parked at Eckie's. Seto and the woman climbed down. Ava saw him say something to Ng, who was still in the Land Rover. The black Nissan was four spots farther along.

Patrick used his cellphone again. "Give them about ten minutes inside and then get Ng," he said. He reached over and opened the glove compartment. Ava saw a semi-automatic in an shoulder holster and several pairs of handcuffs. "We'll need two sets, I imagine," he said as he put on the holster.

"I want to tape their eyes and his mouth before we get them in the truck," she said.

"Just his?"

"Someone has to tell us the entry codes for the gate, and I'm sure the house is protected as well."

He nodded. "There's an alleyway behind the club with an exit leading to it. I'll park the truck there. There's no point in drawing more attention to ourselves than necessary."

They sat with their eyes fixed on the Nissan. At exactly the ten-minute mark the doors opened and two very large men, one the man with grey hair, emerged. They wore black jeans and black T-shirts. Ava glanced sideways at Patrick — he was dressed the same way. Two nights before, both he and Robert had been in black. *They're cops*, she thought.

She watched as the one with grey hair tapped on the driver's-side window of the Land Rover. It rolled down. The cop flashed some ID and motioned for Ng to step out.

Ng didn't move. She saw the cop's neck muscles stiffen as he stepped back. He screamed, "Fuck you, you Asian piece of shit," as he raised a boot and kicked the car door.

Ng stuck his head out the window and said something. The cop pulled his gun and aimed at him. The door swung open and Ng jumped to the ground. Again she could see him talking, and she could imagine what he was saying. She was sure the word *friend* was being dropped.

The Captain's men outweighed Ng by at least a hundred pounds each, and when one of them grabbed him by the collar and ran him towards the club's wall, he hit it with a thud. In the light cast by the flashing Eckie's sign, she could see blood on Ng's forehead and under his nose. She tried to muster some sympathy for him but came up short.

The cop yanked Ng's arms behind his back, handcuffed him, then jerked him backwards, making him fall onto the sidewalk. Then he grabbed him by the hair and hauled him to his feet. Ng's head was turned towards the Toyota. All Ava could see in his face was confusion and fear.

"Are you ready to go?" Patrick said.

"Drive."

He cut down a side street and into the alley. On what looked like a fire door someone had crudely painted ECKIE'S. "Our exit," Patrick said.

They got out of the truck and walked back to the front door. Ava felt a rush of adrenalin.

The club was badly lit, but she could make out a circular dance floor surrounded by booths. There was also a bar, two sets of curtains, and an exit. What little light there was, was trained on the dance floor. At best the booths were in semi-darkness.

"I can't see a thing," Ava said.

"There they are," Patrick said, heading towards the booth closest to the bar. She trailed behind him, almost unconsciously trying to stay invisible.

Seto didn't notice them. He was kissing Anna Choudray, his hand stuck down her blouse, fondling her right breast; the nipple was half exposed. Patrick paused and Ava wondered if he was enjoying the sex.

"Seto," Patrick shouted, holding a badge in midair. "I need you and the woman to come with me."

"What the fuck?"

Ava noted that this was voiced as a demand, not a question, and she knew that her hundred-thousand-dollar investment had been well spent.

"Just get up," Patrick said.

"Or what?"

She could see Seto clearly now. He wore a black suit with a crisp white shirt. She figured he couldn't weigh more than a hundred and thirty pounds. His eyes skittered left and right as if he was trying to figure out if this was a joke. "Don't you know who I am?" he yelled.

"I know exactly who you are," Patrick said. "Now you and the woman get up or I'll come in there and help you."

"Fuck you," Seto said.

Patrick reared back and punched Anna on the side of the head, catching her on the ear and driving her into the back of the booth with an audible thump.

"*Fucccckkkk!*" Seto screamed. "Don't you know who I am? Talk to General Swandas, for fuck's sake. I'm with him. Call him. *Call him.*"

"This has gone several levels above the general," Patrick said. "Now for the last time, get your skinny ass out of there and bring the woman with you."

Seto looked at the gun Patrick was now holding in his girlfriend's face. "You wouldn't —"

"You have five seconds."

Seto slid sideways, bringing her with him.

"Turn around," Patrick said.

Seto pulled the woman to her feet. She held her hand over her ear, tears flowing down her cheeks. Patrick handcuffed him first. When he put the cuffs on Anna, he had to wrench her hand away from her head. "Sorry to do this, but if your asshole boyfriend was more cooperative this would not have been necessary."

"This is a mistake," Seto insisted. "Call the general."

"Here, you call him," Patrick said, holding out his phone to Seto. "If he answers and agrees to help you, I'll shoot both you and the woman right here."

Seto's face collapsed, his confidence gone, the fear visible in eyes that darted around the club looking for help — which wasn't coming. "What do you want?" he said.

"In time, in good time," Patrick said. "First we have to get you out of here."

He led them to the fire door. Ava couldn't help noticing that every eye in the club was focused somewhere else. It was as if they didn't exist.

She had her kitbag in her hand. "Put them against the wall," she said to Patrick when they were outside. She took out a roll of duct tape and wrapped it around their eyes. "Turn him around now," she said. She tore off a small strip and sealed his mouth. "Okay, let's go."

Ava and Patrick helped them get into the back seat.

Anna pressed herself against the window as if she were trying to get as far away from Seto as possible. She was sobbing so hard she was having difficulty catching her breath.

Ava reached back, grabbed the woman's knee, and squeezed until she had her attention. "Listen to me. When we get to the house, you're going to tell us the entry code and whatever information we need to get in the front door. I'm telling you this now so you have time to think about it and be prepared when I ask. I don't want to ask twice."

Anna didn't reply.

Ava squeezed harder. "I need you to say yes."

"Y-yes."

To Ava the drive to the house seemed to take forever; she could only imagine how long it felt for Seto and the woman. Neither she nor Patrick spoke. They both knew how intimidating silence could be.

When they pulled up to the gate, Ava asked, "Anna, is there anyone in the house?"

"No."

"Good. Now tell me the code."

"Eighty-eight, eighty-eight, eight."

"How Chinese," Ava said.

"What do you mean?" Patrick asked.

"Superstition. The number eight in Chinese is pronounced *ba*, and that sounds like the word for wealth. Two figure eights resemble the way "double joy" is written. Having an eight in your address, on your licence plate, or in your phone number is thought to bring good luck, and the more eights the better. Except, of course, for Seto in this instance," Ava said as she punched in the numbers.

The gate swung open. Patrick parked the Toyota next to the Mercedes. "The house code?" Ava asked.

"The same as the gate," Anna said.

They walked to the front door. Ava held the woman by the elbow and Patrick had a firm grip on the back of Seto's suit jacket. The walkway was uneven, making the blindfolded pair stumble; Ava held her charge steady and Patrick yanked Seto straight.

The house was remarkable in at least one way: when they entered, Ava saw a staircase directly in front of her, running straight from the door to the second floor. For anyone Chinese it was an unthinkable design. It would take only a minimal understanding of feng shui to know that it would bring the worst possible luck to the owners of the house. She figured that Seto, or most probably the woman, had bought the house as is.

To the left of the unlucky staircase was a dining room furnished with six chairs and a naked table. No sideboard, no plants, no pictures. It looked as if the room had never been used. The rectangular room on the right was about forty square metres in area, and all it contained was a cheap-looking leather couch, two beanbag chairs, and a large LCD television.

Ava walked towards the kitchen at the back of the house, pushing Anna in front of her. The room held a glass table with three napkins on it and a bowl of fruit, plus a counter large enough for a double sink and a prep area on either side. There was a cutting board and a set of knives in one prep area and the other had a substantial spice rack and jars of flour, sugar, and cereal.

"Bring Seto back here," she shouted to Patrick.

Seto scuffled into the kitchen. The house was air-conditioned but there were beads of sweat on his forehead. “Take off his jacket,” she said.

Patrick undid the handcuffs, removed the jacket, and then put the cuffs back on, adding a hard tug on Seto’s arms for good measure.

Ava set Seto on a chair, lifted his hands over the chair back, and pulled them down behind. She then knelt down and grabbed his ankles. She spread them until they were aligned with the chair legs and taped his ankles to them.

“Pass me the jacket,” she said to Patrick. She quickly went through the pockets, extracting a wallet.

“Now, where is his computer?”

“Upstairs,” the woman said.

“Let’s go,” Ava said. “Patrick, stay with Seto.”

There were four rooms on the second floor. Two were being used as bedrooms, one was empty, and the fourth was a makeshift office. Ava took Anna into the master bedroom, which was furnished with a king-size four-poster bed made of heavy mahogany and matching massive wooden dressers; one wall was entirely mirrored.

The bed was littered with decorative pillows. Ava pushed them onto the floor and then told Anna to climb onto the bed. Then Ava taped her ankles together and taped her mouth. “Now stay here. Don’t move,” she said.

Ava walked into the office and sat at Seto’s desk. It had two drawers on each side and a laptop computer on top. Ava turned on the computer, and while it was booting up she went through the drawers. They were mostly empty, except for one, in which there was a copy of a plane ticket and two cancelled boarding passes. Seto had come to Georgetown from Port of Spain via Miami.

There were also two passports. One was American, in the name of Jackson Seto, and the other Chinese, in the name of Seto Sun Kai.

She opened his wallet. There were four credit cards, all in the name of Jackson Seto, and a Washington state driver's licence in the same name with the address she had visited in Seattle. He also had a Hong Kong ID card under the name Seto Sun Kai.

The computer flickered to life and asked her for a password. That could wait; she turned her attention to the rest of the room. The only things that interested her were six cardboard filing boxes pushed up against a wall.

When she opened the first box, she could see that Seto was neat and organized Everything was filed alphabetically, and when she looked in the Barrett's Bank folder, the paperwork was ordered by date. She took the folder over to the desk and quickly scanned the documents from the oldest — a copy of the signature card from when he had opened his account — to the newest, which included a recent online bank statement. She had her notebook in her kitbag, and the account number on the statement matched the one she had written down.

The account was in the name of S&A Investments. There was only one authorized signature: Seto's. She checked the dates. The account had been open for more than ten years but had been almost inactive until three years ago, when deposit activity picked up. The wire transfers of Tam's money were the largest deposits by far, but Seto had been squirreling other funds away all along, mainly in the range of ten to twenty thousand dollars. Some much larger deposits had been made over the past year; she assumed that was the money Seafood Partners had been scamming from the Indian and Indonesian fish guys.

The two Tam wire transfers brought the account total to more than seven million American dollars. It was the kind of surprise Ava enjoyed.

She went downstairs to join the boys. Patrick sat quietly on the kitchen counter, jiggling his legs to some music in his head. "Did you find what you were looking for?" he asked.

She put Seto's passports, his Hong Kong ID card, and the Barrett's file on the kitchen table. "I didn't do badly." She moved closer to Patrick. "I'm going to speak to him in Cantonese," she said.

Seto was slumped in the chair, his chin almost on his chest. She reached for the tape on his mouth and ripped it off. He yelled in pain.

"Seto Sun Kai, what made you think we would not come after you? And what made you think we would not find you?"

He shook his head as if he was confused, then licked his lower lip. She wondered if it had sunk in that she had used his Chinese name.

"Why would you or anyone else come after me? I haven't done anything." His voice was hoarse, his mouth dry from stress.

Ava took a glass from the cupboard and filled it from the tap. The water was a lighter colour than the hotel's. *Must be the neighbourhood*, she thought.

"Here, drink," she said, holding the glass to his lips.

He hesitated.

"It's your own fucking tap water," she snapped.

He took a careful sip. "Where is Ng?" he asked.

"Gone and not coming back."

"I don't believe you."

"Believe this: You don't have friends here anymore. No one is going to come to your aid. This is strictly between us now, and how it goes and how it ends is your choice."

"Who sent you?"

"I work for people who are friends of Andrew Tam. You remember Andrew Tam?"

"Where are you from?"

"Hong Kong."

He became still. She knew he was now fully aware of his situation. She knew he would be thinking about how to extract himself from it. She knew that when he finished examining his options, he would be left with the one she wanted him to choose. But she also knew it wouldn't stop him from trying other ways out.

"We did business, just business, Andrew and me. There were some problems with customers and I had to step in and salvage what I could, for all our sakes."

"So you're telling me you were looking after Andrew's best interests."

"We had inventory that was shit. I had it reworked and repacked, that's all. It couldn't have been sold any other way."

"And you discussed this with Andrew?"

"There wasn't time. And besides, he was just the money man. What did he know about the actual business?"

"Not enough, I guess," she said. "This product, did you sell it all?"

"I did."

"Did you get paid?"

He paused. She could almost see his mind whirring away, calculating just how big a lie he could safely tell. "For most of it," he said.

"How much did you get paid?"

His head rolled back as if she were holding a knife to his throat. "About three million," he said, squeezing the words out.

"When did you plan to send it back to Andrew Tam?"

"When things settled. I haven't had time; we just got paid."

"But you do plan to send it back to Andrew?"

"Of course, of course."

"Seto Sun Kai," Ava said gently, "you are a thief and a liar."

She reached into her kitbag and removed the stiletto, flicked it open, and pressed its point into his thigh. It pierced his pants and then his skin. It was a prick, not much more. Still, he jumped, startled. His leg twitched. "Don't," he said.

She moved the knife up his leg and stuck the point into his genitals. He flinched and strained to move back.

The knife tracked up his chest and onto his face. Ava rested the tip in the soft flesh just above his eye. Sweat from his brow trickled down his nose and both sides of his face. She was about to say something about the knife but realized it wasn't necessary. Seto understood well enough without the theatrics.

"Seto Sun Kai," she said calmly, "let me tell you what I know and then let me tell you what I need to know. I know why you had a problem with the shrimp. I know the games you and George Antonelli played with it. I know how the shrimp were moved, who repackaged them, and where they were sold. I know how much you got for them. I know about the little bank in Texas where the money was sent. I know that the little bank wired the money to an account in the British Virgin Islands. I have copies of the transfers, so I know to which bank they were sent and I know the account in which they were deposited. I know you are the sole signing authority on that account. Now, there are two things I don't know. Do you want to guess?"

He shook his head, sweat dripping onto her hand and the knife.

"I don't know the password to your computer upstairs, and I don't know the password for your BVI bank account."

Seto grimaced and said nothing.

She waited. A minute passed, maybe more.

"Seto Sun Kai, I'm waiting."

"It isn't that easy," he said.

She felt her first flush of irritation. "I really don't want to hurt you, or the woman upstairs," she said, increasing the pressure on the knife tip.

"The password for the computer is 'waterrat,'" he said in a rush.

"Your zodiac sign?" she asked.

"Yes."

"And for the bank account?"

"Eighty-eight, sixty-six, eighty-eight, sixty-six."

"Thank you."

"It won't do you any good," he said.

She noticed that he was beginning to sweat again and his voice had tightened. This wasn't where she had thought they were going. "And why not?"

"There's a limit to the amount of money I can take out of the account electronically."

"You can access the account through the Internet, yes?"

"Yes."

"You can transfer money out of the account, yes?"

"Yes, but like I said, it's restricted."

"What do you mean?"

"I can only withdraw up to $25,000 per day."

She saw his left foot begin to shake. He was scared, and she began to think he might be telling her the truth. "I don't believe you."

"That's how we set it up. We never had that much in the account until last year, so it was never a problem."

Ava picked up the Barrett's file from the kitchen table. She leafed through it, taking out the monthly statements and the attachments, and read them more closely than she had upstairs. Patrick watched her, confused about what had just transpired.

After ten minutes she said, "There was a withdrawal eighteen months ago of $335,000, and then another ten months ago of $200,000, and then a third just three months ago of another $400,000."

"How many are there for $25,000 or less?" he said.

"Admittedly, a hell of a lot more."

"Anything under $25,000 I did electronically. I was sending money to George's accounts in Atlanta and Bangkok and to my account in Seattle. Those other three withdrawals I did in person."

"What do you mean?"

"I went to the BVI. I went to the bank. I presented a written request for a certified cheque along with my American passport and one other form of photo ID, usually my driver's licence. They drew up a release form and I signed it. They photocopied my passport and driver's licence and dated the copies, and I signed those too. Then they gave me the cheque."

"Who does that anymore?" she said.

"The account was opened before Internet banking took off," he said. "And Barrett's is a conservative bank. They're paranoid about money laundering and gave me a hard enough time just opening an account."

"What if you dropped dead?"

"George has the power of attorney, and that is recorded at the bank. He would need to show up and go through the same shit I did."

"Can't you request a change in the amounts?"

"Only by doing it in person."

Seto was telling her the truth. She knew he was — there was no reason for him to lie. But that didn't help quell her anger: anger about making too many assumptions, about thinking the deal was closed, about having dared google Tommy Ordonez. She had jinxed herself. She had broken one of her own rules and now she was paying for it. The only mistake she hadn't made was to tell Andrew Tam his money was on the way.

"Patrick, look after him for me," she said abruptly. "I have to go upstairs for a minute."

He looked at her questioningly but she was already halfway out of the kitchen.

She went upstairs and checked in on Anna on her way to Seto's office. She was curled on the bed, crying softly to herself. Ava closed the bedroom door so she wouldn't have to listen.

The computer was still on. Ava typed WATERRAT and

the screen opened up. Then she tried to access the Internet and was told it wasn't currently available. She waited. On the fourth attempt she finally got online.

She went to the Barrett's Bank's home page and clicked on ACCOUNTS. She input the account number and then the password. The S&A bank account came to life. She checked the balance: $7,237,188.22. There was a list of options for her to pursue, and one of them was WIRE TRANSFER. She clicked on RECIPIENT DETAILS. She was going to type in Andrew Tam's bank information until she realized she had left her notebook downstairs, so she typed in her own bank data. Under AMOUNT TO BE SENT she requested $50,000. Then she hit the SEND button. The request was immediately flagged.

Ava appeared calm and focused when she walked back into the kitchen.

"What the hell happened to you?" Patrick asked.

"I have a problem," she said.

"I guessed."

"I need to think about it for a while."

"I have good ears if you want to talk it through."

She was about to dismiss the idea when she realized that she was going to need help no matter what she decided to do, so she might as well bring him on side sooner rather than later. "Let's go into the living room," she said.

They sat side by side on the leather couch, which smelled of cigarette smoke, and she told Patrick about her problem. The only thing she didn't — and wouldn't — tell him was the total amount of money involved.

"It sounds to me like you're going to have to take him to the BVI if you want to get that money back," he said. "Or spend the next few months transferring $25,000 a day, though I can't even begin to imagine the things that could go wrong with that idea."

"It has to be done quickly or chances are it won't get done. Is there any other choice?"

"What do you think?"

"I think I'm screwed," she said.

"How's that?"

"As I said, the quicker you move, the better your chances are to succeed. In my business you strike when guys like Seto are vulnerable, scared, and within your control. The longer the process takes, the more they begin to think they can find a way out. But how do I get him to the BVI without getting their Customs or police involved? All he has to do is open his mouth and scream bloody murder. And believe me, it will occur to him — if I can get him there. He'll talk himself into thinking he can get away with this. He'll figure if he can lose me, he has enough money to hide somewhere we can't find him. We always do find them in the end, but the problem is that the money is often gone by then."

"And if you can get him there, how do you deal with the bank?"

"There's no point worrying about the bank unless I can get him to the BVI."

"You need to talk to the Captain," Patrick said.

"What can the Captain do?"

"I'm going to call him," he said. "Don't go anywhere."

She sat in the kitchen while she waited for Patrick to return. Seto kept rotating his head as if he had a stiff neck. She felt like snapping the fucking thing.

The front door opened and Patrick stepped back inside. "I have to go meet with the Captain. I'll be back in a while."

(27)

PATRICK DIDN'T COME BACK UNTIL AFTER TEN O'CLOCK. Ava hated the thought of the two men discussing her business without her. The longer he was gone the more irritated she became, and by the time the door opened again she was really angry. Patrick walked in with the two men from outside Eckie's, the cops who had taken Ng.

"You and I are going to see the Captain," he said. "The boys will look after things here until we get back." He saw the look on her face and said, "I tried to call. Your cellphone was off."

She realized he was right about the phone, and bit back an irritable remark. Then she picked up the Barrett's file and forced it into her kitbag. She wasn't leaving anything behind for them to look through.

"What did he say?" she asked as she climbed into the Toyota truck.

"Who?"

"For God's sake, Patrick, you know who."

"He said he wanted to see you, that's all. I explained the difficulty and he said he wanted to see you. Nothing more than that."

"So this could be for nothing?"

"I can't say for sure, but normally the Captain doesn't waste his time on nothing."

She felt a twinge of hope. "Where are we going?"

"The doughnut shop. It's close by."

The entire area was in utter darkness except for the odd flicker of a candle or flare from a flashlight. The shop, though, was lit up like Times Square. The massive figure of the Captain filled its window, a plate of doughnuts in front of him.

"I'll wait here," Patrick said as he parked the truck.

The Captain gave her a little wave when she walked in. "I ordered you coffee," he said, pointing to a cup. "Patrick said you liked it."

In the bright light he looked even whiter than she remembered. And in the small confines of the shop he looked even larger, a mountain of a man, and she was again taken aback by how startlingly blue his eyes were. If she had been meeting him for the first time, the impression would have been overwhelming.

She steadied herself and sat down. "We have to stop meeting like this," she said.

His eyes twinkled, amused maybe, curious certainly, involved most definitely. "We have a problem, I hear."

She noticed his use of *we*. This was, at the very least, going to cost her money. "We do," she said.

"Unfortunate."

"For no one more than me."

"Seto was either rather clever or rather stupid. Patrick wasn't sure which because he said you spoke to him in Chinese."

"It was necessary for him to understand that I had been sent from Hong Kong."

"And all that entails, implied or otherwise."

"Implied."

"But still effective."

"Normally."

"So you got what you wanted except for a minor twist?"

"If you want to call it minor."

The Captain bit into a chocolate-coated doughnut. "I eat these every day and then rush home to take my cholesterol medication," he said.

"Do you have a way to resolve this minor twist?"

"Yes, I probably do. But as I said to Patrick, what's the point of exerting all that effort — and spending all that money — getting you and Seto there if the bank won't cooperate?"

"I'll handle the bank."

"You sound so confident."

"Just get me and Seto there and I'll find a way to handle the bank."

"You will find a way or you have a way? The difference is not inconsequential. I mean, you're asking to us spend a considerable amount of capital — both financial and personal — assisting you to get to the British Virgin Islands. What if you fail? How do we get compensated?"

"How much do you want?" she asked.

"No, no, no," he said, looking offended by the question. "You're going about this in entirely the wrong way. This is not just about money. This is about making use of friends and contacts whom I don't want to embarrass if things go awry. Friends and contacts whom I don't want subjected to questions from their lords and masters. Friends and contacts I still want to have five years from now."

"So this isn't about money?"

"I said this is not *just* about money."

"What do you want from me?" she asked.

"A plan. I want you to give me a plan for extracting the money from the bank. If I think the plan can work, then we can move on to the other details."

It was, she thought, not an unreasonable request. It was even, she thought, a perfectly sensible request. He could have demanded more money, found a way to shuffle her and Seto to the BVI or somewhere close by, and then washed his hands of them both as he pocketed the funds. The only problem was that he was now becoming a partner, and the cost of business had just skyrocketed. It was a good thing Seto had that extra two million in his account.

"I'll have something by tomorrow," she said, having no idea how.

"Good. Tell Patrick when you're ready to chat and I'll make myself available." He waved his arm at the shop. "We meet here more often than not — we own it. There's a camera overhead and microphones dotted about here and there. I like to bring my political friends here. They think I'm slumming," he said smoothly.

Ava wasn't sure she believed him. If it was true and he thought sharing that confidence with her would earn trust, he was going to be disappointed. In her eyes the Captain was now more dangerous.

"I'd like to go back to the hotel; I don't need the distractions at the house. Can you leave your men there overnight?"

"Consider it done."

(28)

AVA BOUGHT A BOTTLE OF WHITE WINE AT THE HOTEL bar and carried it in an ice bucket to her room. The air conditioning had been turned off again. She swore as she restarted it. Then she poured herself a glass and settled into the rattan chair. "Time to think," she said to herself.

It took her an hour to create a scenario that just might work. She called Patrick. "Where are you?"

"At Seto's house."

"Could you come and get me?"

Ava was quiet in the truck. She could tell that Patrick was anxious to ask her questions. But there was nothing to be said until she had a firmer grasp on the plan, and when she did it would be the Captain she would speak to first.

Seto was sitting in the kitchen, still handcuffed and taped to the chair. She thought he was sleeping until he raised his head at the sound of feet crossing the tiled floor. She touched him on the arm and said in Cantonese, "I need your email password."

"Waterrat."

The man has no imagination, she thought. She had

the Barrett's Bank file in her hand. She opened it and looked at some of the most recent correspondence. Several names and email addresses were involved.

"Who is your primary contact at Barrett's?"

"Jeremy Bates."

"Is he the manager?"

"Yeah. It's a small staff. Jeremy handles most of the clients."

She climbed the stairs to his office. One of the cops sat on the floor outside the master bedroom. "Everything okay?" she asked.

"The woman started wailing a while ago. I had to shut her up."

Ava didn't ask how.

The computer was still online. She accessed Seto's email account and brought up his address book. There was a Jeremy Bates listed. She checked it against the email address she had in the Barrett's file. They matched. She then hit MESSAGES SENT, typed in BATES, and requested a search. There were close to twenty emails that had gone back and forth. She took notice of Seto's style. His tone was more formal than she had thought it would be. Also more candid — Seto hadn't been reluctant to discuss his financial affairs.

She began composing an email to Jeremy Bates.

Hi, Mr. Bates,

I'm coming to Road Town on February 26 or 27. I will be making a wire transfer to Hong Kong in the amount of $7,000,000. I would appreciate it if you could have the paperwork organized for me.

> I will be bringing a Ms. Ava Lee with me to the office. She is the accountant for the firm in Hong Kong that we are doing business with. Ms. Lee is there to confirm the wire transfer in the amount specified. You have my permission to share any and all information regarding the S&A account with her.
>
> Once our travel arrangements have been confirmed I will contact you to set a date and time for us to meet at your office.
>
> Yours sincerely,
> Jackson Seto.

She clicked the SAVE DRAFT icon.

It was lunchtime in Hong Kong. She phoned Uncle. "I'm still in Guyana and I'm still working on getting this project finished," she said quickly. "It's going to be two days more, maybe three, maybe four. I'm getting there, but progress is slower than expected."

"Any specific reason for the delay?"

"I have to go to the BVI."

She could almost feel his grip tightening on the phone. "That wasn't the plan," he said.

"The plan had to be changed. The outcome will be the same."

"Are you going alone?"

"No," she said. "Seto is coming with me, and I'm going to bring Derek down to help."

"Is it that complicated?"

"I just need an extra pair of capable hands," she said. Uncle would be even more nervous now, knowing she had to bring Derek Liang into the picture. He had worked with her on five other occasions, and every one of them had been problematic or worse.

"If you think it is necessary," he said quietly, after a pause.

At the very outset of their relationship, Ava had been present at a meeting between Uncle and a Macau businessman who wanted to hire them. Despite his need for their assistance, he played his cards close to his chest, giving them the absolute minimum amount of information. Uncle had grown impatient with the man's vagueness and began asking questions that became more and more pointed. Finally the man threw up his hands and said, "Believe me, you have enough information. Trust me, trust me — you have everything you need."

Uncle had refused the assignment. As they rode the hydrofoil back to Hong Kong he said to Ava, "Whenever someone says, 'Believe me,' or 'Trust me,' and can't give you a reason to do so that you can wrap your arms around, run the other way. For me they are the most dangerous words anyone can utter; they are the refuge of the weak."

In all the years since, those words had never crossed her lips. The day she had to ask for his trust would be the day she was no longer working with him. And she liked to believe that the same was true in reverse. Even if Uncle was full of reservations, he would never express them. His confidence in her was complete, and even if things went horribly bad — which they sometimes did — he never second-guessed her.

"Yes, I do think it is necessary."

"Is there anything else?

"Do you remember the time I used Fong Accounting as a cover?"

"Yes."

"I need to do it again."

"Do you still have the business card?"

"I do."

"What are the circumstances?"

"When I get to the BVI, I'll be calling on Seto's bank, Barrett's, and I'm going as an accountant. The bank may call Fong to confirm my identity. It's a long shot that they will, but it's better to play it safe."

"What name is on the card?"

"Ava Lee."

"Okay, I'll talk to Mr. Fong and we'll set it up. Is there anything you'd like the office to tell any callers?"

"I'm travelling in the Caribbean — on business, mind you. And you could tell them to offer to provide my cell-phone number if the caller wants to reach me."

"Is that all?"

"No. We'll need to send more money to our friends in Guyana."

He didn't react right away. She could only imagine the questions that were raging through his head. They were already out of pocket more than $100,000 and now she was asking him to send more. Bringing Derek in would cost at least $10,000. If she didn't collect from Seto, how big a loss would they be looking at?

She cut him off before he could speak. "Uncle, I've found more money than Tam is owed — a lot more. We'll get our full commission plus a bonus on top of that."

"What is the amount we need to send?"

"I don't know; I'm still negotiating," she said. "All I know is that Tam's money isn't going to be recovered anytime soon unless we make the investment."

"When will you know?"

"Tomorrow. No later than tomorrow."

"I'll expect your call," he said.

"Uncle, I'm sorry about this. I know you're anxious to get started with Tommy Ordonez."

"He'll have to wait. You look after yourself. You be careful."

Ava next dialled Derek Liang's cellphone number. She didn't reach him until the third attempt. When she did, she could hardly hear him speak over the music that was booming in the background. He was a karaoke junkie and fancied himself as Jackie Cheung, Hong Kong's biggest Cantonese pop star. She yelled at him to go outside.

She had known Derek for six years. They had been introduced by their bak mei instructor, who thought that his only two students should get acquainted. Derek joked that their teacher had visions of them mating and producing the ultimate fighting machine. Even if her sexuality wouldn't get in the way of that happening, Derek would be close to her last choice as a partner. He was the only son of a wealthy Shanghai trader and had been sent to Toronto to get a university education. He had dropped out during his second year and devoted himself to martial arts, customized sports cars, karaoke, and women. She didn't think she had seen him twice with either the same woman or the same car.

But Derek was smart and he was tough — very tough. Over six feet tall, lean and chiselled, well-spoken in English and three Chinese dialects, and a tasteful, conservative dresser when he chose, he made a hell of an impression. He and Ava had posed as a couple several times. Hand in hand, they drew stares everywhere they went. Now they were about to do it again.

"I need you to go to the British Virgin Islands," she said.

"When?"

"Tomorrow, if possible."

"I'll be meeting you there?"

"Yes, but I'm not sure when I'll arrive. Could be a day or two later."

"I'm sure I can find something to amuse me."

"We'll need a suite — a big one, as big as you can get. Someone else will be travelling with us. Can you look after getting the suite?"

"Of course."

"Email me when you've made the arrangements."

Ava paid Derek two thousand dollars a day plus expenses. The first time they worked together he had tried to refuse the money. He said he didn't need it, which was true enough. Ava had ranted at him in Cantonese, which is close to the perfect language for hurling abuse, with its harsh consonants and piercing tone. He took the money and never questioned the arrangement again. For her it was strictly business. If he worked for no money, she would be indebted to him. If she paid, he was indebted to her.

She opened the email she had drafted to Jeremy Bates and read it over. Ava decided it didn't sound authentic and tried again.

Dear Mr. Bates,

I am arriving in the BVI in the next day or two. I am bringing with me a Ms. Ava Lee, who I am introducing to you via this email. She is the accountant for a firm in Hong Kong that we are going to partner with. I am going to be doing a wire transfer in the amount of $7,000,000 to the firm. Ms. Lee will be with me to confirm the transaction, and I would appreciate it if the bank would treat her as my associate. She has complete access to all of our banking records, and by way of this correspondence I am authorizing the bank to provide her with any and all additional information she needs. As soon as our travel arrangements are finalized, I will contact you to set up a time for us to come to your offices.

Sincerely,
Jackson Seto

That's better, she thought, and hit SEND.

It was almost midnight. Ava wasn't tired, so she headed downstairs to find Patrick. He was on the couch, watching television.

"Could you call the Captain for me, please?" she asked.

"Now?" he said, looking at his watch, a Panerai that would have cost about five thousand dollars if it were real.

"Yes, tell him I'm ready to chat. I don't want to wait until morning."

"I'm not sure this is a good idea."

"Give me his number and I'll call him myself."

Patrick lifted himself off the couch with a grunt. "Wait here," he said.

He went outside to phone the Captain. She wondered what they could be discussing that they didn't want her to hear. He was back inside in less than a minute, holding out the phone to her. "He wants to talk to you."

She took the phone. "Hello."

"Go somewhere we can speak in private," the Captain said.

Ava climbed the stairs to Seto's office, closing the door behind her. "I'm alone," she said.

"I didn't expect to hear from you quite so quickly."

"It's mid-morning in Hong Kong. If we're going to wire more money it could be done in the next few hours. Why waste an entire day?"

"So you have concocted a plan?"

"I know how to get back what is owed."

"You are a clever girl."

She assumed he was being sarcastic. "It can be done, and with no fuss."

"Would you like to share it?"

"I have to manage Seto; I have to keep him on ice," she began, and then outlined her plan. "If this works — and I don't know why it wouldn't — it will come down to my ability to convince the bank manager to release the funds. And I think I've already created the framework for that to succeed." When she finished detailing what she had done, she added, "I need you to understand that I'm not about to do anything that will put you at risk with any BVI officials or with Barrett's Bank. It will be my name and my reputation on the line."

"It sounds reasonable," he said, "but it still requires a leap of faith."

"Yes, I know, but I have thought this through. It is entirely doable."

"Ms. Lee, I am inclined to believe you," he said quietly. "Maybe because it's so late and my mind is not fully functional."

Maybe because you stand to make at least another $100,000, she thought. *Maybe because all this stuff about making sure I had a workable plan was just so you could strengthen your bargaining position.* "Thank you, Captain, I really appreciate your support," she said.

He ignored her posturing. "So now we need to talk about the details."

"How do you propose getting us there?" she asked.

She had expected him to sidestep her question but he didn't. "By private plane. Actually a government plane. Nothing fancy — a turboprop — but the airstrip on Beef Island can't handle much more than that. It's about two and a half hours from here. The best time to land would be evening. It'll be quieter, and the fewer people who see you the better. Customs and Immigration will have to be notified of your arrival. We'll look after that, of course. You'll be waved through," he said.

"Sounds good."

"This doesn't mean that anything goes, though. You do understand that?"

"Explain."

"Well, we can't have Seto taped up like a mummy. No handcuffs either. Our friends there expect us to be discreet . . . Can you keep Seto under control without those inhibitors? We can't have him causing a ruckus."

"Seto will be sleeping by the time we land," she said. "A friend of mine will meet us at the airport. His name is Derek Liang. I need you to tell the BVI officials who he is and arrange permission for him to meet me at the plane when we land."

The Captain laughed, a laugh that turned into a cough. "I really must give up these cigars," he said.

"Bless you."

"No, bless you, Ava Lee. You are indeed a clever girl. Does the presence of this Mr. Liang mean you won't need our physical assistance on that end?"

"Not after I get Seto on the plane."

"Can I ask just how you intend to get him to sleep?"

"I had coffee with Patrick at the doughnut shop a few days ago. Check the tape," she said.

"I have," he said.

"So you know."

"I know."

"Then why ask?"

"I wasn't sure I believed it."

"You can."

"Evidently. Well, now that we have landed you safely and you have taken a very passive Seto past Immigration without any fuss or bother, that leaves us with the small matter of money. You can understand that the plane is expensive. And our friends in the Virgin Islands have a grossly superior standard of living. They won't be satisfied with just a few dollars for turning a blind eye to what is essentially a kidnapping."

She had thought of taking a different approach, of giving him a choice between a set fee and a percentage of what she would recover. If she was unsuccessful collecting the money, then giving a percentage would lower the hit she and Uncle would have to take. But that would make it necessary for her to tell him how much money was involved. And if she did, she would tell him the truth; she didn't discount the idea that his BVI contacts were good enough to enable him to find out. And of course, if she was successful he would make even more than he could with a set fee. It would be found money, of course, but it was still coming out of their pockets. It all boiled down to how confident she felt about her chances at Barrett's.

When she was leafing through Seto's records, she had

noted that Jeremy Bates seemed to be a recent arrival at the bank. His name didn't crop up until the past year. Before that Seto had dealt with a Mark Jones. This meant that Bates hadn't been involved in establishing the withdrawal procedures. He would know about them, for certain, but maybe he would find them as cumbersome and old-fashioned as she did. Maybe he'd take a more flexible attitude if she could establish the right framework. It felt right, she decided. It would work.

"Name your fee," she said.

"We'll need $200,000," he said.

"Captain, you're killing me," she said.

"Ms. Lee, this time we are not negotiating with you. That's the sum. Pay it or enjoy your vacation in Guyana with Mr. Seto, because I assure you he is not leaving this country under any other circumstances."

She knew he meant it and she knew she was going to wire the money, but it wasn't in her nature to capitulate so readily. She sighed. "I'll have to talk to my people. I can't agree to this without their permission. Can you give me ten minutes?"

"Take twenty if you need it."

She switched to her own phone, but not before checking the previous calls made on Patrick's. She wrote down in her notebook the number she presumed was the Captain's direct line.

Uncle took her call on the first ring.

"We'll need to send $200,000."

"Same banking information?"

"Exactly."

"It will get done in the next half-hour," he said without hesitation.

"Have the wire confirmation scanned and emailed to me, please."

"It will be done at the same time."

She knew how hard this was for him. "Uncle, this will work," she said.

"How much extra money do you think there will be?" he asked, simultaneously confirming his trust in her and letting her know that his decision to wire the $200,000 wasn't based on a potential windfall profit.

"About two million."

"Do you have any sense of the timing?"

"It will take Derek at least twenty-four hours to get to the Virgin Islands. I can't do this without him, so there's no point in my leaving here until the day after tomorrow. They want us to arrive in the evening, so the soonest I can get to the bank is probably three days from now."

"Keep in touch."

"Every day," she said.

Ava checked her emails for the next half-hour, catching up with her family and friends. The weather was brutal in Toronto, and her mother was making her usual winter threat to move back to Hong Kong. As she was reading her sister's plea for Mummy to stay put — why Marian took these threats seriously amazed Ava, as her mother had no friends there anymore, and besides, if she did show up their father would cut her off financially — an email arrived from Derek. He had booked a flight through San Juan that would get him into Tortola at six o'clock the next day, sooner than she had thought possible. He had struck out with hotel suites but had found a three-bedroom serviced apartment with a one-week minimum stay and had booked it.

An apartment is perfect, she thought. Maybe Derek was going to be her good luck charm. She figured he must have gone straight home from karaoke after her call. She seemed to be the only thing in his life he took seriously. Ava phoned him at home. He didn't seem surprised to hear from her so quickly.

"The place sounds great," she said.

"It wasn't easy to find."

"Derek, I may try to fly into the BVI tomorrow night as well. I would try to structure it so I'd land around ten. That would give you time to get organized."

"What do you want done?"

"I'm coming in on a private plane. I'd like you to meet me on the tarmac with a wheelchair."

"I'm sure I can find a wheelchair somewhere," he said.

"They'll have them at the airport."

"But how do I get to the plane? You know what security is like these days."

"That's being arranged. BVI Customs and Immigration will have your name. They'll let you come and meet me. I don't have all the details yet, but I'll get them and a contact name for you in case you have any problems."

"Sounds simple."

"Doesn't it always — just before things get screwed up."

"Ava, can we trust these people?"

"I'm paying them enough."

"Still . . ."

"They also think I'm triad."

"You mean you're not?" he said jokingly. Even if she wasn't, the idea that she might be connected to the triads was enough to give most people second thoughts about screwing around with her. More than once she and

Derek had been faced with the threat of violence, only to have Ava short-circuit it with, "We're the nice ones. You really don't want to meet our friends."

"Not that I know of," she said. Then she asked him about his departure the next day and said she'd call him before he left to confirm her schedule and to give him the other information he needed.

Now it was time to call the Captain. She punched his number into her phone. No harm in letting him know she could contact him directly.

He didn't answer until the fifth ring, and Ava wondered if he was playing with her. "Ms. Lee, I see you have my number. I'm assuming you also have some heart-warming information for me."

"The money is in the process of being wired. I'll have a copy of the transfer in a few hours. With any luck the money will be in your account tomorrow," she said.

"Do you mean today? It's already well past midnight."

"Today. And I'd like to get out of here today as well. Do you think that's possible?"

"I hadn't counted on your being quite so efficient," he said. "The plane is scheduled to be used by our minister of agriculture today for a quick trip to Port of Spain."

"He can fly commercial. I can't."

"You know, I don't have a reputation for being accommodating," he said, "but for some reason I can't seem to say no to you."

Three hundred thousand dollars so far is a pretty good reason, she thought. "My people in Hong Kong appreciate your help. If you ever need their assistance, all you have to do is ask," she said.

"I can't think why I would ever need them," he said.

"You never know."

The line went quiet. In the background she heard the clink of ice hitting glass. He had been a bit friendlier than usual, jovial almost, and she figured it was the booze. "Captain, can I get out of here tonight?" she said.

"Why not?"

"Thank you."

"Let's talk in the morning, shall we? Call my office around ten and we'll work out the details."

She thought of Derek. "I would like to know the name of our contact in the British Virgin Islands, right now, if possible. My associate will be in transit by ten and we'll be out of touch until I land. I don't want to arrive at the airport and find myself alone with Seto."

"There are two, actually. A chap called Morris Thomas will be at the airport. He is the senior Customs and Immigration officer. We will notify Morris of your schedule the moment it's absolutely firm, and he will make himself available for you and your Mr. Liang. There shouldn't be any difficulties, but if there are, phone Jack Robbins."

She wrote down the number.

"And in case you're wondering, Jack's my younger brother. So you're going to be in very good hands," he said.

After hanging up, Ava sat quietly in Seto's office staring at his screensaver: a photo of a busy seaport. Derek's question about trusting these people resonated in her mind. The problem was that she was in too deep to extract herself without making things worse. There came a time in every case when she had to have faith in her own judgement. This was the time. It was all too easy to imagine everything that could go wrong — she simply wouldn't let herself go there. Instead she said aloud, "The $300,000 is secure. The plane will be there. Seto and I will get to the British Virgin Islands. There will be no issues at the airport. Jeremy Bates will be cooperative. Andrew Tam will be a happy man."

Then she called Derek and told him about Morris Thomas and Jack Robbins.

"See you tomorrow night," he said brightly.

"Tomorrow," she said.

(29)

"YOU PIG, YOU FUCKING PIG!"

Ava walked into the kitchen to find one of the Captain's men throwing paper towels at Seto's feet, where an impressive pool of urine had gathered.

"Couldn't you just take him to the bathroom?" she said.

"He didn't ask."

Patrick wandered in from the den, wiping sleep from his eyes. "We can't leave him like this. He'll stink up the place."

"I'll get the woman," Ava said. "Give me the keys for her handcuffs."

When she entered the bedroom, Anna was asleep. There was dried blood on the side of her head from the blow Patrick had administered. Beneath it Ava could see the beginning of a hell of a bruise. She touched Anna's arm, not wanting to alarm her. The woman woke with a start anyway, fear leaping into her eyes.

"Anna, I'm not going to hurt you. I need your help downstairs with Jackson. Just wait here a minute."

Ava went into the bathroom and wet a facecloth.

The woman was struggling to sit upright but was having some difficulty because of the tape that bound her legs together. Ava peeled it off Anna's ankles and told her to turn around. "Now please, don't do anything stupid," she said as she unlocked the cuffs. She handed her the cloth. "Here, wash your face. There's some dried blood on your right cheek and ear."

Anna winced as she dabbed her face.

"Do you need to pee?" Ava asked.

"Badly."

"Go and use the bathroom. Just leave the door open."

Anna staggered slightly when she stood up. Ava could see that she was completely deflated and wasn't going to cause trouble. "Wash your face a bit more as well, if you want," she said to her.

It took about five minutes for Anna to sort herself out in the bathroom, and by then Ava had made a mental list of everything she wanted her to do. "Let's go downstairs," she said. "Your boyfriend peed himself. I want you to bring him up here and wash and change him. One of the boys downstairs can supervise."

Patrick and the cops were sitting at the kitchen table with disgusted looks on their faces. "Take the tape off his ankles," Ava told the woman. She could have taken the handcuffs off too, but she didn't want to lessen his feeling of helplessness. She didn't want him to think for even a second that there was any chance of a reprieve.

"Patrick, the woman is going to take him upstairs to wash and change. Go with them, will you?"

He looked as if he wanted to argue with her. She turned her back on him and spoke to Anna again. "Do you have a passport?"

"Yes."

"Where is it?"

"Upstairs in my dresser."

"Where is Ng's passport?"

"He keeps it in his room. I don't know where."

"Now listen to me. When you finish with your boyfriend, I want you to pack a small suitcase for him. His toilet kit, change of underwear, shirt, and whatever he sleeps in."

"You don't have to go into the bathroom," she said to Patrick as they started up the stairs.

"Thank you, boss," he said.

She found Anna's passport in the top drawer of the dresser. It took her a bit longer to find Ng's, which was hidden under his mattress. She tore all the pages from both of them, ripped them to shreds, and threw the scraps into a garbage can in Seto's office. Those two wouldn't be leaving Guyana for a while.

She checked her emails. Derek had sent his itinerary. She then signed on as Seto on the off chance that Bates had responded. Nothing. Seto did have about thirty unread emails. She saw the one she had sent from the Phoenix. There were also two from George Antonelli. She opened them; they contained details about a tilapia deal they had been offered.

Seto was standing in the middle of the bedroom. Patrick had removed one of the cuffs and Seto was holding his hands up so Anna could slip a clean shirt on him. He was incredibly skinny, bones protruding through skin. When he was dressed again, Patrick re-cuffed him.

"Do I have to tie you up again?" she asked Anna.

"No . . . please don't."

"We'll leave him here with you. You can take the tape off his eyes when we're gone. There will be someone outside the door and someone else downstairs, so don't get creative. I don't want to see you hurt anymore, and there is nothing, absolutely nothing, you can do to help him. Is that understood?"

"Yes."

"They should be okay till morning," she said to Patrick. "Can you drive me back to the hotel?"

While Patrick told his men what was going on, she gathered up her notebook and kitbag. A quick check showed that Seto's passports, driver's licence, and Hong Kong ID card were still in the bag.

"I assume from the conversation in the house that you'll be leaving us tomorrow?" he said as they began the drive back to the Phoenix.

"That's the plan."

"And you're taking him with you?"

"I am."

"Do you need any help when you're there?"

"The Captain asked me already, and the answer is no."

"Too bad. Not much travelling in my job."

"Travelling is overrated. After a while the planes, hotels, and restaurants all become interchangeable."

"This must have been different," he said.

She smiled. "Different is a good way to describe it."

Patrick's phone rang. He looked at the incoming number. "It's a call from the house," he said.

"I hope nothing's happened," she said, slamming herself for having let the woman stay with Seto.

She could hear the cop's voice but not what he was saying. Thoughts of disaster began to creep into her head.

"No, leave them alone. What's done is done," Patrick said finally, and ended the call.

"Is everything all right?" she asked.

"My guy heard noises from the bedroom, so he opened the door. The woman was giving Seto a blowjob. I guess the handcuffs were a turn-on."

(30)

AVA FINISHED THE BOTTLE OF WINE WHEN SHE GOT BACK to her room. Then she waded into *Tai-Pan*, hoping the turgid writing would quickly put her to sleep. No such luck. She didn't nod off until past 4 a.m., and she was awakened at seven thirty by the clatter of machinery outside. From her window she could see a crew of men fixing potholes in front of the hotel. *If they want to take on the rest of Georgetown too, it could be a lifelong occupation*, she thought.

Tom Benson was in the coffee shop, and this time she didn't avoid him. An entire day stretched in front of her, and it was going to drag. She could use every diversion she could find.

"I'm leaving tonight," she said as she sat down.

"Lucky you. Successful trip, was it?"

"So far."

"I may be leaving soon myself. They told me yesterday that my parts may actually be in transit. Assuming the boat don't sink and the silly buggers at Customs let them into the country, I may have my hands on them in about two weeks. Then it's a matter of a week for installation, and presto, this fucking hellhole has seventy percent of the energy it needs instead of fifty."

"Amazing."

"Isn't it, in this day and age."

"Now if you could only do something about the water."

"I know. Even after all this bloody time I still can't get used to it."

"The only place I can think of that is almost as bad is a town in the Philippines, on Negros Island. I was staying in a hotel where the water had so much sulphur that the entire place smelled perpetually like rotten eggs."

"It wasn't as dangerous as this place, was it?"

"They closed the front desk at ten o'clock at night and turned off most of the lights. They had a soft-drink dispenser in the lobby, and I remember going down one night to get a Coke and being confronted by a guy with a shotgun. His backup was another guy patrolling the entrance with an Uzi. They were the hotel's security system. Now, remembering that this hotel was a dump, what does that tell you about how safe the town was?"

"Did you knock around any of the locals there?"

"I beg your pardon?"

"There's a story all over the hotel about how you beat up two hoodlums who came at you. You're quite the heroine. I'm kind of glad I didn't come on too strong to you." He stood up and held out his hand. "Safe journeys."

"Same to you, Tom."

"You're one I'm going to remember. Can't say that about many I didn't shag."

"I'll remember you too."

Ava sat by herself for the next half-hour reading the local newspapers. The East Indian politicians were calling the black politicians crooks and the blacks were calling the East Indians thieves. *And somewhere*, she thought, *Captain Robbins is pulling everyone's strings.* There had been four muggings, seven break-and-enters, and two attempted homicides the night before. When she left, they could add one kidnapping to the crime statistics.

Jeff was in the lobby chatting up the front desk clerk when Ava left the coffee shop. She waved at him. "Going to be here for a while?" she asked.

"I have a pickup at noon."

"I'll catch up with you before you leave," she said.

Ava changed into her running gear for one more jog along the seawall. That was something about Georgetown she might actually remember fondly. The air was heavy for sure, but it was clear, and the smell of sea salt was almost cleansing. *There is something to be said*, she thought, *for a non-industrial society.*

Her normal run was about five kilometres. She decided to go farther and bought some bottled water in the lobby to take with her.

The doorman nodded to her as she left. "I'll put the word out that you're going for a run — give the baddies a chance to get out of your way," he said.

Ava ran sixteen kilometres, which turned her into a sweaty mess. The air conditioning in her room, for once, was on when she got back. So was the message light on her phone. She threw a towel around her neck and checked the calls. Uncle, Captain, and Marc Lafontaine: a trifecta.

The Captain was at his office and she was put directly through. *The money's arrived already*, she thought. "The payment is in our account," he confirmed. "I admire your efficiency. Patrick will come by the hotel at six. You'll pick up your baggage on the way to Cheddi Jagan. I've scheduled your departure for eight. Good luck to you."

"I'll say hello to your brother," she said, but the line was already dead.

It was late in Hong Kong. Uncle would have already had his massage and dinner and would be settling in to watch replays of the horse races from Happy Valley Racetrack. The phone rang four times and she was ready to give up when he answered with his familiar, comforting "*Wei.*"

"It's Ava. The money has reached them already, thank you. I leave tonight and I'll be at the bank tomorrow morning."

"I'm glad. Let's end this project one way or another as soon as we can. My friend has called me twice tonight, but I've avoided his calls. Tommy Ordonez has called as well. I told him it will be a few days before we can do anything. It is easier when we are dealing with strangers."

"You know Ordonez from before?" she asked.

He realized he had misspoken. "He is a friend of a good friend. They come from the same village. I met him in Jakarta at a conference about ten years ago. Nothing more than that."

I bet, she thought. "I want to end it tomorrow," she said.

"If you can't, talk to me before getting into this any deeper."

"Uncle, how much deeper can I get?"

"No more money."

"I understand."

"And don't put yourself at risk."

She could think of two or three replies, all of them disrespectful. "I won't," she said.

The shower wasn't only brown, it was cold, and after waiting five minutes for it to warm up she gave up and towelled herself off. It was too early to get dressed for the trip so she put on her Adidas track pants and a Giordano T-shirt. She'd save her business suit for the journey.

She sat on the bed and dialled Marc Lafontaine's number.

"Are you okay?" he asked.

"I'm getting ready to leave. I'm flying out tonight."

"Did you get what you wanted?"

"Some of it. I'll know better tomorrow."

"The odds?"

"Fifty-fifty. But the Chinese always say fifty-fifty."

"What do you mean?"

"When my mother buys a lottery ticket, I ask her what she thinks her chances are. She always says the same thing: fifty-fifty — I either win or I lose."

"True enough."

"Only if you have no faith in mathematics."

"So what are your true odds?"

"Ninety to ten, in my favour."

"Good. I'm glad I was able to help."

"Without you I wouldn't have gotten close. Thank you."

"How did you find the Captain?"

She became cautious. "This is off the record?"

"It isn't going anywhere."

"He's a very complicated man, but at the root he is probably completely corrupt and amoral. His only concern is for himself, and that, I think, is the beginning and end of his story."

"Could you be less subtle?"

"If he ever invites you for coffee and doughnuts at

Donald's, don't go. And if you do go, keep your mouth shut. They record every meeting there."

"I've been to Donald's. So has the High Commissioner. He thought it was quaint."

"They record every meeting," she repeated.

"Jesus," he said.

"And there you are," she said. "The last thing he is, is quaint. He's a dangerous man."

"So how did you manage —"

"I paid him a lot of money for something he didn't care about in the first place."

"Jesus."

"He does have some weaknesses. You could exploit them if you decide you ever need to."

"Meaning?"

"He banks with Royal York and has an offshore account in the Cayman Islands. Lean on the bank and they'll lean on him. If you need an account number, I have it."

"Why are you telling me this?"

"I appreciate the assistance I received from the head of security at the Canadian High Commission in Georgetown. In fact, when I get home, I'm going to write to Foreign Affairs in Ottawa to tell them just how good he was."

"You don't have to do that."

"You didn't have to help me the way you did."

"It's my job."

"I haven't met many Canadian diplomats who think that way. Most of them treat you as a nuisance, someone who's trying to disrupt their day."

It was nearly lunchtime and she thought about inviting him to join her. Then she thought better of it; using him just to kill time wasn't polite, and Ava had been raised to be polite. "I have to go now, Marc. I have some work to do in the business centre. Great meeting you."

Ava hung up, grabbed her notebook, and went downstairs. As usual, the business centre was empty. And also as usual, it took her four attempts to get online.

She accessed Seto's email account. Jeremy Bates had replied to the message she had sent the night before. He said he would be quite happy to meet with Mr. Seto and Ms. Lee in the bank's offices. *Bless you*, she thought, and replied that they would be there tomorrow morning around ten.

Next Ava checked her own email account. She had twenty-five new messages, most of which were unimportant. Mimi was wondering when she would be back in the city. There was one from Marian complaining about their mother; she read half before deleting it. She started writing an email to Mimi, Marian, and her mother saying she would see them in a few days, and then she stopped and hit the DELETE button. She wasn't going to jinx herself again by anticipating. One thing at a time.

She checked Seto's inbox again. Bates had responded to her message, confirming the 10 a.m. meeting. *He doesn't get many people dropping in*, she thought.

Ava knew little about the British Virgin Islands, only that the territory was a haven for offshore accounts. She did a quick Web search. A group of small islands close to Puerto Rico, the largest of which was Tortola, and it was only twenty kilometres long and five kilometres wide. The capital, Road Town, had a total population of twenty thousand, and it seemed that at any given time there were as many tourists as residents there. It didn't sound to her like a place where someone could stay inconspicuous for very long. She could meld into most backgrounds, almost disappearing into herself, but Derek was another matter. He walked, talked, and looked like someone who just had to be someone.

It was almost noon and she realized she hadn't heard from Patrick. She called his cellphone.

"Hey, I'm at the house," he said.

"Is everything okay?"

"Fine. We changed shifts this morning and I wanted to make sure the new guys knew the rules."

"Seto?"

"Quiet."

"The woman?"

"She's standing next to me, making us lunch."

"Let me talk to her."

"Hello."

"Are you all right, Anna?"

"Better, anyway."

"Things will be back to normal soon. Now, did you pack Seto's suitcase?"

"I did."

"Good. Let me talk to Patrick again."

"Hi," said Patrick.

"When are you leaving there?" she asked.

"After lunch. I have things to do at the office."

"You're getting me at six?"

"Those are the orders."

"I'll be at the front entrance."

"See you then."

She had one last thing to do online. She went to the American Airlines website. Derek's flight had left Toronto on schedule. So far, so good.

(31)

AT A QUARTER TO SIX AVA WAS IN THE LOBBY WITH her bags. Patrick had arrived early; he was sitting in the lounge with a bottle of Carib and a bowl of peanuts.

She wanted to leave Jeff an extra tip but there was no sign of him. The doorman was still on duty, and she debated leaving it with him. She decided not to and instead asked the desk clerk for an envelope and discreetly put a hundred-dollar bill into it. She sealed it, wrote Jeff's name on the front, and passed it back.

It was just getting dark when she and Patrick left the Phoenix. "Pothole time," she said.

"It gives the city some character, don't you think?" Patrick said. "Rome has the Vatican, London has Buckingham Palace, New York has the Statue of Liberty, and we have the world's largest and most vicious potholes."

"They are memorable."

"You see what I mean."

The Captain's men, Anna, and Seto were sitting at the kitchen table when they got to the house.

"Where's the suitcase?" Ava asked.

The woman pointed to a corner of the kitchen.

Ava collected the bag and put it on the table. She opened it and went through the contents. It contained everything she had requested, and nothing more.

"I assume you know where we're going," she said to Seto. "You can say goodbye to your girlfriend now."

Anna gave Seto a passionate hug. He received it without much enthusiasm. *She is the last thing on his mind*, Ava thought. *But what comes first, money or survival?*

"I need the men to stay with her for another twenty-four hours," Ava said to Patrick. "No phone calls, no Internet. Nothing."

"You heard her," he said.

They bundled Seto into the back of the truck. "I haven't taped your mouth or eyes this time, but one wrong word out of you and I will," she said to him.

For the first time since they had picked him out of Eckie's, she saw something other than fear and compliance in his eyes. He was getting over the shock. He was beginning to think maybe there was a way out for him. She would have to fix that.

It took them more than an hour to get to Cheddi Jagan Airport. The only light was from a crescent moon and the roadway was almost pitch black, forcing Patrick to creep along at thirty kilometres an hour.

She kept looking at her watch. Derek should have landed at six. She called every fifteen minutes until, at seven thirty, he finally answered.

"You good?" she asked.

"Not a problem. The plane was a bit late, but I'm already in a taxi and headed for the apartment. I'll be back at the airport by ten."

"I'm on schedule."

"See you there."

Just before they reached the terminal, Patrick turned away from it. Ava shot a quick glance at him; he looked calm. She waited. He took the road marked FREIGHT, and she relaxed a touch. On the tarmac, under floodlights, she saw a turboprop with GOVERNMENT OF GUYANA stencilled on the side. Parked next to it was a white Cadillac Eldorado that was at least ten years old. She could think of only one person who would drive a car like that.

Patrick stopped his truck directly in front of the plane. As he did so, the driver's door of the Cadillac opened and Captain Robbins got out. Ava could see inside the car — the Captain was alone. She quickly scanned the area around the plane. No one else was visible.

"Let's get out," Patrick said.

She jumped down from the cab and took a few steps in the Captain's direction while Patrick emptied the truck of Seto and their bags.

Robbins lumbered towards them, his size even more imposing in motion than it was sitting or standing. He didn't look flexible or fast, but the power he emanated was overwhelming. Patrick, tall and muscular as he was, looked like a boy by comparison.

"I came to say goodbye," Robbins said.

"Thanks."

The Captain gazed upwards towards the plane's windscreen. The pilot looked down at them and Robbins motioned to him. The pilot joined them on the tarmac.

"This is Ms. Lee," Robbins said to him. "You are taking her and this piece of shit to the British Virgin Islands. She is the boss when it comes to anything to do with him. Stay out of her business. Just land them there safely, drop them off, and get back here tonight."

"Yes, sir."

"Who is your co-pilot?"

"Hughes."

"Make sure he understands as well."

Robbins looked at Seto. "As for you, I think you'd be wise to cooperate."

He turned back to Ava. "Do whatever you want with him when you're finished. I can't imagine we'd miss him," he said with a smile.

She glanced at Seto. His eyes were locked on the Captain. She saw a touch of anger in them and wished Robbins hadn't taunted him.

"Thanks again for all your help," she said.

He shrugged. "Patrick, take him on board. I want to speak to Ms. Lee privately."

Now what? she thought. This could not be good.

Robbins waited until the tarmac was clear before he handed her a slip of paper. "These are the names and cellphone numbers of my daughters in Toronto. Their names are Ellie and Lizzie. I would appreciate it if you could contact them when you get back. I've already told them you're a friend and that if they ever get into any trouble they can call on you for help. I think they would like to hear that from you in person. We do worry about them."

She was surprised by his assumption, and by the level of trust he was displaying. "I would be happy to. We Havergal girls have to stick together."

"Glad to hear it. Now off with you. Good hunting, and say hello to my brother for me."

The plane had been built as part of a commuter fleet;

it was designed to seat thirty-six people in twelve rows of three. It had been converted into an eight-seater, with two rows of four seats facing each other across a table. Patrick had put Seto in a window seat. Ava sat on the aisle, kitty-corner from him.

"Good luck," Patrick said as he left.

"See you around," she said.

The pilot stuck his head into the passenger cabin. "The flight is about two and a half hours long. I'll turn off the seatbelt sign ten minutes after takeoff. There's a galley up front with drinks and snacks. Help yourself."

She had put two bottles of water and two Cokes in her bag just in case. "Any liquor?" she asked.

"A variety."

"That will be just fine," she said.

Seto leaned against the window, his eyes closed. The plane revved its engines and moved onto the runway. Ava braced herself as they taxied, then drew an extra breath when they left the ground, the soft lights of Georgetown twinkling in the distance. After all the crap she had gone through, the departure seemed anticlimactic.

She waited until they had been in the air about an hour before disturbing Seto. He was still slumped against the window with his eyes closed. She didn't know if he was sleeping and didn't care. She stretched a leg towards him and gave him a kick.

His eyes crawled open. It looked forced — he had been awake.

"I need you to listen to me," she said. "Sit up and pay attention."

"Jesus," he said, twisting his neck and shaking the leg she had kicked.

"When we land, I'm going to take off the handcuffs before we leave the plane. We'll be met on the tarmac by a friend of mine. He's tough, mean, and completely loyal to me. One word out of line from you, any bad body language, and he'll lay you out. Our intention is to walk calmly through Customs and Immigration. I'd like you to walk with us, but if we have to carry you, we will. Do you understand?"

"I get it."

"Now, tomorrow will be more of the same. You and I have an appointment with Jeremy Bates at the bank. We're going to wire Andrew Tam the money you stole from him. I'll go over the details with you in the morning. All you have to do is cooperate, and by tomorrow night you'll be on a plane back to Guyana or wherever else you choose to go."

"I get that too. I already told you I was going to give it back anyway," he said.

"Yes, I heard you, and maybe I believe you."

"These cuffs, can you take them off now? What the hell can I do up here?"

"Don't rush," she said. "Tell you what, though, how about I buy you a drink? You want a drink?"

"Sure."

"What do you want?"

"See if they have any Scotch."

Ava walked into the galley. The bar was better stocked than the lounge at the Phoenix. There were three Scotches: Johnnie Walker Red, Black, and Blue — the premium one. "They have Johnnie Walker Blue," she told him.

"I'll take it neat," he said.

She came back into the cabin. "I'll get it in a minute. I have to go to the bathroom first." She took her kitbag from under her seat and went to the washroom. On the way back she stopped in the galley, leaving on the counter two hundred-millilitre shampoo bottles filled with chloral hydrate.

Ava poured herself a modest shot of cognac, a Remy Martin VSOP, and then filled a quarter of a glass with Blue Label for Seto.

She walked back with the drinks and held the whisky to his lips. He slurped rather than sipped. "Give me a break with these cuffs," he said.

"Too soon."

"C'mon."

"Look, I'm sorry it has to be this way. I can't take any chances."

She put the glass to his mouth again. The Scotch disappeared. "You want another?" she asked.

"Why not?"

In the galley she tipped half the contents of one shampoo bottle into the glass and then added the Scotch. The colour was all Scotch. She sniffed. The smell was all Scotch.

Seto was sitting up straight now. The liquor seemed to have revitalized him.

"Slow down," she said. "I don't want you falling-down drunk."

"I can handle my booze," he said.

He followed her advice anyway, and it took him about ten minutes to finish his drink.

She went into the galley and refilled his glass with more chloral hydrate and Scotch. When she brought the refill back into the cabin, he looked up at her a with stupid grin. His eyes were beginning to glaze over, and she realized that the second dose might not be necessary.

What the hell, she thought. *Why waste it?* To her shock he managed to finish the entire glass before collapsing forward. Ava pushed him back against the seat. She figured he'd be out for at least five or six hours.

So far, so good, Ava thought, looking down at the comatose Seto. Another hour and a half and they'd be on the ground, and she'd have Derek to help. Any worries about getting Seto through Customs and keeping him under control were starting to ebb, only to be replaced by anxiety about the next day and the bank. Regardless of how docile Seto was, she knew it was going to come down to Barrett's and her ability to handle Jeremy Bates. She opened her notebook and took the bank files from her bag. The email she had sent in Seto's name had established the framework for the meeting; now she just had to be calm, controlled, and credible. The problem was, she knew that wasn't going to be enough. Somehow, some way, she had to convince Bates to take a leap of faith. Not a blind one entirely, but for a serious banker a leap with a risk, however you cut it.

Ava reviewed the story she intended to spin, making notes as she did. Where were the holes? What questions would Bates ask? *The basic premise seems plausible enough*, she thought, and she had no trouble answering the questions she imagined Bates would ask. Then Seto snorted, and for an instant Ava thought he was having trouble breathing. She watched him until his body eased and he was quiet. She looked at her notebook again, but her concentration had been broken. She was tired, she knew, and the next hour might best be spent giving her mind a break rather than playing out endless scenarios with Jeremy Bates.

She closed her eyes and leaned back against the seat. *One more day*, she thought, *that's all I have to get through.*

(32)

THE PLANE'S DESCENT TOWARDS BEEF ISLAND AIRPORT was rough, and Ava woke with a start, unaware that she had nodded off. She took a hurried glance at Seto. He was dead to the world.

The landing was smooth, the taxi longer than she would have thought necessary for a plane that size. When the engines were turned off, she looked out the window and saw that the terminal was still a hundred metres away. She reached over and unlocked Seto's handcuffs.

The pilot opened the door to the cockpit and came into the cabin. "I called in and they were expecting us. But you can't leave the plane until they get here and give you clearance." He looked at Seto. "Is he okay?"

"He slept most of the way. I think he's worn out."

The pilot went to the exit door and pulled the security handle, then swung the door open and lowered the steps onto the tarmac. Ava felt the warm air rush in, the smell a curious mixture of oils and gases rising from the runway. She put her notebook in her bag, straightened her shirt, pulled back her hair, and reset the ivory chignon pin.

The pilot peered out into the darkness. Ava didn't know what to expect from Customs; she just hoped Derek had acquired a wheelchair and that they'd let him bring it to the plane. She didn't fancy carrying Seto to the terminal. She checked her watch. They had been on the ground for five minutes. What was causing the delay? The pilot must have been thinking the same thing, because he turned to look at her and gave a shrug.

Another couple of minutes passed, and Ava was about to join the pilot at the door when he said, "I see them. They're coming."

She stood and stretched. "Is there a wheelchair?" she asked.

"Yeah."

They were still going to have to carry Seto to the stairs and down onto the tarmac. Ava said to the pilot, "My friend may need help to get him into it." She reached into her bag, looked for her money stash, and counted out four hundred-dollar bills. "Here, this is for you and your co-pilot. Split it any way you think is fair," she said, handing him the cash.

The pilot moved back into the doorway. Ava stood behind, looking around him into the darkness.

Three men were walking towards them. None of them was Derek.

Two of the men were in uniform, one of them pushing the wheelchair. The third man trailed behind, lumbering, the walk an effort. He was massive, a head taller than the others and twice as broad. Ava turned away from the door and leaned against the wall. Where the hell was Derek? *Probably inside the terminal*, she thought, fighting to suppress far more negative thoughts.

"Hello," she heard a voice call. It had a distinct Bajan accent.

"We need some help with one of the passengers," the pilot said. "You'll have to carry him from the plane."

"Not a problem," the same voice boomed.

The pilot moved back and Ava found herself looking into a huge face that was all too familiar. The man had Captain Robbins's bright blue eyes and large, fleshy lips. He lacked the Captain's near-translucent skin, but his dark tan was accentuated by deep furrows that looked like white trenches etched into his brown scalp. The blue eyes flickered around the cabin before they rested on Ava. "You must be Ava Lee," he said. "I'm Jack Robbins."

"Hello," she said.

"You're right on time," said Robbins, pulling himself up the stairs. His head just cleared the doorway, and when he stood inside, it skimmed the ceiling. His frame seemed to fill the front end of the plane. Maybe it was his proximity to her or the close quarters, but to Ava he seemed even more physically imposing than his brother. Maybe not quite as fit, not quite as agile, but certainly just as impressive. His plain white short-sleeved cotton shirt draped like a tent over his gargantuan belly and baggy blue jeans, and his feet were spilling out of unbuckled leather sandals. He glanced at Seto. "Is that the cargo?"

"Yes," Ava said, her eyes now drawn to Robbins's hands, which were covered by clear latex gloves drawn tight around his wrists.

Robbins had to turn sideways to get down the aisle. Ava stepped back, keeping out of his way. He reached down, grabbed Seto under the armpits, and lifted him in the air as if he were a small child. Ava half expected him to carry the man on his hip or over his shoulder. Instead he held him out at arm's length, Seto's head level with Robbins's chest and his feet dangling just above the ground. "Let's get him out of here," he said, turning and walking towards the door.

Ava reached for her bags and for Seto's. She didn't know what else to do. She had no idea what to think. Her confusion was so obvious that the pilot said, "Is everything okay, Ms. Lee? Because if it isn't . . ."

If it isn't, then what? she thought. *You'll take me back to Guyana?* "Just fine," she said.

As she started down the stairs, Robbins was putting Seto none too gently into the wheelchair. The other two men, who were wearing uniforms with the insignia of Customs and Immigration, looked up at her without much interest. "I'm Ava Lee," she said to them. "Is one of you Morris Thomas?"

"Thomas sent them to help. He's in his office. That's where we're heading," Robbins said.

They walked across the tarmac. One of the men pushed the wheelchair while the other chatted to him quietly. Ava was next to Robbins. His face was passive and he was completely silent.

When they neared the terminal, the wheelchair was swung to the left, away from the main entrance. About twenty metres along they came to double glass doors that read CUSTOMS AND IMMIGRATION. EMPLOYEES ONLY. Ava felt her spirits lift slightly.

They walked into a large open office that was deserted and then past a row of desks to the back. MORRIS THOMAS was stencilled on a grey steel door. "Leave the wheelchair outside. One of you stay with it," Robbins said to the men. He reached for the handle, twisted, and swung the door open. "After you," he said to Ava.

A thin black man in a blue shirt sat behind a desk that further diminished his size. *He has to be sixty*, Ava thought, taking in his wiry grey hair, a face lined with worry, and red-tinged eyes with pouches the size of tea bags. "This is Ava Lee," Robbins said to him.

Thomas glanced up at her, his eyes filled with pity, or at best some form of weary resignation. Ava knew immediately that things would not go as planned. "A pleasure," she said.

"Can I have your passport, please?" Thomas said.

There were two chairs in front of the desk. Robbins lowered himself slowly into one as Ava rooted through her bag. "Here you go," she said.

She put her bags on the floor, took the chair next to Robbins, and watched Thomas make a show of turning the pages of her passport. It held forty pages, the largest the Canadian government issued; she'd already filled thirty-two pages and was going to need a new one before the expiry date. "A world traveller," he said, closing it.

"It's the nature of my business," Ava said.

Thomas looked at Robbins, pursed his lips, and reached down to open a desk drawer. Ava watched him slip the passport into the drawer and close it. "You have a friend who arrived here earlier this evening, a Derek Liang," he said.

"Yes," Ava said, struggling to maintain her composure. "Captain Robbins told me he had made arrangements with you for Derek to land. I had expected to see him here."

"There were some problems with his paperwork," said Thomas slowly. His eyes avoided hers and Robbins's.

"What kind of problems?" she asked.

Thomas rolled his head from side to side. "His papers weren't in order. We couldn't let him stay. We picked him up at the apartment he had rented and put him on a plane headed back to Puerto Rico." He looked at his watch. "He left about fifteen minutes ago. And just so we're clear, we notified the Puerto Rican authorities that he shouldn't be allowed to stay there either. I believe they intend to put him on the first flight back to Canada, which should leave around midnight tonight. To Montreal, I think."

Ava glanced at Robbins. His eyes were half closed, a slight grin tugging at the corners of his mouth. "This wasn't what was agreed upon," she said.

Thomas raised his right hand and motioned to Robbins, his part in the proceedings done.

The big man checked his watch, a Patek Philippe that was lost in the folds of flesh around his wrist. Ava wondered if it was real. Then she saw the back of his hands for the first time: red splotches of skin interspersed with black and green scabs. She turned her head away quickly.

"There's been a change in plans, Ms. Lee. My brother is scheduled to call here any minute now, so if you will be patient I'd appreciate it."

"Do I have another option?" she asked.

"No."

"Jack, you don't need me anymore, do you? Because if you don't mind I'll take myself home," Thomas said.

"Say hello to Betty for me."

"I will," Thomas said, rising from his chair.

"Leave one of the men, will you?"

"I'll leave both."

"Only need the one."

"Okay. Just close the door when you go. It locks itself."

When Thomas left, the room seemed suddenly empty. Ava shifted in her chair, and then to her shock Robbins's gloved right hand shot out and grabbed her upper arm. He squeezed, his fingers digging through her flesh until they reached bone. She flinched, more from surprise than pain. "My brother warned me about you," he said. "I'm just telling you it would be stupid to try anything with me."

"I had no intention—" she began, only to be cut off by the sound of a cellphone ringing to the tune of the *William Tell* overture.

"It's me," Robbins said. He listened for a few seconds. "No, it went well. She's sitting next to me." He paused and then passed the phone to Ava.

Ava wiped the mouthpiece against her shirt. "This is Ava Lee."

"Before anything else is said, let me immediately apologize for this untimely departure from our plans."

She heard the clink of ice against glass. He was at home. Drinking. "Captain, what exactly is going on?"

He laughed, or coughed; she wasn't sure which. "I felt it necessary to make some changes to our arrangement."

"So your brother told me, though he was somewhat lacking in detail."

"The thing is, Ms. Lee, you didn't play fair with me."

She sensed at once where this was headed, but she wasn't going to go there first. "As I remember, Captain, I paid you $100,000 for services rendered, and then another

$200,000 for services that so far have been unfulfilled. So in terms of being fair, I think I'm the one who should have be complaining."

"You aren't the least bit curious as to why I feel aggrieved?"

"We have an agreement, one that I've completely honoured. I don't need to know any more than that."

"The thing is," he said again, slurring the *s*, "I've found out that you've been less than forthcoming with me."

Ava closed her eyes. Had this been his plan all along? Had he arranged to get her and Seto to the British Virgin Islands just so he could squeeze her? Had the note with his daughters' names and phone numbers just been theatre? "Captain, I have no idea what you're talking about."

Ice clinked. "I stopped by Seto's house on the way back from the airport tonight and had a chat with his woman," he said slowly. "Don't know why I did it, actually; it just came to me that it was the thing to do. Anyway, she was quite open with me after a little persuasion. It seems that our friend Seto had made quite a score for himself. According to her, he's managed to turn a recent profit in the amount of about five million United States dollars."

She didn't know if she believed a word of it, but her position wasn't going to change. "There was no profit. There was just theft," she said.

"So you concede the amount?"

"Captain, I never misled you about how much money I was chasing. I don't remember ever mentioning an amount."

"And you know, I don't think you did either, so that's true enough. The fault is mine, of course. I couldn't imagine Seto being that successful. But now, belatedly I admit, I find out that he is evidently more clever than I thought. And so here we are, Ms. Lee . . . Let me ask you, given this new information, do you really think it's fair that I should have to settle for just $300,000?"

"Yes, I do," Ava said.

"You disappoint me, Ms. Lee. I mean, really, without our very active and unique support, where would you be? I'll tell you: you'd be sitting at the Phoenix Hotel with no hope of getting at Seto or his money. Yes, I think that's exactly where you would be."

"Possibly," she said.

"And even if you had contrived to get your hands on him, where were you going to go with him? Nowhere, I tell you, although you might have ended up in Camp Street Prison for kidnapping, or worse."

Robbins's voice had risen an octave, his words coming faster. Ava waited for a few seconds, not jumping to respond. When she did, she said as softly and deliberately as she could, "I assume you want to make a proposition."

"Of course I do. I think that we have to revisit our agreement, that we need to make it less one-sided."

"You're looking for more money?"

"It's only fair."

"It isn't my money to give. It belongs to my client," she said.

"That's a quibble. All I know for certain is that the money is in a bank account belonging to Seto. How it got there is your word against his. In fact, the case could be made that you tried to bribe a Guyanese government official to help you fraudulently deprive a Guyanese resident of his hard-earned assets."

Ava bit back the anger that was swelling up from her stomach. Seto had been an idiot to tell the woman. She had probably confessed everything the moment the Captain asked his first question. As for him, well, he was turning out to be exactly what she had feared he was. She just wished he could have been contained for another day or two. But there was nothing positive to be gained in getting angry about any of it. She tried to shift the conversation. "You know, Captain, all this talk about money is still completely hypothetical. There is no guarantee that the bank will release any funds at all to me."

He laughed, phlegm catching in his throat and causing him to cough. "I have absolute confidence in the approach you described to me," he said, catching his breath. "I found it entirely sensible, and when I factor in your persuasiveness and your appeal, well, I think the approach goes well past sensible all the way to irresistible. So humour me, please, and let's talk about money, hypothetical or otherwise."

"What do you have in mind?"

"Half," he said bluntly.

The figure took her aback. He was even greedier, even more aggressive than she'd imagined. "Captain —"

"I want $2,500,000."

Ava held the phone against her neck as she did two quick calculations. The first was how much negotiating leverage she had. The answer was short and brutal: absolutely none that she could think of at the moment, and the moment was all that mattered now. They had her passport and, more important, she was in a place where she had no connections, no support, no backup. All it would take was one quick phone call to the bank from some BVI crony of Robbins and the entire deal would be blown apart.

The second calculation was how much money she would have left if she drained Seto's bank account and paid Robbins what he wanted. Not enough to make Tam whole, but he would get bandaged up. "Captain, that amount is way too high," she said.

"Don't be stupid. I think half is fair for all the trouble I've gone to. In fact, when I really think about it, half is generous on my part."

He'd been under control until then, not pleasant but not harsh either, just confident and insistent. Now she detected the first real threat in his tone. He was drinking, and dollar signs were dancing in his head. *This isn't the time to aggravate him*, Ava thought. *It's time to pull back*. "I've already given you $300,000."

"What?"

"I've paid you $300,000, and I think that needs to be factored into any agreement."

He laughed again, and when he spoke he was back in control. "Always negotiating, aren't you? But you are correct, of course. So where does that leave us?"

Both of them went quiet. Ava had no idea what he was thinking. All she knew was that she had to negotiate some kind of deal or she wasn't going to leave the airport. And there was only one deal on the table. She needed to get into Road Town; she needed to get to the bank; she needed to buy time. "Discounting the $300,000 would mean we pay you $2,200,000," said Ava.

"Are you saying you will pay or you might pay that amount?"

"Will."

"Ah, I knew you were too clever to do anything else."

"I still need to call Hong Kong —"

"No," he said. "No Hong Kong. No calls. You and I have made the deal and we'll leave it that."

"I'm not sure —"

"I'm sure," he snapped. "No Hong Kong. No calls. You go to the bank tomorrow and work your charm. Have them send the $2,200,000 to my account and then you can send whatever you want overseas and explain everything later to your people there. I'm sure they'll understand why it was necessary to do things this way. I mean, a bird in the hand —"

"You know, it isn't going to be as simple as you think," she said as calmly and softly as she could, and then waited for another eruption.

She heard him breathing, and then another clink of ice. "I think you need to explain exactly what you mean by that," he said, the edge creeping back into his voice.

"Transferring the money directly from Seto's account to your account could cause a problem," Ava said.

"Why?"

"Well, I've already established the parameters for my meeting. The banker has been told — by Seto, he believes — that the money is being placed in an investment in China. He thinks Seto and I are going to show up at his office tomorrow morning to execute the paperwork. Instead, I'm the only one who's going to be there. I think I can talk my way around Seto's absence, but even if he thinks I'm credible, he still needs to see Seto's identification and he still needs Seto's signature on a whole bunch of documents. Will he accept the signatures without actually seeing Seto? That's my hope, Captain, but it is by no means certain. He's going to be suspicious enough when I show up without Seto, and even more suspicious when I deliver him signed documents but still without Seto. Now, by sending money to the Cayman Islands, what you want me to do is compound all that uncertainty by changing the terms of the arrangement Seto emailed to him." Ava stopped to let the Captain absorb the information.

She felt Jack Robbins looking at her. He was obviously listening. "Given those circumstances, I can guarantee, Captain, that the moment I tell him we now want only half of the money to go to Asia, and the other half to be sent to a bank account in the Cayman Islands, alarm bells are going to ring in his head. And, Captain, we don't want any alarm bells, because no capable banker can ignore them, and a bank as good as Barrett's will have someone very capable running a branch as sensitive as this one. It's all in the optics, Captain. Change the optics and you change the reaction. Change the reaction and you put the outcome at risk. The optics now are okay — not great, just okay. If we alter the plan now, it would only hurt us both."

She knew none of that would have occurred to him. Now she hoped he wasn't too drunk to think things through.

"If what you say is true . . ." he finally said.

"It is true."

"Okay, assuming it is, and assuming you follow your plan, how do I get my money?"

"We'll wire it to you from Hong Kong," Ava said. "If tomorrow I can get the bank to send us the money, we'll have it the day after. We'll send you your share right away. So we're talking, what with the time change, three days?"

"Three days," he repeated.

"And I'll be here, of course. I'm not going anywhere. My passport is in Morris Thomas's drawer."

"I know where your passport is."

Now is the time, she thought. "So, Captain, as much as I hate to ask, do we have a deal?"

The Captain fell silent. He was making her wait. She knew he was going to say yes, but he had to remind her who was dominant. "I'd like you to give your cellphone to my brother," he said.

"Why?"

"Just do it."

She opened her bag, took out her phone, and handed it to Jack Robbins. "Done," she said.

"What do you think of my brother?"

"You can certainly tell you had the same mother."

"Actually, his personality is closer to hers than mine," the Captain said. "In any event, you'll get to know him better, because he's going to be staying with you for the next three days, or for however long it takes us to conclude our business."

"That's completely unnecessary," she said.

"It's what I want."

"Captain, you have my passport and you have my cellphone. Where exactly do you think I'll go? What do you think I'll do?"

"I don't know what you could get up to. All I know is that you're resourceful, and I don't want to have to worry about you."

"If it has to be —" she began.

He cut her off. "Good. Now put the phone on speaker mode."

She pressed the speaker button and then held the phone out to his brother. It seemed to get swallowed up by the gloved hand. "Go ahead," he said.

"Jack, Ms. Lee and I have reached an agreement that I think is fair. In fact, you could consider us business partners. Now, she has to run to the bank at least once tomorrow. You're the chauffeur and the bodyguard. Make sure no harm comes to her. Make sure that she is well looked after otherwise."

"She'll be fine."

"As we talked about earlier, you'll stay at the apartment they rented. No phone calls. No computer. Nothing. She doesn't communicate with anyone but you, me, and the bank . . . Now, Ms. Lee, please put the phone back on regular mode."

"Okay, it's just me," she said, holding the phone away from her face and wondering what skin ailment forced Jack Robbins to wear latex gloves.

"It's very simple: we have your passport and you're not leaving the islands without it. And to be completely honest, you're not leaving the islands even if you do have it, because Thomas has put your name on a watch list. If you try to leave you will be stopped and detained. I didn't need to say that, but I thought you should know that we're being careful."

"I understand," she said, not pleased to hear how thorough he had been. "What you said to your brother about the computer, though — that could be a problem. How do you expect me to send instructions about a wire transfer to your account?"

"Did you send instructions by computer for my $300,000?"

"I did."

"Are they still in your system?"

"They are."

"Well, when you're ready to send new instructions, show the old ones to Jack and then follow the exact same routine. He'll be watching, of course."

"Of course. One other thing, Captain — something I do have to ask. What happens if, even with my best efforts, I can't convince the bank manager to release Seto's money?"

"That's not the outcome I expect."

"You have too much faith in me."

"You'll get it done."

"But if I can't?" she persisted.

"That's a conversation for another day," he said. Then he went quiet.

Has he gone? Ava wondered. "Captain?"

"I want you to behave for my brother," he said, as if he were talking to a child.

"Of course."

"And Ms. Lee — Ava, I want you to know that I have the greatest respect for you. This isn't personal; this is just business. We — me and you — are professionals, so I know you'll see the fairness in it."

"I understand," she said.

"As for my daughters," he went on, "I meant what I said when you were leaving Guyana. When this is over and we each have our money and you're back safely in Toronto, I'd like you to call them, I really would."

"Captain, don't worry about your daughters," Ava said.

(33)

THE CUSTOMS OFFICER PUSHED SETO THROUGH THE terminal, with Robbins tailing and Ava alongside him, carrying her own bags. A black Crown Victoria idled outside. The window was open and Ava saw a middle-aged man with a tattooed arm dangling out the driver's-side window.

"Davey, help me with this guy and then put the wheelchair in the trunk," Robbins said.

Davey leapt from the car, all five foot six of him. He was scrawny and had a patchy beard. He wore stovepipe jeans, high-top running shoes, and two earrings. The only thing he lacked was a mullet. He opened the back door and watched Robbins shove Seto across the seat. "Put your bags in the trunk and then get in the front with Davey," Robbins said to Ava.

They crossed the Queen Elizabeth II Bridge, which separated Beef Island from Tortola, and wound their way to Road Town. It was a slow trek. The roads were narrow, the car was big, and the route was mountainous. The car was American-made but the steering wheel was on the left-hand side and the road rules were British. It made for awkward turning, especially on the tight corners that came at them every hundred metres. The first time Davey honked his horn as they approached a curve, Ava jumped, anticipating a collision, but he did that before every curve as a precaution.

The car was otherwise quiet. Davey concentrated on his driving. Robbins sat like a lump behind her. Ava glanced into the rear-view mirror and saw him staring at the back of her head; then she imagined his breath on her neck. She tried to clear her mind, tried to start thinking through the mess emanating from Guyana, but Davey's driving was so herky-jerky and the road so potentially lethal she couldn't sustain any level of concentration.

It took twenty minutes to meander their way to the city. Road Town is built at the base of a mountain, and as they drove down towards it Ava saw that the lights were arranged in what looked like a circle. "That's pretty," she said, breaking the silence.

"That's Road Harbour. The town is built around it, like a horseshoe," Davey said.

Ava was surprised by the thoughtfulness of his description. "How many people live there?"

"About ten thousand."

"Looks bigger, but then most cities do at night."

"This place looks okay in the day too. They've done a good job developing it. Your boyfriend picked a nice place for you. It's right over there, next to Wickham's Cay," he said, pointing.

He must have picked up Derek at the apartment, Ava thought, rerunning the timeline since her departure from Guyana. Customs officials must have gone along too, because she couldn't imagine Derek letting just Davey and Robbins kick him off the island. She looked in the direction Davey had indicated but all she saw was a wall of lights. "Any good restaurants near the apartment?" she asked, thinking it wouldn't hurt to make a friend.

"Enough with the chatter, Davey. You aren't being paid to be a tour guide," Robbins said.

They approached Road Town from the east, taking a route that traced the harbour to the west. She saw signs for Wickham's Cay II and the inner harbour as they passed through a combination of residential, commercial, and government buildings. The architecture was Caribbean generic, mainly low-rise white stucco housing with the odd dash of coral pink or powder blue. The homes were to the north, set back from the harbour, while the restaurants, markets, government buildings, and commercial offices, with long lists of tenants posted on their exterior walls, crowded near and around the water. Davey turned left off Main Street, following the arrow to Wickham's Cay I.

Guildford Apartments, a white stucco three-storey building, was right on the cay. To Ava's eye it looked as if it had been built in a week.

Davey stopped right in front of the building. It had a double glass door that looked into the lobby and a reception desk that was unmanned. "How is security?" Ava asked.

"What do you mean?" said Robbins.

"I mean, is there any? Do we really want to be answering questions about Seto's current state? I don't know about you, but I don't want to be drawing unnecessary attention to myself."

Robbins shrugged. "There aren't any guards. They have a small front desk that's open from nine in the morning to nine at night. They lock the doors the rest of the time and you let yourself in with your room key."

"Cameras?"

"What does it matter?"

"How often do they service the apartments?"

"Again, what the fuck does it matter?" Robbins snapped.

"Seto is going to be handcuffed and taped around the ankles and mouth for at least part of the time. We don't want staff wandering in and out."

"We'll ask them in the morning," he said.

Davey opened his door and went to the trunk. Ava followed. She took out her and Seto's bags while Davey hauled out the wheelchair and unfolded it. "That's a creepy-looking guy you've got in the back seat there. Looks like he should be peddling drugs to kids or selling porn," he said.

"He's in the fish business, so you aren't far off," Ava said, thinking that Davey might be trying to make a friend as well.

Robbins got out of the back seat feet first, his arms on either side of the door straining to pull out the rest of his body. He joined them by the trunk and reached inside for a briefcase. "I'm staying the night with the girl," he said to Davey. "Be here in the morning to pick us up." Then he turned to Ava. "What time is your meeting?"

"Ten," Ava said.

"Barrett's, right?"

"Yes, Barrett's."

"Quarter to ten should be fine," he instructed Davey. "Now help us get this guy upstairs before you bugger off."

Davey pushed the wheelchair to the door. Robbins

inserted the plastic room key and then stepped back as he pulled the door open. As they walked into the lobby, a side door opened and a young black woman with a name tag that said DOREEN, RECEPTION almost ran right into them. She looked at Robbins, staring at his gloves, then at Ava, at Davey, and then Seto, whose head was hanging down, his chin on his chest, drool coming from his mouth. "My friend has a terrible case of food poisoning. We need to get him to the room and into bed," Ava said.

"What room?"

"Three-twelve," Robbins said, holding up the key for her to see. "Liang."

The girl hesitated, then said, "Have a nice evening," as she walked out the front door.

As they rode the elevator to the third floor, Robbins asked, "What did you knock him out with?"

"Something that should last another eight hours or so. We'll tape and handcuff him anyway to be safe. I wouldn't want him roaming around or running off in the middle of the night. I'll give him another dose in the morning."

"Do you really need him?"

And if I didn't, Ava thought, *what would you do with him?* "Did your brother tell you what I have to do at the bank tomorrow?"

"I have a rough idea."

"Well, until then I don't know if I need him. If things go perfectly, I don't. In the meantime, we have to keep him on ice just in case he has to make some kind of appearance."

The apartment door opened into a white-tiled living room with a couch, two pine chairs, and the room's main feature, a forty-eight-inch Panasonic Viera television.

On the right was the kitchen, with a wooden table, four flimsy-looking folding chairs, and a sliding door that led out to a balcony. There was one bathroom to the left, the sink visible through the open door. There were three bedrooms between the bathroom and kitchen. "Let's put him in the middle room. If there's a fuss we'll be sure to hear it," Ava said to Robbins.

He looked at her as if she were trying to trick him. "Stick him the middle," he said to Davey.

Davey wheeled Seto into the bedroom and Ava followed with her Shanghai Tang bag. "Throw him on the bed and take off his pants and shirt," she said. As Davey undressed Seto, she went into her bag and took out a roll of duct tape. She wrapped his ankles together and then put a strip across his mouth. The handcuffs went back on. "Could you tuck him in now, please?" she asked.

Robbins watched them from the doorway. When they were done, he motioned to Davey. "A quarter to ten. We'll meet you outside."

Ava stood in the living room and watched the small man leave. Robbins walked into the kitchen and opened the fridge. "Your boyfriend bought some stuff on his way here. Too bad he didn't have time to try it." He took out a Stella Artois and brushed past her on his way to the couch. He spread himself across it and turned on the television.

From where she stood Ava could see bags of chips and nuts on the counter. She hadn't had any dinner and wasn't about to ask Robbins if she could go out. She went into the kitchen and picked out a bag of smoked almonds. She didn't drink beer, so she hoped Derek had bought some soft drinks. To her surprise there was a bottle of Pinot Grigio. She gave silent thanks.

"I want the bedroom with the king-size bed," Robbins shouted from the couch.

Ava turned. He was staring at her from across the room, looking at every part of her except her eyes. Almost absently, his hand reached for his head and he stuck his fingers into the furrows in his scalp and slid them back and forth, the latex gloves easing the path. Ava turned away, repulsed. She put the wine back in the fridge and left the kitchen with her bag of nuts. She picked up her other suitcase and went into the bedroom closest to the bathroom. Two twin beds. She was about to close the door when he yelled, "Leave it open. I need to be able to see you."

She dropped the bag on the floor and went back into the living room. *Enough of this crap*, she thought. "Listen, you fucking jerk. If you heard your brother properly, we're supposed to be partners. I have a big day ahead of me tomorrow and I need to get organized, I need to get my head in the right space. So I'm going to close my bedroom door until I decide I want to open it again. If you have a problem with that, call the Captain and explain to him just exactly why you need to have it open, and then the Captain can explain to me how that is going to contribute to our getting our hands on some money tomorrow."

He barely looked at her. "Whatever," he said.

Ava turned away. She knew she would have to put up with him until the money had found its way to Hong Kong. After that . . . well, she'd play it by ear.

With the door closed, Ava opened her Louis Vuitton suitcase. She took off her watch, undid her cufflinks, detached the ivory chignon pin, and put them neatly inside their pouch. She stripped down to her bra and panties, carefully folding her slacks and shirt and putting them back in her bag with the jewellery. Then she put on her Adidas training pants and a black T-shirt. She looked in her Shanghai Tang bag and found her notebook and a pen, then saw her computer back staring at her. She did a quick visual search of the room for a computer link and saw none. Even if one was available it wasn't worth the risk, at least not yet. On the side and near the bottom of the Tang bag was a zipper. She opened it and reached inside. It was still there: a Hong Kong passport in her name. If the Captain was right about Thomas it wasn't going to do her much good if she wanted to leave the island by air. Not that she was ready to leave anyway. *Do the banking; just get the banking done*, she told herself.

She picked up the notebook and pen and opened the door. Robbins hadn't moved from the couch. Ava went to Seto's bedroom and poked her head in. He was still tucked in bed, his head visible above the covers, looking almost happy.

She closed Seto's door and turned. "There's a balcony just outside the kitchen," she said to Robbins. "I'm going to take a bottle of wine, my notebook, and my pen, and I'm going to sit out there and get ready for tomorrow."

Robbins pulled himself semi-erect, his belly hanging over his knees. His face was pinched; he started to say something and then stopped.

Ava took that as "I don't care" and walked to the fridge. She took out the wine, found a glass in the cupboard above the sink, and slid open the balcony door.

It wasn't a large space: there was room enough for two canvas chairs and a small plastic table between them.

She plopped into a chair and stretched her legs towards the railing. It was a beautiful evening. A light breeze was blowing in from the harbour, carrying a mixture of sea air and flowers. The balcony overlooked the water, and there was enough light from the boats and the surrounding buildings for her to see that the harbour was packed with sea craft of every size. Ava knew nothing nautical, couldn't tell a catamaran from a yacht or a skiff from a sailboat, and was equally lost in terms of the lengths and values of boats. But she was impressed with Road Harbour anyway, because it seemed to have something of everything bobbing on the water. It was soothing, watching the boats, and as she became calmer the reality of her situation began to settle in, moving past shock towards acceptance and from there to dealing with circumstances by priority. The number one priority was Jeremy Bates and Barrett's Bank. Without success there, Robbins's threats were irrelevant and Andrew Tam was toast. She needed to focus on the bank.

Ava poured herself a glass of wine and opened her notebook. For ten minutes she reviewed the strategy she intended to use, again looking for weaknesses and anticipating questions. It wasn't perfect and couldn't be, given Seto's state, but the basic approach she had outlined did make sense, regardless of Robbins's intrusion. She needed to get the bank to transfer the money, and that was all in her hands, under her control. What would happened afterwards, where and how the money would change hands . . . well, that was open for evaluation, and that was what she began to think about.

Since landing at Beef Island she'd been in a state of suspended disbelief, going through the motions, trying to keep the surprise of it all at bay. Robbins had done a good job springing it on her, and she had to acknowledge that she was in a bit of a jam. No Derek. No passport. No phone. Jack Robbins parked on the sofa. But how much danger was she really in? Nothing had changed in terms of Seto and the bank except that Robbins wanted a cut of the money. If that was all he wanted, then it was manageable. And she had to assume that was all he wanted. The only question was how to handle it.

She could, of course, do exactly what she had told Robbins she would do. But there were certain problems attached to that, not least of which was whether she could trust Robbins to be satisfied with $2.2 million. What if, once he knew she had moved the money to Hong Kong, he got even greedier? What if he continued to hold her passport over her head and demanded even more money?

And then there was the ethical issue surrounding Andrew Tam. It was his money. He was entitled to all of it. From a practical viewpoint, she and Uncle had never guaranteed any return, let alone full return, but Ava couldn't lie to herself about the fact that the money was intact and within reach, and that with a little ingenuity she might be able to get it all. Why give Robbins anything if she could find a way around it?

How cooperative, how gullible would Robbins be once he knew she had successfully engineered the wire transfer to Hong Kong? Assuming he was going to be satisfied with the $2.2 million, was he prepared to instruct Thomas to give back her passport and let her leave the country once he had proof that the wire had been sent to his Cayman account, rather than wait until the money actually reached it? He had been willing enough to do that in Guyana. But that was there, and those were much smaller stakes. How much did he actually trust her?

So there would be a Plan A and a Plan B, she decided, and then caught herself before going too far down that road. *Let's focus on tomorrow*, she thought, reopening her notebook. In the back she had taped Seto's Washington state driver's licence. She took it out and placed it at the bottom of an empty page; then, starting at the top, she filled the rest of the page with Seto's signature. By the bottom of the page it was beginning to look authentic.

Ava finished her glass of wine and poured another. Below she saw a knot of ten people on the dock walking towards a boat that looked like a small floating hotel. They looked like couples, old friends, arms entwined or thrown loosely around necks. They weaved as they walked, their voices rising towards her, the happy voices of happy people who had probably just finished a gourmet meal and six bottles of wine. *Well, I have my wine*, she thought, *and a nice evening and a great view. Things could always be worse.* If only she hadn't googled Tommy Ordonez.

(34)

AVA CRAWLED INTO BED FULLY DRESSED, HER MIND jumping back and forth between Jeremy Bates and Robbins. She began taking long, slow breaths and tried to focus on her bak mei exercises. It was difficult to maintain that kind of concentration; it took her half an hour, maybe longer, to finally fall asleep. When she did, her father came to her in a dream. They were in a hotel, ready to leave for an airport. He said he was going to check out and asked her to collect their bags from their room. Except she couldn't find the room. She wandered from floor to floor, her frustration and panic increasing. She was ready to run to the lobby to get his help when someone else entered her dream.

Ava didn't dream that often, and when she did, her father was always in it. The locations, the situations, the other people changed from dream to dream. None of that mattered. It always came down to her and her father and one of countless variations of him leaving and her trying to catch him or imploring him to stay. She never caught him. He never stayed.

Ava sensed a presence, a subtle change in the light triggering her response. She was on her back, arms by her sides, head resting on two pillows. She opened her eyes and saw him standing in the doorway, the light from the living room glowing around him like an aura. She thought she could hear him breathing. Her own breathing had stopped. She lay perfectly still, her eyes unblinking, locked on the doorway. Ava's arms were outside the covers but her legs weren't. She calculated the distance between the door and her bed, and knew that she had the time she needed to react if he decided to come into the room, even if he came charging into the room.

She thought about saying something, and then thought, *No, let him think I'm still asleep. Let him try to do whatever it is he has chosen to do, and then I'll do what I choose to do.* How badly would she hurt him? There was no limit in her mind. Money or no money, she wouldn't let him get close enough to even think he had a chance. Then the Captain could decide which he valued more, his brother or a payday.

Minutes passed, or maybe it was just a few seconds — Ava had no real sense of time. Robbins stood immobile in the doorway, his massive backlit head stretched towards the bed. She couldn't see his eyes and wondered if he could see hers, wondered if he knew she was awake.

Then he moved, turning, one hand reaching for the doorknob. Ava's legs twitched; her body coiled, her mind cleared. He took a step back. Then she heard a deep breath and was plunged back into darkness as the door closed.

Now she could not sleep. She had no idea what time it was and didn't care. She forced herself to think of something other than the man in the next room. Jeremy Bates and Barrett's Bank were her choices. She conjured question after question and threw back answer after answer until the sun slipped between the slats of the blinds that covered her window. The room gradually filled with sunlight and just as gradually dulled her nighttime fears. Ava looked towards the door. That hadn't been a dream.

She slid out of bed, the tiles cold on her feet, increasing her urge to pee. She took out her toiletry bag, walked to the bedroom door, and opened it with purpose. Six empty bottles of Stella sat on the coffee table. Robbins had left the sofa but he hadn't left the room. He was in one of the pine chairs, which he'd pushed against the apartment door. His head was back, mouth open, as he breathed and snored in spurts.

Ava went into the bathroom and locked the door. It took her half an hour to pee, brush her teeth, shower, wash and dry her hair, and put on the lightest touch of makeup. She couldn't remember ever enjoying bathroom time quite so much. As she was finishing up, she heard shuffling in the apartment and knew that Robbins had left his chair. She listened, trying to figure out where he was. She had no intention of opening the bathroom door and walking into him. Then the noises he was making became indistinct and she had two thoughts: he was in his bedroom or he was standing outside waiting for her.

She opened the door carefully and saw him almost at once. He was standing at the entrance to Seto's room. "You need to look after this guy," Robbins said.

Ava had almost forgotten about Seto. She went to his door. He was flailing on the bed, kicking the covers free, revealing a pair of jockey shorts that didn't flatter his stick-like legs. When he saw her, he motioned with his head for her to come close. She pulled the tape from his mouth. "I need to pee," he gasped. His eyes were still glazed from the drug, but she could see that the flash of anger, the hint of growing confidence that had begun to emerge in them the night before had completely disappeared. He was a whipped puppy again, just the way she liked them to be.

"Take him," she said to Robbins, who had come into the room and was standing only a few feet behind her. "Behave," she said to Seto.

"I want nothing to do with him," said Robbins.

"I can't do it, and we can't have him here all covered in piss if I have to bring the banker back."

She watched as Robbins thought it out through his beery haze. "Fuck," he finally said, brushing past her and reaching down for Seto. He picked him up by the armpits again and, holding him at arm's length, carried him from the room. Seto looked back at Ava, his eyes rolling in panic.

While they were in the bathroom she prepared another dose of chloral hydrate in a glass of water. She had only a bottle and a half left. She hoped she wouldn't have to use it all.

Robbins carried Seto back the same way he had taken him and threw him onto the bed from a metre away. Seto bounced and then lay sideways across the bed. Ava helped him sit up and held the glass to his mouth. "Drink," she said.

He shook his head.

"Drink it or I'll get Mr. Clean here to hold your mouth open and I'll pour it down your throat. Look at it this way: you'll be sleeping through a whole bunch of unpleasantness. This is a kindness, not a punishment."

Seto looked up at Robbins, then at the glass Ava held.

His lips parted and he drank. The roll of duct tape was on the bedside table. She tore off a strip and re-taped his mouth. "This will be over soon enough," she said to him.

Robbins followed her from the room, breathing heavily, the stench of beer and body odour wafting from him.

Ava said, "I need to get organized for the meeting this morning. I'm going to get my paperwork and sit in the kitchen. I would appreciate it if you stayed away from there until I'm finished."

"Do I bother you that much?"

"Your smell does."

He raised an armpit, sniffed, and then smiled. "I'm not leaving you alone."

She went into her bedroom, closing the door behind her. She knelt by the bed and said a little prayer invoking St. Jude, the patron saint of lost causes. Given the Roman Catholic Church's stance on homosexuality, Ava had quietly cut her ties with the institution. But she couldn't entirely revoke her childhood. She saw no relationship between prayer and the Church, or between St. Jude and the Church. She prayed to him often when she was working, not because she was involved in that many lost causes, but more because he was also the patron saint of desperate situations, and those were something with which she was more familiar.

Her prayer finished, she laid out her clothes and accessories for the day. She decided on the pencil skirt, thinking that a show of lightly tanned, nicely shaped legs wouldn't hurt. The white shirt fit a little tighter than the other two, and her black bra would be vaguely visible through it. The green jade cufflinks and the ivory chignon pin were musts, as were the Cartier watch and the gold crucifix. They completed the image she wanted to project: professional, successful, and attractive in an understated, conservative way.

She opened the Chanel bag she took to meetings and put the business cards from Fong Accounting and all of Seto's ID into it. Grabbing two sachets of coffee, her notebook, and the Barrett's Bank file she had taken from Seto's office, she left the bedroom and went to the kitchen. Robbins was back in the chair at the door. She thought he was sleeping until his eyes flickered open.

Ava put on the kettle, and while she waited for the water to boil she slipped onto the balcony, leaving the door open behind her. The sun was well above the horizon, beaming down on Road Harbour, the Caribbean a shimmering sky blue with streaks of green and the boat hulls gleaming. It was already warm, at least in the mid-twenties, but a light trade wind ruffled the morning air. Ava decided the balcony was for her. She left the notebook and files on the table and returned to the kitchen to make her coffee.

She drank half a cup standing by the stove, added a bit more coffee, topped up the water, and went back outside. She went through the bank file first, reacquainting herself with the account history. Thank God Jeremy Bates wasn't entirely new. If she'd drawn a manager who hadn't dealt with Seto before, her job would have been that much more difficult, if not impossible. At least Bates knew what Seto looked like.

Then she opened her notebook and reviewed the notes she'd made after Seto had described the procedures for withdrawing more than $25,000 at a time. She wasn't worried about being able to cover the transaction with a plausible paper trail. It seemed to her that Seto's signature on a wire application, along with presentation of the appropriate identification — with copies signed and dated if necessary — would give the bank everything it needed. The important, overriding question was, would the bank insist on seeing Seto actually sign the documents? *But why would they?* she thought. They had his signature on record for comparison. She would be able to present his genuine ID in a couple of forms, with copies signed and dated. Not right away though, not at the first meeting. The worst thing she could do would be to overwhelm Bates with documentation.

The most important thing was for her not to rush, not to appear the least bit anxious. Slow and steady, slow and steady. Spin Bates the story. Establish her credibility. Show him Seto's ID. Establish the relationship. Get Bates primed to organize a wire but don't try to close at that first meeting. It would take two meetings, maybe even three. As long as she could keep nudging him along . . . tiny steps, tiny steps. Let him tell her what they needed and how they needed it. Let him think he was in control of sending the seven million dollars to Hong Kong.

The only problem was that Robbins thought five million was in play. She knew — at least, if he was smart — that he'd want to confirm the wire that Barrett's sent to Hong Kong. If he knew it was seven million his price would go up. She needed to convince the bank to send two wires, and that was doable. The way she figured it, if Plan A worked she'd be able to look after Tam and pocket an extra commission for herself. If things moved on to Plan B, Tam would still recover most of his loss.

She closed her eyes and rested her head against the

back of the chair. The sun was naked in the sky, the heat building. She loved the sun on her skin, but it dulled her senses, lulled her to sleep. *Time to go in, time to go to work*, she thought, pulling herself up from the chair.

The apartment's living room was empty. Robbins's bedroom door was open but she could see no sign of him inside. Then she saw him standing in the bathroom at the sink. He was naked to the waist, rolls of fat rippling like ruffles on a splotchy white dress. He had a cloth in his gloved hand and was rubbing his left armpit. Robbins's eyes flickered in the mirror, staring back at her. Ava avoided his glance and went on into her room. Maybe he wasn't a complete animal after all. Or maybe he just couldn't bear his own stench.

She took her time brushing her hair, fixing the chignon, applying a hint of lipstick, and slipping into the clothes she had laid out on the bed. It was almost a ritual. When she was done, she stood back and looked at herself in the mirror on the dresser. She had left the top three buttons of her shirt undone. She turned sideways and then bent over to see how much breast showed. Too much, way too much for an accountant and too much for the banker. She buttoned one of them. The watch went on last, and she saw that it was already nine thirty. She did one last check of her bag to make sure she had everything she needed and then she was ready to go.

Jack Robbins sat on the sofa, his bare feet up on the coffee table. He had shaved as well as washed and had exchanged the baggy white tent shirt for a baggy black tent shirt. He stared at Ava, making no pretence that her breasts weren't his main interest.

"It's time," she said.

Robbins stopped at the door to shove his feet into his sandals, his hands pressed against his belly so he could see them.

"We need to talk to Reception before we leave," Ava said.

"About what?"

"Maid service. We don't want it."

"I called downstairs already. It's cancelled until further notice."

Ava was surprised he'd remembered.

Davey was waiting for them, the Crown Victoria the largest car in sight. He smiled at Ava as he opened the back door for Robbins.

They left Wickham's Cay and drove into town. In daylight it was at least as pretty as it had been at night, clean and compact, with well-paved narrow streets with actual sidewalks and sections of picket fencing. The town was a mix of British colonial and Caribbean architecture, all on a scale that suited a territory of about fifty small islands and cays with a population of around twenty thousand. Davey kept up a laconic running commentary as they went. He pointed out the two-storey Legislative Council building, with its ground floor fronted by five arches and the second by a balcony that ran its length. "The court is on top," he said.

Ava listened, none of it really registering. It was nice not to be in Georgetown, but that wasn't going to help her with the bank.

Fyfe Street was in the middle of town, the bank housed in Simon House, a four-storey powder blue stucco commercial building. The street was predictably narrow, the sidewalk meagre. Davey drove the car onto the sidewalk and parked it so close to a wall that Ava doubted he could open his door. But then, he didn't have to leave the car. She looked at her watch. It was five minutes to ten. "I have no idea how long this is going to take," she said to Robbins.

"We're not going anywhere," he said.

The bank was only one of a large number of tenants in the building. On the outside wall, on both sides of a white double door with elaborate brass handles, were lists of the occupants. There were two signs in brass, Barrett's and an insurance company. The insurer had the third floor to itself and Barrett's had the fourth. The other businesses, about twenty of them, each had a white-painted wooden sign about the width of a sheet of paper. They all seemed to be involved in offshore registration, providing a legal address and a cubbyhole for mail for God knows how many firms.

Ava stepped through the door into a small lobby with corridors running off on either side. There was an open elevator that looked as if it had been built in the 1950s. She got in, hit the button for the fourth floor, and then waited for the door to close. As the elevator creaked its way upward she realized it wasn't air-conditioned; she felt sweat beading on her forehead. She swore as she wiped at it, not wanting to look nervous.

The door opened onto a reception area that had two red leather couches along the wall to the left and a coffee table stacked with magazines. The wall on the right had pictures of London: Big Ben, Westminster Abbey, the Tower of London. Between the walls there had to be ten metres of Persian carpet. Straight ahead, also about ten metres away, a young woman sat behind a massive mahogany desk that was bare except for a phone and a magazine she was leafing through. Behind her, a wood-panelled wall ran from floor to ceiling. The Barrett's logo — cast in bronze — occupied its centre; it was at least a metre across and two metres high. Behind and to either side of the desk, two steel-plated doors, painted beige to blend with the walls, barred any further entrance into the bank's premises.

There was no one else in the room. There wasn't a sound save for the woman turning the page of her magazine.

It gives the right impression for a private bank, Ava thought. Spacious, unpretentious, elegant in a subtle and solid kind of way, certainly quiet, and no hurly-burly, nothing screaming at you to take out a car loan or refinance your mortgage. It looked like the kind of place where you'd have to know someone before becoming a customer, the kind of place that knew how to keep secrets.

The woman looked up from her magazine and Ava saw that it was *People. The Economist* would have been more appropriate, she thought. "Hello, my name is Ava Lee. I have an appointment with Mr. Bates."

The woman smiled. "Mr. Bates is expecting you. Actually, you and a Mr. Seto."

Not many drop-ins here, Ava guessed. "Mr. Seto is indisposed. I'm here by myself."

"I'll let Mr. Bates know. I'll be back in a minute."

The woman left the desk and walked to the door on the left. She punched in a six-digit security code, turned, and disappeared.

Ava looked through the magazines on the coffee table and found an *Economist* as well as a week-old copy of the *Financial Times*. She was debating which one to read when the beige door opened and the woman reappeared. "Could you follow me, please," she said.

Ava trailed her down a hallway lined with closed doors. At the end, standing in an open doorway, was a tall, slim young man who bore a remarkable resemblance to the actor Jude Law. *That can't be Bates*, Ava thought. The man managing the bank's interests in the world's largest offshore tax haven had to be more senior, tried, tested. Ava had the feeling she was being sloughed off. A ripple of panic danced in her stomach.

"Hello, I'm Jeremy Bates. So pleased to meet you," he said.

Ava took his extended hand, assessing his off-white monogrammed shirt, blue and yellow Ferragamo silk tie, slate grey light wool tailored slacks with their sharp, straight crease, and glistening black lace-up shoes. *Those shoes are handmade*, Ava thought, *and Bates is no working-class boy.*

He was just over six feet, and as he looked down Ava saw that he was eyeing her just as closely. She gave him her shyest smile and said, "Thank you so much for seeing me."

"I was expecting Mr. Seto as well," he said, stepping aside and motioning for her to come into his office.

"He is terribly ill," she said.

"We'll sit at my conference table," said Bates. "Nothing serious with him, I trust?"

"Food poisoning. We ate a hurried meal before getting on the plane yesterday and something did not sit right with him. He's been either in his bed or in the bathroom since we arrived, and either running a fever or experiencing chills."

"So he's here in Road Town?"

"Oh, yes, just not mobile."

She sat, her eyes wandering around the office. It was massive, as large as the reception area, designed to impress. More mahogany in the desk and credenza, another Persian rug spread over wooden floors. A high-backed, heavily padded green leather chair sat behind the desk, with two smaller ones in front of it. There were three picture windows on the back wall and the side walls were lined with bookcases filled with what looked like company minute books. Then her eye caught something a bit more modern. In the upper right-hand corner, where ceiling met wall, she saw a tiny camera. She had no doubt that every meeting in this room was recorded.

"My business card," he said, passing it to her.

"Thank you," she said, noting his title: DIRECTOR, PRIVATE BANKING, BRITISH VIRGIN ISLANDS.

"Now, I have tea, coffee, and water. Do you have a preference?"

"Oh, nothing, thank you," she said, finding herself still taken aback by his youth and good looks. His hair was dark blond, short, receding at the temples. He had brilliant blue eyes set a bit far apart, and his nose was long and slender.

"Fine," he said, pouring himself a glass of water. "Now tell me, Ms. Lee, in what capacity are you affiliated with Mr. Seto?"

She took her business card from the Chanel bag and held it at two corners as she presented it to Bates. "Our firm is the accountant of record for Dynamic Financial Services. Dynamic finances purchase orders and letters of credit and generally facilitates trade among Southeast

Asia, Europe, and North America. One of Mr. Seto's companies, Seafood Partners, has used Dynamic's services extensively over the past six months and the principals have developed a close working relationship. About two months ago, Mr. Seto decided to take an equity position in a scallop and shrimp plant in Yantai, on the northern coast of the Yellow Sea. He used Dynamic to broker the deal, and now we're getting ready to close."

Bates looked at her business card and then back at Ava. She sat tall, Havergal style, her breasts thrust ever so slightly forward. "That all seems very interesting," he said, words she knew meant nothing.

"Well, it's never easy dealing with the Chinese," she said. "Dynamic, though, has extensive experience in that area. They always try, for example, to negotiate terms that leave the investors with exit options in case of problems. Quite obviously, they have contacts inside China that make this possible, contacts they have nurtured over a great many years. The fees they charge for brokering contracts like this, for being the stable bridge between the two parties, are exceedingly reasonable given the level of protection they offer."

He had a pen, a notepad, and a closed file in front of him. He didn't write a single word as she spoke. "Our bank has a presence in Asia, of course, and I have heard how difficult it is to do business there," he said.

"It can be incredibly frustrating," Ava said. "We represented an American firm one time that was negotiating a contract in Shanghai. It dragged on and on for months, and every time they thought the deal was done, some new issue would emerge. Finally they thought everything had been put to bed and were told by the Chinese to bring their senior people to Shanghai for a signing ceremony. A week later their CEO flew into Hong Kong from New York to catch a flight to Shanghai. When he got to Hong Kong, he was met at the airport by his local staff. They had just received a fax from the Chinese company signed by someone none of them had met or even heard of. The fax advised them not to bother coming to Shanghai — the deal was dead. The Americans tried phoning, faxing, and emailing everyone they had met during the course of the previous months. No one would take their calls or respond to any of their communications.

"Dynamic made some phone calls for me and found out that the nephew of the Shanghai mayor had brought a German firm to the table the week before. All those months of work, all the complicated negotiations, all the money expended — it all went down the drain on the strength of a handshake between the nephew and the Germans."

"What a story," Bates said. "You know, if you don't mind me saying, you seem very young to have this level of experience and responsibility."

"I was thinking exactly the same thing about you," she said. "I was expecting to meet some old banker in a tweed suit."

"A tweed suit wouldn't do in this climate, and actually I rarely wear a jacket of any kind," he said, smiling. "As for my age . . . well, Barrett's is very aggressive when it comes to recruiting and very progressive in putting younger staff in positions that place demands on their learning curve. I've just turned thirty-eight and this is my second foreign posting. I was second-in-command of our Paris office before this."

"I had put you as even younger."

"Thank you, I guess, though that's not always good in this business. I get clients coming in here who keep insisting that they want to talk to my boss."

"I get the same thing," Ava said, shaking her head. "I'm in my early thirties and still get treated as if I graduated from university last year."

"I can't say I'm completely surprised. I mean, you do look younger than thirty."

"Chinese genes."

"For someone who is Chinese, your English is remarkably good," he said, and then caught himself. "I didn't mean that to sound condescending."

"I was raised and educated in Canada."

"I love Canada," he said, leaning towards her. "I have a brother living in Montreal and a sister in Vancouver."

"I love it too, but for work purposes I didn't have much choice but to go back to Hong Kong."

"Now, Mr. Seto . . . He lives where exactly?"

"He has a residence in Seattle and another in Hong Kong, and of course he has a home in Guyana."

"Yes, we've most often dealt with him from Guyana."

Ava didn't want to go much further down that path. She opened her Chanel purse. It was time to raise the ante. "Here is the banking information for Dynamic," she said, sliding a sheet of paper to Bates. "You already have their name and address. These are the bank's particulars, including the branch address and the IBN and SWIFT numbers. The account number is at the bottom."

"Mr. Seto wrote that he wanted to send a wire."

"Yes."

"For how much?"

"One for five million, and a second wire for two million."

"Two wires?"

"Yes, the two million is to be sent to the holding company of the scallop plant as a deposit. Here is their data," Ava said, passing over Uncle's banking information. "The five goes to Dynamic. They'll hold it in escrow until the deal closes, and that hopefully will be within the next twenty-four hours."

"Seven million total, then?"

Could that be his only question? He had no concerns about the separate wires? "Yes, seven million."

He opened his file. She saw copies of the emails she had sent from Seto's address on top. They looked bona fide, even to her. "There is sufficient money in the account," he said.

"I assume you'll prepare two wire transfer drafts for Jackson's signature?"

He picked up the two pieces of paper she had given him and put them in his file folder. "Give me a few minutes. I'll get them started right away."

Ava hesitated. He hadn't mentioned the passport requirement or the need to present other ID. She thought about letting it pass and then just as quickly decided not to. Bates might not be entirely up to date with the account safeguards, but someone would be sure to flag them. It was better for her to be proactive, to appear as transparent as possible. She needed all the trust she could generate.

"Excuse me, Mr. Bates, I don't mean to slow things down, but Jackson did mention that the bank normally requires him to present his passport and other forms of ID, and to sign and date copies of them. I brought the originals with me just in case you needed them." She reached into her purse and removed Seto's American passport, Hong Kong ID card, driver's licence, and credit cards. She spread them in front of Bates. "Take whatever you need."

He nodded. "Yes, thanks for reminding me. Marilyn usually handles this kind of detail. I'll take everything to her and she can copy whatever she wants. She'll be preparing the wire transfer drafts as well."

"How long do you think it will take?" she asked.

"You're in a rush?"

"No, no, it's just that I really need to make a couple of phone calls and I left my cellphone at the apartment."

"You can use the phone here if you wish," he said, pointing to the one on the conference table.

"They're long-distance calls."

"Ms. Lee, I think the bank can afford to pay for a few long-distance calls. Any line will do. Dial nine for an outside line, and then 011 and the country code."

"Thank you, I really appreciate it."

"And I'll close my office door. When you're finished, just open it to let me know you're free."

Bates put Seto's passport and other ID into his file. Then he stood up and looked down at Ava. "I must say, this is a nice break from my usual routine," he said.

She watched him leave the room, grateful that he hadn't made her ask to use the phone. Conscious more than ever of the camera at work in the corner of the ceiling, she tried to look as natural and composed as she could. *Just pretend you're calling Mimi*, she thought, as she punched in Uncle's Hong Kong cellphone number, fervently hoping he'd pick up.

"*Wei*?" he answered.

"Uncle, it's Ava," she said.

"I don't recognize this line. Where are you?"

"I made it. I'm in the British Virgin Islands," she said, switching to Cantonese.

"Ava, I've been calling your cell. Why haven't you been answering?" he said, matching her language choice.

"I've made it but I'm having a bit of trouble."

"I thought Derek was there," he said.

"He isn't, and that's part of the problem. But I don't have time to get into all of it, so please listen very carefully to me."

"I don't like this."

"Just listen, please."

"Are you in any danger?"

"Nothing I can't handle, so don't get anxious, please."

"All right, I'm listening," he said slowly.

"I'm at the bank and I'm close to getting Tam his money back, and a sweetener for us. If all goes well today, I'll be able to wire five million to him and two million to your account in Kowloon. Once the wires have left here, and that should be sometime in the next twenty-four hours, I'm going to send you an email asking you to send another $2.2 million by wire to the account in the Cayman Islands we've already sent $300,000 to — except I don't want you to send the wire. What I want you to do is get your friends at the bank to dummy one up. When our accountant gets it, I want him to scan it and send it to me and to another email address I'll provide."

"Ava, this is all a bit more complicated than you expected, no?"

"Uncle, will you have any problem getting your bank to dummy the wire?"

"No, it is owned by friends of mine. But why are we sending more money to the Caymans, or pretending to, at any rate?"

"It's a shakedown. I don't want to get into the details right now. Just believe that it is something I need done."

"I can get the bank to do it. That won't be a problem," he said.

"Great. When I send you the email requesting the wire, I'll include the guy's email address and fax number so you can copy him when it's issued."

"What makes you think he will accept the wire at face value?"

"Well, he has before. And he's not Chinese, so I'm assuming he has some faith in banks."

"That sounds thin to me."

"Uncle, I don't have time to explain everything. I'm using someone else's phone because I don't have mine, so let me finish what I have to say."

"I'm listening, I'm listening," he said.

"All I'm hoping the dummy wire will do is buy me the time I need to get out of here. As I said, I'm not going to ask you to send the dummy until I know for sure our money is secure. So if for some reason this guy doesn't bite, we just might have to send him his share. The extra two million I got covers most of it, and Tam can eat the rest."

"How will I know what is what if I can't reach you?"

"When I send the first request — the one I want you to dummy up — I'll sign off simply as Ava. If I really need you to send the money, I'll send a follow-up email asking for confirmation that the money has been sent and sign off as Ava Lee. If you don't see my full name, don't send anything."

"I don't like this," he said.

"Uncle," she said quietly, still conscious of the recording device, "this guy is trying to take us for a ride. I don't like it, and I'm not about to roll over and play dead. I want Tam to get his money, all of his money. And I want us to get our share and then some. I know you're not taking a cut from Tam's end, but there's no reason you shouldn't have half of anything extra we collect. I mean, you did front $300,000."

"What if the guy there catches on?"

"I'll tell him there was a glitch in the system and send you the second email. All it should mean is that I'll be stuck here for a few extra days."

"You're confident about this?"

"Enough to try it."

"And I still won't be able to reach you?"

"No, and don't bother. I can't use my cellphone or my computer on my own. Right now I'm in the banker's office. I should be able to email you the wire request soon. If you don't get it within the twenty-four hours and you don't hear from me, send in some troops. I'm staying at the Guildford Apartments in Road Town. The room is booked in Derek's name."

"You know," he said softly, "I wish I hadn't talked to Tam's uncle about taking this job."

It's a bit late for that, she thought. "*Momentai* — no problem, Uncle. Now I have to go. I'll email you when I can, and hopefully I'll be talking to you sometime tomorrow."

As she hung up she felt suddenly quite isolated. When was the last time she and Uncle had been out of touch through any reason not of their own choosing?

What other option did she have, she wondered as she phoned Derek.

His cellphone rang four times, and she was preparing to leave a voicemail when he answered, his voice defensive, as Uncle's had been. "Who is this?"

"Derek, it's me, Ava. I'm in the British Virgin Islands. Where are you?" she said, again in Cantonese.

"I'm in Montreal. I'm catching a plane back to Toronto in a few minutes. Do you know what happened?"

"They told me your papers weren't in order."

"Bullshit," he shouted.

"I know."

"I walked through Customs with absolutely no problem, caught a cab, and stopped at a market near the apartment to load up on some food and drinks. I was in the room for barely ten minutes before they came knocking — two customs officers and a guy who looked like a walking mountain. I tried to argue with them but they wouldn't listen. If they hadn't been customs officers I would have resisted. Sorry, Ava, but I just didn't see the sense in doing that."

"No, Derek, you did the right thing, absolutely the right thing. No point in making things worse. They told me they shipped you back to Puerto Rico and then put you on a plane to Montreal. I'm glad you made it."

"Hey, how about you? You okay?"

"Not so bad."

"You need help?"

"That's why I'm calling."

She heard voices in the background noise behind him. "They're boarding my flight," he said.

"This won't take long. Do you have a pen and paper?"

"No. Let me see if I can find something."

"Wait, don't bother," Ava said quickly. "Turn off your cellphone when we hang up. I'll call back and leave a voicemail with some names and phone numbers. Derek, listen to me — I need you to be completely available over the next twenty-four hours. I may need you to pick up something for me, so keep your cellphone charged and on. If I have to call in the middle of the night, I want to know I can reach you. Right now you're my lifeline."

"I don't like that word," he said.

"I'm just being dramatic," Ava said with a light laugh.

"But you're not joking about my being available."

"No, I'm not," she said.

"Shit, Ava —"

"Okay, Derek, enough. Go catch your plane and turn off your phone, and if you don't hear from me, don't worry and don't be disappointed."

She hung up and waited, giving him two full minutes. When she connected with his phone again, she was put right into voicemail. Ava explained, slowly and carefully, what she wanted him to do.

(35)

AVA SAT QUIETLY FOR A MOMENT, TRYING TO COMPOSE herself, conscious of the camera tracking her every move. It was time to focus her attention back onto Jeremy Bates. The meeting had gone well, but she knew that was the easy part. There were still so many things that could go wrong. All it would take was one small doubt on his part and the words "I really do need to talk to Mr. Seto" and all the scheming in the world wouldn't do her much good. *Why did I think this was going to work?* she thought. She shook her head, caught herself, and rubbed her eyes. It was becoming a struggle to stay in the moment. There were all the things that could go wrong with Bates, and then of course there was Robbins. Had she overplayed her hand by calling Uncle? No, she told herself, she at least had a backup plan now, and Uncle never failed her. The thought of Uncle reminded her of Tommy Ordonez. Uncle hadn't had a chance to mention him during their talk, thank God, but now he intruded into her mind — the jinx that lingered. She pushed him away.

One thing at a time, she thought. *Get off the chair. Walk to the door. Open it.*

There was no one in the hallway, but she could see an open door halfway down the hall and hear Bates's voice saying, "That looks just fine." She turned and went back to her seat, her spirits improved already.

Bates wasn't far behind her, the file folder in one hand, a clutch of papers in the other. "Here we go," he said, putting the papers on the table in front of her. "I had everything done in triplicate. One set for Mr. Seto and you and two sets for me."

Ava leafed through the documents. The two draft wire transfer requests looked perfect. All they needed was Seto's signature. They had copied his passport, Hong Kong ID card, and Washington state driver's licence. That meant fifteen signatures. She tried not to think about how difficult that would be.

"I'm hopeful I'll be able to get these back to you within the next few hours," she said.

"Ms. Lee —"

"Please call me Ava."

"And I'm Jeremy," he said with a slight smile. "What I was about to say, Ava, is that it would be ideal if Mr. Seto could accompany the documents in person."

The fact that she was prepared for the request didn't make it any easier to hear. "Jeremy, I'll obviously do everything I can to make that happen. I just can't predict what kind of shape he's going to be in."

"Well, we can wait, you know," he said. "This doesn't have to be done today."

"Yes, it does," Ava said matter-of-factly. "We can't miss the closing. If we miss the deadline, the Chinese will see it as a sign of weakness. We'll be forced into yet another round of negotiations and will probably face a higher cost."

"This is quite difficult. From my end, I mean," he said.

There was no threat in his tone, just a kind of sad resignation, but to Ava the message was clear enough. Jeremy Bates had drawn his banker's line in the sand. No Seto, no money. She knew from Bates's side that it was the right thing to do, and the only thing that gave her any comfort was the subtle way in which he had chosen to tell her. She respected him for his tact, and at heart she respected the fact that he wasn't willing to discard his sense of duty — even for her. "I'll get Jackson out of bed and over here if I have to carry him myself," she said.

"That would be best, Ava," he said.

She gathered the papers together and put them in her Chanel bag. "Well, I guess I should get going."

"I'll walk you to the elevator," he said, standing up.

"That's not necessary."

"I insist," Bates said.

They walked side by side, Bates more awkward than she. "Where are you staying, by the way?" he asked.

"The Guildford Apartments."

"Nice."

"Yes, nice enough."

"When do you leave?"

"If we wrap up today, then tomorrow."

He pushed the elevator button for her. "Now, would you let the bank buy you and Mr. Seto dinner tonight?"

"I can't imagine he'll be up to it."

"Then how about just you and me?" he said, not missing a beat.

"I would like that very much."

He paused, his eyes wandering away from her. "You'll call me, I trust, when Mr. Seto has signed the documents. We can arrange another appointment then. My afternoon is quite open, so there won't be any delay on my end."

"I'll call," she said.

"Excellent, and when you do, we can confirm a place and time for dinner."

"Of course," Ava said, with more enthusiasm than she felt.

The elevator was still hot and still slow, but her mind was preoccupied with signatures and the very unconscious Jackson Seto.

The Crown Victoria was where she had left it, with Davey in the front seat, window open, bobbing his head to the sound of Neil Diamond's "Cracklin' Rosie." It made Ava think of Bangkok and Arthon. How long ago was that? And what was up with all the Neil Diamond? Robbins was sleeping, his head flung back, his mouth wide open. As she stood on the sidewalk she could smell the aroma of fresh bread coming from a bakery across the street. She suddenly felt hungry and realized she had eaten only a bag of almonds since noon the day before. She looked up and down the street and spotted a fish-and-chip restaurant a few doors down from the bakery.

She walked to the front passenger side of the car and stuck her head in the window. "I'm going to eat at that fish-and-chip place. If he wakes up, tell him where I am," she said to Davey, and then turned and left before he had a chance to say a word.

The restaurant was plainness itself — linoleum floor, plastic chairs and tables — but it was clean, and the smell of cooking oil was muted. "I'm surprised you're open," Ava said to a tall, skinny man dressed entirely in white.

"Cruise ship docks in about half an hour. We'll get swamped."

She scanned the menu, her fish-and-chip experience limited to the occasional after-club foray with Mimi and Good Fridays with her mother and Marian when the girls were small. She couldn't remember whether haddock or halibut was the premium choice, so she asked.

"Take the halibut," he said.

"With chips and gravy," Ava said.

"Mushy peas?"

"Why not?"

She felt a touch guilty when the plate was put in front of her. Loading up on grease was something — Guyana and KFC aside — she rarely did voluntarily. Now she put malt vinegar and salt and pepper on the fish and chips. A dollop of tartar sauce went on one side of the plate and ketchup on the other. She cut into the fish, the batter golden brown and surprisingly light, slathered a piece in tartar sauce, and ate it. The fish melted in her mouth.

Ava ate quickly, but she was still only halfway through the meal when the front door opened and Robbins lurched in. His eyes danced around the restaurant as if he were expecting to see something other than her sitting at a table. "What are you doing?" he demanded, his voice husky with sleep.

"What does it look like?"

"You should have asked."

"You were sleeping."

His hand went to his head. Ava turned her attention back to her food, not wanting a glimpse of his fingers sliding in the furrows. But the vision was already in her head. She ate a few more chips, a sliver of fish, and a forkful of bright green mushy peas, then put her utensils down. "That really was excellent," she said to the man behind the counter.

He nodded as if he was used to hearing such compliments.

As she left the restaurant she said to Robbins, "I need to find a place where I can make some copies of documents."

Davey had moved the car to in front of the fish-and-chip shop. Ava climbed in. "I need to make some photocopies," she repeated.

Davey looked back at Robbins. "Go to Quickie Copy," Robbins said.

They drove back through town, past the turnoff for Wickham's Cay II, and continued around the southwest corner of the harbour. The copy shop was on Main Street, in the end unit of a small strip mall. Ava went inside with Robbins tagging along. She made an additional two copies of each of the papers Bates had given her. Her Jackson Seto signature was passable, she thought, but the extra copies gave her some insurance.

Back in the car she said, "And I wouldn't mind stopping at a grocery store on the way back to the apartment."

"Jesus Christ, this is getting stupid," Robbins said.

"I can't exist on nuts and potato chips."

"There's a market just around the corner from the apartment. I saw it as we were leaving this morning. It's right on the way," Davey said.

"Okay, okay, but that's it," said Robbins.

As Davey pulled up in front of the store, Robbins's cellphone rang. "Wait," he said to Ava. He listened for no more than a few seconds. "Here, it's my brother for you," he said, passing her the phone.

She held it away from her mouth. "I left the bank about half an hour ago," she said, knowing that was why he had called. "Nothing is finalized, nothing is agreed. It was step one, that's all."

"I was going to ask if you slept well," the Captain said.

"And then you were going to ask me about the bank."

"That is incorrect. I was also going to ask if my brother was good company."

"And then you were going to ask about the bank."

"True enough." He laughed. "So if it is just business you want to discuss, tell me how it went."

"I didn't get thrown of their offices, if that's what you mean."

"That's the last thing I would have imagined."

"You may be expecting too much of me, and it's way too soon to know how this will end. The banker, Bates, is very sharp and very conscientious. He's insisting on talking to Seto," Ava said.

"And you're trying to tell me that could be a problem?"

"What do you think?"

"I see the potential risk."

"That's an understatement."

"Oh, I'm sure you'll be able to handle it, Ms. Lee. I have nothing but confidence in you."

Ava saw no reason to pursue such a pointless conversation. "Look, I have to go. I have papers to sign and things to organize."

"What is your schedule?"

"I'm going to talk to Bates again this afternoon. If he'll accept at face value the documents with my version of Seto's signature, I'll attempt to get the money wired to Hong Kong today. If that happens, and after I have confirmation, I need to email my end to initiate a wire back to you. Obviously I need to use my computer to do that, so you'll have to instruct your brother accordingly."

"That won't be a problem."

"Landing here wasn't supposed to be a problem."

"Ms. Lee, don't be churlish," he said.

"Assuming we get to the point of sending a wire from Hong Kong — and I'm not guaranteeing we will — I'll ask my people to email you a scanned copy of the wire as I did before. And to be doubly safe, I would like to send you a fax copy. Do you have a fax number that's secure?"

"My brother has that number."

"I don't want to ask him for even that much," said Ava.

"Ah. He does lack charm, I admit. All right, I'll email it to you."

Ava saw Jack Robbins stiffen and realized that he could hear what his brother was saying. That gave her pause. She had been about to nudge the Captain about returning her Canadian passport and calling off Morris Thomas after he received the wire transfer notification. Suddenly and completely, that felt like one of the worst ideas she'd had since leaving Toronto. *God, don't appear the least bit anxious*, she thought. *And don't give him time to think about doing it. Try to catch him when he's just been told he's about to pocket two million dollars.* "Thank you," she said. "You understand this means I have to get into my computer?"

"As long as it's related to our business and Jack is watching you, I have no objections."

"Aren't you generous."

"Ms. Lee, you honour your commitments and I'll honour mine."

She handed the phone back to Jack Robbins. "I'm going to buy some food. Here, you talk to your brother."

Robbins caught up with her as she was putting two bottles of sparkling water into her basket. "Stop running out on me," he said.

"Just trying to save time."

"My brother wasn't finished with you."

"Tough," Ava said, and held out the basket. "If you're going to follow me around you might as well carry this."

Robbins stared, his eyes for the first time really looking into hers. They weren't entirely lifeless, she saw, more like disinterested, as if she was completely insignificant to him. She knew that goading him wasn't the best approach, but she couldn't bring herself to make nice. "Let's go," he said, ignoring the basket.

Ava walked down two more aisles, adding rice crackers, cheese, a jar of olives, and a small plastic container of hummus. Robbins stayed close behind her, his gloved hands jammed into his jeans pockets, saying nothing.

Outside the store she could see that the apartment building was no more than a couple of minutes away; she asked Robbins if they could walk. He opened the car door and said, "Get in."

Davey dropped them in front of the building. "Do you need me later?" he asked.

"If I do, I'll call," said Robbins.

Doreen, the young woman they had met in the lobby the night before, was behind the reception desk. She stared, rather rudely, Ava thought, as she and Robbins entered and walked to the elevator. What lurid thoughts were running through her mind?

The apartment was as they had left it. Ava went to

look in on Seto. He had rolled over onto his side, kicking the bedcovers clear. His hair was dishevelled and starting to look greasy. Drool had dried on one side of his mouth. She covered him, hoping it wasn't going to be necessary to clean him up.

Ava heard a clatter from the living room and looked out to see Robbins clearing the Stella empties. She walked towards him as he deposited the bottles in the kitchen trash bin. "I need this space," she said. "I have a lot of papers to sign and I need to concentrate, so I'd appreciate it if you could leave me alone. I don't want the television on. In fact, I don't want any distractions at all, so it would be ideal if you could hang out in your room until I'm done."

She saw his body tense; this time he wanted to argue. Before he could react she brushed past him and sat at the kitchen table. He stood near the sink, staring down at her. She tried to ignore him, extracting from her purse the documents Bates had given her, setting out the extra copies she'd made, and laying out Seto's passport, Hong Kong ID card, and driver's licence in a row. "I need to work," she said, not looking up.

"Cunt," he muttered.

Ava heard it clearly enough but pretended she hadn't. She searched in her purse for one more document, a copy of Seto's last withdrawal request from the bank, and then put it next to his other identification. She opened her notebook. "I need to work," she said.

He took two steps towards the living room, stopped to look back at her, and then shuffled across the floor to his room.

Ava sat quietly at the kitchen table for a few minutes, collecting herself. Robbins was becoming a distraction, and she blamed herself for letting him annoy her. She opened her notebook and looked at the signatures she'd penned the night before. *Not bad*, she thought, *not bad at all.*

There were a lot of things for her to like about Seto's signature. It was short, for one thing, simply *JSeto*. It also wasn't identical from document to document. Similar, of course, and recognizable obviously, but with minor variations. It gave her a little wiggle room. Despite those positives, she sat quietly at the table for a few minutes, gathering her nerve. She had done this often enough in the past and never failed, but her perfectionist streak could always find flaws. The truth was, any reasonable facsimile normally worked. She was just afraid of running into someone as anal as she was.

She started with a blank page in her notebook and began to practise. The signature was basically a big looping J, the bottom loop curling into the upper, and a relatively straightforward S, followed by a straight line that tailed off to a dot. The J was dominant. If she got that right, imperfections in the rest would pass. The proportions were tricky, though, between the top and bottom loops, and when they were out of sync the signature looked contrived.

Ava began to write J's — just J's. She had filled almost the entire page before she managed to get three in a row that looked similar to the ones in front of her. She closed her eyes, envisioning it. *I have it*, she thought.

She started with the copies of his ID. With one eye fixed on the bank document he'd signed and the other on the paper in front of her, she wrote *JSeto* nine times in rapid succession. When she had finished, she discarded only the last two — the J was out of whack. *Take a break*, *step away*, she thought. She got up and turned on the kettle. While the water boiled she looked out onto the harbour, amazed by the level of activity.

Ava drank half her coffee on the balcony, clearing her head, and then went back to the table. She had written two more lines of J's in her notebook before she recaptured the balance she wanted. Then quickly she redid the two signatures that looked suspect and moved on to the wire transfer requests. Those went smoothly, the signatures indistinguishable, even to her paranoid eye, from what the bank had on record. *There, the easy part is done*, she thought, as she organized the paperwork into matching sets.

It was too soon to call Bates. There was no value in letting him think Seto had been well enough to affix the signatures so promptly. She'd wait. It was almost eleven thirty. One o'clock — no, one thirty worked better. *Give him time to have some lunch*.

She gathered the documents and slid them into their folder. Out of nowhere came a yawn, and Ava realized she was tired. She'd been awake since God knows when, and the morning had been draining. She had time to kill, and a rest couldn't hurt.

Ava didn't say anything or look into Robbins's room as she walked past to hers. If he couldn't figure out that she had finished working, that was his problem. She closed the door behind her and lay on the bed fully clothed. Her mind was more of a jumble than she would have liked. Bates was more than enough to occupy her, but Robbins — both Robbinses — kept intruding. She tried to shut everyone out, thinking bak mei, crane position: her foot poised to strike, her hands moving faster than light.

When she woke, it was with a start, her eyes darting to the doorway. It was closed. She was on her bed, still dressed, nothing out of place. She lifted her left hand and looked at her watch. Two forty-five. She sat on the edge of the bed, composing herself.

She opened her bedroom door and saw Robbins back on the couch, watching television. She went to the bathroom, locking the door behind her, and washed her face with cold water, slapping at her cheeks. Then she undid her hair, brushed and coiled it again, and put the ivory chignon pin back in place. She reapplied her makeup. Her eyes looked a bit puffy from sleep, but there wasn't anything she could do about that.

Robbins turned towards her as she re-entered the living room. "I need to call the bank," she said.

"Use that phone," he said, pointing to the only one in the apartment, which was on the wall near the kitchen.

She called the number on Bates's business card, assuming it was his private line. Instead, the receptionist she had met earlier answered with a rolling "Barrrrrett's."

"Mr. Bates, please. Ms. Lee calling."

He came on the line quickly, and she guessed he had been waiting for her call. As he'd said, she was a diversion from his usual routine. "Ava, how are things progressing?"

"Hello, Jeremy. Well, not bad at all. Jackson has signed the draft requests and all the other documents that are needed."

"Wonderful. So when will I see the two of you?"

She heard the emphasis, however slight and subtle, on the word *two.* Ava drew a small breath. She knew for certain, knew totally and completely, that no matter how she spun things, Jeremy Bates wouldn't be sending any wires until he actually saw Jackson Seto. Suggesting anything else, no matter how creative she could be, wasn't going to fly. She could try to charm him, of course, but she knew there were limits to charm, and when charm had to compete against money, it lost its lustre pretty quickly.

"Unfortunately, Jeremy, there is that continuing problem with Jackson. Frankly, I'm having a tough time getting him from the bedroom to the bathroom, let alone dressed and out the door to visit the bank. In fact, I may need to ask you for the name of a doctor."

"Ah," he said.

To Ava's ear, that simple interjection was filled with hesitation, questions, doubt. She felt a slight touch of panic, and spoke before he could shut any doors on her. "There is another way, though," she said, in as low-key a manner as she could manage. "Why don't you come here to collect the documents? I know Jackson would like to see you to say hello."

He didn't respond immediately, and for a second she thought she had misjudged the situation. "You know, that's not a bad idea," he finally said.

"The sooner, the better," she said. "He's exhausted and keeps nodding off."

"About an hour?" he asked.

"Perfect. We're in apartment 312."

"See you both then."

(36)

AVA TRIED TO PUT HERSELF IN BATES'S POSITION. EVERY transaction he conducted was a candidate for scrutiny, a potential target for the only person who might scare him: the bank's auditor. All the good bankers she had known made it a religion to cover their tracks, regardless of the size or nature of the transaction. Following banking regulations had become second nature to them. So to her mind, dinner invitation or not, Bates wasn't going to treat her differently from any other customer. It was her job to make sure he had everything he thought he would need if an auditor came calling. And she thought she had done that adequately.

He had the email from Seto saying that he wanted to send a wire and bringing Ava into the picture as a trusted associate. He had met Ava, and she seemed to be the person Seto had described. She knew, given the time difference, that he hadn't had a chance to call the accounting firm in Hong Kong to confirm her position, and from the way he had looked at her card and at her, she knew he wouldn't. He had seen all the originals of Seto's identification, and they matched everything they currently had on file. Now he was going to get the signed original copies of the wire transfer requests and signed and dated copies of the same ID. It was, all in all, Ava thought, a paper trail that would satisfy any auditor.

But there was still the important matter of Bates actually meeting Seto, actually witnessing him signing the necessary documentation. It was a chink in the due diligence process, she knew, that might cause Bates problems if he had to explain the situation later. But that would be later, when hindsight would make it easy to adapt what had actually occurred into what was supposed to have transpired. And even then, he could say with all honesty that he had seen Seto. The fact that he was comatose could be explained. Seto was ill, after all, and Bates had made the point of physically going to his apartment to meet with him. He couldn't be blamed for the fact that Seto was sleeping at the time. Due diligence had been done. The bank couldn't reasonably expect more of him.

It's going to hold, Ava thought as she stood up, feeling satisfied.

"We're going to have a visitor, and I need your help," she said to Robbins.

"Huh?"

"The banker is coming to meet me and Seto. We need to get organized."

"Like how?"

"Come with me," she said, heading for Seto's bedroom.

He was still out cold, but it had been more than six hours since she'd given him the previous dose of chloral hydrate. She wasn't about to take the slightest chance that he'd wake up when Bates was there. "Sit him up and see if you can revive him enough to drink," she said.

While Robbins grabbed Seto under the arms and hoisted him up, Ava rooted through the toilet kit Anna Choudray had packed for him. She found a toothbrush and a hairbrush. She threw the hairbrush on the bed and left the room with the toothbrush.

In the bathroom she mixed another dose of chloral hydrate and set it aside. She soaked a facecloth, put toothpaste on his brush, and with a towel under her arm went back to join the two men.

Robbins was shaking Seto as if he were a rag doll. Seto's eyes rolled open, but for only a few seconds at a time before closing. They were blank, uncomprehending. Ava wondered if the dose would be necessary, a thought that was banished when he slurred, "What the fuck . . ."

"Hold his mouth open," she told Robbins.

Brushing Seto's teeth was nearly impossible because his head kept moving around, but at least when his mouth was open there was now a faint smell of toothpaste. When she was done, she took the facecloth, wiped away the remnants of paste, scrubbed the dried drool from around his mouth, and then for good measure opened the cloth and rubbed his entire face. "I'll be back," she said.

Seto seemed to have nodded off again when she returned. "He needs to drink this," she told Robbins.

Robbins pried open Seto's mouth again. She poured. He gagged, and she slowed down the process until he was taking little sips. He got halfway through the glass before he couldn't swallow anymore. She stopped; a drowned Seto wouldn't do her any good. "Hold him upright for just another second," she said.

Ava went to work with the hairbrush. When Seto

finally looked decent, she reached behind him to undo the cuffs. "Lay him down."

She unwrapped the tape from his ankles. Fortunately neither they nor his wrists were marked to any degree. She pulled the bedcovers halfway up his chest, leaving both arms out, resting comfortably along his sides. She stepped back. He was thin, wan, pallid — like someone who was very ill but was being well looked after.

His suitcase was still on the floor where she had dropped it the night before. She put it in the closet. "That should just about do it," she said to herself.

Ava went into the living room, closing Seto's door. "I can't have you here when the banker comes," she said to Robbins.

"I'm not leaving," he said.

"Then we have a problem. Do we need to call your brother?"

"I'll go to my room. The door will be closed. But I'm not leaving the apartment."

Ava tried to think of a convincing argument that he was being unreasonable and failed. "Just be quiet, then."

"I didn't bring my drums," he muttered.

She carried her file folder to the kitchen, opened it, and placed Bates's two sets of documents on the table. She checked the signatures against the passport and the Hong Kong ID card. The only way they wouldn't pass, she thought, was if the person looking at them had predetermined they weren't genuine. They weren't perfect, she knew; they were just good enough. And if Bates, God forbid, questioned any of them, she could always use Seto's illness as an excuse.

"Hello, hello," a voice said from the intercom by the door. "There's someone here to see a Ms. Lee."

Ava looked at her watch. Bates was early. She walked to the intercom. "Send him up, please."

Robbins rose from the sofa and walked silently to his room.

Bates looked slightly uncomfortable when Ava opened the door. She hoped the idea of being in the apartment alone with her — well, almost alone — was behind it.

"I've never been in one of these apartments before," he said. "I've heard good things."

"Well, they give you value," she said, directing him towards the kitchen. "Can I get you anything? Bottled water, coffee?"

"I'm fine."

"Let's sit then."

He looked at the documents on the table.

"They're all signed. Two sets for you, one for us."

Bates sat at the table and began to peruse them. He went through both sets, which surprised her. Then he took a copy of one of the wire transfer requests and placed it alongside the copy of Seto's passport, checking the signatures. He did it far more intensely than Ava would prefer, and she felt a quiver of doubt.

"It all seems to be in order," he finally said.

"Are you ready to meet with Jackson?" Ava asked.

"That would be excellent."

She led him to the bedroom door, gave it a light tap, and listened. "He may be sleeping," she said, rapping harder. She counted to ten. "I think he's sleeping. We'll go in anyway."

Seto's covers had slipped a touch. She tiptoed towards

the bed. Bates followed behind her, looking uncomfortable again and doing his best to be quiet. Ava leaned down. "Jackson," she whispered. "Jeremy Bates is here. Do you want to say hello?"

"He looks very pale," Bates said.

Ava nodded as she gently shook Seto's shoulder. "He's terribly dehydrated. I've been making him drink as much water as he can handle."

"Food poisoning can be debilitating," said Bates.

"Jackson, Jeremy Bates is here. He wants to say hello," Ava said more loudly.

"Oh, leave him, please. Leave him," Bates said. "I have everything I need."

Ava backed away from the bed, bumping into Bates and stumbling. He reached out to steady her, his right arm slipping under her breasts. That's when she heard a thud. To her it sounded as loud as a bag of bricks being dropped three metres onto a tile floor. She flushed.

"Sorry about that," Bates said. "I thought you were going to fall."

"I might have," she said, scarcely believing he hadn't heard the noise.

She led him out of the bedroom, closing the door behind her. "You mentioned earlier you might need a doctor?" he said.

"I don't think that's necessary now. He's slowly coming around. I've had food poisoning myself, and it's usually twenty-four hours of misery and then another twenty-four to forty-eight hours of recovery. I just hope he'll be okay to fly. We're supposed to leave tomorrow night. I may have to postpone if he isn't feeling up to it."

"There are worst places to be stuck," Bates said.

"Admittedly," she said with a little smile.

They walked back to the kitchen table and the documents. Bates gathered up his sets. "Do you think it will be possible to send the wires today?" she asked.

"I don't see why not," he said casually.

"Wonderful. We would really appreciate it."

"You will want copies of the actual transfer, I presume, and confirmation that they've been sent?"

"Yes, I would. We need to let Hong Kong know as soon as possible that it's a go from this end."

"Why don't I bring them with me tonight when we meet for dinner?" he asked.

That was smooth, she thought. "Jackson won't be up to it."

"Well, we'll have to manage without him, won't we?"

"Yes, we will. I'm looking forward to it," Ava said, not missing a beat.

"There's a French bistro called Les Deux Garçons on the first street before the bank. Are you comfortable with French food?"

"I eat everything."

"Fantastic. Do you need me to pick you up?"

"No, please don't. I'm going to spend the rest of the day sightseeing. I'll find my own way."

"Seven o'clock, then?"

"Yes, perfect. I'll see you at seven."

She waited by the door until she heard the elevator close. She was walking towards Robbins's room when he emerged.

"Dinner?" he said.

"What the hell was that noise?" she said, cutting him off.

"You handled it, right?"

"If he had had any suspicions at all —"

"But he didn't, or it sure didn't sound like he did. Dinner at seven, huh?"

"I had no choice."

"We'll drive you and we'll wait outside. And don't give me any story about having to go back to his place for a drink."

"There's no chance of that," Ava said. "It's dinner and out. I just want to get this thing finished and get myself on a plane back home."

(37)

THEY LEFT THE APARTMENT AT QUARTER TO SEVEN. Ava had spent the rest of the afternoon and early evening going back and forth between the balcony, bedroom, and kitchen, her restlessness even getting on her own nerves.

Davey knew the restaurant and drove her to within a hundred metres of it. Ava looked up and down the street, not wanting Bates to see her getting out of the car. When there was no sign of him, she got out and moved away from the door. Robbins rolled down his backseat window. "We'll be right here," he said.

She got to the restaurant door at seven on the dot. There was no sign of Bates at the entrance. She stuck her head inside. It was a small place, only about fifteen tables, and unless he was in the washroom he hadn't shown up yet. A short, round, cheery-looking woman with a menu cradled in one arm glanced at Ava, waved, and then walked towards her. "Ms. Lee?"

"Yes."

"Mr. Bates called for you. He wants you to phone him at this number."

Ava's paranoia kicked in. *This can't be good.*

"I'll have to use your phone. I left mine at the apartment."

"Certainly," the woman said, pointing to a phone on the hostess stand.

Bates's phone rang six times, and Ava was ready to give up when he answered.

"It's Ava," she said.

"Sorry, I didn't recognize the number. I should have known you'd call from the restaurant."

"Is there some kind of problem?"

"Ava, apologies. Actually there is."

There was only one obvious question, and she wasn't going to ask it because she didn't want to hear the answer.

"A very important customer from New York dropped in unexpectedly with a long list of things he wants done, right away, of course," he said. "He's insisted I join him for dinner at his hotel at eight. And I'm not in a position to refuse."

Ava could feel her tension melting. "That really is too bad."

"You know, you can join us if you wish. I'm sure he won't mind, since we've concluded most of our business already."

"I can't leave Jackson alone that long."

"I understand," he said slowly.

She paused. "Jeremy, did my wires get transmitted in the midst of this other activity?"

"Of course. They went out late this afternoon."

"Wonderful. Thank you."

"My pleasure."

"And the copies for our records?"

"They're right here in front of me. You're only a

couple of minutes from the bank. Would you care to walk over?"

"Sure."

"There's a night bell in the lobby. Ring it when you get here. I'll have to come down and let you in."

She left the restaurant and retraced her steps to the Crown Victoria. Robbins stood outside, leaning against the car. "What's going on? You get stood up?"

"He can't make it — some other business — but the wire has been sent and I'm going over to the bank to get a copy of the confirmation."

"We'll drive you."

"I'll walk. You know where I'm going. Follow me if you want."

She took her time, enjoying the fresh evening air, the breeze from the Caribbean drifting inland. *In a different time, under different circumstances, I might actually enjoy this place*, she thought.

The Crown Victoria passed her on Fyfe Street, drove past the bank, and parked about twenty metres past the double doors to Simon House. Robbins stared at her through the rear window.

Ava walked into the lobby; the corridors to the left and right were closed off, sealed by what looked like fire doors. She pressed the night bell next to the elevator, stood back, and waited. It took Bates a couple of minutes to reach her. She had half expected him to bring the documents with him, but he was empty-handed except for the plastic card that activated the elevator during off-hours. "Let's go upstairs and we'll get things sorted," he said.

Sorted? She wasn't crazy about his word choice. Neither was she comforted by his body language, which seemed stiffer, more awkward. *Something's happened*, she thought. She just couldn't think what.

Bates led her past the Barrett's reception desk and into his office. The bank was deserted.

They sat in the same chairs they had occupied that morning. It seemed to her like a very long time ago. There was a brown envelope on the table. Bates placed a hand on it.

"Ava, there is something I need to discuss with you," he said, his eyes averted. "I wouldn't do this normally, but I think we have struck up a good enough relationship that I feel I can share some information that has come to my attention."

She saw that he was tense, his lips tightly drawn. She fought back a sense of foreboding, flashing an encouraging smile in his direction. "Please, Jeremy, feel free."

"I received a phone call from a bank in Dallas late this afternoon, just after we sent your wires. It's the bank that recently sent us electronically two very large transfers from Jackson Seto. The call was in confidence — a courtesy, one bank colleague to another — and I have to ask you to honour the spirit in which it was made."

"Of course. You can be assured of my discretion," Ava said.

"The bank . . . the banker advised me that they were contacted by an investigator from the U.S. Treasury Department about a week ago with regard to Mr. Seto. The Treasury official said that Mr. Seto was being investigated on suspicion of money laundering."

"Good God, I can't imagine —" she began.

"Ava, how long have you known Jackson Seto?" Bates asked. His eyes were full of concern.

"A few months, no more than that, and only because Dynamic introduced us and wanted us to help with the financial side of this transaction."

"I think it's only fair to tell you that I ran some checks on Dynamic and your accounting firm after that phone call."

"That's understandable."

"Both companies, of course, reported well — long-standing, excellent reputations — so I'm not suggesting even for a second that either would be involved in some illegal operation."

"I should think not," Ava said.

"Seto is another matter," Bates said. She noted that the honorific had disappeared. "His account has been a minor concern for some time, and I say minor because until recently there wasn't that much money going through it. I went through some of the bank's files. We've had calls from lawyers and the like before, asking questions about him and his account. There were claims that he misappropriated funds. There was no proof, of course, and the chap who was here before me let the matter slide. Even if he hadn't, of course, the bank would hardly be able to just give the money back."

Ava sighed. "I had no knowledge of any of this, and I'm sure Dynamic doesn't either. As far as I can tell, Seto was referred to them, and vouched for, by a cousin of the CEO."

"Well, now you've been warned."

"Has the Treasury Department taken any action?"

"No, not according to the Dallas banker, and he should be in a position to know."

"So it's supposition at this point?"

"Precisely."

"Still, I'm going to speak to my boss and make sure he talks to Dynamic. Knowing him and them as well as I do, I imagine they will distance themselves from Seto as quickly as they can. We are committed to concluding this transaction, but after that I can't see them conducting any more business with him."

"I'm of the same mind," Bates said, a trace of anger in his voice. "My bank has an operating code of ethics that is the very first thing new recruits have drummed into them. We have survived and thrived for more than two hundred years by doing business completely within the letter of the law. If the U.S. government ever charged Seto with money laundering and our bank was somehow implicated, I can tell you it would end the career of everyone who had put a finger to it."

He's worried, genuinely worried, Ava realized. "Jeremy, I'm absolutely sure nothing will come of this," she said softly. "Money laundering is easy to say and hard to prove. Has the Treasury Department contacted you yet?"

"No."

"There you go. If they were really bearing down on Seto I'm sure they would have contacted you by now. The Dallas bank told them where they sent his money, yes?"

Bates nodded.

"So the fact that a week has passed and they haven't followed up with even a phone call does tell you something. You won't hear from them. I'm sure of it."

"I thought that as well."

"Anyway, Treasury Department or not, we will cut ourselves free of him after this."

"As will the bank. I'm going to close his account as soon as your wires clear. When you see him, tell him I need to talk to him privately. He can come here or I will come to the apartment."

Ava sat back. "Jeremy, do you think you could delay doing anything until I leave? This is quite uncomfortable for me. I was going to stay with him until he was well enough to travel, but now I have to call Hong Kong and probably adjust my plans. I would appreciate it if you could hold off until I have some direction."

"Of course," Bates said, his hand reaching across the table as he passed over the envelope.

Ava touched his fingers and then pulled back. She looked at the brown envelope. "Are those my copies?" she asked.

"Yes, of course. Forgive me for getting distracted," he said.

She opened it and took out the confirmations. Both had been registered at 4:15 p.m. "Thank you so much."

"It was my pleasure. I'm just sorry about dinner. Maybe tomorrow night?"

"If I'm here — and I think I will be — I'd love it."

He walked her to the elevator, his hand lightly touching her elbow, a display of interest that confirmed what she had already decided: it was time to leave Tortola.

As the elevator door closed, Jeremy Bates left her life as completely as if he'd never been in it. During the ride down and halfway across the lobby, the Robbins brothers consumed all her attention. But it wasn't until she was nearly out the door that it dawned on her she was taking some things about them for granted. She stopped, opened the envelope, and took out the wire confirmation for the two million that had gone to Uncle. She folded it into a small square and tucked it inside her underwear.

The car was where she had last seen it. Davey saw her first and said something to Robbins. The big man whipped his head in her direction, his eyes drawn to the envelope. Ava gave thanks to whatever impulse had made her remember the second wire.

She climbed into the front seat and said, "I'm starving. I need to eat."

"Was the money sent?" said Robbins.

"Yes, I told you it was."

"Is that the confirmation?"

"Yes."

"I want to see it. Pass me the envelope."

"Do you have your brother's permission?"

His voice rose. "You need to stop fucking around with me."

Ava turned around to face him. "I'm not fucking with you. I'm doing business with your brother. I'm not showing this to anyone unless he tells me to."

Robbins stared at her. Ava could see that he was trying to make up his mind whether she was being respectful towards the Captain or pissy towards him. "I'll call him," he said.

"That's the wise thing to do," she said.

He climbed out of the car and crossed the sidewalk to a white stucco wall. He leaned against it, the phone appearing in his gloved hand. Davey looked sideways at her as if to say *Be careful*. Ava realized it was the first time she'd actually been alone with the driver. "Why does Robbins wear those gloves?" she asked him.

"Ugly, huh?"

"Certainly not pleasant."

"Nothing freaky, if that's what you're worried about.

He got what he thought was eczema a few weeks ago. It comes and goes, except this time it didn't go. The doctor told him he's got some kind of ringworm. He got some medication but he has to wear the gloves for a few days."

"It hasn't done anything for his disposition."

"Hey, with or without the gloves, Robbins is a piece of work."

"How long have you worked for him?"

Davey laughed. "What makes you think I work for him?"

"I assumed."

"He's got his own day job and I got mine. This is just a short-term gig for me. I crew for a living. This is the busiest charter port in the Caribbean. I'm off again in two or three days. We got some honeymooners going island-hopping for a week."

"What does he do?" Ava asked.

"He's a cop."

"I should have guessed."

"Why? He sure as shit doesn't look like one."

"And what does your typical cop look like?" Ava asked.

"Not like the Michelin man."

Robbins lumbered towards the car. Davey said, "Best for us not to talk so much. He's a suspicious son of a bitch."

"My brother wants to speak to you," Robbins said from the door, holding his phone over the back of the front seat.

"Captain," Ava said.

"I understand congratulations are in order, Ms. Lee."

"The money has been sent."

"Well done, very well done. Now do me a favour and pass the confirmation to my brother. He'll need the phone back as well."

Ava handed them both over. The big man retreated to the wall again. She started to speak to Davey, but he turned his head away.

She watched as Robbins read the wire details to his brother. When he was done, he climbed into the car, a fat, sloppy grin spreading across his face. He handed her the phone.

"Yes, Captain," she said.

"I imagine you're eager to inform Hong Kong of your success?"

"You know I am."

"I've told my brother that you're free to use your computer. Please show him the transfer requests you did before and then follow the same model."

"The only difference, obviously, is that I'm going to ask our accountant to fax and email you directly a copy of our bank's wire transfer to your Cayman account."

"That's understood. I must say, Ms. Lee, it's a pleasure doing business with someone who values efficiency as much as I do."

"Well, speaking of efficiency," Ava said, "while I'm on the computer I wouldn't mind booking a flight out of here for sometime late tomorrow."

"I guess that won't do any harm," Robbins said slowly. "But until things are concluded, you understand, our current working arrangement will remain intact."

"I didn't expect anything different."

"Good. Now let me speak to my brother again."

Jack Robbins listened for a minute, closed his phone, and said to Davey, "Take us back to the apartment."

"Hey, I need to eat," Ava protested.

"We'll have something delivered."

(38)

AVA REALLY DID HAVE TO EAT. THE MEMORY OF THE fish and chips was long gone, and the rice crackers and hummus she'd snacked on during the afternoon hadn't done much to fill the void in her stomach, a void that had expanded as the tension of doing business with Jeremy Bates and the bank subsided.

She wanted Chinese. Robbins told her there wasn't any in Road Town, and when she said that was impossible he turned to Davey. "Tell her, will you?"

"There ain't none."

"How about Italian?" she asked.

"You like pizza?" Davey asked. "The Capriccio is good," he said to Robbins.

"Drop us off at the apartment and then head over there. Better get three large, with sausage, mushrooms, and olives. That okay with you?" Robbins said to Ava.

"Thin crust?"

"Two regular, one thin crust. Call when you get to the building. We'll come down and get the food."

As Ava and Robbins walked back to the Guildford she could feel that he was less tense now as well. She wondered if his brother had said anything in particular to him. When they got into the apartment, he said, "Where do you want to set up the computer?"

The cable connection was in the kitchen, next to the phone. While Ava got her computer and notebook from her bedroom, Robbins went into the fridge for a Stella. He was sitting at the kitchen table, the bottle already half empty, when she came back and started to get set up.

The connection was good and Ava quickly got online. "I'm going to sign into my email account now," she said.

He came over to her side, his head almost touching her shoulder. "Don't crowd me, please," she said. He pulled back about six inches.

Her inbox had more than thirty messages. "I have to open that one from your brother. It has his fax number in it," she said, ignoring the others. She opened her notebook to the Guyana page where she'd recorded the Captain's bank account information, and wrote the fax number underneath. Then she hit the MESSAGES SENT tab, scanned down, and found her first email to Uncle with Robbins's bank information.

"There, that's what I sent before," she said to Robbins, not remembering exactly what she had written in addition to the bank details. Not much, it turned out. At least no editorializing, nothing negative about the Captain.

"Okay," Robbins said.

Ava clicked on the COMPOSE button, typed in Uncle's email address, and then copied the email she had shown Robbins, changing only the amount of money to be wired and adding a request that a copy of the confirmation be emailed and faxed to Captain Robbins at the address and number provided. When she had finished, she said, "Here, read this and make sure it's all right. In fact, why don't you call your brother and read it to him? That way neither of us has to worry about being accused of screwing up."

"That's not a bad idea," he said.

"Good. While you do that, I'm going to the bathroom," she said, standing up. He pulled back to let her pass. She didn't know which she needed more, to pee or to get out from under the hovering Robbins. Even in mute mode he was still oppressive.

Ava was about to sit on the toilet, skirt pulled up and panties around her knees, when the copy of the second wire transfer fell to the floor. God help her if she hadn't remembered it back at the bank. She would have been hard-pressed to talk her way around that problem. It would have cost her more money at the very least, and more important, it would have destroyed any trust the Captain had in her. She picked it up and tucked it back into her underwear.

When she came out of the washroom, Robbins was at the table again, a second beer freshly opened. "Did you reach your brother?" she asked.

He nodded. "You can send the email."

"I want to change first. I don't feel like eating pizza in these clothes."

"Whatever."

She took off her jewellery first, putting everything neatly away. Then she slid off her skirt and reached into her panties for the folded piece of paper, which she put in the pocket of the Shanghai Tang bag that held her Hong Kong passport. She unbuttoned her shirt, thinking that with any luck she was done with dress shirts for a while, and reached for her last clean T-shirt.

"Your brother did tell you that I can stay online and book a flight after I send this email?" Ava asked as she re-entered the living room and walked towards the kitchen.

Robbins nodded and then got to his feet to stand behind the chair where she'd been sitting. Ava resumed her place. The email was still exactly as she had drafted it. She hit the SEND button. "There we go — the easiest two million dollars Captain Robbins ever made," she said.

The apartment intercom sounded. Davey's familiar voice said, "Pizza man."

Robbins went to the door and pressed the button. "Can you get in?"

"Not without a key."

"Okay, I'm coming downstairs," he said and then looked at Ava.

"I'm looking for flights. I'm not going anywhere," she said.

He hesitated.

"What am I going to do, for God's sake, jump off the balcony?"

"Be back in two," he said.

Ava found an American Airlines flight to San Juan. From there she could catch the midnight flight to Montreal or any one of a number of connections to Toronto through Miami, Chicago, or Newark. She did a rough calculation. If they moved fast in Hong Kong, Robbins would have his copy of the wire by morning — the middle of the night, actually. That might allow her to get a morning flight to San Juan, an early afternoon flight to the U.S., and a connection that would get her into Toronto in the evening. *Why not?* she thought, as she signed off on that itinerary.

Just as she finished, Robbins was back with three large pizza boxes in hand. He put them on the counter, the aroma filling the small kitchen. He opened the top one and put it aside. "That's yours," he said.

Ava salivated as she took a plate from the cupboard. As she did, Robbins took her place at the computer. He hit the MESSAGES SENT tab. The email to Uncle was top of the list. He switched to DELETED MESSAGES. Nothing. Ava forgot about any growing notion that Robbins trusted her, even in the slightest.

She watched until he was finished. When he stood up, she leaned down and turned off the computer. *It's almost over*, she thought, as she put three slices of pizza on her plate, poured a glass of sparkling water, tucked her notebook under her arm, and headed for the balcony.

(39)

AVA DIDN'T SLEEP WELL. SHE HAD GONE TO BED EARLY, way too early. She hadn't been tired, just bored. With Jeremy Bates out of the way, the money sent to Hong Kong, and the Captain at least half managed, her mind was now purring along in low gear. Robbins had parked himself in front of the television and she wasn't about to join him. She had no phone and didn't want to have to ask permission to turn on the computer again. That left the view of the harbour from the balcony, but bobbing boats have their limitations, especially in the dark. Around nine she went to check on Seto. He was still sleeping, but she figured the chloral hydrate would wear off soon, so she taped his ankles and mouth again and reapplied the handcuffs. Then she went into her bedroom and opened the James Clavell novel.

She had been reading for no more than ten or fifteen minutes when her eyes began to close. The first time she woke it was just past midnight, and she was on top of the bed with the lights on. She opened the bedroom door and saw that Robbins had fallen asleep on the couch, the television still running, four empty beer bottles on the coffee table. She made a quick bathroom run, turned off the lights, and crawled under the top cover.

Sleep was now more difficult; thoughts about the day ahead kept intruding. She pushed them aside, only to have Tommy Ordonez slip in through the gaps. She hoped she wouldn't have to spend any time in the Philippines. Guyana had offered enough hardship to last her for a while. And then Captain Robbins intruded on her consciousness. Had she overplayed her hand with him? No, she thought, his greed aside, they had connected at some level. He was a man who understood how things really worked, what motivated people to do things they wouldn't normally consider voluntarily — the right things for the wrong reason, although his definition of what was right might differ sharply from hers. Still, they had connected. They had some measure of mutual respect, respect that had nothing to do with approving what the other actually did. It was more for the manner in which each operated. Style points, Ava thought — they gave each other credit for style points.

The next time she woke it was two thirty. For ten minutes she fought to get back to sleep and then gave up. She turned her light on and picked up James Clavell again. She read for more than an hour before sleep encroached enough for her to turn off the light and give it another try.

It was dawn when she opened her eyes. She looked at her watch: ten minutes past six. She closed her eyes and began to pray to St. Jude. She had barely started when the tones of the *William Tell* overture interrupted. It went on and on and then cut out. She went to her door and opened it a crack. Robbins was still asleep. The volume on his cellphone was louder than she remembered, but not loud enough to wake him.

She started her prayer from the beginning, only to have *William Tell* start up again. “Answer the phone,” she said under her breath. As if on cue, the tune ended and she heard him say, “What is it?”

She was almost finished when he knocked on her door.

“Yes?” she said.

“My brother needs to speak to you,” said Robbins.

Ava thought about the time, and an immediate feeling of disquiet crept through her. Why would he call so early? Had something gone wrong on the Hong Kong side? No, she thought. Uncle never failed her. “I’m coming,” she said.

A few last words to St. Jude, the name Robbins in her prayers for the first time, and then she went to the door.

“Here,” Robbins said, handing her the phone, and then turned and walked to his bedroom.

Ava went to the kitchen and sat facing the balcony, the harbour glittering in the morning sun. “Good morning, Captain.”

“Good morning, Ms. Lee.”

“It’s rather early for a phone call.”

“Well, I’m too perturbed to sleep.”

Ava felt a surge of worry. “How so?”

“The Hong Kong wire.”

“You didn’t get it?” she asked, her disquiet expanding.

He paused. “I got a copy of a copy. I got it by email and fax.”

“Was the amount wrong? The date? Did they make a mistake with the bank information?”

He said, slowly and carefully, “You know, Ms. Lee, I don’t know which annoys me more, the fact that you tried to play me for a fool or the fact that, even though you've been caught, you keep trying to play me for one. At this very moment I think it's the latter, and I warn you not to persist along those lines."

Ava closed her eyes. *Why did I try it? How the hell did he catch on so soon?* She wished him away, wished away her attempt to keep the money, but she was not yet ready to concede a single thing. "I can't even begin to respond to that until you tell me what the problem is."

"There is no money."

"I beg your pardon?"

"And there you go again with your bullshit," he said, his voice harshening.

"I don't understand," she persisted, glad he couldn't see her, the sweat beading her upper lip.

"You didn't send the money."

"Captain —"

"My relationship with my bank is as strong as the one I imagine you have with your bank in Hong Kong. They give me twenty-four-hour service, something I never thought I needed — until I started doing business with you. Well, when I couldn't sleep this morning, I called them, gave them the wire transfer number, and asked them to check its progress. Ms. Lee, they had no record of the wire, nothing anywhere in their system. Nothing, absolutely nothing."

Ava drew a deep breath, struggling to keep her voice even. "I can't understand how that's possible unless there was a glitch during the transmission process. Let me contact Hong Kong and check it from that end," Ava said. "I assure you —"

"— that it is shit. The only thing you can assure me of is that every word you've said to me is shit."

"Captain —"

"My bank called your bank," he said with finality.

God, she thought, *surely no one actually told them about the dummy wire?*

"A very friendly young woman on the international desk at your bank told the friendly young woman from my bank that there was no record of the wire on file. No record, no wire. Simple enough, I think."

That wasn't the worst thing he could have been told, she thought, her mind spinning, searching for an explanation, any explanation, that would at least buy her a little time. "Given the nature of the transfer, my people may not have used standard procedures," she said. "You need to let me call or email Hong Kong."

Robbins went quiet. *He's thinking*, she thought, with a glimmer of hope. "Yes, I think we both know that you need to contact Hong Kong, and this time to tell them to actually send the money," he said slowly. "The one thing I grant is that you know how to stick to a story. The thing is, the more I listen to it, the angrier I get."

"Captain, please —"

"What? You thought this would actually work? You thought so little of me as to try something this stupid?"

Oh God, Ava thought. When was the last time she had misjudged a situation quite so badly? When was the last time she had misjudged a man so badly? "I can fix this," she said, still not wanting to admit culpability, not wanting to bring up Plan B.

He ignored her, and Ava felt him slipping away. "You know, you shouldn't have tried this. We had an arrangement and I was fully prepared to honour my end. Now you've changed all that, and I have to decide what I'm going to do."

"I can fix this," she said.

"Yes, I have no doubt you can fix it, but the details may change. I'm not going to rush into anything with you, so have no fears about my being rash. I'm going to take some time to think this over. In the meantime, you need to do some thinking about what you've done. I think you need to make penance. You need to be punished, Ms. Lee. You need to be taught a lesson."

"Captain, I can't even begin to tell you how bad I feel about the way this process has been mangled. Just give me the chance to get it fixed."

"That half-hearted apology doesn't quite make up for the transgression," he said.

She knew what he wanted, but she just couldn't give it to him. It was one thing for him to be ninety-five percent sure of what had happened and another for him to be one hundred percent certain. She had to leave a shred of doubt. She couldn't prostrate herself. "I'm sure that as we talk this through —"

"No, we're finished talking for now. I need to think and you need to reconsider your position and your attitude towards me. I have spoken to my brother and asked him to help you rethink everything. His ways may be a little rough but I expect you to take it like a big girl, and when he's finished we can look at this again through fresh eyes."

"That is —" she began, but he was gone, the phone line dead. She put Robbins's mobile on table, her mind in a muddle. *What the hell is he talking about?* she thought. Then she screamed as the back of her neck and her right shoulder exploded. The pain brought her to her feet, but before she could turn her left leg collapsed and she fell forward against the kitchen wall.

He was behind her, a thick leather belt in one hand, a baton in the other. How had he managed to move so quietly? she thought. She twisted to press her back against the wall. She knew it was the belt that had hit her shoulder and the baton that had jabbed into the soft flesh behind her knee. For some reason the details became important. He held the belt by the buckle so that he could hurt her without scarring her flesh. The baton was close to a metre long, longer than any she'd ever seen, and it was made of fibreglass, a high-tech innovation hardly necessary for the purpose it was meant to serve.

"It's never a good idea to screw around with my brother. He isn't a turn-the-other-cheek kind of man," Robbins said.

"No one screwed your brother."

"That isn't what he thinks, and that's all that matters to me. He told me to strap you, and that's what I'm going to do," he said. "If you're cooperative it'll be over before you know it."

She shook her head.

He held up the baton. "I know how to use this but I'd rather not. The belt won't break anything, but this might, so I advise you to lie still for the belt. It's your choice, though."

She flexed her leg. It ached, but she could move it.

He was at least two metres away, the distance giving him time to react to anything she might try. The baton was poised and the belt hung by his side, waving back and forth. "You need to think about the big picture," he said, enjoying the sound of his voice. "I give you a bit of a beating and my brother plays nice with you again. Not such a bad deal, the way I look at it."

She shook her head again.

The belt lashed out, catching her across the top of her thigh. Ava shifted her feet.

Robbins took a step back, cautious. "Don't let my size fool you. I can still move quickly," he said.

She slid slowly to the ground. He stared down at her, his eyes now tightly focused on her for the first time since she'd met him. Ava lowered her head. Her arms fell to her sides. Slowly she pressed the small of her back firmly against the wall, tightened her glutes, and pushed her hands into the floor. "This isn't necessary," she whispered.

"My brother thinks it is, and I agree with him. You are a sneaky little cunt, a cunt who got caught," he said, raising the belt.

"Don't," she said.

"I'm losing my patience," he said, the belt drawn completely back.

She sensed rather than saw the motion, and when he took the necessary step forward to hit her, she uncoiled. The belt went flying past Ava's face as she left the wall, her right heel driving into his groin. He groaned and staggered but didn't fall, the baton flailing in her direction.

The kitchen was cramped and Ava was still hemmed in against the wall, vulnerable to even the wildest of swings. She jumped to the right, the baton grazing her left arm. His head was turned and all she could see was his right eye. She thrust. He moved at the last second, too late, and her fingernail pierced it, drawing blood almost instantly. He screamed, his belt hand going to his eye, finally giving her room and time to manoeuvre.

She moved farther right, away from the still-thrashing baton. Her right hand formed a fist, the middle knuckle of her index finger extended like the end of a pile driver, and then she leapt, the knuckle driving into his ear. He rocked on his heels, backing up some more.

Ava couldn't believe that he hadn't collapsed, though he was staggering now and looked disoriented. The last blow had moved him completely out of the kitchen and into the living room. She circled wider, to the side where his vision was impaired. He hadn't dropped either the baton or the belt, but the belt hand was still held to the eye she had damaged, blood trickling through his fingers. She moved in on him from behind and jumped onto his back, her fingers digging into his neck, searching for a carotid artery.

He yelled and shook his upper body. She could not believe how big and strong he was; she was hard-pressed to hang on. Robbins swung the baton over his shoulder, trying to catch her head, but she had it pressed against the side of his neck. Then he swung it around behind his back and found her, the stick catching her repeatedly on the calf. Ava tried to move her leg out of the way but started to slide down his back. She had no choice but to recover her grip, ignore the pain, and hold on even harder. "Where is that fucking artery?" she shouted, her fingers lost in the mounds of flesh that protected his neck.

Robbins turned sideways and started to back up. Ava saw he was going to try to drive her into the wall. Her fingers pressed deeper, harder. She hit the wall and felt it give, but the momentum wasn't strong enough to dislodge her. He lurched forward. Ava could finally feel his legs starting to buckle. She clenched her fingers with every ounce of strength she could concentrate in them.

When they hit the floor, Robbins's head bounced with the impact. Ava slid off to the side and did a complete roll, coming to rest on her back about a metre away from him. Her leg was sore where he had beaten her with the baton. Her neck and shoulders ached from the belt strike; she knew there would be a welt. Her fingers felt stiff.

She turned to look at him. She'd never taken on anyone bigger or stronger. He twitched. *No*, she thought, *lie still.* He twitched again. His eyes opened, the bloody one nearest her, staring blindly. *What does it take?* she thought. He raised his head, shook his shoulders, and started to get up.

Ava scrambled to her feet and grabbed the baton, which had been jarred free when he fell.

Robbins was halfway up, his attention moving back and forth between her and the baton. "Don't make me use it," she said.

"Cunt," he said, forcing himself to his feet.

She took out his left leg, the baton smashing into the kneecap with a sickening crack. He fell to the ground as if he'd been shot, letting loose a screech that tore through her head.

Ava's duct tape was in Seto's room. When she went in, he was awake and sitting up. His eyes bulged like a raccoon's caught in a flashlight, sweat pouring down his face. "Lie down and don't move," she said.

Robbins was still on the floor when she came back, but he was moving, trying to crawl towards his room. Ava got behind him and, avoiding the kicks from his good leg, grabbed his ankles and taped them together. That at least slowed him down. She thought about taping his wrists but wasn't sure she was strong enough to hold them together long enough to do it. She also wasn't sure that, even if she did manage it, he wouldn't eventually force the tape apart.

She went back to check on Seto. He looked even more panicked. "You can sit up now, and turn around," she told him.

He struggled to a sitting position, mumbling beneath his tape. She thought she could hear him saying, "Don't hurt me, don't hurt me." She undid his handcuffs and quickly taped his wrists together. Then she pushed him back onto the bed. "Stay there and you'll be fine."

Robbins wasn't moving as much. Maybe the effort to crawl had exhausted him, Ava thought. Still, she approached him cautiously, looking to see where his hands were. She slid one of the cuffs over his right wrist. It barely fit. Then she lifted his left arm and moved it across his back. He flinched and she felt the arm begin to resist. Quickly she yanked it towards the other, slipped the second handcuff on, and closed it. Then she reached again for his neck. He tried to twist away but she persisted, and finally she managed to put him completely out.

On her knees, Ava pushed herself back towards the bedroom. Easing into a sitting position, she leaned her back against the wall. She took deep, slow breaths, trying to calm herself down. But even as her body's tension eased, her mind raced with an anger that was directed mainly at herself — for having taken the Robbins brothers too lightly, for letting herself be blindsided. *Calm yourself*, she thought. *The worst is over.*

Then the doorbell rang.

Ava struggled to her feet. She had no idea who was there, but she wasn't going to open the door for anyone.

She looked through the peephole. A young man in powder blue pyjamas was standing at the door looking concerned.

"Hello," Ava said through the door, her voice hoarse with emotion that hadn't completely dissipated.

"I'm from the apartment next door. Is everything okay in there? I heard a horrible racket. I was just about to go downstairs to get someone," he said, his face clouded with confusion.

"Please don't," Ava said. "My husband, he's epileptic. He had a fit, that's all. It was a bad one, even for him, but he's all right now. He would be mortified if he thought strangers were looking in on him."

"It was a hell of a noise."

"He's a big man and he hit the wall. It's passed. Please believe me, there will be no more trouble."

She watched him through the peephole. He looked at least partially convinced. "Thank you for your concern, though. It's really appreciated," she said.

He took two steps back and looked around as if waiting for someone else to voice a complaint. "Okay, no worries then. Like I said, I'm next door, in 310. If you need anything, let me know."

"Thanks again," Ava said, watching as he moved away, glancing back at the door.

She took a deep breath and turned. The apartment was a disaster. There was blood in several places on the floor and a cracked crater in the drywall she'd been backed into, and sometime during their struggle the coffee table had collapsed, two of its legs broken. There was no point in trying to clean it up. Robbins was on the floor and Seto was in the bed, and they weren't going anywhere. Ava knew she had better things to do and not that much time in which to get them done.

She had to step over Robbins to get into his room. A gun and a police badge were on top of his dresser. He was a sergeant, and still active. She figured he'd been crawling towards the gun. Her cellphone was in the bottom drawer, resting on some very large men's underwear. She took it out, turned it on, and walked into her own bedroom. Then she picked up her notebook and pen and took three sachets of coffee from her bag. The clock said six forty. She needed her morning coffee. She needed to think. The morning had barely begun, and Ava didn't need the day to get any more dramatic.

(40)

AVA STOOD BY THE STOVE WATCHING THE WATER BOIL, the mindlessness of it comfortably distracting. She made her coffee and went out onto the balcony. The sun was creeping up the side of the building and soon she'd be engulfed in it. She was thinking how pleasant it was outside when the *William Tell* overture called from the kitchen. She stuck her head through the door and looked at Robbins's phone until it went quiet. It was only a short reprieve, she knew. The Captain would call back soon, and she'd better be prepared to talk to him.

She sat on a chair and hoisted her legs onto the railing. She knew if she rolled up her pants the bruising would already be visible. *What a mess,* she thought. *What a fucking awful mess.* When was the last time, she thought again, she had misjudged a situation so badly? When was the last time she had misjudged a man so badly? Why hadn't she simply sent him the money in the first place and avoided all this chaos? Because it wasn't her nature to give in so easily, and besides, she hadn't trusted him to honour his commitments. And why hadn't he given her a chance to resend the money without all that unnecessary violence? Because that wasn't his nature, she answered herself again. He needed to hurt her. He needed to be dominant.

Ava finished her coffee and went back to the kitchen for another. She put two sachets into her second cup to really get a jolt. Then she picked up Robbins's phone and her own and returned to the balcony. She placed his on the table and pressed her voicemail key. There were more than twenty messages, most of them old. Uncle. Uncle. Uncle. Derek. Derek. Her mother. Mimi. Her mother. Uncle. Uncle. *He's worried*, she thought.

And then Andrew Tam. "I need to hear from you," he said, his voice a mixture of fear and anticipation. "I have a meeting with my bank tomorrow morning, and I don't know what to tell them. You need to give me something, anything, that can help me hold them off. Please, Ava, call me. Call me." Ava checked the time of his message. It had come in the middle of a Hong Kong night, right around when she was showing Seto to Bates, a few hours before Bates had sent the wire.

She scanned the other messages quickly. More of the same, until she got to Tam again. He sounded as if he was bouncing up and down. The five million had reached his account two hours before his meeting with the bank. As he was speaking, his emotions overcame him and he began to cry. *Well, at least some good has come of this*, Ava thought, listening to him say "thank you" over and over again. As Uncle always said, they didn't just get people's money back, they got them their lives back. Now all she had to do was take care of her own.

The last voicemail was from Derek. "I don't know if you have access to your phone yet. Just a heads-up — I have the information you wanted. Call whenever." *You darling*, she thought, reaching for her notebook before calling him back. Then Robbins's phone jumped to life again.

The *William Tell* overture was rapidly becoming the most annoying piece of music she'd ever heard. She thought about not answering, even turning off the phone, and then instinctively knew that either of those choices would be wrong. Nothing good could come from putting him off. The last thing she needed was for him to go crazy on her, to do something unpredictable like calling in the cops or Morris Thomas and his boys. She needed to slow things down, not force his hand and have him speed them up. So she had to deal with him. She left the balcony, went into the kitchen, and sat down, her eyes looking out towards the harbour.

"This is Ava Lee," she answered.

"Ms. Lee?" he said.

"Yes, it's me."

"I would like to speak to my brother," he said.

He was cool, she gave him that. "Your brother is indisposed."

"I'll wait. Ask him to come to the phone."

"Not that kind of indisposed."

"I would still like to speak to him. Ask him to come to the phone."

"He isn't in a position to walk."

He paused. "Then take the phone to him."

"There isn't much point in that either, because I don't think he can talk."

A longer pause. "You're a nasty little thing, aren't you?"

Ava said, "There is a French saying that applies to my situation: 'Be careful of that animal — it is very vicious. When you attack it, it defends itself.'"

"We could have a debate about who attacked whom, but I don't think that would help this situation," Robbins said. Then he added, "Is he alive?" as casually as if he were asking whether she had eaten breakfast.

"I think so. I haven't checked in the past ten minutes."

She could hear him breathing through the phone but he didn't sound particularly stressed, and again she had to give him credit. "Ms. Lee, I hope you don't think this mistreatment of my brother changes your position in any material way," he said.

"I wasn't thinking that far ahead when he was swinging a belt at me and threatening to break my bones with a baton."

"Maybe that was ill-advised on his part."

"He was simply doing what he was told."

The Captain drew a deeper breath. "You shouldn't have lied to me."

There goes any concern for his brother, Ava thought. "I accept that as a fair criticism, and I apologize for it. I also, if you remember, offered to fix the problem," she said, offering her first peace token.

"It was perhaps silly of me not to accept, but I do have my pride and you did breach my trust."

"And it was silly of me to have done that."

"Is this the start of renewed negotiations?" he asked carefully.

"That's up to you."

"Well, I think it could be. Forgive and forget, Ms. Lee. Let's both of us forgive and forget."

"I think that's best."

He paused and then said slowly, "Excellent. Now, of course, I still want my money."

"That's a given, and I'm prepared to make that happen. I just need time to get hold of my people in Hong Kong and set things in motion . . . in proper motion."

"The full amount we agreed?"

"Of course."

"Plus I'm going to have to look after my brother —"

"Nothing extra," she said curtly, knowing she had to maintain some pretence of control on her end.

He didn't argue, but Ava knew she might not have heard the last about that. "By my reckoning, it is sometime in the evening in Hong Kong. When exactly do you think you can execute the transfer?"

"You aren't the only one with a bank that provides out-of-hours service. The straight answer to your question is that I don't know until I talk to my people there. I have to reach them and they have to get to the bank."

"Give me some rough idea of a time frame."

"It may be a couple of hours before I know."

"I'll give you an hour to reach them and get back to me with a schedule. When we have that, then we reassess our position."

"I'm not sure what I can accomplish in an hour, but I'll go along with you as long as the door doesn't slam shut when the time is up."

"I said we could reassess."

Ava knew she wasn't going to do any better. "That will do, thank you."

"It's a good start anyway. Puts us back on the rails, so to speak," Robbins said. "But now, Ms. Lee, I do have to say that we can't have a repeat of last night's document farce."

"I understand that only too well."

"I also don't mean to be overbearing or repetitive or unnecessarily threatening, but you have no passport and you aren't leaving the BVI without one. In fact, you aren't leaving until Morris Thomas says you can leave, and you can be certain that direction will come from me. You also have two men in your apartment, one who has been kidnapped and the other one — a local policeman at that — in what I presume is a deprived physical condition brought on by you. On top of those abuses, you have engaged in a fraudulent scheme with one of the leading banks on the island. Road Town is a small place. One phone call and you're minutes away from quite a pile of unpleasantness."

"I do understand my situation," Ava said.

"Still, there's no harm in my making it clear. I trust there's no offence taken on your part?"

"None."

"So where does that leave us?"

"With me calling Hong Kong to urge them to get that wire out to you as fast as they can."

"Exactly. And of course you'll call me the moment you have the details, and by the end of an hour even if you don't."

"You'll hear from me either way."

"Ms. Lee, I await your call."

Not a word of concern about his brother after the topic changed to money, Ava thought as she hung up. Blood ties must run pretty thin in Barbados.

She sat quietly for a minute. It had gone about as well as could be expected. He still had dollar signs dancing in his eyes, and he wasn't going to ease up on her until he had his money. He thought he had serious leverage, and in some respects he did, but only if she let time work for him. And when he got the money, was he capable of reneging on her? She had no doubt that it was, at the minimum, in the back of his mind. The thing was, she had no intention of hanging around to find out if she was right or not.

She went into her bedroom to fetch her toilet kit. She needed to get clean, take a quick shower, brush her teeth and hair. Dealing with the Robbins brothers made her feel dirty.

When she stripped, she saw that the red welt on her shoulder and neck was longer and wider than she'd thought. It would turn black and blue eventually. The side of her lower leg was throbbing and already discoloured. Thank God, she thought, he didn't catch bone, or she would be trying to deal with a break. She stepped into the shower, turned her face into the stream of water, and tried to think more pleasant thoughts.

Ten minutes later she was in the bedroom. She put her toilet kit into her bag, checked her cash stash, and headed for the kitchen. She made a coffee and then sat at the computer and began to search the British Virgin Islands and its Caribbean neighbours. She didn't have to look far.

It wasn't quite seven thirty when she sat on the balcony to call Derek, her notebook open to a clean page.

"Hi, Ava," he said, his voice sleepy.

"I got your voicemail, thanks."

"You're using your own phone again. Everything okay?"

"Looking up, anyway."

"I was worried. Uncle too. He called to find out what happened to me. He said he had some guys in New York on standby but was waiting to hear from you before doing anything."

"I'll call him after we're finished."

"I located the girls."

"I figured as much. Tell me what you found out."

Derek had been thorough. As Ava reviewed her notes after they were finished, she began to feel that an element of control was finally back in her hands.

The cay below her window was beginning to come to life. Small offices were strung around the piers, most of them advertising charters and cruises. They were just starting to open up. *Hong Kong first*, Ava thought.

"*Wei*, Ava," Uncle said breathlessly. "Where are you?"

"Still in the BVI."

"You are using your own phone."

"Our situation has improved."

"I was worried," he sighed.

"I know you were. Sorry for that, Uncle. Now, did you get the two million I sent?"

"Yes, it came in yesterday morning, and Tam got his money too. My friend is grateful, although not as grateful as Tam . . . But what about you? Did the phony wire work?"

"No."

"Ava, I told you it was risky . . . So now what, your Plan B?

"There's a Plan C now."

"Do we still send money to the Caymans?"

"No. Money isn't going anywhere."

"Do you need my help in any other way?"

"No, I think I can manage."

"Be careful."

"As always."

"I have men in New York, no more than eight hours away."

She could imagine them. Two or three small Chinese men, tattoos peeking out from under their shirt collars, broken English, and U.S. passports that might or might not pass rigorous examination. "I don't need them, but thank you anyway."

"Need them or not, you have to keep in touch with me, because if you go missing again for more than twenty-four hours I'm sending them in."

"No worries, Uncle. I'll stay in touch."

"When do you expect to leave that place?"

"Today, soon. I'll call you once I'm organized."

"Any time. I'll leave my mobile on."

(41)

THE CHARTER OFFICES ALL LOOKED ABOUT THE SAME, and all of them seemed to offer identical services. So Ava chose the largest one, figuring that had to increase her chances of getting a boat.

"I'm spending the next week of my holiday on St. Thomas, and I thought I'd like to get there by sea," she said to the weather-beaten little man behind the counter.

"There are cruises you can join," he said.

"I'd rather go alone."

"More expensive."

"I don't mind."

"You want a bareboat?"

"A what?"

"You going to sail it? Skipper it yourself?"

"Of course not."

"So you need a crew?"

"I need someone to sail the boat."

"One way?"

"Yes."

"We'd have to charge a two-way fee."

"That's okay."

"You care what kind of boat?"

"What do you mean?"

"You want a sailboat, a motorized boat?"

"I want to get there quickly."

"A motorboat then."

"If you say so," Ava said.

"When do you want to leave?"

"Well, how long is the trip?"

"We're only going about fifty kilometres, so around two hours."

"Then I'd like to leave this morning."

"You need to be more specific."

"Ten o'clock?"

He opened a ledger that was on the counter. "Sure, but the only thing I've got available then is a Bavaria 35. It's expensive."

"How much?"

"Round trip, figure six hundred dollars plus a tip for the skipper."

"Cash okay?"

"Cash works."

"Perfect. I'll be back here at ten."

"I need a name."

"Lee."

"And contact information."

She gave him her cellphone number.

"You'll need your passport to land on the U.S. side."

"Not a problem," she said, reaching into her Chanel bag. "Here's two hundred dollars as a deposit."

The hour she had bargained with Robbins was almost up and she didn't want to call him from outside the apartment. She hustled back, taking a minute near the front door to see if there were any occupied cars lingering nearby, any people idling about. The area seemed clear.

The hour wasn't quite over when she settled into the kitchen. She used Robbins's phone to make the call. The Captain answered on the second ring. "I can't tell you how pleased I am that you are prompt," he said.

"I've been back and forth with Hong Kong, and the money is being organized as we speak. They tell me they're expediting it on an urgent basis."

"What does 'urgent' mean?"

"They're saying it should be in your account by five o'clock this evening. Not in transit, mind you, but physically in your Cayman Islands account. But Captain, you can't hold me to that; I'm just repeating what I was told. I can tell you, though, that I stressed and re-stressed the importance of its actually happening."

"All very businesslike."

"I insisted on having a timeline. I didn't want to have to give you generalities."

"I think, Ms. Lee, we are back on common ground."

"I certainly hope so."

She waited for him to ask for a copy of the new wire, her reply ready. Instead he moved on. "How is my brother?"

Ava looked at the large, still body lying prone on the floor. He hadn't moved since she'd cuffed him. "Resting."

"Will he need medical care?"

"Perhaps, but not until the money is in your account and you've given me the green light to leave Road Town."

"You have things in proper order, I'm glad to hear."

So much for Jack Robbins, Ava thought again. "I still need to make some plans," she said. "The flights out of here seem quite busy. There's one leaving for San Juan tonight at nine o'clock with some seats available. If you don't mind, on a contingency basis I'd like to reserve a seat on it."

"I don't see any harm in that. What's the flight number?"

"American Airlines 4866, departing at eight fifty-five."

"Fine."

"And I'd appreciate it if you could let Mr. Thomas know that those are my plans and arrange for him to have my passport dropped off later today at the apartment."

"Once the money is in my account, I'll talk to Thomas."

"I understand."

"And you should probably assume you'll have to pick up your passport at the airport. He isn't a courier service, you know."

"No problem."

"Well, this has been a much better conversation, I must say."

"For me too."

"So now you have the rest of the day to kill. Do you have any plans?"

"I have to get out of this apartment for a while. I find that looking at your brother and Seto for hours on end is more than I can handle. I'll go for a walk, get some lunch. I'll keep your brother's phone with me in case you want to contact me."

"Don't stray too far."

"Have no worries," Ava said.

When she hung up, she went online and booked the American Airlines flight to San Juan. Then, using a different credit card and a different address, she bought a seat on American Airlines flight 672, leaving St. Thomas at two thirty and arriving in Miami at five twenty, connecting with American Airlines flight 646 from Miami to Toronto at five past eight. She figured she'd be home just after midnight.

(42)

AVA DECIDED TO TRAVEL COMFORTABLY, IN HER RUNNING shoes, track pants, and the black T-shirt she'd slept in. She packed carefully, putting her jewellery and cash in the Chanel bag and then the bag into the bottom of the Louis Vuitton suitcase, surrounded by dirty clothes she'd neatly bundled up. The only expensive accessory she wore was the ivory chignon pin.

When she packed the Shanghai Tang bag, she remembered that she still had some chloral hydrate and the switchblade. She emptied the shampoo bottles into the sink. The chances were slim that anyone would have examined them, but it was foolish to take chances. She slipped the blade under the mattress of her bed.

Her Hong Kong passport and other loose ID went into the back pocket of her Adidas pants, which she sealed with the Velcro tab. The cash she needed for the boat, taxis, and meals en route was stuffed into her front pants pocket.

By nine thirty she was ready to go and saw no point in hanging around the apartment any longer. She left her bags by the door and paid a visit to Seto.

He was awake, his eyes opening and closing sporadically from the lingering effects of the drug. She sat him up. He motioned for her to remove the tape from his mouth. "No, it has to stay on," she said. He looked panicky again.

"Now listen to me carefully," Ava said. "I have to go out for a little while. The big guy you saw — Mr. Clean — he's in the next room, so if I were you I wouldn't make too much noise. Nod if you understand me."

He nodded.

"This is going to be over by tomorrow. I'm leaving then, and so is Mr. Clean. We'll call the staff after we're gone and tell them where to find you. So until then, you behave yourself."

He nodded.

"The last thing, and maybe the most important, is that you have to forget about me, about Andrew Tam, and about this entire affair. It never happened. You say one word and we'll find you and we'll hurt you. Do you believe me?"

He nodded.

Ava patted him on the cheek. "And if I were you, I'd find another business. There are enough creeps peddling fish without you and that fat pervert of a friend of yours in the mix."

As she left the apartment Ava took one last look back at Robbins. He still wasn't moving. Ava thought about dragging him into his bedroom but wasn't sure she was strong enough, and besides, what difference did it make where they found him? From the doorway she couldn't tell if he was actually breathing. Was he alive? She tiptoed close and reached down to feel the pulse in his wrist. It was racing along, maybe too fast. Well, it wasn't her problem anymore.

Downstairs, Doreen was in the lobby behind the desk. "I'm leaving today, heading for San Juan," Ava said. "My friends are still in the apartment but they don't need any maid service until tomorrow. Could you make a note of that, please?"

"That will be three days."

"Just doing what they can for the environment," Ava said.

She walked to the charter office and paid the man in cash, showed him her passport, and at five minutes to ten was aboard a Bavaria 35 heading out to sea. Ava looked back at the Guildford Apartments as the boat powered its way out of the harbour. She felt bad for the room maid who would stumble across Robbins and Seto next morning. Hopefully it wouldn't alarm her too much.

Road Town began to shrink into the distance. It was a pretty city, the white stucco buildings nestled against the greenery of the mountains encircling the deep blue harbour. She doubted she'd see it again. Revisiting old job locations was never a good idea.

She went below into the cabin when Road Town had become just a dot. About an hour and a half later the boat engines eased and Ava climbed back on deck to watch as they pulled into St. Thomas.

The U.S. Customs officer in St. Thomas hardly glanced at her passport. She took a cab from the pier to Charlotte Amalie and boarded American Airlines flight 672 at two fifteen. At six o'clock she was eating a bowl of gumbo in the TGIF restaurant at Miami International.

She waited until seven to call Uncle. He was up

already. Ave could hear Lourdes, his Filipina housekeeper of more than thirty years, asking if he wanted another cup of tea. "I'm in Miami," she said. "I'll be in Toronto by midnight."

"Thank goodness you are out that place. I didn't sleep well."

"I told you, no worries."

"Between you and Tommy Ordonez it has been a hard two days."

"Don't mention Tommy Ordonez," Ava said. "I'm not home yet. I need to get home and I need to rest for a few days. So please, Uncle, not another word about Tommy Ordonez until I feel I'm ready."

"All right," he said, his reluctance obvious, but he knew how superstitious she could be.

"I just want to finish the Tam job, and it won't be finished until I'm in my own bed again."

"Speaking of Tam, call him, will you? He wants to thank you personally."

"He left me a voicemail already."

"Ava, please. The man just wants to say thank you. You saved his business, his family's capital. Let him be appreciative."

She reached Tam at his apartment. "It's Ava. I got your voicemail. I'm just calling to tell you that I'm pleased things worked out."

There was a long silence from the Hong Kong end. "Andrew, are you there?" she asked.

"Sorry, Ava, I'm still in a bit of shock from yesterday. I was only a couple of hours from total disaster when the money came through. I had no idea it had been sent. I mean, you didn't communicate with me."

Was that a complaint? she thought. "I wasn't in a position to communicate directly. The best I could do was give Uncle at least an indication that the money was on its way."

"He didn't pass that on."

"What do you want me to say?" Ava asked. "You got your money — what else matters?"

"Nothing. I'm sorry if I sound unappreciative."

"In a day or two I'll send you our bank information. You can remit our commission then."

"Yes, yes," he muttered.

She felt another flash of irritation. They were always eager to agree to pay the fee when they thought it was their only chance to recover their money. Then when they had the money back, they tried to cling to every dollar of it. "The fee is only half what we normally charge. Uncle waived his portion out of respect for your uncle."

"We'll pay the fee, and Uncle's part as well, if you want," Tam said quickly.

Ava knew she'd overreacted. Her nerves were still on edge; she needed to get home. "No, just pay my part, but you should understand that Uncle did more than just waive his fee for a friend. At one point he advanced $300,000 U.S. without any guarantee he would ever see it again," she said, knowing that Tam would tell his uncle, knowing that the uncle would be forever indebted.

"They swam from China together," Andrew Tam said, as if that explained everything.

Maybe it does, she thought.

(43)

IT WAS A MISERABLE NIGHT IN TORONTO. AS THE PLANE approached Pearson Airport from the west, Ava looked out and saw a sea of white slashed here and there with ribbons of highway that were struggling to stay black. As they started the final descent, the plane's windows became wet with sleet; the lights lining Highway 401 illuminated falling snow.

She coasted through Customs and Immigration, flashing her Hong Kong passport, and grabbed a limousine. The highways were slushy and the driver was being careful, not talking, focused on the road. The only time he spoke was when they hit a pothole pulling onto the Don Valley Parkway. "Sorry about that," he said.

She thought about Guyana and smiled. "No problem," she said.

Jack Robbins's phone had been turned off since she left Road Town that morning. She had thought about calling the Captain from Miami and quickly dismissed the idea as foolhardy. She needed to be on home ground, as far from him and his influence as she could get. She turned it on as the limo headed south on the Parkway, and was greeted by a barrage of messages. Ava checked the incoming numbers. All except one were from the Captain.

She opened the Shanghai Tang Double Happiness bag and took out her notebook, then hit CALL RETURN on Robbins's phone. "Where are you?" he screamed.

"I'm riding in a car . . . in a snowstorm actually."

He paused. "I don't believe that."

"I'm in Toronto, in a limo, trying to get home from the airport. I figure I'm about ten kilometres almost directly east of Olive Street."

Ava could hear ice clinking on glass. He was drinking, his nighttime ritual. She waited for him to speak, waited for him to acknowledge the Olive Street reference. When he didn't respond, she began to read from her notebook.

"Ellie and Lizzie live in apartment 816 at 1415 Olive Street, about two blocks from Havergal. Ellie is in grade twelve, Lizzie in grade eleven. Ellie drives a blue Honda Accord, licence plate number BDAC 685. They leave for school at eight in the morning and are normally home by four thirty. My friend Derek, who, you might remember, did not meet me in Road Town, has been keeping an eye on them. If you need to know about their social lives, boyfriends and the like, sexual experiences even, he can find out. They seem like nice girls, Captain. It would be a tragedy if anything unfortunate were to happen to them. There isn't any reason for that to occur that I can think of, unless of course I find my life disrupted in any way . . ."

She could hear him breathing as he absorbed this new reality. "Where are you?" he said deliberately, the rage tempered.

"As I said, I'm in Toronto, and I really am only about ten kilometres east of Olive Street."

"How did you get out of Road Town, and —"

"What does it matter?" she said.

She could hear liquid pouring, the clang of ice swirling around his glass. Then he sighed as if he was giving in to something inevitable. "There's no reason to involve my girls in any of this," he said.

Ava said, "That's my preference and, in my absence, Derek's. We don't want any reason to act otherwise. Although we would if the need arose, and you need to believe me when I say we would."

"Leave my girls alone and you will never have to fear any action on my part."

"You'll need to pass that message along to your brother too."

"When he's functioning again, I will."

"They found him?"

"Oh yes, they have him. When I didn't hear from you by nine, I sent in some of his men."

"Is he okay?"

There was a long silence. "He may be blind in one eye."

"Yes, perhaps," Ava said.

"He can't hear out of one ear."

"That may pass."

"And he's not going to be walking for a while."

Ava thought about Jack Robbins standing over her with the belt and the baton, and moved on. "How was Seto?"

"Groggy, confused. He says he can't remember how he got there or who brought him."

"What do the police think happened?"

"They can't get anything out of him that makes sense."

"Captain, I think it's best that your brother be equally confused. I don't want to have to deal with long-distance police enquiries."

"My brother won't talk to anyone unless I tell him to, and then he'll be following my advice."

"And what kind of advice do you think you'll give him?"

"Seto has set an example that I think he should emulate."

Ava looked out the limousine window as they exited the Parkway onto Bloor Street. The snow was falling harder now, the wind picking up. "It seems we have an understanding, Captain."

"Yes, I think we do, Ms. Lee . . . But tell me — humour me, please — where is the money that was supposed to have been sent?"

"There is no more money, you know that. You were paid $300,000 for services rendered. Be content with that."

"Did you ever intend to send it?"

"You know, there was a chance that it would have been sent," Ava said slowly. "I honestly hadn't decided what to do until your brother tipped the scales. In effect, he — in reality, you — made that decision for me."

"You were never going to send it. It was always a game with you," he said.

"I don't see any value in second-guessing each other, Captain. You are $300,000 richer and I have a happy client. Let's leave it at that."

"Yes, Ms. Lee, maybe we should."

"There is one last thing, Captain. I would very much like to have my Canadian passport back. I hate the idea that it's in someone else's possession and could be used for mischief."

"Give me your address and I'll —"

Ava laughed. "Yeah, sure. Look, have it sent to the bank in Kowloon to be held for pickup. And considering that I've already paid you $300,000, don't send it COD."

Robbins hesitated and then said slowly, "Ms. Lee, I have to tell you that I wish our business relationship had ended on a more congenial note."

"The only way that would have been possible from your end is if you had gotten your two million dollars. Me, I'm happy enough with the result as it is," Ava said.

"You aren't entirely wrong about the money —" he began.

"Goodbye, Captain."

"Ms. Lee, if you're ever back in my neck of the woods —"

"Not a chance, Captain. Not a chance," she said, closing the phone.

Ava saw the limo driver looking her in his rear-view mirror, and she realized that her end of the conversation must have sounded strange. "What's the weather forecast?" she asked him.

"More of this," he said.

She opened the window far enough to be able to stick her hand out. It was turning colder, the snow sticking to the ground. She tossed the phone out onto Bloor Street. It bounced twice before the back flew off. Traffic would take care of the rest.

Read on for a preview of the next thrilling Ava Lee novel, *The Disciple of Las Vegas.*

AVAILABLE NOW

(1)

WHEN AVA LEE WOKE UP, THE FIRST THING SHE FELT WAS A sharp pain shooting through her neck and shoulder. She stretched, causing the pain to become more intense, and then slowly relaxed her muscles. She knew from experience that the lashing she had endured wasn't going to cause any long-term damage.

She turned her head to look at the bedside clock. It was only 6 a.m. She had flown home to Toronto around midnight and had been in bed for less than five hours. She had thought that two melatonin capsules and a glass of Pinot Grigio would see her through the night, but the pain and a mind that was still a jumble of emotions were gnawing at her.

She lay quietly, hoping she could drift off again. After ten minutes she gave up and pulled herself out of bed. She kneeled to say a short prayer of thanks to St. Jude for her safe return, and then headed for the bathroom. Pulling off her black Giordano T-shirt, Ava turned so she could see her back in the mirror. The belt had hit her on the side of her neck and across her right shoulder, and then again on the same shoulder and partway down her back. The marks were a deep black and blue, yellowed at the edges. They actually looked worse than they felt, and in a few days they would start to fade.

Ava went into the kitchen, made herself a Starbucks VIA instant coffee, and sat down at the small round table set against the window overlooking Cumberland Street and Avenue Road. She lived in the heart of Yorkville, the ritziest neighbourhood in downtown Toronto. Despite the early hour, the traffic below was barely moving while the January weather tried to decide if it was raining or snowing.

Normally she would have the *Globe and Mail* newspaper spread across the table, but she had been away for more than a week — travelling to Hong Kong, Thailand, Guyana, and the British Virgin Islands, tracking down and retrieving more than five million dollars that had been stolen from a client — and had cancelled the paper until further notice. So she opened up her laptop and turned it on so she could read the news online. That was a mistake.

After she signed on, Ava opened her email program, expecting to see messages from friends, a bit of spam, and not much else. She froze when she saw Uncle's name in her inbox. Uncle was her Hong Kong–based partner, a man in his seventies whose idea of high-tech communication was a Chinese knockoff iPhone he had bought for less than forty dollars at the Kowloon night-time street market and used strictly for making calls. He had sent her two messages in the past eight hours; she couldn't remember receiving that many from him in the past year. She opened them. They were identical, simply stating that he needed her to call him. He didn't say it was urgent. He didn't have to — that he had sent two emails conveyed that fact well enough.

Ava groaned and went over to her hot-water Thermos and made another coffee. She knew what he wanted to talk about. While she was in Guyana they had been offered a job by a Filipino-Chinese businessman named Tommy Ordonez. Ordonez was the wealthiest man in the islands. They had put him off so they could finish the job they were on. Ava had hoped he could be put off longer, because that job had turned nasty, with unforeseen complications. What was supposed to have been a straightforward tracking and retrieval of misappropriated funds had turned into extortion. She had prevailed, but not without difficulty, as the bruises and welts demonstrated, and not without stress, some of which still lingered.

Ava had turned off her cellphone the night before and thrown it into the bottom of her purse. She had intended to leave it there for a few days, or at least until she felt her head was in the right place. She went to retrieve it and saw that Uncle had called as well. She sighed. She had to call him back. She couldn't ignore two emails and a phone message without insulting him. Insulting Uncle was something she had never done — and never wished to do. It was just past six in the evening in Hong Kong, and Ava knew she'd probably catch him at a massage, an early dinner, or his Kowloon apartment.

"*Wei,*" Uncle said. Ava could hear his little dog yapping and his Filipina housekeeper, Lourdes, telling it to be quiet. He was still at the apartment.

"It's Ava."

"You are in Toronto?"

"Yes, I got in late last night."

"And you are okay?"

"Yes, I'm fine."

"Good, I was worried about you . . . It is early there."

"I couldn't sleep, and then I turned on my computer and saw your emails."

"We need to talk."

Ava wondered if he thought she was being critical of his persistence, and felt a bit uneasy about being perceived as even mildly rude. "No problem, Uncle. Is it about Tommy Ordonez?"

"Yes, he and his closest adviser, Chang Wang, each called me twice yesterday, after calling me twice the day before. I have been telling them they need to be patient."

"And how did they react?"

"Impatiently."

"Uncle, you did tell them we never do two jobs at the same time, and that I was still working on one?"

"Of course, but it only seemed to frustrate them more. Especially Ordonez. He is a man who does not think he should ever have to stand in a queue or have someone else's interests take precedence over his."

"Did he say that?"

"He didn't need to. Ava, the last time I spoke to him he could barely contain himself. I could feel him eating his anger, and I know that if he had been talking to anyone but me he would have exploded."

Ava finished her second coffee and, holding the phone to her ear, went to the counter and emptied another sachet into her cup. "What do we know about the job, Uncle?"

"Not that much. Just that it is a lot of money, and that one of Ordonez's younger brothers is involved. They want to meet us face to face to provide the actual details."

"Is it a firm contract?"

"If we want to accept it."

"You haven't committed?"

"I thought it would be best for us to hear the full story before signing on."

"What I don't understand, Uncle, is why, with all the resources and power they have, they need us in the first place."

She had asked that question when the job offer was first made, and it had generated an awkward response from Uncle. Now he was just vague. "They will explain everything when we are in Manila."

"So you want us to go?"

"I told Chang Wang that we would discuss it with them, and they are insisting on doing that in person . . . I'm told the sum of money involved is more than fifty million dollars. I think that is worth a trip to Manila, don't you?"

"Yes, of course it is," she said, and then realized that Uncle had twice referred to Ordonez's right-hand man by both his family and given names. It was a form of respect he rarely used for clients, and she guessed there was some kind of bond between the two men. "This Chang, Uncle, do you know him well?"

"He is from Wuhan, like me, and over the years we have done each other many favours. I would still have ten men rotting in Filipino prisons if it wasn't for him, and he would still be waiting for permits to build cigarette factories in Hubei province if it wasn't for me."

Ava was accustomed to Uncle's Wuhan connections. He had been born and raised in a village on its outskirts, and he and the other men from there who had escaped the Communist regime had remained intensely loyal to each other. "And Chang hasn't confided in you about the nature of Ordonez's problem?"

"His first loyalty is to Ordonez, and we need to understand and respect that."

"Earlier you mentioned that Ordonez restrained himself when he was talking to you. I didn't think you knew him."

"Chang introduced us once, years ago, when I was at the top of my heap and he was scaling his. It was a passing encounter that seems more important to him than it is to me. I did not even remember the meeting until he mentioned it."

Ava was now standing by the kitchen window. The falling rain was beginning to freeze on it. She watched a car skid into the intersection below and slide into a SUV. She hated this kind of weather. At least Manila would be warm. "Can you buy us an extra day or two?" she asked.

Uncle hesitated. She knew he didn't want to push her too hard. "I would like to get there as soon as possible. But if you need to spend more time in Toronto, then I will deal with Chang Wang and Ordonez as best as I can."

"Would they walk away from the deal if we delay?"

"I really don't know."

"Well, I guess that's something we shouldn't risk," Ava said.

"No, we should not. Their impatience could get the better of them."

She did a quick calculation. "If I catch the Cathay Pacific flight late tonight, I can be in Hong Kong the day after tomorrow, early morning your time. That at least will give me all of today to get caught up here, and I'll have a sixteen-hour flight I can sleep through."

"Good. We can leave for Manila the morning you arrive. I will have those flights booked," said Uncle. "I will let Chang Wang know right away that we are coming. Ordonez's office is near the Ayala Centre in Makati City. The Peninsula Hotel is nearby. I will have them book us rooms."

"Okay. I'll call you when things are confirmed on this end."

"Fine. And Ava, I think this is the right thing for us to do."

She shrugged. "Ordonez is a big man and it's a lot of money."

"That does not mean we cannot still say no," Uncle said. "We will go and talk to them, and then you and I can talk about what we want to do . . . I have to tell you, though, I have a feeling that it will be worth it in the end."

"Yes, Uncle."

"Now I have to call Chang," he said.

As she hung up the phone, Ava tried to remember if she'd heard Uncle mention Chang's name before, and came up blank. That wasn't unusual. He had a network of friends and associates that spanned Asia, though his closest contacts were those who shared those long, deep Wuhan roots.

Is Ordonez from Wuhan as well? she wondered. She knew he was Chinese-born, but nothing more specific than that. She'd find out soon enough, but her interest was far more aroused by the kind of problem a man as rich and powerful as Tommy Ordonez couldn't handle himself.

ACKNOWLEDGEMENTS

Ava Lee and her story came to me unexpectedly. When it was finished, I had no idea whether Ava and her life would be of interest to anyone else. To find out, I imposed her upon my children and friends, all avid readers. Their input and encouragement were invaluable, and I need to thank them.

Ava then found her way to Westwood Creative Artists, where she found support from Bruce Westwood and Carolyn Forde. Their enthusiasm was instrumental in helping Ava find a home. I owe them both a great debt of gratitude.

Home for Ava is House of Anansi Press. I want to thank publisher Sarah MacLachlan and the rest of her team for believing in Ava and for deciding they wanted to introduce her to the world.

Finally I must thank Janie Yoon, Senior Editor at Anansi, for her contribution to the final product. Janie is smart, dedicated, talented, persistent, and polite, much like Ava herself.

There is one attribution I need to clarify. "People always do the right thing for the wrong reason" is referred to as one of Uncle's credos. In reality, I heard these words spoken many years ago by Saul Alinsky, the great Chicago community organizer, and they have stayed with me.

ABOUT THE AUTHOR

IAN HAMILTON is the author of the Ava Lee series: *The Dragon Head of Hong Kong: The Ava Lee Prequel*, *The Water Rat of Wanchai*, *The Disciple of Las Vegas*, *The Wild Beasts of Wuhan*, *The Red Pole of Macau*, *The Scottish Banker of Surabaya*, *The Two Sisters of Borneo*, and *The King of Shanghai*. *The Water Rat of Wanchai* was the winner of the Arthur Ellis Award for Best First Novel, an Amazon.ca Top 100 Book of the Year, an Amazon.ca Top 100 Editors' Pick, an Amazon.ca Canadian Pick, an Amazon.ca Mysteries and Thrillers Pick, a *Toronto Star* Top 5 Fiction Book of the Year, and a *Quill & Quire* Top 5 Fiction Book of the Year.